ELVIS IS ALIVE

James LeCroy

ISBN: 10 069254562X
ISBN-13: 9780692545621

DEDICATION

This book is for all the unsaved people in the World, and believers as well. It is my hope that all people who read this book are inspired by the Holy Spirit. And lead to accept Jesus Christ as your personal Savior

CONTENT

Acknowledgments	vii
Forward	ix
Chapter One	1
Chapter Two	5
Chapter Three	35
Chapter Four	41
Chapter Five	54
Chapter Six	62
Chapter Seven	69
Chapter Eight	92
Chapter Nine	114
Chapter Ten	130
Chapter Eleven	147
Chapter Twelve	156
Chapter Thirteen	164
Chapter Fourteen	193
Chapter Fifteen	218
Chapter Sixteen	241
Chapter Seventeen	250
Chapter Eighteen	261
Chapter Nineteen	290

Chapter Twenty 297
Chapter Twenty One 328
Chapter Twenty Two 342
Chapter Twenty Three 353
Chapter Twenty Four 372
Chapter Twenty Five 382
Chapter Twenty Six 398
Chapter Twenty Seven 411
Chapter Twenty Eight 422
Chapter Twenty Nine 448
Chapter Thirty 463

About the Author 495

ACKNOWLEDGMENTS

I would like to acknowledge my Lord and Savior first and foremost. The day I accepted Jesus Christ as my savior is the day my life changed. Knowing the Lord is the most important thing in my life. His knowledge and grace as been my biggest inspiration. The Lord gives me strength, wisdom, love, patience and the capacity to love others.

I would also like to acknowledge my dearest friend in Christ Jesus, the late Archie Morris. I think of him every day. He was a person I confided in almost on a daily basis. He was also a person that was saved from the horrible addiction of alcoholism. He attributed his success in being set free from Alcoholism to Jesus Christ. We were baptized together in March of 2000. We enjoyed twelve years of ministry together. His knowledge of the Word of God and world history was astounding. I learned more from him about Christ and history than any teacher, person, or anyone else. He was very astute and practical with a lot of common sense. During and after my relationship with him I was able to appreciate and value using and making common sense applicable to my life. Being able to use and apply common sense in my life is far more valuable than anything I learned in school and life. He was able to make me aware that the Word of God is all about common sense and allowing the Word of God to work in my life.

The knowledge I received from this man has made me a better person in understanding my life, and the life of others and how I can apply the Word of God in any situation and make it better. Archie wrote the first page and a half of Chapter 4 in this book. His contribution to this book allowed my fire to burn brighter and I was able to gain more insight into how the novel should flow. By knowing Archie it enabled me to not prejudge anyone, not even a bum on the street. Everyone can be valuable to society not just the rich, famous or privileged. The lowly person lying on a park bench (like Jesse, a character in this book) can be valuable to the lives of others. We just have to open our eyes and allow God to work through our hearts, eyes, soul and spirit so that we may recognize the lowly people and the value they can offer in our lives and the world.

And as always I would like to thank my mother Irene "Crickett" LeCroy for loving me and being there for me all of my life.

FORWARD

Audubon Park was empty, except for a morning mist that hovered low to the ground and a few leaves that blew along the gravel path up to the old man on a park bench playing a harmonica. To the knowing ear, the tune was the old gospel hymn "Oh how I love Jesus," but to the general public, it was a simple, cheerful tune that transformed the park from the everyday to a mystical playground of curiosity and emotional intrigue.

The lowly old man was clothed in a ragged military jacket looked as if he hadn't bathed in quite some time. A dirty hat pulled low over his face as he played his harmonica. As the song ended, he lowered the harmonica and looked up towards the heavens from under his hat.

A short distance away, the mist swirled up into a small cloud and almost hid the partially nude man kneeling at a pair of bronze feet that was situated on a high throne, the one on the throne had fiery eyes and the eyes pierced the soul of the partially nude man and then a thunderous voice of many waters sounded, "where are your crowns?,".

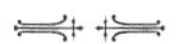

"Crowns? What do you mean? I have none." Said the man lying at the bronze feet. Wrapped in an old blanket and covered with sweat and dirt, the man was shivering violently as if he was in shock. Upon closer inspection, tears could be seen streaming down his face as he reached out to touch the brass feet. He turned to see the voice that spoke to him, and upon turning he saw 7 golden lamp stands and in the midst of the lamp stands, there was the son of man, clothed with a garment and a around his chest was a golden band. His hair was white like wool, and his eyes like a flame of fire, his feet like fine brass, and his voice was like many waters. In his right hand seven stars, out of his mouth went a sharp two edged sword. Drawing a ragged breath, he looked up into the fiery eyes, and began to speak. "I have no crowns, I'm bare before you. My shame is exposed. I'm sorry for what I've done. I'm sorry I didn't take advantage of the blessings bestowed upon me when I was alive. You blessed me with so much talent, Lord, I was confused. Please give me another chance to use my gift and show you that I love you with all my heart. I want to be an ambassador of all that is good and noble. Please give me another chance to receive the Crown of Life" He stopped and took a deep breath, as if he needed to summon all his strength to continue. "My soul is crying out to you, Lord. I'm in so much pain. I've fallen short and hurt so many people by not being true to you and to them, Lord. Please let me do your work so that I may redeem myself and win souls to accept your loving grace. Please hear my prayers…please…"

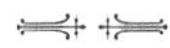

He dropped his head to hang over the bronze feet, presenting a perfect picture of dejection and sorrow. The mist continued to swirl around him as the eerie harmonica music began again off in the distance. Then, from out of the mist came the voice of many waters, "Do not be afraid, I am the first and the last, I am alive forevermore. I have the keys of Hades and of Death but you shall not see either, your salvation has been granted for accepting me as savior, however to receive the Crown of Life you will have to do my works, faith without works is dead, after 40 days you shall return to me, according to your deeds on earth and you shall be rewarded the crown of life, your redemption is granted.

Depart from me until you return.

CHAPTER ONE

The 57' Olds Cutlass convertible buzzed down the interstate at a steady 65 miles per hour under the hot rays of the golden desert sun. Clouds of dust kicked up as it flew along the wide open road. With the top down, the arm of the costumed driver hung out over the edge of the car door and an ornately bejeweled hand was keeping time with the music belching out of the car. Every finger hosted an imitation diamond ring, and the white suit was covered with rhinestones.

"Don't Be Cruel" blaring from the converted cassette player, the Cutlass pulled up to a whitewashed, cinderblock building on the outskirts of Vegas. The Elvis impersonator was about 36 years old and slightly out of shape, filling out his costume with a few extra rolls for good measure. His dark complexion stood out against the pasty white of his suit, giving him a look that more closely resembled a flashy matador than Elvis. The long characteristic sideburns and the sunglasses made his get-up look even like a caricature. With no lack of self-confidence, however, Sunny Carlisle unfolded his long legs from the Cutlass and hopped over the side of the door. A puff of dust rose from under his black San Remo boots when it hit the dirt, and he stretched and strode without any sense of urgency to the door of the establishment.

Leaving the door open behind him, Sunny took the stairs to the second floor two at a time. At the top of the stairs was an open room with all the recognizable accoutrements of an aging office. Piles of paper were stacked on filing cabinets, an old wooden desk on one side of the room, a broken coffee table in front of the two overstuffed leather office chairs next to the desk. An assortment of Old coffee cups were scattered around the room and stacked up by a coffee pot that didn't look like it had seen the inside of a dishwasher since it had been taken out of its box.

Magazines and newspapers were stashed in almost every conceivable location, and a clothing rack on one side of the room held a dozen or more Elvis costumes in several different styles, some hanging haphazardly on their hangers.

Having worked out of this office for over two years, now, Sunny took no notice of the clutter and threw his keys down on the coffee table then plopped down into one of the chairs and put his feet up.

"You're late, Sunny!" a voice came from the other side of the office.

"So what." Sunny responded in irritation. "Hey, can I get a brew before I die of thirst?" A younger, rather skinny man looked somewhat uncomfortable; he was sitting in a chair adjacent to the desk. An older man late 60's moved behind the desk, opened an ancient Frigidaire, and retrieved a dark brown bottle with a silver label. Moving across the floor and handing it to Sunny, the man stood and watched Sunny as he took out a pack of cigarettes and a lighter and lit one up.

"Make yourself comfortable, Sunny, it will be your last beer in here" the man said sarcastically.

"What?" Sunny replied, not really listening as he worked to pop the cap off the bottle.

"I said, make yourself comfortable, Sunny," the man repeated. "It's your last beer in this place."

Sunny looked up at the man and said, "What?" again. "Do I have to be an asshole to get you to understand me?" The man barked "You're done here. Today's your last day." This time Sunny took notice and stood up to face the man with a cigarette dangling from his mouth, "What are you talking about?" he asked, slightly alarmed. "Are your firing me, Jack?" "You can call it whatever you like," the man answered, turning and heading toward the desk. "You're always late, everything is on 'Sunny time' ----and you don't impress the clients anymore. You don't look the look, and you barely walk the walk."

Sunny just stared at the man, completely caught by surprise. "You can't fire me! You need me" "Not by a long shot, buddy," answered his boss. "It's all about you lately, Sunny, not the act, and now people are requesting that I not send you on the gigs when they call."

He sat down heavily at the desk behind the young man who was still seated rather uncomfortably on the corner. "I can't carry that kind of dead weight. I need the best man for the job, and you're no longer the best man." Sunny just stared at the man in a mixture of surprise and disbelief. "You can't fire me! What about all the gigs we have lined up for next weekend?"

"I've already replaced you," was the reply from behind the desk. "Meet Chuck....your replacement. Chuck...meet Sunny, your predecessor."

"You've got to be kidding me!" Sunny exclaimed, giving the other man a once over. "He's skin and bones! He'll never fill out the suit!"

"Sunny, he's already been fitted for a suit, and he actually fits in it better than you do," answered the older man with irritation.

"Besides, the Elvis everyone fell in love with was slim and trim in black leather," Smiling sheepishly after his devilish reply. "It was the paunchy Elvis that everyone loved" Replied a frustrated Sunny. "Sunny stop giving me shit! What's done is done! "He would be better at impersonating Stan Laurel than Elvis," Sunny Challenged. "Sunny," roared his boss. "Enough! Get your stuff and get out of here!"

Sunny shook his head in disgust, took a last puff from his cigarette, and flicked the butt in his boss's direction with a classic Andrew Dice Clay look on his face. Then he turned his heel and sauntered to the top of the stairs as if he didn't give a shit that his livelihood had just been yanked from beneath him. Before he left the room he threw one last jab over his shoulder. "You think that clown is going to cut it? He doesn't look a damn thing like Elvis!" he jumped down the stairs and exited the building, slamming the door behind him. He jumped back in his car and turned it on, preparing to back out into the roadway. The window above him opened before he could move the car, his boss shouted, "Sunny! Where're you going with that costume? I need that back!" Sunny waved at him as he peeled backwards in the Cutlass.

"You'll get it when I get my final paycheck, asshole!" And with that, he sped off, leaving a cloud of swirling dust in his wake. The dust billowed up to the window, causing the man to cough and gag before he could get the window closed. It was an inauspicious end to an inauspicious beginning.

CHAPTER TWO

Sunny and the Cutlass drove back out of town to a small bar that hugged the side of the highway. An out-of-the-way place with a nondescript external décor, the only telltale sign that it was a bar was the neon Budweiser sign in the window next to the metal door with peeling blue paint. Obviously designed as a pit stop for weary travelers who did not have any discriminating taste at all, the grimy outward appearance, the scattering of oil-stained parking spaces diagonally across the front and down each side of the blue building, and the small gravel lot ringed with weeds and brush next to it told a story of tired truckers who needed a place to have a beer and talk a little smack to a listening ear, as opposed to ambience.

Sunny pulled into one of the spaces out front and hopped out of the Cutlass. He leaned into the back seat and pulled out an old duffle bag. With the duffle bag in hand, he entered the building. Inside was a bit more esthetically sound than the outside appearance of the bar, other than the obvious neglect from day to day wear, some of the pictures on the wall of James Dean,

Frank Sinatra and Marilyn Monroe were a bit crooked and the floor looked as if it hadn't been cleaned from the night before. Sunny moved toward the bar, removing his sunglasses, paused for a moment to allow his eyes to adjust to the reduced light in the dark murky place. Cigarette smoke, the smell of booze, and the faint odor of last night's vomit that obviously had not been cleaned from the floor yet, permeated the air.

Sunny moved toward the bar slowly, looking around noticing that he was the only one in the bar other than a silhouette of a person in the corner near the juke box. He then glanced down at his watch and noticed that it was only 3pm in the afternoon. Dropping heavily onto the torn leather bar stool at the bar, Sunny growled "I'll have the usual." The bartender looks closely at Sunny.

"You don't look too good, Sunny."

"I'm about as thrilled as any other dude who just lost his job," Sunny scowled as he accepted the beer the bartender offered him. "Other than that, I'm just great!"

"The old guy finally gave you the ax, huh? The bartender mused. "The freaking asshole!" Sunny muttered vehemently. The bartender laughed, wiping down the bar with a rag and gathering dirty glasses and bottles and disposing of them behind the bar.

"He replaced me with some Stan Laurel lookalike who probably sings as well as William Hung and will send the ladies screaming for the exits instead of throwing their underwear at him!"

The bartender stopped his cleaning momentarily. "You can get another Elvis gig somewhere else, Sunny. Vegas is full of agencies that need Elvis impersonators."

Yeah, I know, but I'm freaking burned out on all this Elvis crap!" Sunny declared, slugging down a big gulp of beer. "I mean, the guy died over 3 decades ago. It's time to let him go!"

"Nobody's going to just let him go, Sunny," the bartender countered. "Not when there's millions of dollars to be made off him. Christ! He's worth more dead than alive!"

"Yeah, but I'm tired of parading around as a dead guy," Sunny countered. "I'm 36 years old and have nothing to show for my life except my car and a duffle bag full of Elvis costumes! I want to do something different!"

"What else is there?" asked the bartender.

Before Sunny could answer, a woman about his age came up from behind him and began to massage his back. He jumped slightly and looked over his shoulder to see who it was. Not exceptionally pretty, the woman had a painted look that suggested that she had been using her wiles to attract men for many years. Without a skipping a beat, she leaned forward, put her arms around his chest and said,

"Hey, baybee…how's your day going?"

Sunny took another gulp of this beer before saying, "Not so hot, baby. Not so hot."

"Oh?" purred the woman, "What's wrong with my little Elvis?"

Sunny removed her arms from around his body with a burst of energy and stood up.

"Stop calling me Elvis! I'm not anyone's Elvis after today----least of all, yours!"

The woman pouted a bit and looked hurt. She tried to put her arms around him again. "You'll always be my Elvis, honey….."

Sunny pushed away her advance again. "No, the old guy fired me today. I'm done with it!"

"Oh, baby…you'll get another gig somewhere else," the woman crooned. Sunny looked imploringly over at the bartender who was watching the scene with a grin. The bartender just shrugged and kept on working behind the bar.

Sunny looked back at the girl, and put his hands up as if in self-defense. "No! I don't know, I mean, I'm tired of all this Elvis shit!" He closed his eyes and rubbed his temples as if he felt a migraine coming on.

"How 'bout you come over to my place so I can make you feel better, Sunny?" the girl mooned over him, running her hands over his chest provocatively. "I can always make you feel better, right, my little Elvis?"

Sunny sighed in exasperation and once again removed her hands from his body. Backing away from her, he retorted, "No, baby. Not this time! I've got a lot of thinking to do, and you're not helping!"

Sunny grabbed his beer, slammed down the rest of the bottle, picked up his duffle bag off the floor and backed up until he could turn and escape into the men's room in back of the bar.

Closing himself into a stall, Sunny stripped off the offending Elvis costume and swapped it out for a standard pair of worn-out jeans, a black T-shirt, and plain black cowboy boots. Shoving his worn, hole in the soles, San Remo boots in the duffle bag, along with his sequined fabric, he then ran his fingers through his hair in front of the mirror with his free hand before exiting the bathroom and furtively headed for the door. At a quick glance he noticed the woman he had offended looking dejected standing by the juke box, as he passed by, he dropped his duffle bag, pulled her into his arms roughly, and kissed her long and hard. Her knees buckled slightly and she felt backward for the jukebox to steady herself. When Sunny let her go, he whispered "Consider that a down payment on a future rendezvous baby!"

Then he picked up his duffle bag and walked toward the front door, putting his sunglasses on as he went without a glance backwards. Kicking a trash can out of the way as he grabbed the door handle, Sunny hesitated for a moment looked down at his bag full of Elvis stuff and tossed it hard in the trash can making it rattle. Taking a deep breath and firmly planting in his mind that Elvis is a thing of the past and he vowed to himself that he would never masquerade as Elvis again. He stood and smiled at the sunshine momentarily and said out loud. "Its time for a new life"

The Sun was creeping down on the Princeton orange sky leaving a radiant glow, the cutlass cut through the cool crisp dust air headed east. A Sunoco station was perched on a rising crest to the left of the highway; it blended in well with the sky creating a picturesque view. The screeching sound coming from the brakes along with a cloud of dust settled in around Sunny and the Cutlass, he jumped out of the car slammed the door and perched himself on the car hood and laid back across the windshield with his arms folded behind his head. Staring into the sunset and taking in the beauty of the sky he started thinking about his life. "The last 20 years have been a blur, where the hell did they go? What the Hell am I going to do now? I'm too old to go back to school, the young people would look at me like I'm a loser, I'm not going to put myself through that shame. My resume of a dead rock singer over the past decade isn't going to get me too far in the entertainment industry. After all, there only 85 to 90 thousand Elvis's around the world these days. The irony of having to claw my way to the top of the heap in Vegas, is a cut throat mission, destined for failure. I have got to find a new direction, but what?? What the hell can I do? I'm not trained to do anything else other than Elvis. This Elvis crap all started back in high school on a dare from my buddy to perform Jailhouse Rock at the senior talent show," "Louis I ought to cut your throat." Laughing profusely "Who knows where I would be today if it weren't for that Dare.

Probably sitting at a desk balancing ledger sheets in Uncle Benny's insurance agency in Reno. Geez, I'll take the Elvis gig anytime over that." Laughing out loud, Sunny gazed out into the sky that had turned from Princeton orange to a midnight blue backdrop with a canopy of stars over it. Sunny inhaled his last cigarette, threw the bud down on the ground, jumped off the car and crushed the bud with his black studded calf high boots. He jumped in the cutlass and headed back west toward Vegas. No further ahead in his quest to find direction, Sunny was feeling a bit defeated at this point. Trolling along in the desert at night was not doing anything for his mood, and he was beginning to wonder if the road would ever lead to the city lights again or if he was doomed to this purgatory of indecision and uncertainty.

"I guess this is where a normal person would say a prayer asking for strength and guidance," he thought. "I guess I never saw the point, but it sure would come in handy to have someone tell me what I need to do next right about now."

Contemplating a higher power for the first time in his life he felt a little hypocritical. He had, after all, resisted all the religious rhetoric his family had tried to shove down his throat since he was a little boy. "Giving in" to the religious establishment at this point-even as crappy as he felt at the moment-was a bit over the top for Sunny. Surely he could make a career switch on his own without heavenly help!

Sunny was just beginning to realize just how far out he had driven in his purple haze of thought when off in the distance to his right he saw a flash of light. "Lightning," he thought instinctively. "But that's weird…there's no clouds, no wind, no nothing!"

He saw another flash; this time a little brighter---again off to his right, and off some distance in the desert.

"Man! He said out loud. "That's not lightning! Must be some kind of explosion or something!"

It only took a split second for Sunny to decide that he needed to follow his gut instinct and find out what it was. The only problem was the lack of roads leading out over the desert in the direction of the light display. After a moment of indecision, Sunny simply turned the steering wheel and stepped on the gas, flying out into space as his car launched itself off the road and into the desert dust with a screech and a thud!

Without losing any speed, Sunny sped off toward the light, trying as best as he could to avoid rocks and large brush. His headlights provided some small defense against these kinds of obstacles, but didn't always give him enough time to truly avoid running into things that he knew he would pay for later. Even so, nothing could deter him as he raced toward the continuing flashes of light.

As he got closer, he noticed that the night sky above him had become blocked by a rather large, black cloud that was billowing overhead like a thunderhead in formation. The thick black and purple cloud was difficult to see except when the lighting (or whatever it was) flashed, and it looked ominous and disturbing.

"What have I gotten myself into?" Sunny began to doubt his decision to drive out into the desert alone in the middle of the something so obviously strange and sinister. The flashes of light were still occurring, but there still were no bolts of lightning headed to the ground anywhere, so maybe he was ok. He couldn't tell if it was going to rain, or if it was the beginning of a tornado. "Looks like it's no terrorist attack or explosion," with a disappointed look on his face. Sunny finally stopped the car, and put up the soft top in case the heavens decided to open up on him. Little did he know that the heavens were about to open up, but that rain was not in the forecast!

Suddenly, with what sounded like a large crack of thunder, the cloud above Sunny seemed to split into two parts. With very little time to react, Sunny watched a very bright beam of light start from the split in the cloud and slowly make its way down to Earth. The light was so intense that Sunny had trouble looking at it. Instead, he focused on some shrubbery a ways off from the Cutlass and watched the beam descend with peripheral vision.

After almost a minute, the beam literally collided with the Earth, sending out a shock wave that hurled Sunny up in the air and backwards for a good ten feet before he hit the ground with a large cloud of dust. The bright beam enlarged upon impact, completely enveloping Sunny, the car, and several feet beyond in a large circle of light that completely blinded Sunny and made him unable to move.

He could feel the intensity of the light on his face and knew that it was burning his skin, but he could not turn away. Shielding his eyes from the light with one hand as best as he could, he tried to look around him to see what was happening, and possibly figure out how to escape the onslaught of the beam.

As he began to regain his vision, he spied the silhouette it appeared to have a gaze blank and pitiless as the sun, its glare was blinding. The figure was moving slowly. A sphinx appearing as a man in the distance walking toward him through the light.

"Whoa," he thought. "That's messed up!" He shut his eyes as if to blink away the hallucination, but when he opened them again just enough to squint at the spot where he thought he saw someone, he definitely could still see someone walking toward him.

"Holy crap!" Sunny said out loud this time. "This is nuts!" He scrambled up and opened the door of his car, which now had the cover on, and slid into the driver's seat, slamming the door behind him. Locking the doors, he tried to start the car, but nothing happened.

"Damn!" he swore, hitting the steering wheel with the palms of his hands in frustration. "This freak storm must have shorted something out!" He looked up, and from the shelter of his overheating car, he watched the figure get closer.

Somewhere in the dark recesses of this brain, something clicked about the figure. It was becoming more distinct and the shape and the way it was walking began to trigger some sense of recognition in Sunny. It was obviously a man, not a woman, and something about the shape, with the broad shoulders and narrow hips, and the obvious sense of self confidence as it approached with a slight swagger to its step triggered some vague memory for Sunny—he had seen this person before somewhere.

Less fearful than he had been at first, Sunny leaned forward and became almost entranced with the figure that walked toward him, still unable to see any details because of the bright backlighting, but still firmly convinced that he had seen this person—or something like this person—somewhere else.

As he watched, he almost didn't notice that the circle of light was getting smaller and smaller and that the car itself was no longer in the middle of it. As the light receded, the figure began to be more visible. Sunny could make out the dark leather pants, a dark button-down shirt under a leather jacket, and dark loafers, and after a few moments he could tell that the man had dark hair and was wearing sunglasses. Suddenly, as the light continued to recede, the identity of the man walking toward Sunny became crystal clear—but Sunny couldn't believe his eyes!

The man walking toward him out of a surrealistic beam of light in the middle of the Nevada desert was none other than the King himself—Elvis!

Sunny's mouth dropped open and he stared at a man he had made a living impersonating for the last 15 years, blinking repeatedly as if it would magically change the identity of the person who was now only about 20 feet from his car.

"No Way!" he said aloud as he stared almost trance-like at the man who had supposedly been dead for the last 40 years. "This cannot possibly be happening!"

Sunny scrambled around in the front seat, found his cigarettes and lit one as quickly as he could. As he did so, the beam of light narrowed to a man's width and slowly retreated back into the clouds, leaving Sunny, the Cutlass, and a dead man alone together in the desert. As Sunny looked up from lighting his cigarette, he realized that the man had disappeared as well. Thinking he had hallucinated the entire episode, Sunny exhaled loudly and tilted his head against the headrest in relief.

No sooner had he relaxed, however, he heard a seemingly loud tap on the window, just inches from his left ear. He jumped violently, and turned very slowly to peer at the source of the thunderous tapping sound. He saw Elvis staring at him outside the car window, motioning for him to roll the window down. With his hands shaking Sunny rolled down the window only an inch or two and stopped. He managed a weak smile at the King, and then turned his head away quickly, and found himself observing out of the corner of his eye that Elvis was dressed the way he looked at his 1968 concert, rather than as the jumpsuit-wearing, overweight guy who had died of a heart attack in a bathroom at Graceland in 1977. He definitely looked older than the youthful Presley of 1968, but he was much healthier and could even be considered 'cool.'

"Uh, hello?" the apparition outside the car spoke for the first time. Sunny turned his head and stared at him.

"Uh...I need a ride into town," the Ghost of Elvis Past leaned down to speak through the 2-inch opening in the window. "Can you take me?"

Sunny nodded dumbly, and watched as Elvis moved around behind the car to the other side. Elvis tried to open the door, but it was locked. Sunny was oblivious to the finer points of the situation, so Elvis tapped on the window again.

Sunny looked over at him, and Elvis shouted through the glass. "The door is locked. Can you let me in?"

Jolted out of his trance, Sunny quickly leaned over and unlocked the door, and Elvis—the King of Rock and Roll supposedly dead for 40 years –slipped into the passenger seat of Sunny's Cutlass and offered Sunny his hand in a handshake. Sunny, still a bit stunned, shook Elvis' hand, and noticed that it was quite warm and normal for a dead person. "I'm Sunny" Sunny uttered in a reserve tone of voice.

Elvis noticed Sunny's surprised look and chuckled with his famous warmth. "What's the matter, Sunny? You look like you have seen a ghost!"

Sunny smiled weakly and just sat there in the driver's seat staring at Elvis. Elvis smiled and said, "You know, the car will drive MUCH better if you start it first."

Sunny found his voice at last and choked a bit, swallowed hard "I tried to start it when you, umm, when you first….appeared in all your majesty and glory…. (Cleared his throat)….but for some reason it would not start during your heavenly descent. (Cleared his throat again) he then turned his head slowly to see the reaction on Elvis' face.

Elvis chuckled again, "I think if you try it again it will work just fine," he said with a wry smile. "The heavenly transportation system I use sometimes paralyzes electronic equipment, but I assure you it's only temporary."

Sunny turned the key in the ignition, and sure enough, it started immediately. He grinned despite his nervousness, and slammed the car in reverse with a riveting jolt. Uncertain of his wear-a-bouts Sunny hesitated, he couldn't remember which direction the road was. Elvis noticed the uncertainty written on Sunny's face. Elvis leaned forward and stuck his head out the window and looked toward the sky. Pointing at a rather bright star, he instructed Sunny. "Keep your car heading toward that bright shining star and I will lead you to the promise land" Smiling with a light chuckle. Sunny looked at Elvis with a half crooked smile on his face, that turned to a hint of frustration.

His patients for humor at this time was running a little scarce, not to mention his blood pressure was through the roof and his hands were still shaking from this close encounter of the heavenly being that was seated next to him in his Cutlass.

Sunny remained focused on the bright shining star and feeling a bit humiliating doing so, "I feel like the 3 wise men following the northern star to see the baby Jesus" Sunny whispered. "You have a premonition of the future I see" Elvis responded. "Premonition of the future? Are you kidding me?" "Not at all" Elvis looked at Sunny with a grin. "This is so surreal.... Unbelievable" Sunny concentrated on the dodging the obstacles on the desert plain the only sound coming from the tire's hitting the rocks, which rattled the car making it appear it was going through a war zone.

With an attempt at humor to mask his continuing nervousness, Sunny asked "So, are you new in town?"

Elvis chuckled, "Yeah, you could say that."

"Uh, you're the last person I expected to see dropping out of the sky in the middle of the desert." Sunny finally exhaled. "As a matter of a fact I don't think I expected to see anyone drop out of the sky in the middle of the desert..." 'He looked over at Elvis again....but least of all YOU." Elvis continued to look out the window at the passing scenery.

Sunny's curiosity finally began to get the better of his nerves and he began to ask some questions. "What happened out there? Why are you here? Didn't you die 35 or 40 years ago or something? Where the hell have you been?"

Elvis grinned that famous, irrepressible grin and shifted slightly in the seat to better face Sunny. "Okay, I'm sure you have lots of questions. Let's just start with this: I did die 35 years ago.

I've been in purgatory all this time, but I have seen Jesus, as a matter of a fact I had to plead to Jesus to give me a second chance at winning souls to Christ. Jesus granted me my wish so here I am…" "But why me of all people? In the desert of all places…I don't get it" Sunny questioned. "I don't know, it's all coincidental, I have no idea really." Elvis retorted. "But I only have 40 days to get the word out before I have to return to this same spot we just left to be raptured up to the judgment seat of Christ again Sunny looked confused. "40 days? Why 40 days? Why do you need to help us?"

A frown came upon Elvis' face for a second then the usual Elvis relaxed look returned to his expression. "Sunny?"

Sunny looked a little surprised by the question. "Uh, no, not particularly, although after tonight I'm beginning to question a lot of things."

"Well questioning things and questioning yourself is a good thing." Elvis continued, "But so is faith."

"Faith in what?" Sunny challenged. "God? I think you're wasting your time, bud. My parents tried to drill that crap in my head but it just didn't stick with me because every time I believed it for a second reality would hit me upside the head like an 18lb sledge. But a lot of people are believers so you probably won't have a hard time getting people to believe you, especially since you're the King …I mean since you're the one and only Elvis…." Chuckled Sunny. "No, I don't mean believing in God, Sunny," Elvis answered. "You can believe, and even tell others you believe, but the world is in pretty bad shape even with all the so-called 'believers,' people have to have hoped that Jesus is coming to save them from this messed up world."

"Wow," said Sunny, "You're getting pretty intense their buddy, this is a little over my head." Elvis let out a light chuckle, "Well you will certainly agree that the world is messed up … right?"

"Oh hell yes, What kind of fool wouldn't agree to that?" "Exactly, people have begun to lapse into a state of lawlessness and self-centeredness, not to mention the P.C. crap that's going on, it's gotten to the point where there is almost no return to the kind of goodness and charity that God expects from us."

Sunny sat still for a moment, to let this sink in.

"Sunny," Elvis started in again. "Do you remember the Bible story of Sodom and Gomorrah?"

"Uh, isn't that the one where it rained for 40 days and 40 nights," Sunny started. "Or wait; was that the one where the little guy beat the Giant?"

Elvis shook his head. "Obviously you are no reader of the Bible."

"No," Sunny answered sheepishly. "I never could figure out what it was saying. My grandma made me read the verses along with the pastor at church on Sundays, but I could never understand what they meant.

Why can't they write that stuff so regular guys can understand it?!"

"It's not about making it easy for you, Sunny." Elvis said, "You're supposed to have to think about it. That's the trouble with this world now-nobody wants to think-about anything!"

"So?" Sunny answered. "What's wrong with that? We have computers to think for us! Isn't that what 'progress' is all about?"

"I think that's why I'm here," Elvis replied pensively. Sunny was beginning to feel confused and stopped talking for a few moments. Then his curiosity got the best of him.

"So this Sundam and Gonorrhea thing," he asked. "What's that all about?"

Elvis smiled as he watched the scenery, but didn't make a point of commenting on Sunny's tasteless remark.

"Sodom and Gomorrah were two cities in ancient Jordan that had fallen into dishonor with God because of the demented lifestyles of their citizens and the way they treated visitors," Elvis explained. "God warned them that if they didn't change their ways, he would destroy them. Well, they didn't listen and the rest is history."

"He really nuked them?" ask a surprised Sunny.

"Well, it was fire and brimstone, actually," answered Elvis, "But yes, he 'nuked' them."

"Wow!" Sunny exhaled in surprise sarcastically. He looked over at Elvis with a question in his eyes. "So what you're saying is that you're here to warn people about their behavior?"

"Well, yes but I just want a chance to make things right with Jesus by doing a better job this go around of winning souls to Christ, I think I fell a little short the first go around.

But I have no standing set of instructions to follow so your guess is as good as mine but I do have an intuition that I have to go to Memphis, Tennessee.

"Memphis?" Sunny quipped. "Yeah Memphis, got to go to my mother's grave in Graceland." "I've been to Memphis several times for ETA contest there during Elvis Week. Your birthday week is pretty rocking people from all over the world come there to celebrate your birth." "Yeah should be a little calmer this time of year." Elvis answered.

Elvis took a sidelong glance at Sunny, who was driving with both hands on the wheel as if deep in thought. "Penny for your thoughts," he said softly.

Sunny just looked at Elvis before retreating back into his thoughts as he guided the Cutlass down the road with the lights of a nearby diner coming into view from a distance. The Cutlass veered from the road and came to yet another nondescript bar, the accent colors were different and the neon signs in the windows were older, and some were flickering, the place looked busy with quite a few cars parked in the parking area. Sunny whipped the cutlass into a parking space grabbed a pack of cigarettes and opened the car door but before he could land his black jack alligator horn backs on the dusty ground.

"Hold on" Elvis spoke.

"What?" Sunny questioned, looking down at Elvis' hand on his shoulder. Elvis pulled his hand back. "Can you bring me a glass of water? I'm not going to come in with you."

"Why not?" Sunny demanded.

"I'm not sure the world is ready for me yet," Elvis remarked with a wry smile. "We're gonna have to ease into this thing,"

Sunny finished his wayward motion from the car, and looked back briefly. "Whatever you say. You're the King!" and with that he strode quickly into the bar, looking back over his shoulder once or twice as if he had to reassure himself that the frowning mirage in his car wasn't going to fade from view as he left the car behind him.

Once inside the building, Sunny walked up to the bar. There was no one standing or sitting at the bar, and Sunny leaned on the bar and looked around the room waiting for the barkeep or someone to show themselves. The diner was dark but not unclean like the previous place he was at in Vegas. Several of the tables were full but unlike most desert bars there were no truck drivers, or road scum hanging out but regular everyday people and some bikers. A girl looked at Sunny and smiled, Sunny grinned and winked at the girl, he then noticed the guy next to the girl giving him a hard look and he turned his head swiftly toward the sound from the bar. "Uhh….can I have a glass of water?" Sunny asked. The bartender sized him up, nodded wordlessly, and began to fill up a glass.

Sunny continued to look around the room. The customers were huddled in several sections, the obvious biker types and their babes in tight jeans and leather, the cowboy collection with their Dixie chicks, and a few older folks who looked bored and a bit out of place. A couple of the leatherettes at the jukebox in the corner.

Behind Sunny, the bartender set a glass with ice water on the bar and went on about his business. Never one to miss an opportunity with the fairer sex, Sunny picked up the water and raised it to the one of the leatherettes standing by the juke box. The woman grinned back and raised her bottle of beer in return before she turned away and began whispering to the woman next to her. Sunny was aware that he would have to find a way to get her attention other than with a glass of Ice water.

"Get me a beer," he barked at the bartender before turning back to the ladies. After standing at the bar for a long five minutes or so with no second looks from the leatherettes, Sunny instinctively went for the shock factor. Sunny cleared his throat so he could talk louder than usual. "This glass of water is for the King, ya know," He spoke over his shoulder so he could keep an eye on the leatherettes. Not getting any response he tried again. "The King….the King of Rock and Roll."

At this the bartender looked up, "For who?" he asked. "You know, the King of Rock and Roll…Elvis!" Sunny continued to talk over his shoulder.

The bartender looked at Sunny for a long moment before he shook his head and went back to work. "Yeah, whatever!" he scoffed. Emboldened by one of the leatherettes who finally started glancing his way a few times, he continued.

"Yup. This here ice water is for none other than Elvis himself." The bartender shook his head as he continued to dry glasses behind Sunny. Sunny turned his attention to several of the women in the diner. "How many of you were Elvis fans growing up?" The patrons in the bar began murmuring to each other as they watched Sunny, who was beginning to get into the moment as he realized that interest was mounting.

"How many of you would be crazy excited if he reappeared after 30 years or so...or however long it's been since he died." Again, the crowd murmured, but this time leatherette #2 put her hand up and up and waved it as if she were truly a fan.

"Okay, ladies," Sunny sauntered over to the leatherettes, despite the glares from the dudes the women were supposedly with.

"What would you say if I told you Elvis is in my cutlass right now this very minute?"

"Seriously?! Elvis is incredibly cool!" The leatherette purred....... "I love Elvis impersonators." The bartender studied the conversation briefly to make sure nothing got out of hand. Sunny leaned in closer to her, obviously not caring about the reaction he was getting from the guys in leather situated just beyond the juke box at the table. "No not me." Sunny answered with a wicked grin. "The real Elvis. He's in my cutlass outside."

"Okay, okay," the bartender spoke from across the room with a warning tone in this voice. "Enough is enough, buddy. I don't want any trouble!"

Sunny turned toward the bartender while still keeping his attention on the two women, who were obviously enjoying every minute of the attention as well as the growing reaction from the men in leather.

"Don't sweat it bartender, I'm just having a friendly conversation with the two ladies here." Sunny was in full showoff mode as he continued to smile at the young women. The bartender was visibly irritated by Sunny's remark. Sunny leaned toward leatherette #1

"What's your name, darling?" he asked in his best Elvis drawl.

"Shawna" answered the woman, who leaned back from Sunny just a little as he came closer.

"Well, Shawna," Sunny continued. "Would you and your friend here like to meet the King of Rock and Roll today?"

At this point two of the leather-clad monsters from the corner stood up as they took a particular interest in the girls' answer. The bartender also had enough and moved to the jukebox to grab Sunny's shoulder and pull him around to face him.

"Okay, hot shot!" the bartender barked, "I think you better be moving along and take your Elvis crap with you!" Sunny looked stunned. "Elvis crap?" He moved toward the bartender. "Excuse me, but I'll have you know that Elvis is sitting right out there in the car!" Sunny put on his best Elvis face and glanced around the room, "Thank you, thank you very much!"

Shawna and her friend moved quickly to the window, prompting several others to stand up as well with anticipation of joining them. The bartender grabbed Sunny's arm again. "I said, take your water and get the hell out of here!" as he tried to force Sunny towards the door.

Shawna squinted through the window at the Elvis-shaped figure in the passenger seat of Sunny's car. A bit disappointed, she made her way back to her seat while the other patrons waited for the verdict.

"It's just another impersonator," she said, not a little disappointed.

"Well, what did you expect, the real Elvis?" the bartender snapped at her. Shawna and her leatherette companion began talking to each other again and ignored Sunny completely.

"Wait!" implored Sunny, who was still trying to keep her attention. "I'm serious-that's Elvis out there in my Cutlass!"

Although Shawna sat down with her crowd and blew him off, several others looked like they might want to go have a look themselves. The bartender again tried to force Sunny out the front door with his glass of water spilling on the floor.

"I told you to get the hell out, now get the hell out before I call the cops!"

Just then, the door swung open to reveal the silhouette of Elvis, his 6'0" frame easily filling the doorway. All action in the bar ceased instantly, and they could have heard a pin drop as everyone stared at the dark form as it paused before entering the room.

Elvis stepped forward without a sound, taking in the scene and silently observing Sunny in the process of being pitched out the door, the bartender doing the pitching, and the patrons all in various stages of sitting and standing.

"What's going on in here?" Elvis' voice echoed through the bar, resonating in everyone's ear a familiar tone.

The entire place remained silent as the observers of the Elvis clone tried to reason with the rationalization that although he was a dead ringer for the dead superstar, there was no way on Earth this man standing in the doorway of the bar could actually be Elvis, the King of Rock N' Roll.

"What is going on in here?" Elvis repeated, completely unaware of the analytical stares from the patrons. He looked at Sunny, who was still holding the now half-filled glass of water. "Is that mine?" Sunny turned to the mesmerized bartender. "See? What did I tell you people?"

He shrugged the bartender's hand off his arm and handed the glass of water to Elvis, glaring at the bartender as he did it. Elvis, taking the glass but looked at it with some reservation, glanced around the bar and spied a Juke Box, Elvis walked over to it, and after peering through the dusty window to try an see inside he slammed it twice with his hand. As everyone stared, the jukebox cranked up "Love Me Tender" Elvis turned around and faced the room. Sunny grinned and walked over toward Elvis, "And you all thought I was nuts!"

Suddenly, the quiet in the room was shattered when Shawna got up quickly from her seat and moved over to Elvis.

"Oh, my God! I am such a fan! Where have you been? Why are you here?" she cried. Elvis looked at her with amused affection, so self-confident and assured in his stance that he obviously was used to excited women and their rantings. He smiled and placed a hand on her shoulder to calm her down.

"Look, hon…it's a long, long story," he started. As he was trying to explain himself, many of the other patrons got up and starting to mill around Elvis. The movement jolted the bartender out of his mesmerized state of mind, as he was contemplating how the Elvis song was played over the jukebox because to his knowledge there were no Elvis songs in there. Hesitantly he moved in the direction of Elvis. "Hey!" the bartender started, "I don't know who the hell you are, but there is no way you are Elvis and I want you out of my bar!"

"Sir," Elvis quipped.

"Shut up!" the bartender growled. "Just take your buddy and get your impersonating asses out of this joint before I call the police!"

Elvis placed a hand on the bartender's shoulder in a slightly patronizing gesture of humility, and said "Mr., you don't know who you're talking to."

"Oh, yeah, I do. A couple of punks trying to stir up trouble in my place, and I can't afford to have any more crap happen in here. They'll shut me down!"

The crowd filled in where the bartender was once standing, and Sunny veered in that direction as well. The bartender quickly moved behind the bar and picked up the phone. Elvis was enjoying the attention of the women in the room who were clamoring to find out where he'd been and why he'd come back. The scene was becoming chaotic, with Elvis responding to the music and the women cheering him on. Sunny tried to get his attention as he watched the bartender on the phone, obviously calling the police. Unable to get his attention visually, Sunny ducked through the small mob and pulled on Elvis' arm. The first couple of tugs didn't work, and with a quick desperate look toward the bar, where the bartender was finishing his call, Sunny grabbed Elvis by the shirtsleeve and pulled him forcibly to the front door. A few women squealed in frustration as Elvis and Sunny fled the building, but only one woman was there with them when they reached the car.

"What are you doing?" Sunny exclaimed when he realized Shawna had joined them at the car.

"I want to come with you!" she exclaimed, not able to take her eyes off Elvis. Elvis smiled at her and as if no one else was in the parking lot. Sunny sighed and shook his head in dismay as he realized that they were either going to get arrested, or they were about to become a threesome. The monster leathered clad bikers spilled into the parking lot, looking none too pleased about Shawna pleading to join them.

"No Way!" Sunny shouted, as he flung his door open, jumped in, and slammed the door. Shawna ran over to the passenger side to hang on Elvis' arm in an attempt to hop in the car.

"He's right, hon." Elvis said as he disengaged Shawna's arm from his and opened the door. "Your friends over there are going to be a problem!" Elvis slid into the passenger seat and Sunny turned the car on at the same time. Shawna looked ticked off and gestured to her gang members as Sunny did his classic spin away with the car tires squealing as they hit the pavement.

As he peeled out from the parking lot unto the road, a cloud of dust arose and covered the patrons who were standing in the parking lot.

Shawna stood in the mist of the lingering cloud as she starred into the horizon to hold onto a mental image of a guy who looked uncannily like the King of Rock n' Roll.

As Shawna watched Sunny's cutlass disappear into the night, a black and white screeched into the parking lot, sending the bar patrons scattering in all directions. Two local deputies stepped out of the car, looking eerily like Andy Griffith and Barney Fife; they both looked around the parking lot as if the culprits might be waiting for them. The locals were either re-entering the bar or standing on the gravel scowling in small groups, and paying no attention to the Keystone cops who were standing there.

The bartender burst out of the door and headed toward the two deputies with a waving of his hands.

"Here! Here!" he called as he tried to get their attention.

"They went that way!" he gestured toward the road headed east.

"Whoa, now..." said the Andy Griffith deputy. "Who went what way?"

"The Elvis clone and his sidekick went that way!" once again pointing east.

"Hey..." started the other deputy. "Let's start from the beginning. What do they look like?"

"THEY LOOK LIKE ELVIS!"....Geez...murmured the bartender.

"That's what Elvis impersonators look like!Daaah..."

"So they're Elvis impersonators..." mused the first deputy. "That's a start..."

"Yeah," said the other. "Now let's interview a few witnesses and see if they can give us some more details." Completely exasperated, the bartender threw up his hands. "How can you possibly catch them if you spend all night talking to these bimbos!" he yelled.

"Wait," said Deputy Barney. "You mean they're on the Iam?"

"What?" exclaimed the frustrated bartender.

"They're running from the law? On the Iam? You know..." Said Deputy Andy.

"Yes, yes, and yes!" the bartender shouted. "Now, go after them, or you'll lose them!!" The two deputies looked at each other for a moment before dashing to their squad car, stashing their notebooks, and starting the car. Without even looking around, Deputy Andy threw his car in reverse, pulled the car around to face east, and peeled out of the parking lot in the direction that Sunny and Elvis had just disappeared.

Throwing his hands up in exasperation, the bartender strode back into the bar and the patrons in the parking lot began to disperse-either back into the bar or to their cars to spread the word of what just occurred. Elvis…outside of Vegas? Thirty-five years after his death? Unthinkable. Sunny looked in his rear view mirror and saw a cop car creeping up on him in the distance. That age-old feeling of dread grew up from the pit of his stomach and rose quickly to almost strangle his voice.

"We got company," Sunny began. "What do we do?"

"Wait for them to get a little closer," replied Elvis. Somewhat distractedly. Sunny looked at Elvis sharply.

"What?" he asked in disbelief. "What do you m mean?"

"I said, wait until they get a little closer," Elvis repeated without looking at Sunny or the squad car that was approaching from the rear. Sunny looked confused as if he didn't know whether to be afraid or upset. Continuing to focus on the rear view mirror, Sunny kept tabs on the progress of the police as they continued to gain on the Cutlass.

"Uh…umm…." Sunny started as the distance between the two cars began to narrow rapidly. "What exactly should I do when they pull us over? I don't think I can take another ticket. It hasn't exactly been a good year for me."

Elvis looked over at Sunny and chuckled.

"So I hear," he said with his famous lopsided grin. "You aren't going to have to worry about it this time." Sunny looked sharply at Elvis with a questioning look.

"What are you talking about? They're almost on top of us" he barked.

"When I give you're a sign, just hit the gas as hard as you can." Elvis instructed, still with a bit of a grin on his face.

"Are you crazy?" Sunny was incredulous as he watched the police cruiser bring the gap between them to a couple hundred yards. "We'll never outrun them!"

"Just wait for my sign and trust me," Elvis soothed.

"We didn't break any laws," Sunny rationalized. "Why don't we just stop and tell them the truth."

"Because I have a feeling they'll try to take us in," Elvis answered, finally watching the cops out the back window of the Cutlass.

"What, did God tell you that or something?" Sunny scoffed grumpily as he contemplated the scene that was about to unfold. Elvis looked at him with a wordless smile and caught Sunny's eye for moment before looking back at the police care, which had finally gotten close enough to see the faces of the officers in the front seat.

"Just trust me, Sunny," Elvis cautioned. "And do what I tell you."

"Okay," Sunny did not look completely convinced. "I guess I have to put my faith in you since you came down from Heaven and all…"

Ignoring that statement, Elvis put his hand up as if he was waiting for something to happen. Sunny looked at him and held his breath expectantly. For a breathless moment or two, all three of them were caught in suspended animation as Elvis watched the squad car make its final approach. Finally, after what seemed like an eternity, Elvis brought his arm down and shouted "Okay, floor it". Almost instinctively, Sunny slammed his foot onto the gas pedal and the car launched forward at an unbelievable speed, throwing both of them back against the seat and forcing Sunny to grab the wheel to keep from going off the road from the force of the take-off.

"What the..?!" Sunny roared over the sound of the engine in overdrive. "I can't control it!!!!! Aaaaahhhh!" Elvis, thrown back against the seat, never lost composure as the car hurtled forward at a breakneck speed, handily leaving the older cop car literally in the dust.

"Just hold on and lock your arms," he shouted to Sunny.

"The rest will be taken care of."

The Cutlass broke land speed records as it hurtled down the desert road and away from the pursuing cruiser. Dirt and gravel flew in all directions and the dust cloud behind them rivaled that of a Formula race car taking off from the starting line. Sunny hung on for dear life, not letting go of the steering wheel and praying fervently for the strength to hold on until the car, which was completely out of this control at this point, decided to slow down.

After what seemed like an endless amount of time, Elvis sat forward and the car immediately dropped its speed and slowed to what Sunny felt was a crawl, but after a look at the speedometer, he realized it was still going over 100 mph. With a quick look in the rear view mirror, he recognized that the cops were nowhere in sight and visibly relaxed his hands on the steering wheel. The car was back under his control and he steadied it as he brought it back to a more reasonable 70 mph before he looked over at Elvis.

"What the hell was that?!" he croaked as he tried to steady his nerves.

"That my friend was an exit strategy," replied Elvis, who showed no sign that he was at all concerned about the car-rocket interval. "We needed to lose them, and we did!"

"Uhh…are you going to tell me what exactly 'took over' my car?" Sunny's terror had quickly changed to irritation.

"Does it really matter, Sunny?" Elvis was even-toned and unflustered as he looked over at the driver. "Isn't the definition of faith the substance of things hoped for but the evidence not seen?

"I think I witnessed plenty of evidence that what happened was unbelievable," Sunny replied,

"I shouldn't have to prove anything to you for you to believe that I just got us out of a situation that could have derailed our mission."

"And what exactly is our mission?" demanded Sunny crankily.

"To warn people that Jesus is coming soon," Elvis replied, looking back at the road ahead.

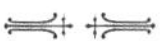

Outside the bar where Sunny and Elvis had caused such a disturbance, the last of the police were getting back in their vehicles and leaving for more interesting and productive cases. All that remained were the two deputies, back from their hair-raising ride through the desert.

The News truck, however, didn't show any sign of leaving the area. Rather, it looked like it was taking up permanent residence in the parking lot, as bar guests and the bartender were eager to tell their stories. Getting on the local news made you an instant celebrity in these parts, and nobody was going to give up an opportunity to see his or her name or face on the 7pm news broadcast if they could help it!

It didn't hurt that the reporter was a very attractive young woman who was obviously bucking for a promotion to desk anchor-dressed to kill, and in heels to boot, she was a knock-out (borrowing a phrase Sunny would utter) wearing a windblown, half-wild blouse whose inhabitants hadn't seen anything like her in quite a while!

The bartender, so surly and antagonistic when he was trying to bounce Elvis and Sunny out of the bar, was suddenly fawning over the reporter and jumping in to get his share of the spotlight at every turn.

"Like I said before, this guy comes in here, harasses my customers and brings in this Elvis impersonator as his sidekick," the bartender was quick to say. "The Elvis dude hits my Jukebox and starts to sing Elvis tunes in the middle of the whole thing-what an idiot!!

"Now, sir…" started the reporter. "How dangerous can someone be who is dressed like Elvis and sings Elvis songs to the ladies in your restaurant? Surely you are overreacting!"

"Uh, NO!" retorted the bartender. "It was a nice quiet evening before the two of them showed up! My 'guests' were enjoying themselves and everything was running like clockwork. I don't know what their problem was, but…" The reporter turned away as if the story was elsewhere, and looked for someone more interesting to interview.

"Wait!" the bartender was determined to get his moment of fame, and possibly impress this amazing young lady.

"There's something else you should know."

The Lois Lane lookalike turned back in irritation, "What?"

"There aren't any Elvis tunes on my Jukebox!" the bartender added importantly.

"So?" the reporter replied and turned away again, but the bartender grabbed her arm and gave it a good yank. The reporter was now obviously annoyed and just a little unhappy about the rough handling.

"I TOLD you, he hit the Juke box and it played an Elvis song "Love Me Tender" and I do not have that song in my Juke Box!!!!" The reporter just stared at the bartender for a moment as if she had to process the information she just heard.

"AND," the bartender continued. "I don't know how he could have pulled that off, it was like a magic act or miracle I don't know which.

"Show me!" the reporter ordered the bartender, who promptly propelled the disbelieving journalist toward the open door of the bar. The restaurant swallowed them both into its internal darkness while the rest of the crowd swirled around the news truck and police car in the parking lot.

Less than thirty minutes later, the reporter stood in front of the camera with the bartender, several patrons, and one of the sheriff's deputies standing off to the side. The bartender and patrons whispered back and forth to each other and eyed the camera expectantly, hoping the viewers would get at least a glimpse of them back at home. Deputy Andy, on the other hand, stood clasping and unclasping his hands in a painfully nervous gesture as he waited for his cue from the reporter.

"There you have it Jim," the reporter directed toward the camera using a lapel microphone. "An Elvis impersonator plays tunes that don't exist on a jukebox and causes quite a stir here in Townville."

"How does this happen? We may never know. Deputy Andy has some remarks he'd like to make at this time," the reporter continued. "Deputy Andy?" Deputy Andy stepped up the mic, tripping over AV cords on his way to the podium and fumbling in his shirt pocket for his notes. The small crowd of townspeople and bar patrons, camera crew, and the other deputy waited as Deputy Andy wiped his brow and looked nervously at the cameras.

"Uh..umm…just a second," he started as he tried to unfold his notes and adjusted the mic so he could speak into it better.

"We have a person of interest in this case," he spoke hesitatingly into the mic. "A witness took down the license plate number of the kid driving the getaway car. Its Nevada plate number PJY4816, registered to a Sunny Carlisle of Farmington Street in Vegas. An APB has been issued for the car and a warrant has been issued for Mr. Carlisle for evading arrest and excessive speed on state roads. He is also a person of interest in the aforementioned disturbance at this here fine rest-a- raunt."

Deputy Andy stopped and looked over at the bar as if to acknowledge that his comment was indeed a respected establishment, and then looked back at the camera nervously.

"Well, I guess that's about it, then."

The reporter stepped quickly back into the camera's view and tried valiantly to wrap things up professionally.

"There you have it, an Elvis impersonator gets the jukebox to play an Elvis song that doesn't exist and then squeals out into the desert in a car that somehow can outrun the police." She paused for dramatic effect. "We will continue to investigate this incident and bring you updates as they happen. This is Jan Bullock reporting live from KTNV, Channel 13. Back to you, Charlie."

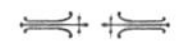

CHAPTER THREE

"I can't believe you talked me into driving all the way to Memphis!" Sunny complained, after hours in the car and a full complement of dust coating. "What I would give for a hot shower and a cool drink!

"All in good time, my man." Elvis replied wearily, looking out the passenger window at the lush countryside quite a different plateau than they'd been used to, having driven all the way from the desert lands of Nevada.

"Easy for you to say," Sunny retorted. "You probably don't have to eat or drink. I figure you're on some kind of perpetual, heavenly food product!"

Elvis looked over at Sunny as if to check whether or not Sunny was joking or serious.

"Heavenly food product? Are you serious?" Elvis smirked. "Do you think I don't eat or drink?" Sunny was just tired enough that his sarcastic humor was showing some signs of true irritation.

"I don't know what to think about much of anything right now, bud, "he said. "To days ago I was unemployed Elvis clone and then suddenly I'm his chauffeur! Too much like a bad sci-fi movie."

Elvis signed and shifted in his seat. "You gotta take the good with the bad, Sunny," he commented wearily. "A few hours ago we left the Keystone Cops in the dust and you were okay with that whole scene."

"Whoooohooo, yeah that was awesome!" Sunny was obviously well over his shock of the rocket car episode. "So tell me, EL.... VIS, did God teach you how to do that, or did it just come naturally?" Elvis sat silently without any intention of replying. Sunny, in his travel-numb state, could not let it go that easily. Looking over at the quiet superstar, he cajoled "Come on, tell me! How did you do that?"

We left those suckers in a different time zone, man! It was really cool! That was the best high I've had in a VERY long time!!

Elvis continued to look out the window in apparent disinterest, which of course just spurred Sunny on in his weary, dust-filled negative space.

"Aren't you going to say anything?" he spat out finally, as he realized that Elvis wasn't going to respond to any line of questioning that involved supernatural or other-worldly activity. The reflex of the power nod jolted Sunny back to reality just in time to see the "Welcome to Memphis" sign fly by on his right. With a quick glance at Elvis confirming that the ghost of rock and roll past was awake and aware of where they were, Sunny gave in to a yawn and rubbed his eyes.

"I'm gonna have to stop real soon," he shared, slapping himself on the cheek playfully in an effort to sharpen his senses. "We need to find a place to get some shut eye." Elvis grinned wryly with a silent nod.

"Any suggestions, or do you want me to just pick a place?" Sunny had very little functioning brain power left at his deposal, but knew that his passenger might have better taste than he did, even in his best moments.

"The sky's the limit, my man." Elvis answered without moving his eyes off the road ahead. "Let's drive downtown before we stop, though."

Sunny groaned, legitimately desperate for some sleep and not sure how much longer he could hold out. But, sensing that his guest was on a mission of some kind, he grit his teeth and turned the radio up a notch to help him stay focused. The two men in the Cutlass wound their way through a maze of city streets, getting ever closer to the Mississippi River. Just when Sunny thought he couldn't possibly drive another foot, Elvis spoke without warning.

"Turn here," he ordered. Sunny turned down Union Ave toward the Mississippi River in a knee-jerk reaction without even taking note of where he was. Quickly recovering from the quick change of direction, Sunny checked out his surroundings and noticed a rather extravagant, ornate brick domicile that took up a full city block rising up in the distance. Navigating through the increasingly busy traffic, Sunny spent almost as much time peering out the windows at the small bars and deli shops along Union Ave. as he did driving. As they approached the monumental framework, Elvis grew noticeably excited, and by the time they reached the architectural beauty, he sat forward and said, "This is it. Pull in here."

"Pull in where?" Sunny replied awkwardly.

"Right up here," Elvis gestured over at several liveried men on the right under a rather large awning that covered the expanse of the sidewalk in front of the edifice. As Sunny pulled in, and watched in surprise as a uniformed man came around to the driver's side door, Elvis donned a pair of dark sunglasses and a baseball cap and pulled the collar of his jacket up as if to hide from the strangers lurking along the sidewalk. Stepping out of the car, Sunny took in the opulence of the ornate architecture and the obvious prosperity cascading from the domicile and the people associated with it. In complete awe, Sunny stood in the arm of the car door while Elvis consulted with a well-dressed man on the sidewalk.

"Ahem," came from a man that appeared before him instantly, and suddenly Sunny came back to reality and realized that the uniformed man was waiting for him to move away from the car. With a look at Elvis, who was pressing several large bills into the other man's hand, Sunny's eyes widen as he stepped back from the car door and made room for the car attendant to take his place.

With barely enough time for Sunny to grab his bag out of the back seat, the attendant zoomed off with the car, leaving both Sunny and Elvis standing on the sidewalk staring up at the awning over the obviously expensive digs. With a quick look around, Elvis dug in his pocket and pulled out more cash. Quickly flipping through the bills, he pulled off a large number of them and handed them to Sunny.

"What?" Sunny exclaimed in surprise, backing away a step. "What am I supposed to do with that?!" "Get a room, take a shower and get some shut eye, and wait for me," Elvis ordered. "I have to make a side trip-alone."

Sunny digested this for a moment and then looked around him as if confused. "Okay, where's the Model 6?" he asked.

Elvis smirked and just stood there looking at him. Sunny trying not to scrutinize to hard over the fact that he was holding a wad of cash and his heart pick up a pace.

"Seriously….what am I supposed to do with all this?"….Elvis looked up at the awning above his head and then at the door to the Peabody of Memphis hotel. Sunny followed his gaze and his mouth dropped open when the enormous wooden doors opened up to reveal a resplendent decorated lobby with liveried doormen at each door handle.

"You want to stay here?!" the disbelief was all but palpable in Sunny's voice. "You have to be joking!!"

In obvious direct contradiction of Sunny's exclamation, Elvis gestured toward the wad of cash in Sunny's hand and closed Sunny's hand firmly around the cash, to prevent it from falling to the ground, as Sunny stood glaring at the doorway with his mouth open.

"Like I said," Elvis repeated. "Go in, get us a room…preferably a suite, and take a shower…nap...Whatever you want…while I'm out." Elvis turned away and melted into the crowd while Sunny continued to stare at the doorman, who was now beckoning him inside. When he came to his senses a moment later, he looked around quickly, and discovered that Elvis was nowhere to be found.

"Hey, how will you know…?" he shouted, realizing at that moment Elvis was long gone and he felt a bit awkward, while the doormen were gazing at him with a bewildered look on their face.

With one last look around-as if to make sure that there wasn't a Motel 6 in close proximity- Sunny stepped forward and went up the steps into the luxurious lobby of the Peabody Hotel. Sunny moved hesitatingly to the front desk and quickly discovered that his cash stash was impressive enough to easily secure a tree-room suite on the top floor, with an infinite departure date. His heart picked up pace once more, just thinking about it. "Paying in full for a week?" beckoned the manager with his eyebrow raised, and Sunny being unaware that a lovely admirer of the female persuasion was passing by as he was wrestling through the wad of cash.

"Hey, how are you...." a alluring but very definite female voice asked as Sunny was picking up his keys and receipt. Sunny, never one to miss an opportunity to converse with the fairer sex, turned around quickly to see who or what owned that voice. Standing in front of him, was the loveliest set of long, libidinous legs he'd ever seen, attached quite coincidentally to a very conservative waist and biggest tats he'd seen in months!

"Uh…hey!" he remarked in surprise, looking her up and down in typical testosterone- induced appraisal. "And who are you?"

"Name's Elisha, and I've been sent from heaven to make sure you get a proper Memphis welcome!" the voice came from a beautiful heart-shaped face with dark brown eyes and dark tone skin with a radiant complexion framed by a luxurious, wavering long onyx mane. Sunny's grin grew from ear to ear as he realized what a full package this babe really was.

"Sent from the heavens, huh?.." Sunny replied. How Ironic another heaven sent angle in less than 24 hours, Sunny paraphrased to himself in thought. He looked back at the woman, this time noting the fish net stockings, 4-inch heels, and the mini skirt that barely covered the keister.

"And what exactly IS a 'Proper Memphis welcome?" he asked as he offered his arm to the woman.

"First, a shower, then some fresh clothes, and then we'll see what else is in store…" she answered with a sly smile.

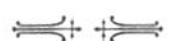

CHAPTER FOUR

He could have been perfectly content to remain seated on that wrought iron bench forever. . The evening sun had finally retired behind the stately old oaks, and running ivy. Early evening was now beginning to make its way through the thick coarse air that one almost needed a reminder to breathe. The incessant chirping of the cicadas blended with the almost intoxicating scent of the newly opened magnolia blossoms around him. Yet when the summer breeze had decided to pass through, bringing with it all the raw and muddy smells, it never failed to refresh and rejuvenate ones' body and soul. Even the rising cacophony of the traffic could not break the reverie of the moment. One thing was certain. He found himself once again in the bosom of the beloved south. Only steps away from his cherished meditation garden that he often visited in the past.

He had almost forgotten all the things about the old South that he loved growing up. The smells and sounds of his youth, and the birthplace of life's fondest memories.

Exactly how much time had passed since he had taken this seat, after being almost overwhelmed by the beauty and visions of yesteryear dancing in front of his eyes, he didn't know. But finally, coming to his senses and realizing where he was, he knew he had something he needed to do.

Elvis rose from the bench, walked slowly across the crushed gravel that covered the well-manicured walkway, and came to a stop at the foot of several gravestones. Minnie, Elvis, Vernon, Jessie, Gladys, and Ebony's double.... In times past, this had always been an excruciating and unbearably painful experience. His very soul cried out, his heart breaking to the point where he feared that he would surely die. Certainly he would drop where he stood, or fall over as he knelt. This time, however, as he stood and waited for the pain and the tears to come streaming down his face, waiting for the ground to come rushing up as he fell to his knees, he realized that neither was happening.

Not only was he not crying or fighting the almost physical pain he felt whenever he visited the grave site before, he was actually smiling and both feet were firmly planted on the ground with no threat of buckling. As he stood there, he found himself enveloped in perfect peace, slightly incredulous at the reality that was taken place, he realized the reason for his euphoria, and there was no reason for remorse, guilt or any of a myriad of emotions which usually assaulted people at these times. The souls of those resting here- people he had missed insanely and whose absence had threatened his very existence at times-where in heaven and happily awaiting his return! Hadn't he spoken to his beloved mother only hours ago? How radiant she looked in the fullness of health, and how supremely joyous she was. . He now found himself giggling out loud, struggling to fight a full blown belly laugh. It wasn't every day that one stood at the foot of his own grave. That's right. His very own grave. But the urge to get going rose within him again. There was no reason for him to remain here-he had a job to do. Besides, Elvis being spotted at his own grave would certainly be something for the tabloids to chew on for weeks-it wouldn't be in his best interests to be seen here, at least not yet.

Sunny eyed himself appraisingly in the mirror, admiring the new shirt and dress pants he was sporting in the entryway of the fancy hotel suite he'd been lounging around in most of the afternoon. "Lounging" is one way to call spending the afternoon with a lovely woman who had soaped him up, introduced him to Memphis in as many carnal ways as he could handle before he passed out, and then called for these great new threads while he was sleeping off all the hours he'd been on the road.

Sunny picked up the whisky and water he just made himself at the wet bar and glanced at the clock on the stereo as he slid his feet into the brand new hand crafted all leather Kressler Wingtip's from Italy, along with a Giorgio Armani Taylor made suit, "haven't had one of these before, just my style." He murmured as he admired himself in the mirror. "The money was well spent, cause I'm sure Elvis doesn't want his chauffeur to have cheap cloaks. " Justifying his choice to satisfy himself.

Now, if that infernal woman would just get out of the shower-they were going to be late for dinner! Sunny allowed himself into the bedroom he and Elisha had been sharing all afternoon and knocked on the bathroom door. There was no sound except for the running shower. He knocked again. Again, no sound. Slightly irritated, Sunny barked "Hey girl! What's taking you so long? Our reservations are for 7pm!"

When he heard nothing, he opened the door, peered around the corner as steam from the hot water wrestled around him, he blurted out, "Hey baby how about I dry that hot steamy body of yours off?" No reply, he then pulled back the shower curtain, which revealed an empty shower stale with wafts of steam and water that immediately made his face break open in a heated sweat, he urgently looked around the bathroom and noticed a white towel laying on the floor and Elisha's clothes were glaringly absent from the room. Cursing angrily, Sunny ran through the bathroom and went promptly to the patio doors. A quick look around, No Elisha. First impressions indicated that she might have taken off, but it wasn't outside the realm of possibility that she was just playing a prank on him. They'd had quite and enjoyable time together, and a harmless prank would be just something Elisha would try—after all, they'd hit it off so well that they'd made plans to have dinner and see a bit of the city tonight. Surely she was just messing with him…

Sunny looked in the closets and under the bed. With a sinking feeling in the pit of this stomach, he began to realize he'd been scammed. He whipped out his wallet and opened it up… empty!! His license and other cards were there, but all the cash Elvis had given him was gone.

"Damn!" he yelled, shoving his wallet back into his pocket. "Elvis is going to be pretty ticked off, I lost all that cash," he thought to himself. "Thank goodness the room was paid for!"

Sunny grabbed his room key and the new Georgio Armani sports jacket the two of them purchased at James Davis, and left the room in a burst of anger and humiliation. The ride downstairs in the elevator a tense one, as Sunny shifted his weight back and forth in frustration and irritation. The elevator door opened as Sunny stepped out and looked around the lobby anxiously, hoping that he would see Elisha and she would still be lurking around looking for another victim. "Of course she's not here, what I'm I thinking about?" he muttered to himself. "She's long gone! Only an idiot would hang out after stealing hundreds of dollars from an unsuspecting scumbag in a hotel!"

Sunny slammed his Jacket to the floor, and drew the attention of other hotel patrons who looked at him with a thinly disguised alarm. Sunny sighed and picked up the coat, brushed it off, and slumped into a chair in the lobby.

"Guess I'll wait here for the King of Rock and Roll to show up," he grumbled dejectedly. "That is, if he DOES show up." The absurdity of being in fancy new clothes in a high class hotel, losing all his money to a beautiful con artist, and then waiting to be rescued by a dead pop idol began to catch up with him, and he started to laugh with a touch of hysteria in his voice. This again drew the attention of a few passing by, and he tipped an imaginary hat to them as he continued to chuckle and shake his head.

Just as he was getting ready to go back up to the suite and rummage through the wet bar for some crackers or other munchies, he spied a mane with a familiar onyx shine, that the sunlight hit at just the right angle to catch the corner of his peripheral vision, without a thought of what he may look like he jumped up out of his chair and raced to the lobby's main entrance and pushed his way through incoming patrons and took one giant leap to the sidewalk. He noticed the black hair beauty trying to flag down a cab, "Hey!" he shouted to the retreating brunette as he began running down the street after her. The woman looked over her shoulder briefly, recognizing the proceeding victim, Elisha began to walk in the opposite direction of Sunny with a fast brisk pace, trying desperately not to trip in her brand new maniac suede platform pumps, with a skin tight leather moto-skirt and a leather detail scoop neck top that complimented her physic well and made her standout in a crowd. Elisha trying desperately to weave in and out of people on the busy sidewalk. Sunny was in full speed stride as he came within only a couple of yards of

Elisha, he slowed down, reached out and grabbed her arm and pulled her around to face him. "Where do you think you're going!!?" he demanded, breathing heavily trying to get his wind back. Elisha gracefully put her hand on her hip and retorted. "What the hell do you want?" as she looked furtively around for a way to escape.

"Give me my money!" Sunny ordered, still gasping for air.

"What Money?" Elisha replied haughtily, "I don't know WHAT you're talking about!"

"You know EXACTLY what I'm talking about," Sunny was almost a ghostly white with anger. "The money you took from my wallet you were supposedly in the shower!"

"You're out of your mind!" She turned to leave, but Sunny grabbed her arm again and wheeled her back around to face him.

"Leave me alone!!" shouted Elisha, as people started to take notice walking by. She knew she had an audience. "You're hurting me, Please stop!" trying to scream loud enough to draw attention.

"Sure I am," snarled Sunny. "Keep it up and I'll really give you something to whine about! Now, where's my money?"

He reached for her purse, but she lifted it up and behind her to keep it out of his reach.

"You took ALL of my money, Bitch!" Sunny yelled. "It wasn't even mine! I want it back, and I want it back now!"

Elisha took a step back and began to put on a show. "I don't know what you're talking about." She raised her voice even higher. "Get away from me, please someone help me!!" Shouting even more loudly than she did before. Several people looked as if they were ready to save the woman in distress; Sunny noticed the attention and tried to tone things down a bit.

"Look, we had a great time together. If you don't want to go to dinner, that's fine, but that money you took isn't mine. I need to give it back to the guy it belongs to!" he said firmly, but much more quietly.

Elisha didn't budge. Her eyes darted to the bystanders, and she stepped up the panicked note in her voice, "If you don't stop attacking me I'm going to scream!!" Elisha stepped back ready to let out a loud scream, then suddenly she felt a warm body behind her. Before she could turn around to see who it was, a voice in her ear said "Be quiet and move with me back into the hotel, and we'll settle this quietly." The voice sounded hauntingly familiar, and has a result had a calming effect on Elisha. With a quick gaze at Sunny, who had backed off a step or two yet was also eyeing her warily; Elisha moved slowly toward the front door of the Peabody and entered the lobby with the stranger's arm guiding her from behind.

As they entered the hotel, she whirled to face the owner of the mysterious person escorting her back to the hotel, and came face to face with a man that looked eerily familiar, but not enough for her to recognize immediately.

"Thanks, man..." Sunny spoke first. Elvis shut him up with one blistering glance. Elisha didn't miss the exchange, and looked at Elvis with suspicious eyes.

"Who are you?" she asked cautiously.

"Who I'm I is not important," Elvis answered, "What is the problem? Why is Sunny arguing with you?"

Elisha seized the moment to capitalize on Elvis' apparent concern. "I have no idea who this 'Sunny' guy is," she started. "I was leaving the hotel and he came up behind me and tried to take my purse!"

Sunny couldn't take it anymore and jumped into the exchange. "She is so full of bullshit! She stole my money...YOUR money...the money you gave me for the ROOM!"

Elisha disagreed, with a look of shock. "He's crazy! I have no idea what he's talking about!"

Elvis gave both of them a signal to quiet down, and led them to a spot further away from the main desk. "You're not going to get away with this con game, lady!"

Sunny's whisper-shouted directly at Elisha. Elisha made a face at him and folded her arms without saying a word. Elvis started to laugh, and both Sunny and Elisha looked at him with amazement and confusion.

"First of all," Elvis started, looking pointedly at Sunny, "It's just money, that's not the problem. Let her have it, Sunny's mouth fell open as Elvis turned to Elisha. "…and all three of us know where you've been this afternoon, who you've been with, and what you took. And I don't care about any of it."

Elisha expression mimicked Sunny's as Elvis continued. "Now, we're going to pretend that none of this happened, and go enjoy that dinner reservation-I'm starving!" Elvis finished up, offering his arm to Elisha and motioning with a nod of his head for Sunny to follow. Elisha glared at Sunny, and then accepted Elvis' arm with a toss of her hair as the two of them walked toward the hotel's restaurant. Sunny growled as he stared at them, grabbed his sports jacket, and followed them reluctantly.

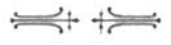

Elvis put down his fork and observed yet another member of the wait staff ogling him from behind the staff divider. All evening, the pointing and gesturing when they thought he wasn't looking, and it was beginning to be noticeable. Even restaurant patrons were looking more closely at the three of them as they had dinner, and Elvis knew the evening at to draw to a close rather quickly.

"Okay," he started. "This has been great, but it's time to get down to business."

Sunny looked startled. Perhaps Elvis was finally going to take the con artist to task for her little game this afternoon! Served her right, acting like she was all that and then turning out to be nothing more than a call girl with an attitude! Thought Sunny.

"There are some things I need to do, and I need to get started. No more time to waste." Elvis explained, playing with his teaspoon as he waited for the cup of coffee he'd asked for quite some time ago.

"Well, I'm sure this doesn't involve me," Elisha started to get up and gather her purse. "Thanks for dinner, and I'll see you around."

"Wait!" Elvis stopped her. "This most certainly involves you dear. Sit Down!."

Elisha looked surprised and sat down immediately, as if she were stunned that Elvis addressed her that way and told her to 'sit down.' She thought about the demand and started to grow a little angry and just walk away despite the rude demand. But the charm of Elvis' calming voice lured her attention and captivated her curiosity and she quickly lost the thought of bitterness. Elvis ask her about herself, and she spun an elaborate story of a sales girl who spent her off hours in different cities trying to find gentlemen to have dinner with. Sunny sat in sullen silence, still smarting about how Elvis had just trivialized his entire experience and then flaunted the perp in front of him all through dinner-a meal he had planned when he intended to spend the evening with Elisha himself.

Sunny hadn't missed the way Elisha was growing more and more drawn to Elvis, and he was ticked off that this evening was turning out the way it was. Elvis had little to say other than to comment quietly on aspects of Elisha's well-rehearsed story, and Sunny couldn't believe that Elvis seemed to take the con queen's scam at face value.

"He's either and idiot or completely naïve!" Sunny thought to himself as he finished up his last bit of steak and waited for whatever nuggets of brilliance were going to come out of the man who kidnapped him and subjected him to the humiliation of being cheated by a fishnet-wearing con artist.

"There's something I need to do," Elvis continued. "And I need your help to do it--both of you."

"Ummm…I don't know either of you," Elisha Started.

"And I don't think I'll be hanging out with you anytime soon. Thanks for dinner!" She began to rise out of her seat once again, but Elvis put up his hand and she slowly sank back into her chair.

"You don't have to 'hang with us," Elvis said the words as if he was unfamiliar with the terminology. "But, can I ask if you will work with me and help me accomplish the project I need to complete in the short amount of time that I will be here."

Elisha stared intently out the window for a second then drawing her attention back to Elvis before the realization hit her. "Oh! I get it….I'm so sorry to hear that you're terminal. My uncle just passed from cancer of the pancreas, and I know it can go downhill so quickly!"

Elvis looked surprised and confused as well, as he observed Elisha's dramatic flair. "I know what you're going to say." Elisha continued, laying a hand softly on Elvis' arm as if in sympathy. "And I'm so sorry your having to go through this horrible ordeal." I'm sure we can help you find a good home for the rest of your money. There are many good people out there who could use your help, and I'm just the person to find them for you…"

She looked pointedly at Sunny, who sent a smoldering look back at her before almost exploding with laughter. "You're serious!?" he snorted. "You think he's dying and you're going to just 'help' him spend all his money. I'm sure you'd just LOVE that!"

Elisha's confidence looked a bit shaken as she looked back at Elvis and she retracted her hand from his arm as if she realized that she might be a victim of a scam this time. Elvis chucked.

"I declare a truce," Elvis smiled at the both of them. "You really are very much alike, you know." Sunny and Elisha looked warily at each other, as they had been doing all evening, but not at all convinced that they had anything in common other than irritation and distrust.

"Look," Elvis began again. "Sunny already knows some of this stuff, but I'm only here for another 38 days, and I have a rather significant message to get out to the general public in that amount of time. I need the world to realize who I am, get some concert dates, and spread the word."

Elisha didn't speak. She looked at Sunny and then back at Elvis. Sunny forgot that he was ticked off at Elisha. His focus was on Elvis and what he thought of what was yet to come.

"Okay, let me get this straight," he leaned toward Elvis.

"You came back to do some more concerts…getting low on cash up there?" he pointed to the ceiling with barely concealed sarcasm.

"Does everything in the world revolve around money for you?" Elvis asked Sunny, and then looked over at Elisha, who returns a blank stare at Elvis, as if she was mesmerized by the conversation. Elvis continued, "I realize you are in need of some training, but sometimes you surprise me."

Sunny wasn't about to let that go, "Excuse me, but you drop out of the sky, looking like you've lost a few pounds but otherwise you're the same old, out-of-date rock star you were when you croaked, and you want to go on tour right away. What are we supposed to think?"

Elisha's face showed her obvious surprise at Sunny's retaliation toward Elvis and Elvis held his composure his face flickered with silent irritation for a moment before he took a breath and answered.

"Okay, let's see if we can start at the beginning," he tried to keep his voice level. "When I picked you up in the desert," he began, "I told you that I had a job to do, and I only had 40 days here to do it. Do you remember that conversation?"

"I remember that I picked YOU up in the desert," Sunny retorted. "After that, it gets a bit fuzzy."

"Well, I'm sure it's clearer than you think," Elvis continued.

Elisha swallowed before trying to speak. "You're…you're… Elvis? The Elvis? How can it be? "She whispered, almost reverently. Elvis looked at her and smiled briefly in affirmation before refocusing on Sunny.

"I need to get a message out to the world, Sunny. I've been chosen to do this because of my ability to appeal to the largest audience possible, but I need your help to get it done in the next 38 days," Elvis explained carefully. "If the lure of easy money serves as a carrot to get you to jump on the bandwagon and help me out…" Elvis glanced at Elisha as he spoke," then I'll take that help any way I can get it at this point. We have a lot of work to do."

Sunny sat back taking it all in, it was his turn to be astonished by what Elvis was suggesting. And Elisha, not one to lose control of a moment that might benefit her financially or any other way, leaned forward to speak. "I'll do whatever I can, but I need to earn a living while we're doing this …whatever this is," she fished for whatever words she could to sound like a willing participant in the venture.

"Thank you, Elisha, for being brave enough to take on a venture like this." Elvis smiled at her, putting his hand over hers. I will reward you handsomely."

Elisha smiled back at him and retracted herself in the chair and appeared more at ease. Obviously, the idea of a sugar daddy was comforting to her. Sunny looked over at her with a smirk on his face as if he could read her mind.

"Now, I suggest we retire upstairs and start thinking of ways to get started," Elvis motioned to the waiter for the check. Then, looking back and forth at Elisha and Sunny, he added "and I expect the two of you to work together as if there were no history between you. We don't have time for distractions."

CHAPTER FIVE

Back at the Peabody overlooking the city of Memphis, Elvis sat deep in thought. Completely focused, he tapped his fingers rhythmically on the small cherry table as he pondered his circumstances and the road set out before him. Even for someone who was obviously used to the surreal, this adventure was so far out of the ordinary that it required some subjective thought to make sense of it all-or at least to stay upright and not falter in the face of what he was being asked to do.

Elisha had the remote and was flipping through the channels on the 65-inch plasma that threatened to take over the room. Sunk into the cream-colored overstuffed suede sofa, and her feet up on the ornate mahogany coffee table that graced the space between the couch and the huge television, Elisha's bare feet with impeccably painted red toenails were moving in almost the same rhythm as Elvis' tapping. Even with the TV muted, it was like the two of them were following the same drummer or listening to the same music. All that was missing were the earphones connected to IPods.

Sunny was stretched out on the matching cream-colored suede sofa that sat at an angle to the one on which Elisha sat, snoring softly as his body tried to recover from days of driving. As weird and whacked out as this situation was so far, he had finally succumbed to exhaustion and were dreaming wild dreams of Arthur Fonzarelli falling out of the sky into Arnold's diner with four vivacious girls clinging to him. Muttering to himself off and on as he snoozed, the rest of the room's occupants seemed oblivious to him and whatever was spilling out of his overtired mouth.

Suddenly, Elvis got up, grabbed some hotel stationary and a pen from the roll-top desk near Elisha's couch and returned to the dining room table. Sitting back down, he began scribbling furiously, still without saying a word. Elisha looked up briefly as Elvis breezed by, but then resumed her channel-surfing as soon as he was back at the table.

After a few moments, Elvis looked up and spoke for the first time in what had seemed like hours. "We have to find someone who's willing to go on the record and confirm who I am," he started. "That's what we have to do." Elisha looked over at Sunny, who chose that moment to roll over noisily, mumbling about Mrs. Cunningham's cooking. Looking over at Elvis, who was still scribbling like crazy, she poked at Sunny with her fare foot. When that didn't elicit a response, she jabbed at him harder. Only on the third try did she get a reaction, when Sunny swung his body around in a sleep-induced reaction and fell off the couch onto the floor with a thud.

"What the f---?!" he grunted loudly and pushed himself up on his elbows to look around for his assailant. The first face he saw of course was Elisha's, and his confused look quickly changed to one of barely concealed contempt. Elisha's pretty blues glared right back at him for several moments before she motioned toward Elvis with a nod of her head.

"And you woke me up for....?!" Sunny growled as he looked from Elisha over at Elvis. Sitting up on his knees, he waited as if he might somehow get a response to that question from the owner of the steel toes before getting to this feet and navigating around the couch to approach Elvis at the table.

"What do you want?"

"I think I know what we need to do," Elvis answered distractedly, and we need to start by finding someone in the music industry that will recognize me, understand that it is indeed me, and then go on record to help me convince the rest of the world."

"On record- that's funny!!" Sunny guffawed, starting to slap his thigh in mock humor before realizing that Elvis wasn't laughing. Stopping his guffaw in mid laugh, Sunny pulled out another chair at the table, slumped into it, and watched Elvis as he continued to scribble on the hotel stationary pad. For some reason, he found himself resenting the entire situation.

"And how do you expect we'll do that?" Sunny asked. "Especially in 36 or whatever days?"

"That's your job, Sunny." Elvis dropped on him absently, still writing.

"My job?" Retorted Sunny. "Now look, chump! You drop out of the sky into my miserable worthless life and start telling me I have 40 days to convince the world that you're you. Has it occurred to you that I haven't got a clue how to do that?"

Elvis looked up calmly for a moment. "I think it's your destiny to help me, Sunny."

"Destiny, my ass!" Sunny choked. "You can talk about your destiny and quests and visions and whatever the hell you have to do, but don't talk to me like you know anything about me!"

Sunny stopped talking, as if he realized he was out of line, and sat there sullen and brooding. Elvis just observed him for a moment before speaking again. "Sunny, I know that your destiny is not preordained. And it's not even guaranteed that you will help me. What I do know, however, is that I have faith in you and the path that you will take, and I believe that it will lead you along the same journey I am taking"

Sunny's expression lightened somewhat as he found himself mesmerized by a man who until about three days ago had been dead and buried and immortalized by millions. The guy certainly had a strange effect on people.

"Whether or not you continue down the same path after my time here is done remains to be seen," Elvis continued as he folded his paper in half. "But I think you're going to surprise yourself over the next several weeks.'

Sunny glanced over at Elisha, who was still flipping through the channels as if she had nothing better to do. Where was the cold, calculating woman who had taken off with all his cash just a few hours ago, anyway" She certainly didn't act like she understood how significant it was that she was sharing a hotel suite with the King of Rock and Roll. "What about her, then?" he asked Elvis. "Is she 'walking the same path' too?"

"That's up to her," Elvis answered. "We each walk separate paths, Sunny. Whether or not we walk them side by side is up to you and Elisha, not me."

Sunny shook his head. "All this philosophy crap..." he muttered, "way too touchy feely for me!"

"You may change your mind one of these days, Sunny," Elvis grinned as he got up and pushed in his chair. "Every man is changed by the people he meets-and the people he helps."

"I think you have got the wrong impression of me," Sunny responded. "I've never helped a soul in my life. It's all about me, you know. But I'm sure you already know that. If I help you, it's because I can see something in it for me. That's all!"

Elvis smirked as he started searching in desk drawers.

"Whatever you say, Sunny. Help me find a phone book."

Surprisingly, Sunny got up immediately to help him and caught himself instantly, covering a wry smile as he realized he hadn't hesitated in the slightest when Elvis asked for help. After a brief search, a Memphis phone book was located in a kitchenette drawer and Sunny tossed it on the table. Bringing the phone with him, he placed it where Elvis had been sitting then Elvis motioned for Sunny to retake his seat.

"What?" Sunny questioned before following Elvis' directions.

"I need you to find me a radio station." Elvis instructed. "… one that has a soft spot for me and some dead air space to fill."

"Seriously?!" Sunny frowned at him. "Now I'm your booking agent?"

"Whatever you want it to be, Sunny." Elvis smiled. "You can tell them you're my agent, my lawyer, or my best friend. Just call them."

Sunny sat for a moment before grabbing the phone book, as he started to flip through the Yellow pages. Elvis walked slowly over to the cream-colored couch and stood behind Elisha as she watched an infomercial. His hand reached forward as if to touch her hair, and then he paused, as if he wasn't sure it was an appropriate move. Elisha froze, and Elvis dropped his arm and he continued toward the large picture window at the far end of the room. Elisha visibly relaxed and Elvis stood by the window looking out over the city of Memphis. "This is exactly what I had a problem with before; I couldn't keep my hands off of women.

Was it because I was being tempted by Satan or just my carnal ways? I don't know but I do know for sure that I can't even think about a woman in that way, I have to deny my flesh during this tenure or I surely would be condemned to Hell….I promised

Jesus, I have to keep my promise to Jesus, there will be no more chances after this. I'm sure." Elvis contemplated to himself while looking out the window at the skyline of Memphis. Sunny's voyage through the Yellow Pages was the only sound in the room for several minutes before he finally spoke.

"I found it!" he nearly shouted. "This is the station we want."

Elvis looked over at him from the window. "What makes you think that?" he asked. "Which station is it?"

"WHAL," Sunny answered. "Gospel."

Elvis smiled. "I appreciate your zeal for finding your inner Elvis, but don't you think a current rock and roll station might be a better first choice?"

Sunny grinned mischievously as he swiveled around in his chair to look at Elvis and Elisha. "current rock and roll stations won't touch Elvis tunes, my friend," he chuckled.

"You may be the King of Rock and Roll, but most of the current generation won't listen to your stuff--it's out of date!"

Elvis frowned briefly before looking at Elisha. "What do you think, Elisha?"

Elisha turned on the couch and looked at them both.

"You're asking me?"

"Yes."

Elisha stared back at them as they waited for her reply, obviously trying to figure out what to say. Finally, she went with her gut reaction.

"I have no idea what station to start with, "she shrugged.

"I'm just the resident 'ho!' Call them both and see what reaction you get and go to the one who laughs the least!"

Elvis smiled, obviously pleased with her answer. "I agree," he said, turning to Sunny. "Call whoever comes first in the phone book and keep calling until you find someone who takes us seriously."

Sunny snorted in a mixture of frustration and sarcasm.

"Yeah, like she knows anything about anything!" He turned back to the Yellow Pages and flipped the pages back and forth for a moment before grabbing the phone and dialing. He only had to wait a minute for someone to pick up.

"Uh, hell," he started. "My name is Sunny Carlisle, and I'm calling to talk to your station manager about scheduling an on-air interview with Elvis." Sunny listened to the person on the other end for a moment before replying. "Yes, ma'am. THE Elvis!!!. I'm his manager…" Sunny looked over at Elvis, who smiled. "… and he's looking for an interview on a Memphis station within the next 12-24 hours."

Another moment went by and then Sunny slowly placed the receiver back on its cradle. He looked over at Elvis and then Elisha, both of whom looked back at him expectantly.

"I don't think they took me seriously," he explained, lowering his eyes. "Guess I'll try the next one." Sunny picked up the phone several more times and replaced the receiver each time with increasing frustration. "Dammit!" he swore after the fifth call. "This just isn't going to work!"

"Keep trying, Sunny," Elvis replied. He came over to stand by Sunny at the table and Elisha turned off the television and walked over to the table to watch the progress.

"Is this some kind of test?" Sunny asked Elvis as his hand reached for the phone again... "If it is, I can tell you right now that I'm going to fail. They think I'm full of shit! And I don't blame them!"

"All we can do is try," answered Elvis confidently.

"Yeah, right," Sunny answered.

Another couple of phone calls and he slammed the receiver down. "That's it! They think I'm nuts!" Sunny got up, grabbed his jacket, and headed for the door. Elvis and Elisha stood watching him—Elvis with concern, Elisha with a self-satisfied smirk on her face.

A shared glance with Elvis, however, and Elisha wiped the smug look off her face and looked away.

"Sunny! Where are you going?" Elvis called after him.

"Me? You mean 'we'!" Sunny turned, opened the door, and stood waiting for them. "We're not going to waste any more time on the phone. If I can't make them believe me on the phone, we have to change the plan."

"If the mountain won't come to Muhammad..." Elvis began.

".. Then Muhammad must go to the mountain," finished Elisha. With a shared grin, Elvis and Elisha each grabbed their coats and left the room ahead of Sunny, who closed the door behind him with a resounding thump.

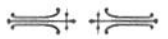

CHAPTER SIX

Sunny's Cutlass pulled up in front of a three story brick walk-up with a small sign out front with the call letters "WHAL" scrawled across it in faded red ink. Obviously this radio station had seen its share of struggle-either that or nobody gave a rat's ass about first impressions!

Sunny hopped out of the car without opening the door and headed around the car toward the front of the building.

Elvis opened his door and stepped out of the car, but turned to pull the seat forward for Elisha before following Sunny into the building. Sunny entered the building without waiting for his two companions and began walking through the offices, looking for someone to talk with. Gold and platinum albums, concert posters a variety of acts graced the walls of the station, and Sunny couldn't help but be a bit impressed at the photos of many famous faces that were framed and nestled in between the records and posters. Obviously this station had been around for a while.

A young Girl Friday, jumped up from a desk as Sunny strode through the office, obviously unnerved by his appearance in the otherwise quiet studio.

"Excuse me, sir," she started, trying to stop him from making his way through one office after another. "You can't just help yourself to the office. You need to make an appointment..."

Sunny paid no attention to her as he continued on his search, nimbly casting the receptionist aside as he went. One more closed door, and he had found what he wanted. Standing in the doorway for a moment, Sunny observed a dark haired man about his own age synching up CDs and making notes in a logbook.

Obviously the DJ of the hour, the jockey looked like he'd just stepped out of the cast of HAIR, and was absorbed with what he was doing and didn't realize that Sunny was watching him.

Suddenly the receptionist pushed past Sunny into the small room and stood with her arms crossed in front of Sunny, who wasn't paying her any attention.

"You have to leave now," she ordered, and pointed a finger back out the door. "You have NO RIGHT to be in here!"

"Oh, I have every right to be here," Sunny answered, finally looking at her for the first time. The small frame receptionist didn't look a day over 15 years old. Her reddish hair with dark highlights and little freckles scattered about her face. She wore a tight fitting white halter top with the top three buttons undone revealing a hint of her brandish little teats and a cute black and red checkered skirt with white stockings and black heels to boot. "I've been trying to talk to the station manager for over an hour and obviously the only way to get his attention is to drive over here and meet him face-to-face." "We have rules!" the young Girl Friday, shouted, finally attracting the attention of the man behind the thick glass of the station's studio. "You need to leave before I call the police!"

"Go call the police, little lady," Sunny smirked and then smiled sheepishly realizing how cut the girl was, then suddenly masking his smile with a serious look "That will give me time to talk to the gentleman behind you."

The young Girl Friday looked over her shoulder and exchanged a glance with the DJ before shifting her hands to her hips. "I'm sure you'd like that," she growled. "...but you're not getting any closer."

"Sunny made eye contact with the DJ and arched one eyebrow. "This isn't a hold up and I'm not a crazy fan," he barked without dropping his eyes to the girl. "I need to schedule a station interview with my client, and I need it to happen today!"

"Your client?" the DJ asked as he slipped out from behind the glass and approached Sunny and Girl Friday. He was obviously being cautious, but also seemed interested in diffusing the situation if at all possible.

"Yeah," Sunny answered. "My client wants to be interviewed on the air, and you're his first choice. Why, I have no idea, but you are."

The DJ looked intrigued, and extended his hand slowly to Sunny. "I'm Solange Ledoux. the station manager here."

Sunny shook the DJ's hand briefly before he looked back at the young Girl Friday, who was still clearly in a defensive posture between the two men. Solange gave her a look, and Girl Friday after looking back and forth between them several times as if to read the situation for herself, she dropped her arms and sneaked past Sunny to leave the small room.

"I'll be right outside," she murmured, with a pointed look at Solange as she left. Sunny laughed a little under his breath being slightly amused by the little Girl Friday. It seems so strange her looking like a kid but having an attitude of a furious Lion.

"So," Solange began, motioning Sunny over to a small desk just outside the studio windows. "Who's this mystery client that is so insistent on speaking with me?" Sunny moved to the desk with him, but showed no interest in sitting. Instead, he took a quick look behind him, wondering where Elvis and Elisha had ended up, since they had obviously not followed him into the studio.

"I know you're going to think I'm crazy," he began, "but I've teamed up with this guy… a guy you'll recognize, but you won't believe it's him."

Solange sat on the edge of the desk and looked at him expectantly, waiting for him to continue.

"Uhh… anyway, this guy has an announcement that he needs to get on the air," Sunny paused for a moment, trying to find a way to introduce Elvis without sounding like a lunatic.

Just then, however, Solange attention was slightly diverted. His eyes widened and then a frown played with his eyebrows as his whole body focused on something just over Sunny's shoulder. He looked quickly at Sunny and then back at the doorway, and Sunny knew immediately what he was staring at.

"Solange?" he announced without even a glance over his shoulder. "May I introduce you to Elvis?"

Solange's mouth dropped open, and Sunny wasted no time as he went for the kill. "I'm sure you will want to discuss terms with me now," he started, "now that you understand the full ramifications of this situation."

Solange got up from the desk and moved slowly over toward where Elvis stood in the doorway. As he moved, he stared intently at the singer, as if sizing up every feature as he drew closer. Elvis, seeming to understand the DJ's need to analyze the moment, remained motionless, his eyes locked on Solange. Finally, Solange stopped directly in front of Elvis and made eye contact for the first time.

"Hello,." Elvis broke the silence.

"My God!" Solange breathed, as he realized the voice and intonations were genuine.

"No, not God." Elvis responded with his characteristically crooked smile. "But God did send me here with a message, that I really need your help to deliver. Can you help us?"

Solange chuckled, not moving his eyes from Elvis' face. "Right!!" he scoffed, and then just as quickly realized that nobody else in the room found that funny at all. "Uhh, seriously, what's this all about?"

Solange looked closely at Elvis, trying to determine how much of him was genuine and how much was a cleverly engineered fake. There was just no way that this was the real deal! Elisha and Sunny watched Solange, both their faces registering amusement as they let him go through the motions just as they had only hours earlier.

Solange stopped studying Elvis, yet didn't seem convinced of his authenticity.

"Solange," Elvis began. "I need a few minutes of your time and your airwaves. Think you can help me?"

Solange looked startled. "What are you talking about?"

"I have a message I need to get out to the public, and radio is my best option at this point. Can you help me out?"

"What message?" Solange asked, suspicious.

"Do you believe in God, Solange?" Elvis asked softly.

Solange stared at Elvis without answering.

"Do you, Solange?"

"Well, yeah! It's the Bible Belt – everyone believes in God." Solange answered with a snort.

Elvis frowned but continued. "If you believe in God, then you believe in miracles, too."

"I guess so, but get to the point! I don't have all day and I certainly can't put you on the air without knowing who you are and what this message thing is all about!"

Elvis put his hand on Solange shoulder and looked briefly at Elisha and Sunny before addressing Solange again.

"Whether you believe it or not, I am who you think I might be. I was sent here from Heaven to spread the Word that Jesus will be returning soon to rid the world of greed and vice and corruption." Elvis stopped for a moment as Solange began to look more skeptical. "I'm like the warning shot from God, man. This world is messed up and I have 40 days..."

Elvis looked at a calendar on the wall. "...make that 36 days... to make sure as many people as possible hear that they have this last chance to redeem themselves before he comes back."

Solange backed away a step or two as he took this all in, not sure whether or not to believe anything he was seeing or hearing.

"Okay, man... this is just a bit too much! You're way out on a limb there," Solange started. "Jesus? You sent back from Heaven? Naaahhhh..."

Sunny stepped forward. "Look, guy. I'm kinda struggling with this whole deal myself, too. Some of it just seems surreal, ya know? But he's the real thing. There's no doubt in my mind. Once you get past that, it's easy to hear the rest, even if you don't really get into it."

Solange looked at Sunny and then back at Elvis, still struck by the reality of the King of Rock and Roll standing in his radio station. After a few moments of silence as he absorbed all the information, Solange's face broke out into a wide smile.

"Okay, okay," he acknowledged. "Either you're the real thing and how you got here is going to take lots of grey matter to understand, or you're the best damn fake Elvis I've ever seen in my life!" Solange moved over to his glassed-in studio and opened the door. Over his shoulder he said "Whichever it is, I have a bombshell that the world should hear about. We'll set everybody on their ears and let them figure it out!"

Elvis looked over at Sunny and Elisha as if to say "get lost" and moved to join Solange in the small studio. Sunny and Elisha faded back into the depths of the radio station with Girl Friday and Elvis focused on his introduction to the world.

"A couple of things..." Solange started, as he settled Elvis into the only other chair inside the studio. "You're gonna have to sing a song or two so they know it's you... and that whole 'message from God' thing. You're gonna have to tone that down a bit. Don't hit them over the head with it. Believe me, you're gonna need to ease people into it!"

"You got it,"

"I got it," replied Elvis.

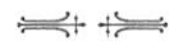

CHAPTER SEVEN

In the hustle of the Memphis Police Department, no one noticed the hum of the fax machine on Sergeant Yalom's credenza. The paper threaded itself through the equipment like a snake winding its way through the treetop canopy of the Amazon jungle. When the machine stopped, the sheet of paper lying face up in the tray showed a photograph of a late model Oldsmobile Cutlass with a beat-up license plate showing amid the clouds of dust that were kicked up around the car. The name "Sunny Carlisle" was typed across the top, right under the words "All Points Bulletin."

A few minutes later, a young female officer, Miss Adamczak, was parading around once again in a tight mini skirt and every head turned each time she had to bend over—obviously more interested in the cell phone call she was on than what was going on in the office—picked up the stack that was laying in the fax machine's paper tray and tossed it on another officer's desk without even looking at it. Sunny's car stared up at the ceiling for all to see... for anyone who was looking, that is.

The station, the big burly Sergeant with extra rolls of fat around his mid-section, a big conk and a receding hair line and all the officers obviously had more important things on the mind, than some want -a -be Elvis Impersonator doing doughnuts at some rinky –dink pub outside of Vegas. Sergeant Yalum's reputation was built on fighting thieves and murderers, as the Chief of organized crime at the NYPD Shomrim Society, not some show off punk who is in desperate need of attention. He grabs the fax paper from Officer Dudley's hand, "You're not working on this you hear me, and I want you on the Henley murder at Tobey Park." "Yes Sergeant," quipped the officer.

Sergeant Yalom walked straight to his office and slammed the door behind him. He thought to himself," I've got a bunch of numb brains in this precinct, Lord Help me please, Time for some relaxation."

He places his ear buds from his MP3 player in his ears, and leans back in his recliner as soft sounds of Mozart resonate through his brain.

While drifting in a dream for a moment, he heard the telephone ring and opened one eye, "Lord Jesus, can't I just get a little peace around here?" He reluctantly picks up the phone. "Hello Sergeant Yalom at your pecking call."

"Sergeant Yalom this is Captain Andy Parker from the Las Vegas Police Department Did you receive the APB over the wire yet? We have reason to believe the Elvis Imposter is in Memphis." "Yes Captain Andy Griffith we have everything under control." "Excuse me Sergeant but my name is Andy Parker, not Griffith."

"Oh my apologies Captain I had you confused with someone else." Sergeant Yalom pulled the phone away from his ear and he could hear the Captain gabbing on through the receiver, he stared at it a few more seconds and then slammed the phone down. "Damn I'm getting tired of hearing about all this Elvis crap, there is more important stuff going on in this world than an Elvis Impersonator on the loose, give me a freaking break." He places his ear buds back in ear, kicks back and continues to enjoy the religious overtones of Mozart.

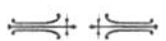

Sunny and Elisha were comfortably ensconced on a couch in the outer office of the studio, listening to Elvis knock out Blue Kentucky Rain over the interoffice studio feed. Elisha seemed to be asleep, but her foot was beating a rhythm to the tune, but Sunny seemed a bit tenser. His pencil-tapping was about to drive Girl Friday crazy, and she told him so.

"Sorry," Sunny muttered, sitting up to hunch over the pencil as if he was getting ready to jump up out of his chair. He was coiled like a spring, waiting for Elvis to start back up with his "message." The whole situation was feeling a bit surreal to him again, and Solange's words about "easing into the message" had struck a chord with him.

"Ali, you awake?" he whispered to Elisha so Girl Friday couldn't hear him.

"Don't call me 'Ali'," she replied quickly.

"Whatever. Do you think this whole Jesus coming back thing is a little too much?"

Without moving a muscle, Elisha replied "It's not up to us to decide if it's too much or not. We promised to help and that's what we do. We don't analyze."

"Yeah, but don't you think it's a little embarrassing to be fronting a guy who has such a ridiculous claim?" Sunny pressed on. "I mean, I have to worry about credibility. I'm not sure the 'hit them with it all at once' approach is gonna work for him."

Again without moving, Elisha answered "He only has 36 more days. I don't think he has time to be subtle."

"Yeah, but I don't think he has time to hit them over the head with the whole 'you have X amount of time to clean up your act or you will face the wrath of God' and then clean up all the pieces of that before they believe him, either," Sunny retorted.

"Leave it to him, Sunny." Elisha warned. "We're just the worker bees, remember?"

Elvis finished singing and the interview started back up. Elvis had already explained how he was the genuine Elvis Presley and had returned from Heaven to spread a message of God's love and understanding in a time of trial and turbulence. Sunny knew that, as strange as that sounded, it was the least of the craziness that he was about to discuss, and Sunny braced himself for the announcement.

"Okay, Mr. Elvis," Solange began after Elvis finished the song. "You mentioned that you had a message for the people of the world. What exactly do you mean?"

Elvis looked pensive for a moment as he took Solange's warning about being too blunt into consideration, and then decided against fancy words and explanations. Plunging right into the heart of the matter, Elvis began.

"I have been sent by God to foretell the second coming of Christ," he said. Solange's face registered a moment of panic, knowing what a furor that would instantly create for him.

"Our world is racked by corruption, greed, selfishness, and hatred," Elvis continued. "The Son of God is returning to deal with all of it, but he has sent me back first to warn those who transgress that they have a finite period of time to mend their ways."

"Mend their ways?" Solange repeated, ignoring the lights that were starting to blink on his phone system. "Like, what do they have to do?"

"My job does not involve telling people how to behave," Elvis answered, with just a hint of frustration. "I simply am here to deliver a message through words and music. People will just have to use the information and the sentiment with which it's offered and make their own way."

Solange leaned back, engrossed in the concept for a moment, before speaking again.

"So you're just spreading a message -- say, of hope and redemption -- before the heavy hitters arrive to start meting out justice and sentences?"

"I can't tell you what will come after me," Elvis replied patiently. "I can only tell you that I have been sent here on a mission. I am here to spread the word that what is happening here at this time is flawed and headed for disaster, and that humankind should take some time to reassess its path and chart a different course before it's too late."

"Wow!" Solange breathed loudly enough for the microphone to pick it up. "This is pretty heavy stuff for this early in the morning!" He glanced at his phone system, which was flashing like the lights on his grandmother's Christmas tree. Knowing he would never be able to recover if he started to take calls, he grasped at a way to stall that piece of his job and still keep the King of Rock and Roll at his microphone.

"So, Elvis. What is your plan for telling the world about what you're doing," Solange asked quickly, "And how are you going to deal with the hordes of people who aren't going to believe that you're really the King?"

Elvis smiled his crooked grin confidently and leaned back a bit in his chair before he leaned toward the mic to reply. "Once they see me, and see me perform, there will be no more questions about my authenticity," he answered.

"Well, folks…" Solange decided to wrap up. "I think we'll conclude this interview with a final song. I apologize for not taking your calls, but I'm overwhelmed enough with all that has transpired today. I'm not sure I can handle the drama of fielding questions today on top of it all. Mr. Elvis?"

"I'd be happy to," Elvis replied. "How about 'How Great Thou Art?"

"Whatever floats your boat, man!" Solange said with a grin as he sat back to listen.

Less than 30 minutes later, Elvis and Sunny stepped into the hallway outside the studio with Solange and Elisha close behind. Girl Friday was valiantly trying to answer phone calls from the desk in the front room, and not having much luck. Elvis turned to face Solange as Sunny walked the short distance to the front door on his way to get the car.

"Thank you so much for agreeing to interview me," Elvis began, holding his hand out to Solange, who grasped it warmly for a shake.

"The pleasure was all mine, Mr. Elvis," Solange answered. "I hope everything works out for you… and your crew," he said, with a nod toward Elisha and the retreating Sonny.

"It's 'Elvis,' and I have no doubt that my mission will be successful," Elvis replied. "Especially when I have the help of professionals such as yourself."

Solange chuckled and glanced back at the intern who was still struggling with the phones. "Well, sir, I'm not sure how much help I was. The calls we're getting peg you somewhere between a freak show and a reincarnation! I'm not sure what you are, but you sure seem like the real deal to me."

"Thank you, Solange." Elvis smiled. "You'll be hearing from me again before it's all over, I'm sure."

"It would be my pleasure," Solange grinned as Elvis and Elisha turned to head toward the outside door. Solange watched them walk down the hallway to the front door of the building before stepping back into the studio office to face his assistant. The look on her face said it all. What had just happened?!

After a moment of silence, Girl Friday spoke first. "You don't really believe that he...."

Solange interrupted immediately. "I don't have a clue what I believe!" he snapped quickly, and ducked through the doorway to escape to the solitude of the studio and the barrage of calls and emails he was sure he would find waiting for him there.

Elvis and Elisha stepped out into the bright sunlight from the dim space in the interior corridor of the office building, they blinked rapidly and tried to shield their eyes while they fished out their sunglasses. They didn't see the small crowd of 10 or 15 people who were gathered on the sidewalk at the foot of the stairs.

"Elvis, Elvis!" started almost instantly, and completely caught them off guard. "Is that really you?!" one woman screamed, and Elvis looked startled as she started up the stairs as if to touch him. Just at that moment, Sunny pulled up in the Cutlass, somewhat scattering the small group as he did so.

"Get in!" he hollered at Elvis and Elisha as he swung open the passenger side door of the vehicle. "Let's get out of here!"

Elvis and Elisha wasted no time jumping down off the brick steps and into the car, brushing off several people who clung to them on the way down. "Don't go!" shouted a woman, and a man grabbed onto the side mirror as if to prevent the car from leaving. It was all a bit too surreal for Elisha, who scrambled into the back seat of the car as Elvis pried the man's fingers from the mirror and then flashed a look to Sunny that gave him permission to floor it!

Sunny reacted with split second timing, planting his foot on the gas pedal without hesitation and peeling out of the space in front of the studio as if his life depended on it.

The car sped away, leaving the jilted fans choking on dust and exhaust as they came to grips with the fact that they'd just seen a ghost.

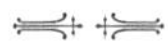

The trio of travelers entered the hotel suite shortly thereafter, and both Elisha and Sunny immediately claimed spots on the couches in front of the Vizio monstrosity on one side of the large living area. Elvis stood in the entryway of the large room, watching the two of them as they seemed to be settling in for a lengthy stay.

"Don't you DARE turn on NASCAR!" Elisha warned Sunny when he grabbed the remote before she could get to it. "I watched enough of that last night to kill a cat!"

"You loved it and you know it!" Sunny retorted as he kicked off his boots and put his feet up on the coffee table.

"Yeah, right!" Elisha would give no quarter this afternoon. "I put up with all those endless left-turns all afternoon yesterday. It's MY turn to use the equipment!"

Sunny and Elisha glared at each other for what seemed like several minutes before Sunny finally gave in. "Whatever!" he snarled, and pulled his arm back as if he was going to toss her the remote.

"Elisha." Elvis' soft but resonant voice cut through the room like a knife through butter, stopping both Sunny and Elisha like statues before they could even exchange a look.

"Elisha." Elvis spoke again.

"Yes?" Elisha answered, looking straight at him. "Is something wrong?"

"Let's go for a ride," Elvis answered, without any elaboration.

"Uhh... what about the radio show?" Sunny responded, not sure what this was all about. "Aren't we supposed to wait for a phone call from a promoter?"

Elvis looked at Sunny with a wry smile. "Do you really think anyone is going to call me with a concert proposal after one radio show?" he asked as if he found Sunny's question a bit silly. "All we did this afternoon was break the ice. It's back to the phones for you, I'm afraid."

Sunny groaned and dropped the remote on the couch cushion beside him as he got up off the couch. Walking around the couch and back toward Elvis in the doorway, he tried valiantly to change the dynamics in the room.

"So, this is where the rubber meets the road," he started. "I get to stay here, working my ass off with nimwits on the phone who think we're crazy at best and possibly some kind of alien invaders at worst, and you two are gonna take a joy ride in the countryside?! I don't think so!"

"Let's go," he ordered, turning around to leave. Elisha picked up her purse off the coffee table and moved to follow him out the door without argument. Elvis looked over his shoulder at Sunny as he opened the hotel room door and said, "I expect you to have several more shows lined up for tomorrow by the time we get back."

Elisha looked back at Sunny as Elvis exited the room, and Sunny wiggled his eyebrows at her in a knowing way, as if he was insinuating what Elvis' real motives were for taking Elisha away from the hotel. Elisha reddened and frowned back at him before turning with a flip of her hair and following Elvis out of the room.

Sunny waited for a moment after the door closed before kicking out at one of the chairs in the dining area in disgust. "Damn!" he growled. "Leave it to a broad to get out of all the work!" Obviously disgusted by the turn of events, Sunny paced over to the window and watched the busy Memphis street below as he fidgeted with nervous energy. After a few minutes, however, he visibly relaxed and moved back over to the kitchen. Snagging a cold beer out of the fridge, Sunny picked up the phone book he had been using earlier and the remote he had let drop on the couch, and sauntered over to the spot where Elisha had planned to take up residence for the afternoon. Phone in hand, phone book on the coffee table, and several swigs of the beer already ingested, Sunny picked up the remote and switched on the television.

"No NASCAR, huh?" he said under his breath as he hit the mute button on the remote. "It's my room this afternoon, so it's MY rules, baby!"

And with that, he flipped open the phone book to the dog-eared section he had been working through earlier that day when everyone he called had laughed at everything he had had to say. This time, however, he expected it to be different.

Elvis was silent as he led the way outside the hotel lobby onto the sidewalk. Elisha wasn't sure what they were doing or where they were going, so she was silent all the way down in the elevator and across the lobby out into the sunshine.

The first thing that caught her eye once they were outside, however, was a gorgeous Eagle Rider parked against the curb, as if it was waiting for someone. Two helmets were sitting on the seat, and the key was in the ignition.

"Wow!" she exclaimed without thinking. Elvis smiled and led them straight to the bike.

"Is this yours? Where did it come from?" she asked, almost breathless.

"The Lord works in mysterious ways," Elvis answered with a twinkle in his eye. Elisha gave him an "I can't believe you just said that" look as he picked up the two helmets and tossed one to her. "C'mon, let's go have some fun!"

"This could cost you," warned Elisha.

"I doubt that," Elvis answered with his famous smirk. "But if it does, I'm sure it'll be worth it."

The miles flew by on the motorcycle, with Elvis' songs piped into the helmets through the state-of-the-art sound system on the Eagle Rider. The streets of the city had finally given way to the country highways outside of town as they sailed along at a steady speed.

Elisha had no idea where they were going, only that she was enjoying the ride and was finding herself drawn to this mysterious leather-jacketed ghost who seemed very real to her right now. Her arms were wrapped around his waist as they screamed down the country roads outside Memphis, and he definitely "felt" real to her. There was nothing ghostly about this man, at least not at the moment.

Finally, after what seemed like an eternity, but practically was probably not more than 20 or 30 minutes, Elvis turned off the main road onto a dirt road with no street sign. The road led to what looked like an old farmstead, with a pond to one side and several outbuildings nestled in amongst very tall live oak trees and some smaller but stunted magnolia trees twisted with wisteria vines.

Elvis maneuvered the bike to a stand of younger trees near the pond and brought it to a stop. Kicking the stand into place, Elvis waited for Elisha to dismount the bike before swinging his leg up and over the seat and taking off his helmet. Without looking at Elisha, Elvis took a look around as if he hadn't seen the place in years.

"This was my favorite place in the world for most of my life," he started. "But unfortunately I didn't really realize it until after I was gone."

Elisha was startled to realize that he meant after he had died in 1977, and once again the surrealistic intensity of the situation hit her in the face. She stared at Elvis and felt as if she was drowning in his easy sensuality. Every move he made exuded an aura of confidence and focus that complemented his trademark charm and flirtatiousness. The combination was hard to resist, and Elisha found herself studying the man for the first time since they'd met.

"Penny for your thoughts," Elvis said quietly, and Elisha realized that he knew she'd been staring at him. A bit flustered, Elisha looked down quickly at her hands, but when she looked back up, she found Elvis watching her with that quirky upturned smile that women had found so irresistible for decades. Completely disarmed, Elisha smiled back, and when Elvis held out his hand to her, she put her hand in his without any hesitation.

Elvis turned away from Elisha then, and still holding her hand, began to walk toward the pond and outbuildings. They walked in silence for a few minutes before Elvis finally spoke.

"You know, Elisha…" he began, looking over at her with that crooked grin of his. "I know more about you than you realize."

Elisha looked over him in surprise. "What do you mean?"

"I've known many women over the years," Elvis answered, swinging her arm with his as they walked around the pond.

"I love women. I love them in every shape, size, color, and economic class. It's like a hobby for me—getting to know women and helping them feel good about themselves."

"Really," answered Elisha, with a sarcastic bite to her words. "I'm sure it is. They certainly threw themselves at you for years and years… from what I heard, anyway."

"Yes, women have 'thrown' themselves at me for years, as you say," Elvis frowned. "Actually, if you spent any time watching any of my old reels, you'd see that it was less of an assault on their part, and more of an invitation on mine."

Elisha looked at him with a bit more interest. This wasn't the kind of conversation she was used to with men, and it certainly wasn't progressing the way she had expected.

"Anyway, I wanted a chance to talk with you away from the drama of Sunny's issues," Elvis continued. "You're such an incredible person, and I really want you to learn to love yourself."

"I can learn to love you!" Elisha batted her eyes at him, and swinging her arm back and forth playfully. "Actually, I can make you learn to love me!"

Elvis smiled at her. "I'm sure you could," he laughed. Elisha broke free of him and skipped ahead lightly, teasing him over her shoulder as if she wanted him to play with her. He picked up his pace, caught up with her and grabbed her around the waist. Giggling, Elisha played coy at first, breaking away from him and waiting for him to catch up with her several more times before she turned to face him with a serious expression on her face.

"I wasn't really joking, you know," she started. "I can do anything you want." She began to stroke his back and move more provocatively. "What do you like? I can make you a very happy man."

With that, she leaned in and kissed him warmly on the lips, and felt him respond to her almost immediately. Feeling emboldened, her kiss grew more urgent and before long, they were both locked in an embrace that could have set off fire alarms. Elvis seemed to be as lost in the moment as Elisa was, his hands creeping up and entwining in her hair. Elisha's head dropped back and Elvis began kissing down her neck and lower until Elisha started to moan.

It was that moan, totally instinctual and animalistic, that stopped Elvis in his tracks. He buried his face in her shoulder and slowly pulled her arms from around his neck and held them down at her sides until he was more recovered.

Elvis took a deep breath and lifted his face to look into her eyes, smiled at her, and then very gently dropped her arms so that he could cradle her head between his two hands. Elisha looked confused, not understanding why he had stopped and worrying that he hadn't been impressed enough.

"This is wrong," he whispered. "I can't do this."

"What's wrong?" she whispered back. "Just tell me what you like and I'll make it happen."

Still trying to collect himself, he took both her hands in his and gazed into her face.

"Elisha," Elvis began. "First, my life is not my own, I can't live by my flesh the way I did before, the only reason I am here is to warn people about the final days, and secondly, You are such a beautiful woman, inside and out, yet you don't believe it yourself. What will it take to convince you that you are worth more than you give yourself credit for and start showing the world what you have to offer?"

"I don't know what you're talking about," Elisha responded, dropping his hands and turning away from him for the first time since they had arrived. "I don't have any self-confidence issues. I am happy with who I am."

"No, you're not," replied Elvis. "You think you are, but your manufactured self-worth is a mirage, shimmering above the reality of what lies below. I can see it much more clearly than you think."

"What I think, is that you just don't like the package because I represent things your Christian filter can't handle," Elisha snapped back at him. "Well, I like who I am, and you're wrong about me!"

"Am I?" Elvis asked quietly, turning her around to face him. "Have you heard of the seven deadly sins, Elisha?"

Elisha looked a bit wary, but nodded her head. "I've heard of it, but don't know what they have to do with me."

"The seven devils are negative aspects that cloud our vision at the seven energy centers or chakras within our bodies," Elvis explained. "The seven demons include pride, lust, envy, anger, covetousness, gluttony, and sloth."

"Well, maybe I suffer from a little pride and maybe even a little anger," Elisha mused. "But I don't understand those others, let alone own any of them."

"Oh, you definitely know them all. You not only know what they are, you exhibit most of them so often that people can't get to know the real Elisha."

Elisha frowned in frustration. She truly didn't know what he was talking about, in that clouded, veiled way that people who do not understand their own actions often exhibit.

"Here's another way to look at it," Elvis searched for a way to explain it in terms she could understand.

"You were raised in a family that had just enough for the basics, but never enough for the fun stuff, am I right?" Elvis started. "And you never went hungry, and always had clothes and school supplies, but there was never enough money for designer jeans, jewelry, trips, or nice cars. Sound familiar?"

Elisha nodded.

"You grew up wanting things you could not have, and watching your friends get the things you wanted," Elvis continued. "You determined at a very young age that when you were old enough, you were going to make sure you got what you wanted, regardless of what it took to get there."

Elisha nodded again, and then looked away as if she could sense where he was headed with the analysis of her life.

Elvis kept painting the scenario that she had buried for years. "You started off shoplifting jewelry and clothing at the local malls so you could look like your friends and 'fit in' with the popular crowd, then you realized that sleeping with boys got you more attention than just flirting with them. It wasn't long before you found out that sleeping with older men gained you more than the attention you enjoyed from the boys your age."

Elisha began walking again, and Elvis fell in step beside her. "Am I wrong?" he asked. Elisha shook her head.

"It wasn't long before the benefits of your new lifestyle became something you not only wanted, but couldn't live without—money, power, lavish lifestyle, and the luxury of not having to work terribly hard for any of it." Elvis took her hand as they continued to walk slowly along the path at the edge of the water.

"Gluttony is your excessive partying lifestyle, lust is your uncontrolled appetite for money and power, covetousness is your love of money and penthouse living, and you are proud of your, uh… talents with men." Elvis stopped Elisha and turned her to face him. "What you may not immediately realize, is that you exhibit sloth with your unwillingness to work an honest job for a living, you envy other women who do not have to sell themselves or their integrity for the nice things they enjoy, and you are angry at yourself and the world for actually living the way you do."

"You add all those up into one neat package and you end up with a self-destructive life journey with no hope of redemption," Elvis continued. "That's where you are right now."

"I am not!!" Elisha replied defensively. "You don't know anything about me or where I've come from!"

"Oh, yes, little lady," the King replied quietly. "I've seen it all, and then some. Women constantly sell themselves short, getting wrapped up in destructive behaviors, and convincing themselves that their lives are the envy of all their friends, when they are, in fact, the envious ones."

Elisha tried to wrench her hand away from Elvis, but was unable to do so. "You may think you know me, but you don't!" she protested. "There's no way you could." she jerked her hands away from his steady grip.

"My dear, I'm not just any man," Elvis replied, reaching out for her again and pulling her closer to him. "I knew many women when I was here before, but while I've been gone I've developed a unique perspective that you can't even imagine.

You have a beautiful soul, Elisha, and you have smothered it with seven energy-clouding traits that prevent you from being the person you should be."

Elvis pulled her to him and folded her into a large, warm embrace… something Elisha hadn't experienced in years.

"My journey here will not be complete until you realize your own personal potential and shed all these negative energies that have consumed you for so long…" Elvis said softly. "Promise me you will work to become a better person while you are with me so that when I leave I will know with certainty that you will fulfill your destiny on Earth."

Elisha felt some of the tension in her body releasing as she stopped fighting his embrace, and rested her head on Elvis' shoulder. All of a sudden, she saw herself through his eyes with more clarity that she had ever had in her life. She stood up straight so quickly that Elvis was almost knocked off balance. Elisha gave him a startled look, as if acknowledging her newfound vision about the quality of her life. Looking away as she tried to make peace with what he had revealed, she couldn't make eye contact with Elvis.

"You have no reason to be embarrassed with me," he soothed. "I love you. I just know who you could be as well, and you are amazing!"

Elvis took her head in his hands and turned it toward him so he could kiss her lovingly on the forehead. Elisha closed her eyes as he kissed her, and when she opened them, her face shone with emotions she had not felt in years.

Feeling that they had sidestepped a moment where both of them could have made an unrecoverable mistake, Elvis turned to walk back toward the motorcycle with Elisha's hand in his. He could not see the mosaic of emotions flitting across Elisha's face as they made their way back to where they had started.

It was obvious to any observer, had they been there, that she was experiencing conflicting responses to all that had happened (or hadn't happened) between them in this place. Although her face sported a smile, her brow was furrowed and her eyes were bright, as if she was fighting back tears. As they walked back down the path toward the motorcycle, she watched him with a wary look as if she wasn't sure how she would handle herself if he turned to look at her. Luckily, he did not, and she was able to get her emotions under control by the time they made it back.

Elvis grabbed their helmets and turned to hand Elisha hers. She smiled at him, almost wistfully, as she accepted the helmet, but when he turned back to the bike, it was easy to see the love radiating from her face as she watched him put on his helmet and straddle the bike.

Taking a deep breath and putting the helmet on her head, Elisha climbed onto the back of the bike and clasped her hands around his waist to ready her for the bike to start moving. Kick-starting the motorcycle, the vibrations of the rumbling machine rattled Elisha's body; she gasps lightly with excitement when the trembling bike aroused her. Elvis rolled it onto the gravel drive and pointed it in the direction of the city. Elisha laid her head against his shoulder and tightened her grip around his waist, closing her eyes as she anticipated the bike's departure, and they roared back toward the city.

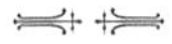

Back at WHAL, Solange was sorting through his song lists and watching the phone system lights, which were still pretty busy. It had been about 8 hours since what looked uncannily like Elvis – the

King of Rock and Roll – had walked through the doors of his studio and announced to the world that he had returned from the dead. Solange still did not know what to think of the whole situation, and had even pinched himself several times to make sure he wasn't unconscious!

Girl Friday in the front office wasn't much help, either. She had no memory of the real Elvis from years past, being at the tender age of only fifteen years old, so it was much easier for her to believe that the man who had visited the station earlier was a clever impersonator.

The intercom button on the phone began to buzz, and Solange picked it up a bit reluctantly. He expected it would be yet another request from Girl Friday for him to help field the phone calls, and he just couldn't find it within himself to keep trying to explain what had happened in his studio. He let the phone buzz two or three times before he groaned and reached over to find out what Girl Friday wanted this time.

"Yes, Girl Friday," Solange answered the line.

"Mr. LeDoux," she started. "There's a Mr. Clinton on the line for you."

"A Mr. What?" Solange replied. "Can't you just take a message? I think we talked about this just a few minutes ago…"

"No, Mr. LeDoux. This one is different. He says he's a promoter and he needs to speak with you about finding Mr. Elvis."

Ugh. A promoter! Just what he needed, thought Solange? What was it about long-lost superstars reappearing that brought out the best in people?! Did this guy really think he could make a dime from a dead dude? This was about to get completely "Jerry Springer" for everyone involved.

"Okay, I'll take it," grumbled Solange, flicking off the intercom and locating the correct phone line to take the call.

"Hello?" he began when he hit the phone line button on his phone unit.

"Uh, yes Mr. LeDoux," said the disembodied voice on the other end of the line. "My name is Clinton Robertson and I'm calling about the gentleman you had on your program earlier today."

"Yeah, you and everyone else!" replied Solange.

"What?" asked Robertson?

"Nothing. Sorry." Solange recovered. "What do you need to know, and frankly, why do you need to know?"

"I would just like an opportunity to speak to the individual myself," Robertson answered. "I liked what I heard, and I want a chance to find out for myself if he has potential for becoming part of my stable of performers."

"You're STABLE?" Solange retorted. "Do you know who you're talking about? I doubt he's interested in any stable – unless, of course, he's planning on taking that tall drink of water he brought with him on a trail ride!"

"Mr. LeDoux," Robertson ignored Solange's sarcasm as if he hadn't even heard it. "I heard a potential celebrity this morning on your station, and I would like an opportunity to speak to that individual as soon as it is logistically feasible. Can you help me?"

"You know it was the REAL Elvis, don't you?" Solange countered. "NOT an impersonator."

"Elvis is dead, Mr. LeDoux," Robertson replied. "I'm sure he looks authentic to the untrained eye, but…"

"The untrained what?!" Solange blew a fuse. "I've been working with artists and interviewing them for over 35 years, Mr. Robertson. I think I know Elvis when I see him!"

"Nonetheless, I need to arrange a meeting with the individual you interviewed this morning." Robertson persisted. "Can you make that happen for me?"

"I'm not sure," Solange replied. "It's not like he left me his resume, or anything." The promoter waited silently for Solange to make up his mind.

"Okay, okay. I think he mentioned the hotel where he is staying," Solange hedged. "I'll try to track him down for you."

"Thank you," said Clinton Robertson. "I appreciate your assistance."

"Yeah, whatever," Solange murmured. "Leave your contact information with my intern and I'll have someone give you a call if the man wants to talk with you." And with that, he put Robertson on hold and clicked the intercom button.

"Girl Friday," he called.

"Yes," she answered.

"Get this guy's number and email and put it in a safe place for me, k?"

"Yes, sir," she replied, and clicked off the intercom system.

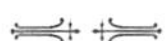

Sunny woke from a sound sleep when the phone lying on his chest began to ring.

"What the fuck?" he yelped as he grabbed the receiver. He must have dozed off while making calls, because the phone book was on the floor in a jumbled mess of yellow and white paper. He found the receiver and put it to his ear, not completely conscious as he did so.

"Uh, yup..." he started, assuming it was Elvis or Elisha.

"Elvis?" the voice on the other end asked.

Sunny sat up quickly, much more awake now. "No, actually. This is Sunny Carlisle, his manager. Who the hell is this?"

"Solange. Solange LeDoux from WHAL. Mr. Carlisle, you and Elvis came into my studio this morning, right?"

"Oh yeah," Sunny was putting it back together. "Yeah. Sorry about that. I was... my mind was somewhere else... yeah, I remember. What's up?"

"I received a call from a concert promoter this afternoon," Solange was not sure this Sunny character was the one he should be speaking to. "His name is Clinton Robertson, and he would like to speak with your Elvis."

Sunny bristled a bit. "He's not MY Elvis, he's THE Elvis," he retorted. "And he's not here at the moment."

"Oh. Well, I told this guy I'd get him some contact information so he could get in touch with you guys."

Sunny thought about that for a moment before replying. "I think it would be better if you gave me his information and I'll pass it on to Elvis when he gets back."

Solange sounded a bit unsure, "Do you think Elvis won't want to talk with this guy?"

"I don't know what to think," Sunny answered truthfully. "This isn't exactly your standard run-of-the-mill situation. I've learned over the last few days not to second-guess him at any time."

"Okay. I'll give you the guy's number," Solange answered. "To tell you the truth, he sounds a little smarmy to me. Like he's not completely on the up and up. My advice. Don't trust the SOB as far as you can throw him."

"Thanks," Sunny agreed. "I'm not sure of anybody in this situation so far. Even Elvis." Just saying his name sounded strange to Sunny. He hadn't had an opportunity to use it until now and somehow it sounded strange rolling off his lips like that.

Solange listed the number for Sunny and the brief phone conversation was over. Sunny stared at the phone number and wondered what the rest of the day was going to bring. Just then, the phone rang again. This time Sunny was prepared for it.

“Yes?” he answered it. After a pause, “Yes, thanks for returning my call. Mr. Elvis would definitely like to book an interview. What does tomorrow look like for you?

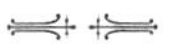

CHAPTER EIGHT

Zion Tabernacle a Romanesque church that stood alone in the midst of the shadows cast by trees surrounding the immense ziggurat. The large country style doors where open to let in a cool unusual crisp breeze for a summer morning in the outskirts of Memphis. A couple older model cars and trucks parked in a scattered formation in the gravel circular drive way that outlined the majestic edifice. Cherri Smith flowers were growing wildly alongside the north end of the church and the cool summer breeze rustled the tallest stalks of brittle grass that stood up in random clumps. It was obvious that the small congregation was finishing up its service, but less obvious that some of the people where not happy to be there. A few children were playing with homemade paper airplanes in the vestibule. Young boys with tan khaki pants and long-sleeve white Oxford shirts were obviously bored with the service as they stood facing the long winding road leading up to the church.

Just inside the country style doors were about 40 men and women standing and facing the podium, the men were dressed in similar khaki pants and long sleeve white shirts as the boys out front, and the women were in simple cotton dresses of every conceivable pastel shade. Most held Bibles clutched to their chests and some swayed as if keeping time to some invisible metronome.

In a back room, several young girls of varying ages were watching a number of much smaller children, all of whom were dressed exactly like their parents. The girls were trying hard to keep the youngest members of the congregation busy and quiet at the same time.

Behind the podium, one single light came down from the ceiling and descended upon the head of a tall man with rounded shoulders and a black beard. He stood in an extremely erect position and was wearing an Indian style white robe over long, loose, white pants.

His hands were pressed together as if in prayer, and his eyes were shut.

Suddenly he spoke, in a loud, mesmerizing voice that mystically prompted all the church members to close their eyes and raise their faces to the heavens.

"It has come to pass; he started slowly, with this voice resonating throughout the room. Even the small children and young girls in the back room hung on his every word. ".......that a false prophet has come among us."

"This man," the bearded leader enunciated, "has been known to us before, in another life. Now he has gotten the attention of the world again by creating a reincarnation of himself, and hopes to persuade us of a mystical allusion that will not come to pass.

The man in the white robe raised his hands above his head and spoke in a slow measured tone. The people stood before him, swaying to the symphony of his words, obviously lost in his voice.

"This false prophet has come among us as someone we knew and loved in a world before today! He is dangerous. He threatens our very existence. We must not be caught off guard. We must protect ourselves from his devilish deceit.

The leader standing before his congregation lifted his face to the heavens and continued. "This is a strange and complicated situation. If we do not deal with this false prophet, he will lead many astray. We must expose his fraud.

Members of the congregation opened their eyes in surprise and looked at each other in panic. Zorzi looked out over the congregation, stepped forward to the front of the podium, and swept his hands out in front of him, encompassing the group.

"I need volunteers to accompany me as I pursue this false prophet and lay him bare before the world. Those who can join me will be my disciples….doing God's work at a time when our world needs us the most!"

Zorzi waited, looking out over the congregation. He observed the murmurings and the look of panic in the eyes of his children. "Ahhh," he said to himself. "Just as I had expected."

A soft breeze kicked up dust and swirled it into tiny windstorms on the floor of the church as the congregation stood in reverent silence before its leader. Hands slowly rose, as both men and women felt the call. Zorzi nodded slowly and a smile grew on his bearded face as he saw the adoration on the faces of those who were offering to follow.

And it was good.

Sunny was snoozing in the chair by the phone when the front door opened and the two joy riders entered the hotel suite. Noticing that Sunny was asleep, with his hat tipped down over his face; the two exchanged a glance before Elisha walked quietly over to the sleeping Sunny and leaned down to his level.

"Hungry?" Elisha asked him as close to his visible ear as possible without actually touching him. Sunny woke up with such a start that the chair he was sitting in fell over backward, landing him, the phone book, the phone, and the chair in a tangle on the floor. Elisha burst into laughter at his expense, while Elvis watched from the open doorway.

"What the..." Sunny stuttered, trying to scramble up off the floor in the midst of phone, books, and his long legs. "What's going on? Where have you been??"

"Never mind where we've been," Elvis answered calmly. "We came back to see how much you've gotten done and perhaps steal you away from all this to get some grub."

Elisha couldn't stop laughing, as Sunny continued to extricate himself from the mess and get everything back into its place. Sunny glared at her and shoved his hands into the pockets of the sun washed blue jeans he'd been wearing for 3 days now.

"Thanks for nothing, girlfriend!" he shot at her, as if it were she who was initiating the conversation rather than the gentleman in the doorway.

"I just couldn't resist," laughed Elisha. "You were asking for it, all balanced and snoozing like you were. You were supposed to be working!"

"Yeah, and I suppose you were 'working' this afternoon, too!" Sunny snarled, looking at Elvis out of the corner of his eye, trying to get a sense of any change in their relationship.

Sensing nothing new or out of the ordinary, Sunny relaxed just a bit. Maybe they had just taken a ride after all...

Elisha looked surprised by the remark, and some of her merriment faded as everyone seemed to remember where they had left off earlier in the day.

"Okay, you two," Elvis interjected. "Let's get a bite to eat and talk about what Sunny has lined up for us. I'm sure he has a full schedule for us over the next couple of days."

Sunny grabbed his jacket off the back of the couch and slung it over his shoulder. "Yes, let's get out of here. I could definitely use a change of pace!" He stormed past both Elvis and Elisha, through the open doorway and down the hallway toward the elevators. Elvis held the door open as if in invitation for Elisha, who followed Sunny into the hallway. Elvis offered her his arm, and Elisha made brief eye contact with him when he did so. His smile disarmed her, and she smiled back hesitantly for a moment before she took the offered appendage and they both headed down the hallway after Sunny.

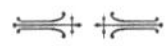

Zorzi sat in the leather wingback chair in his office and stared silently at the 52-inch television that was barking at him in that annoying, national news channel kind of way. What was holding his attention, however, was not the story they were covering, but a headline in the ticker that was running at the bottom of the screen. Apparently, a man claiming to be Elvis was making the news there, and a local radio DJ named Solange Phillips had broken the story the day before. It wasn't quite national news yet, but CNN felt it was interesting enough to introduce at the bottom of the screen. It was their way of tantalizing their viewers and making them wait around to see if there were any further developments.

"Damnation!" Zorzi exclaimed finally, sick and tired of watching for something that was obviously not going to happen anytime soon. "Do they not know how important that news byte is?!" he shouted.

A woman in a white dress, barely covering her thighs, flew into the room to see if her leader was okay, and Zorzi threw her a scorching glance as she entered the room.

"Sir, do you need anything?" Amanda asked.

Zorzi got up and switched off the television and growled at Amanda. "I thought I told you all that I wasn't to be disturbed."

"Well, we heard you yell…"

"There is nothing any of you can do for me," Zorzi answered angrily. "I need solitude so I can decide what our path should be from this point forward. Constant interruptions are not going to help!"

"So sorry, Sir," Amanda answered, retreating almost as quickly as she had entered.

Zorzi paced slowly across the floor of the room, stroking his beard with one hand and muttering under his breath. After several minutes, he came to a stop, put both hands on his hips, and gave one powerful nod of his head. Turning around abruptly, he moved to the door with purpose.

Entering the large meeting room, Zorzi surveyed the faces of the 15 or so men and women who were gathered there. Several of them were asleep, and those who were awake had dark circles under their eyes and looked like they hadn't eaten or slept in days. They were a simple, but rag-tag bunch who were obviously running on adrenaline and expectation rather than food, drink, or sleep.

Zorzi moved to stand in front of them. Those who were awake nudged those who were not and everyone slowly sat up and faced their leader.

"God has spoken to me," Zorzi started in his best cult leader resonance. "And he has shared with me our calling."

Several in the group looked at each other before facing Zorzi again with heightened interest.

"I have been briefed on the false prophet. He is among us, although he is not here." Zorzi looked almost menacing as he stirred the energy of his followers. "I pray hourly for continued guidance. God will show us the way to this devil man and once he does, we will seek out this false prophet, capture him, and make him one of us."

The group began to murmur amongst themselves as their excitement grew. "He must not be allowed to teach his wicked ways to our brethren in this world!" Zorzi continued. "His path is the wrong one, and it is up to us to correct that path!"

"But Sir," a young man spoke up suddenly. "How will we know this imposter?"

Zorzi glared at the young man. "I already know, and you all will know soon enough. He has come to us as someone the world reveres, which increases the danger for all of us who follow the true teachings of God."

Zorzi paused for a moment, as if to gather his thoughts. The pregnant pause only heightened the intensity in the room. "This man is the Anti-Christ! God has warned me against him. He is evil and intends harm to all who do not believe in him."

The group in the room tensed at his words and began to look at each other as if suddenly afraid of the work they had set out to do. "Do not fear, my children." Zorzi softened his tone for a moment. "He is harmless in the face of my greatness and your devotion to the true light. We will draw him in, contain him, and harness his energy for our own design. You will rise above him because we are the true believers. It is our duty to save mankind from his destructive powers. And we will prevail!"

Sunny finished his double whopper in about six monstrous bites and then began working on the supersized fries and giant cherry coke, as Elisha and Elvis watched.

"You act like you haven't eaten in a week!" Elisha observed with a moderate amount of sarcasm in her voice. "Didn't we just have surf and turf last night? Oh, and a full continental breakfast this morning?"

Sunny glared at her over the top of his drink, fries still in his hand awaiting consumption. "I don't criticize how you eat, or what you wear, or who you hang out with..." he replied with just as much attitude, looking over at Elvis for emphasis.

"There's nothing wrong with the way I dress!" retorted Elisha, angry now. "At least I have some kind of fashion sense and don't spend every day in the same pair of jeans and..."

"Enough! Both of you!" Elvis finally interjected, showing a considerable amount of both restraint and patience. "Now that our basic needs have been met, it's time to have a serious conversation about our next steps, and how far Sunny got today with his phone calls."

"Well, I don't know about YOUR basic needs," Sunny replied with his mouth full of fries, "but I still need about a day's worth of sleep! Every time you all sleep and play, you expect me to be making and taking phone calls. At some point, my mouth and brain are going to stop working and I will be of no use to anyone!"

Elvis pondered Sunny's statement for a moment before answering, studying the Sunny's face for insight before continuing with his own thought process. Seeming to find what he was looking for, Elvis smiled at Sunny and nodded his head before continuing.

"You know, Sunny," Elvis started. "You're right. When we get back to the hotel, you take a shower and go to bed. We can handle everything that needs to be done tonight."

Sunny looked a bit surprised at the apparent change in policy, but nodded back at Elvis. "I appreciate that," he acknowledged. "I'm seriously not going to be any good to anyone without some shut eye."

"I totally understand," Elvis answered. "Now, we need to know what you were able to accomplish while we were out this afternoon. Did you line anything up for the next couple of days? Did anyone call about a concert?"

Sunny did nothing to conceal his surprise. "How did you know about that?" he exclaimed.

"About what?" Elvis questioned.

"About the concert promoter," answered Sunny, wiping the salt from the French fries off his hands.

"I don't know what you're talking about," Elvis repeated. "What concert promoter? I thought you were just calling radio stations all day today."

"Shit, man!" Sunny exclaimed. "You just asked about a concert, so I thought you pulled that out of your extraterrestrial sixth sense or some shit! You mean you really don't know?"

Elvis directed a stony look at Sunny that indicated he wasn't too happy with the tone of the conversation. "If I knew, would I have asked?"

"Never mind!" Sunny dropped his eyes and gave up. "Some dude named Clinton Robertson called Solange this morning after the broadcast. Seems he's a shady sort and Solange said not to trust him."

Elvis brightened considerably at the man's name. He obviously knew who Sunny was talking about, and seemed pleased about it.

"You know the guy?" Sunny inquired tentatively. "I can see it rings a bell somehow."

Elvis didn't reply, as he seemed lost in his own thoughts for a moment or two. Elisha watched him carefully, as if any minute would bring an axis-altering decision.

Both Sunny and Elisha held their collective breath as they waited for any kind of a response from the man who had been calling the shots for them for several days now.

Looking at both of them briefly, Elvis cleared his throat. "I am aware of the danger of going down this path. Solange is right to be wary of this Clint Robertson. However, it is a path I must follow. It is our destiny to attempt a relationship with this man. I accept the challenge."

"Dude," started Sunny. "What challenge? I'm sure there are other promoters who will come out of the woodwork once they realize who you are! Why screw around with a guy that is shady at best?"

Elvis gazed at Sunny with his classic half smile on his face. "Sunny, one day you will realize that taking the more difficult road builds character – the kind of character that will carry you through both the good and the ugly. If you only learn that lesson through all of this, I will be satisfied."

Sunny sat back in his chair, unsure of what Elvis meant, but unwilling to pursue it any further.

"Well, if you want to talk with the guy, we should go get started," he groused. "I have some shut eye to work on while you are saving the world!"

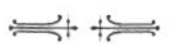

The TVs in the sports bar sported a headline news program running in the background, the patron chatter making volume unnecessary. Nobody was watching it anyway. It just made the bartender feel cerebral to have the news on instead of the game of the night, regardless of the sport of choice. It was a busy place, with regulars crowding the oak-topped bar and dinner patrons at almost every table. Saturday nights were always the busiest, with shoppers and tourists steaming in for that last normal meal before the all-nighter at the casinos.

"Hey! Can we get the game on?" shouted a burly guy sitting at the end of the bar with an entourage of other men and women who were dressed for a night on the town. "Who watches the news in a bar anyway?"

The bartender groaned inwardly. "Here we go again," he muttered, as he fished around for the remote control. Stalling, as if he couldn't find it, he hoped the customer would drop the issue. Yes, he was a strange beast, not wanting to watch yet another contest between overpaid, overweight, steroid-injecting thugs who couldn't form a coherent thought during an interview to save their lives. Was it really too much to ask for one night of something different? Silence was preferable to any game in any sport, but sadly, the life of a bartender required the sham of being a sports addict – being "up" on all the insider information on every team in every sport, so that he could carry on the "therapy" with the customers that his job required on a nightly basis.

"Hey, tender!" the customer barked again. "Sometime tonight, maybe?!"

"Okay, okay," he barked back. "Let me find the remote…" and finished under his breath "you oversexed, half-witted oaf!" He grabbed the remote, which had been right where he left it, and turned to face the TV to make the change.

Just at that second, however, the newscaster's background picture changed to a photo of Elvis with a diagonal graphic that read "Alive???" He paused for a moment, and watched the picture change to men and women gathered outside a radio station in Memphis, Tennessee. They were waving Elvis memorabilia and jumping up and down as if they were waiting in line for autographs.

Rather than change the channel, the bartender turned the volume on the TV up to hear what the broadcaster was saying.

"… Reports of Elvis on radio programs in the Deep South. Although these reports are unconfirmed, rumors are spreading like wildfire that the man claiming to be Elvis on the radio knows far too much about the dead singer's life to be an imposter," the suit on the TV intoned. "No one has reported actually seeing this new Elvis, but there have been several reports of an Elvis lookalike being spotted from Vegas to Memphis."

The background picture became the focal point of the broadcast and switched to a small, roadside bar in what looked to be a Nevada-looking landscape. Several patrons were gathered outside while a rather agitated man with an apron on gestured down the road as he spoke to a reporter. A sheriff's deputy of some sort stood near the man, very obviously more interested in the camera than in what the other man was saying. The station switched the audio to the scene just as the reporter got the deputy's attention and dragged him over to the microphone.

"Uh… we have a person of interest in this case," the deputy started, looking at a crumpled piece of paper in his hands. "A witness took down the license plate number of the kids driving the getaway car. Its Nevada plate number PJY4816, registered to a Sunny Carlisle of XXX Street in Vegas…"

The customer at the end of the bar shouted something that the bartender didn't even register. He waved his hand over his shoulder as if to say "Wait a minute…" and turned the volume up a little.

"An APB has been issued for the car…" and the audio switched back to the newscaster in the studio. "Our reporter is on the scene, talking with witnesses, who all share similar stories about a man who looks exactly like the late Elvis singing songs to them in this roadside bar karaoke-style and then discovering that those songs do not exist on the establishment's jukebox.

All very mysterious, if you ask me," he continued. "We have similar reports of Elvis sightings in Memphis in recent days. We will continue to follow this rather unbelievable story as it unfolds."

The bartender watched a bit of banter between the newscaster and his attractive, blonde female co-anchor before pressing the mute button on the remote. As he did so, he immediately noticed the silence in the room behind him. Turning around, he was shocked to see all the customers at the bar staring at the TV with open mouths.

"Hey, turn that back on!" ordered the same customer at the end of the bar that had wanted the game on. "What was he saying?"

The bartender smiled and turned the volume back on. "Let's just watch this a little longer and see what else they tell us." His night was going to be okay after all!

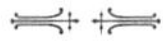

The trio drove through town on their way to yet another radio station, "Hound Dog" began cranking up on the station they were currently tuned into.

"Hey, can you turn that up?" Elisha shouted from the back seat. She was valiantly trying to paint her toenails as they were driving, and not having much success. As Sunny reached over to increase the volume in the back seat, the music faded into the background as the DJ began to speak.

"On any other day," he started. "Playing a song like this would just bring back memories of the good old days of Rock and Roll! But today, we can't help but think about the last 24 hours of revelation with the reports of Elvis doing radio shows in the Memphis area."

Sunny and Elvis looked at each other with a grin.

"Is Elvis really back with us, and if so, how and why? These are all questions that Elvis fans – and the rest of us – are all asking this morning. And I, more specifically, am wondering why this radio station hasn't gotten a visit from him yet. Does that mean he doesn't really exist and these reports are just a publicity stunt? If so, I take issue with the tactics of my competitors. Raising an icon from the dead just to sell ad time is not very cool, even by today's standards. If not, I challenge this Elvis character to spend some time with ME on my program. I'd like my own chance to determine if he's the real thing or just an imposter!"

Again, Sunny and Elvis looked at each other. "Are you thinking what I'm thinking?" Sunny asked his partner. Elvis nodded with a grin. "Elisha!" Sunny called into the back seat. "Find the address of this station on your Phone – it's our next stop!"

Elisha glared at Sunny over the top of her dark sunglasses, and continued to paint the toe she was working on.

Hearing no response, Sunny tried again. "Elisha! I need an address for this station, please." Again, there was no response.

Elvis turned around and looked at Elisha without saying a single word. No judgment was present on his face, but Elisha sensed a change in the air and looked up to meet his gaze. Without dropping her eyes, she put the cap on the nail polish and fished out her phone. Elvis turned back to face the road while Elisha silently accommodated their request.

As she was tapping the keys on her phone, Sunny's phone blared a karaoke version of "All Shook Up" that he had recorded at one of his last gigs.

"Ugh, that's me," he groaned and reached for the interfering piece of equipment. Elvis smiled at Sunny's frustration.

"Yeah," Sunny answered the phone.

A man's voice on the other end of the line asked "Hello, is this Elvis?"

"Uh, no!" Sunny replied. "But I'm his manager. Who is this?"

"My name is Clint Robertson," the disembodied voice answered. "And I would like to speak with Elvis, if you don't mind."

"Well, actually, I DO mind," Sunny began to take on a warning tone in his voice. "Elvis doesn't take calls from just anybody. If you want to talk with him, you'll have to talk with me first."

Clint Robertson sighed with irritation. He was used to gatekeepers when working with big name artists, but he had to admit he hadn't expected this purported Elvis wannabe to have a handler already. Damn! This had all the makings of a difficult situation.

"Okay, then. Who am I speaking with?" he asked Sunny.

"Sunny Carlisle," Sunny answered, and Clint immediately recognized his name from the news broadcast he had watched last night on TV. "And we've been expecting your call."

Clint chuckled. "You've been expecting me, have you?" he started. "I suppose you're psychic as well as resurrected, then?"

"No, asshole," Sunny growled. "A certain DJ that we're mutually acquainted with informed us that you were inquiring about my man here."

"Well, that clears everything right up," Robertson snarled back. "I suppose he's the reincarnated one and you're just the lackey. Do I get to speak to him this morning, or do you do all his talking for him?"

"Elvis only talks to people who are respectful and genuinely interested in what he has to say,"

Sunny returned the volley a bit more calmly after catching a warning look from Elvis. "I talk to all the people like you who treat him otherwise."

With that, Sunny hung up and tossed the phone into the back seat.

"Whoa!" Elisha grabbed it in mid-air as she passed her phone up front.

"I don't want it back!" barked Sunny, still pissed off at Clint and his smug attitude.

"It isn't your phone," interceded Elvis as he took Elisha's phone and looked at it. "Elisha has the address of the radio station. Elisha, hand Sunny back his phone. We need to be ready when Mr. Robertson calls again."

Sunny looked at Elvis. "What do you mean we need to be ready? I think he's a creep!"

"Well, creep or no creep, we need his help to get to the next level," Elvis replied quietly. "I only have 30 more days and I'm not going to get done what I need to get done by driving around Memphis for a month."

Elvis gave a sullen Sunny the directions to the radio station. Just as he finished, Sunny's phone rang and he took the device from Elisha's outstretched hand with an almost inaudible growl.

"What?" he sneered into the phone.

"I don't even need to ask if this is Sunny," the voice on the other end said. "May I please speak with your Elvis person?"

"No you may not," Sunny exaggerated his formal politeness for Clint's benefit. "Elvis is indisposed. Whatever you need to talk with him about, you can talk about with me."

Clint Robertson sighed inwardly so Sunny couldn't hear his exasperation. "Okay. I would like to find out for myself if this Elvis everyone is talking about is for real or not. Once I know for sure that he's the real thing, I might be interested in promoting a concert to reintroduce him to the world."

Sunny looked over at Elvis with his mouth open in surprise, and then focused back on the phone as if he was about to fire off an insult for Robertson insinuating that Elvis was a fake. Elvis grabbed the phone before Sunny could do any irreversible damage and spoke into it.

"Mr. Robertson, this is Elvis. What can I do for you?"

There was silence on the other end for a moment or two before Robertson collected himself enough to respond.

"Wow. You sure sound like the real thing," he managed finally. "Let me ask you a question – as a form of reference check... Should your middle name be spelled with just one "A" or with two?"

Elvis chuckled.

"Either answer is right, Mr. Robertson," he explained. "My birth certificate has it with one 'A,' but the world has always wondered if that was a mistake or not. Some think that my parents named me Elvis 'Aron with one A' by design, so that it matched the middle name of my twin brother, Jesse. I tried to have it changed to be spelled with two 'As' – as it is in the Bible – before my death, but discovered in the process that the state had already recorded it with two 'As.' When I asked my Daddy why it was spelled with one 'A' on my birth certificate when the state had it listed with two, he just said 'a lot of people around Tupelo didn't spell right back then.'"

Robertson laughed on the other end of the line, realizing instantly that no one but the real Elvis could have been that self-deprecating about something as significant as the spelling of his own name. As weird as it might sound, this Elvis had to be the real thing!

"Wow!" Robertson said without thinking. "I don't know if I believe what I'm hearing!"

"If you don't believe me, Google it!" Elvis responded, not particularly fond of the constant disbelief people exhibited about his reappearance.

"No, no, I just meant it's hard to believe that it's really you… Elvis… that I'm talking to!" Robertson answered back. "I mean,

I'm not sure I will fully understand it until I see you in person, but nobody else would have answered that question that way!"

Elvis relaxed and the trademark half smile played across his face for a moment or two.

"Well, Mr. Robertson, what can I do for you today? We have to make a stop in a few minutes, so let's get down to the reason you called."

Robertson didn't waste any time. "Okay, I would really like to organize a comeback concert tour for you. I am assuming you are interested in getting back on stage, right?"

Elvis looked over at Sunny, who could still hear most of Robertson's side of the conversation, and grinned.

"Yes, Mr. Robertson. I am very interested in getting my message out to as many people as possible between now and the end of the month. Can you help me with that?"

"Absolutely! Can you get yourself to Vegas in the next 24 hours? I can get started with the details while you're on your way," Robertson gushed, finally letting down his reserves.

"Mr. Robertson. While I am very interested in gaining stage time in Vegas, I have some requirements that you will have to manage for me if we are going to be working together," Elvis interjected.

"Sure, sure," Robertson was eager to maneuver himself between Sunny and Elvis as quickly as possible. Seeing the incredible potential of becoming both concert promoter for the biggest act in rock and roll history and his manager at the same time, Robertson was willing to promise almost anything.

"I would like to perform at the Stardust Theater, and I would like Wayne Newton to introduce me to the audience. He has worked hard since I've been gone, and he doesn't get enough recognition." Elvis was nostalgic for a moment as he pondered the possibilities.

Robertson leaned back in his leather office chair as he considered the impact of Elvis' requests. He wasn't quite sure how to react, and even more unsure how he should respond.

He was, however, even more convinced that Elvis was the real thing. It was the only explanation for why the singer had asked for the impossible.

"Uhh.... Elvis..." he began. "I'm not sure how to tell you this, but the Stardust Hotel was demolished in 2007, and a hotel called Resorts World is there now." He waited for Elvis' response.

Elvis was silent as he pondered the news.

"And, there's more..." Robertson continued. "Mr. Newton hasn't had a show in Vegas for quite a few years. Elvis still said nothing as both Sunny and Robertson, on opposite sides of the conversation, waited for some response from him.

Rather than wait forever for a reaction from his famous potential new client, Robertson forged ahead.

"If I can make a suggestion," he started. "Why don't I try to book the Las Vegas Hilton? It's certainly is a big part of your story. They even have a bronze statue of you out front!"

Elvis looked over at Sunny and nodded. "Sounds like a great second option. I agree."

Robertson relaxed a bit. "What about Newton?"

"I don't know yet," Elvis replied. "Let me think about that while you're making the other arrangements."

"Okay," the promoter concurred. "So how fast can you get to Vegas?"

"Give us a couple of day, we have some more business to attend to here before we head out. "Good," Robertson was pleased. "That will give me enough time to get the venue booked and figure out who will perform with you. Your original backup singers and band are spread out over the four corners of the Earth by now!"

"Over the four what?" Elvis questioned, looking confused.

"Never mind," Robertson laughed. "We probably won't be able to find any that are left, that's all."

"Oh, okay. I can work with new artists. That's the least of my worries."

Robertson felt a twinge of uncertainty for a moment. He couldn't risk losing this client – this one was going to put him on the map. He would be as famous as the Colonel. And, if Elvis was the real thing, Robertson could see the financial advantage of being on the receiving end of the man's generosity.

Elvis could feel the greed seeping through the phone line as he wrapped up the conversation, but he steeled himself to finish the call and hung up.

Sunny looked over at him as they headed through Memphis to the radio station. "Vegas in two days, huh?

Elvis grinned back at him. Sunny's eyes widened as he tough about returning back to Vegas as the risen Elvis' manager.

Elvis continued to grin at Sunny as they pulled up at the radio station. "All you need to know is that we have time for several more radio shows before we have to start our road trip."

Sunny groaned as he parked the car. "Heaven help me!" he whispered. Then he looked upward quickly. "Oh yeah, I keep forgetting!"

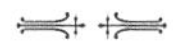

Zorzi sat pensively at a large walnut desk in the middle of his office, surrounded by photos of himself and various top-name evangelists and politicians. Books on the Anti-Christ and Revelation filled the floor-to-ceiling bookcases behind him, as he pondered the whereabouts of his newest nemesis.

"Now where would the so-called King of Rock and Roll go after being resurrected," he mused out loud. He looked out the window of his office. Walking across the courtyard of his complex was a young man wearing a Memphis Tigers basketball jersey and he jumped from his seat.

"Of course!" he shouted. "He's in Memphis! Why didn't I think of that earlier?!"

Zorzi grabbed the phone receiver, punched the button for his assistant's extension and tapped his heavy fingers on the desktop as he waited for him to pick up. He didn't have to wait for long.

"Alonzo!" he barked. "Find out where The Elvis is staying at here in Memphis.. No… no… don't argue with me. Just find out now!" He slammed the receiver back down and almost tipped his chair over as he pushed it back to stand up. Pacing from the window to the desk for several minutes, it was obvious to any observer that he was agitated and anxious to take action.

Twisting his signet ring rhythmically, Zorzi kept an eye on the door as he wore a path into the expensive Turkish rug between the desk and the windows.

"Alonzo!" he called after a few minutes went by without any movement from outside the door. "What's taking so long?" Getting no answer, Zorzi went behind the desk and slumped back into the chair, switching from ring-twisting to finger-tapping as he waited not so patiently. After another few moments, unable to stand still, Zorzi bolted upright and strode to the door. Just as he reached for the doorknob, however, the door opened, and Zorzi had to jump backward rapidly to avoid it.

"Mr. Zorzi," the young Latin American began. "It seems he is at the Peabody hotel sir."

"I will write him a letter to get his attention; I will invite him to our sanctuary". Thank you My Dear Alonzo"

"Sir!" Alonzo looked shocked.

"Thank You God Bless you, your services are never taken for granted" Zorzi revised his order after seeing the look on the younger man's face. "I apologize for my 'enthusiasm' a moment ago—I'm just very anxious to get going and I don't have much patience for delays."

The young Arabian looked cautiously appeased with the change in tone, but kept a wary eye on his boss as the conversation continued.

"Sir," he tried again. "The parish bank account only has about $3,500 in it, and the rest of us are supposed to be traveling with you. We have to be concerned with raising more money for the church and perhaps not as concerned about the Elvis Character."

"Quiet!!" roared Zorzi, in his best bigger-than-life cult leader voice. "It is imperative that I find this imposter before he has done any more damage! Pray, Pray, Pray, My dear Alonzo and the truth will be revealed to you! He is the Anti-Christ! Give me some time to reflect and get this letter together!"

"Sorry, sir," Alonzo backed out of the office, looking down as he went. "I'll do it right away, sir."

"Revelations 13:1-8 read it and study it!" Zorzi ordered as the door was closing.

Alonzo shut the door behind him as he left the office to head to his room to study. Zorzi, still fuming, began gathering his things and throwing them into a missionary's bag. As he did so, the corners of his mouth slowly turned upwards until he broke out into a devilish grin. The delight of figuring out where he needed to look first was pushing all else from his feverish brain, and Zorzi was now singularly focused on Elvis and how to end what he had started. It is good!

CHAPTER NINE

The lobby of the Peabody Hotel was quieter than normal, but still bustled with visitors coming and going every few minutes. The toiletry shop was doing a brisk business and the restaurant had a small crowd in for the pre-dinner hours. The famous Peabody Ducks that made their daily entrance from the roof of the Peabody to the lobby and a red carpet laid out along the floor waiting for their arrival as they marched to the beat of John Phillips Sousa's King Cotton March. The hotel always attracted an eclectic clientele from all over the world on a regular basis, but nothing had prepared them for the tall, imposing figure of Zorzi when he entered the lobby.

His dark hair contrasting with the long, white, formal robes and sandals were head-turners for most everyone within eyeshot of his entrance. He approached the front desk with the posture of a world leader, and stood waiting for someone to recognize that he was there.

The young woman behind the counter finally hung up the phone and looked up with a smile.

"Can I help you, sir?" she asked.

Zorzi looked down at her the way a Pharaoh looks down at the slave who is washing his feet.

"Where can I find the Elvis Imposter?" he asked in an imperious tone.

"Excuse me, sir?" the young woman asked, clearly confused but still the picture of happy helpfulness.

"I said, where can I find the Elvis Imposter?" Zorzi repeated in the same intonation. "There is a man staying here that looks like Elvis staying with another man who looks like Elvis. I have business with them."

The reservations clerk's smile faded a bit as she struggled to digest what Zorzi was asking. There were so many Elvis impersonators in Memphis these days that the hotel staff had long since stopped noticing specific ones as they checked in and out.

"I'm not sure who you mean exactly," she tried to be helpful. "We have Elvis look-alikes in here all the time. Do you have a specific name I can look up for you?"

"No!" roared Zorzi. "Tell me where he is! It is imperative that I locate this Imposter and bring him to justice!"

The clerk looked visibly shaken and pressed a button under the counter for assistance.

"Sir, I don't know who you are talking about, but if you can give me some more information, I can try to help you. I can't help you if I don't have a name."

Zorzi looked disgusted and turned to sweep his gaze over the rest of the lobby.

"I know he is here," he muttered, as he surveyed the room. "The trick is to find him."

At that moment, two security guards approached Zorzi and the hotel manager joined the reservations clerk behind the counter. After a quick consultation with the clerk while Zorzi's back was turned, the hotel manager spoke.

"Can I help you?" asked the hotel manager, meticulously clothed in a Lord & Taylor suit with hotel-issued tie and tie clip. "I hear you are looking for someone."

The security guards flanked Zorzi when he turned to face the counter again.

"I am looking for the Elvis Imposter, but your worker here is either incompetent, or she is protecting him," Zorzi spoke directly to the manager. "I want to locate this demon and save the world from his manipulations, and I need to find him before he escapes."

The hotel manager exchanged a look with the clerk, and then motioned to the security guards. "We will not be able to help you find the person you are looking for. Even if you had his name, our first priority would be to protect the safety and interests of our guests. We wouldn't give out locations of guests to strangers for any reason."

A myriad of emotions flickered across Zorzi's face as he stared at the hotel manager and it finally registered that he would not get anywhere with the hired help. Standing motionless for another moment, he barely noticed the two security guards moving closer.

"You need to remove yourself from the premises, sir," said the hotel manager while making contact with the guards. "You are not welcome here unless you are willing to become a guest of our establishment. I must warn you, however, that even if you register for a room, I cannot provide you with any contact information for any of our other guests."

Zorzi continued to stand silently, pondering his options as the security guards stood at attention, waiting for the signal to pounce. Finally, after about another 30 seconds of the stand-off, Zorzi dropped his gaze.

"Check... mate," he said softly, raising his eyes to look at the hotel manager and the several staff members who had joined him at the front desk. "But I will find a way to discover this Imposter which I seek, with or without your help."

Zorzi backed away from the desk, bumping into the two security guards as he did so. Locking eyes with the young registration clerk, he moved backward very slowly, until there were about 8 feet between he and the staff.

"I know you are misguided in your attempts to protect the wizard," Zorzi said as he stopped briefly. "You don't know the truth, and if you did, you would behave differently. But, you are innocent in your deception and therefore you will eventually be saved. Go with God!"

And with that, Zorzi broke off eye contact with the young clerk, turned around, and exited the lobby to the street outside. The security guards followed him to the door and watched as he walked up to a young Latino man.

After a few subdued words, the two men turned and headed down the street. After assuring themselves that Zorzi would not try a repeated entrance into the hotel, the security guards walked toward the rear of the hotel and the service entrance. The hotel manager waited until they had cleared the scene before leaving the desk area in the competent hands of the registration clerk.

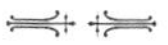

Clint Robertson swung his chair around to face his desk, still pondering his newfound luck in discovering what seemed to be a reincarnated pop idol! No one that he knew had ever found themselves in this position. Who would have thought it was possible to "discover" an act that already had the kind of guaranteed appeal that this one did.

Of course, there was still the possibility that this guy would turn out to be a scam. After all, Clint hadn't met him in person yet, and it could all still be a giant hoax. but, the possibilities that existed even if it was a hoax were endless!

"I mean, even Simon Cowell knows how to take a marginal or outright terrible act and turn it into a novelty with a schtick that appeals to millions!" Robertson mused silently. "If he can do it, so can I."

Armed with the knowledge that he could still use this new act to his advantage even if it turned out to be a fake, the promoter picked up the phone and dialed a number.

"Margie, this is Clint. Is Roger there?" Robertson inquired. "Great, thanks."

A moment or two passed with Robertson tapping his pen on the desktop--the kind of energy that most Type A personalities unknowingly exhibit. It wasn't long before the voice he wanted to hear answered the phone on the other end.

"Hey, Roger. It's Clint. Yeah, I'm great! How are Camryn and the kids? Great, great..." Robertson looked out the window as he played the Pleasantries Game with the guy on the other end of the phone. A few moments into the game, however, he turned serious.

"Listen, Roger, I need a favor," he started cautiously. "I need the theater for an event... as soon as possible... I can't really explain why, let's just say it's an 'Elvis' event with unprecedented commercial appeal... I know I'm being vague, just humor me."

Robertson shifted his weight in his chair, leaning forward to put his elbows on the desk.

"Why am I being vague?" he countered. "Because not all the details are in place yet, and I'm being very cautious about letting the world know what I'm doing before I vet the performer and make sure everything is confirmed."

Robertson listened to the voice on the other end for a moment before breaking in. "Roger! You have never asked me to provide all the details of a show to book an event before, and I've never booked an event that flopped… yes, I know that talking about Elvis in Vegas is a mixed bag and that Elvis shows are a dime a dozen, but trust me… this one will be different. And if it's not different, I'll eat the cost of the room rental… yes, I'm serious… and I'll let you in on all the details once I have them solidified."

Robertson got the answer he was looking for, secured the date for two days off, and hung up, feeling immensely pleased with himself. After all, what was the point in working 25 years as a Vegas concert promoter if you couldn't pull a few strings and grab some space on a moment's notice?

The older man sat back in his chair and relaxed for a moment. Everything was coming together. The next two days would be a blur of preparations and public relations, but the firm stood to make a fortune if this ghost Elvis turned out to be the real thing. Robertson took a minute to daydream about the possibilities. What would Elvis look like after 40 years? He didn't sound elderly on the phone, but if he had just been in hiding all this time, he would over 80 by now, wouldn't he? Could he even handle a concert at his age? And where had he been for the last 40 years? There were so many unanswered questions, but Robertson knew that he had to move forward with the concert preparations without getting bogged down in the surrealism of the situation.

Picking up the phone, Clint began the long list of phone calls he needed to make to pull together a showstopper Elvis concert in less than 48 hours.

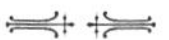

Elvis, Sunny, and Elisha burst through the door of the hotel room with an energy that was palpable as they started grabbing their things.

"We have about 30 minutes to grab our stuff and get back in the car," Sunny directed, looking over at Elvis. "Unless, of course, you have a magic packing spell that will pull it all together for us in just seconds!"

Elvis grinned. "No, Sunny. I'm not Sabrina the Teenage Witch. You'll have to do your own packing!"

Sunny looked disappointed for just a second before darting into the suite's bathroom to toss a few things into a grocery bag. Growling at the flimsy bag's inability to hold his stuff, Sunny went through the drawers of the bathroom and tossed the small complimentary soaps and shampoos and a roll of toilet paper into the bag with his two or three items. As he stood up, he caught his reflection in the mirror and stopped to look at himself reflectively. The bags under his eyes that had been there for years were almost gone, and his skin had a sort of glow that he had never noticed before. His hair, however, was a bit on the greasy side and longer than it had been in a while.

"Wow, I need to get a haircut!" he mused, still amazed that his face looked more relaxed and rested than it should after the wild, whirlwind weekend they had just completed in Memphis. As he was reflecting on the change, he heard a knock on the suite's door, and it jogged him into finishing his quick packing job. Entering the living area of the suite a few minutes later, Sunny noticed 2 small, wheeled suitcases standing by the door of the suite. Looking for Elvis, who was sitting on the couch, Sunny flashed him a questioning look and tipped his head toward the suitcases.

"What are those for?" he asked as he set his plastic grocery bags on the dining table.

"For you and Elisha," Elvis replied, with a smile. "I could tell you weren't exactly prepared for a road trip."

"I'm not exactly prepared for any part of this 'trip'," Sunny snorted. "But I've done a pretty good job of improvising this week."

"Yes… yes, you have," Elvis nodded. "I've been impressed so far."

Sunny went over to select a suitcase. "Sounds like you had a pretty low opinion of me at first," he pouted. "Why the hell did you pick me out there in the desert, then? I can't imagine it was an accident that I was the only one out there that night!"

Elvis smiled as if were keeping a secret. "Sunny, none of this was preordained. I came here knowing I had a message to spread and a job to do, but after that, nothing was planned. I think you being in the desert that night was a total fluke, but I had to play the hand I'd been dealt."

Sunny picked a suitcase, rolled it over to the table and began transferring his meager belongings into the empty bag.

"Why didn't you just move on to someone more your style after we got to civilization, then?" Sunny asked as he worked.

"I don't have a 'style', Sunny," Elvis sighed. "Do you think you are somehow to be excluded from hearing and accepting the truths that I was sent here to share?"

"Me?" Sunny sounded surprised. "I'm just the driver! You can spread any message you want, but don't keep me around just because you think you can pull me into some cult mentality about you and Jesus. I'm just not into that shit!"

Elvis got up off the couch and walked over to the table where Sunny was finishing up his packing.

"It's not a matter of being "into" anything," he started. "I have no interest in starting a cult of any kind. I am here to get the public's attention before it's too late for them to help themselves, and open their minds and hearts to the beauty of accepting God's word again.

You may be one of my biggest challenges, but I am determined to teach you to trust a higher power and put your destiny into the hands of something bigger than you."

"Well, plan on a lot of overtime, then," Sunny retorted, getting frustrated with this line of conversation. "Long motorcycle rides might win over 'Chickie' in there, but they're not really my style. You'll have to cook up something much more creative to make me believe in any of that stuff. I'm just the driver on this crazy, messed-up thing we're in the middle of!"

Just then, Elisha came back into the room with a suitcase in tow, and stopped when she realized she was interrupted a rather serious conversation. Sunny glanced at her suitcase in surprise.

"Hey! I thought those two suitcases were for me and her!" he exclaimed.

"What? You didn't think I needed one, too?" Elvis asked, without taking his eyes off Sunny.

"Well, I kinda had the impression that divine beings traveled a lot lighter than mere mortals," scoffed Sunny. "Besides, I haven't seen you carrying any stuff around with you."

"We went straight from the desert to Memphis, Sunny," Elvis dropped the smile. "I'm long overdue for a shower and change of clothes myself, and that suitcase is full of everything I need to make that happen. If you'll excuse me, I'll get that done and join you and Elisha in the lobby in thirty minutes. Order the car and wait for me."

Elvis retrieved the remaining suitcase, which definitely rolled like it was full, and retreated into the room that Sunny had just vacated.

Once the door was shut behind Elvis, Sunny looked over at Elisha, who hadn't moved.

"Did I interrupt something?" she asked, without the perpetual sneer in her voice that had been present since the money-stealing incident.

Surprised, Sunny answered without any attitude. "He was just pounding away at me about Jesus and God as if I'm his newest pet project, that's all. It wasn't a big deal."

"You aren't at all swayed by what he has to say?" Elisha asked, moving her suitcase to the door and getting her coat out of the hall closet.

"Hell no!" Sunny was emphatic. "I didn't sign on because I believe in God, I signed on because I don't have anything better to do and he's paying the bills for a month!"

Elisha was quiet, but busied herself with her coat and suitcase as if she was uncomfortable with Sunny's answer. Sunny zipped up his suitcase and joined her at the front door.

"You didn't really think I would just dive into whatever this is without looking, did you?" he asked her. "Are you already a convert after one ride on his bike?"

"I don't know what you mean," she said, in obvious discomfort, not making eye contact.

"I mean," Sunny's voice had an edge to it. "You go off with him, not any more indoctrinated than I am, and come back all quiet and shit... like something has changed. Are you under some kind of spell, or did something else happen while you two were off on your jaunt?"

Elisha slipped around him and headed toward the kitchen. "Nothing has changed. We had a long talk, that's all. I think he's an amazing man, whatever his story is."

"So something did happen," Sunny followed her. "You haven't been the same. What's wrong with you? Are you in love with him?"

"That's none of your business!" snapped Elisha, pulling bottled water out of the refrigerator. "And nothing happened except

I have realized he is an exceptional human being and I have great respect for him."

"Sure you do!" Sunny sneered. "I can see the signs. You're completely under his spell now and I'm all alone on the reality train! Thanks a lot!"

"I'm here to help him just like you are, Sunny Carlisle!" she answered angrily. "You do it your way and I'll do it mine!"

"Yeah, well make sure you're using birth control while you're doing it," Sunny shot back at her. "Or you'll be single-parenting a half-mortal long after this dude goes back to wherever he came from!"

"You really don't believe his story, do you?" Elisha challenged him. "You told him you would help him, and you don't buy into any of it!"

"I don't have to believe everything he says to stick around for the paycheck," Sunny defended himself. "You started all this for the same reason, admit it!"

"Maybe I did, but he's the real thing and I can see that now," Elisha was not quiet now. "You can believe or do anything you want, but you have no right to question what I believe or don't believe! Just keep your opinions to yourself and we might be able to work together for 30 more days without me killing you!"

Sunny chuckled. "You started it, babe. Rest assured I won't bother you with my opinions anytime soon." He strode to the door, grabbed his suitcase, and opened the door. Before he left the room, however, he turned to her one final time.

"Just be careful, sister," he warned. "Don't get all sucked into whatever this is until you understand it. It'll bite you in the ass if it ends up not being what it seems."

He turned and headed toward the elevators. Elisha just watched him go and waited for a minute so she wouldn't have to share the ride to the lobby with him before she left the room as well.

The light streaming in the window over the hotel-grade HVAC system that was bolted into the wall illuminated a man in quiet prayer. Kneeling at the corner of the king-sized bed that filled the small bedroom, Elvis' head was bowed and his eyes were closed as he silently mouthed the words he was saying. The almost palpable silence in the room emphasized the ambient noise from within and outside the suite. The honks and reverberations of the traffic on the street below, combined with the constant low hum of the fan embedded in the air conditioner under the window, created a low-amp white noise that added surrealism to the scene.

Coming to the end of his meditation, Elvis opened his eyes, looked upward for a brief moment, and then rose to his feet, gathering the towel and toiletry bag that he had dropped on the end of the bed. His hair was still damp from the shower, and his skin shone with a luster from the steamy bathroom he had just exited. As he stood, he caught his reflection in the mirror on the opposite wall from the bed, and stopped for a moment to ponder the figure he presented. With dark trousers and a white button-down oxford shirt, his 40-ish years reflected well on his trim and healthy body.

"I wish I had looked like this at the end," he mused silently as he observed his stature for the first time since he had returned. "Maybe I'd still be here in the flesh."

He chuckled and switched to thinking out loud. "Well, I am here in the flesh... just not the way I expected!"

Elvis moved to the dresser, still watching himself in the mirror, and took a horsehair brush out of his toiletry bag. Dragging the brush through his thick, black hair, he noticed a hint of gray in it that surprised him. His brush poised in mid-stroke, he picked at his hair with his other hand, playing with the smattering of gray strands that had appeared at his temples and near the roots. Smiling at himself in the mirror, Elvis finished brushing his damp locks and put the brush back in its bag before buttoning the last couple of buttons on his shirt.

Standing before the mirror for another moment, Elvis chuckled. "This is definitely not the Elvis that anyone remembers," he spoke with a grin. "Not fat, not young, but something in the middle."

With one last look, he picked up the small bag, inserted it into the suitcase that was waiting by the door, and exited the room, pulling the suitcase behind him.

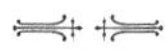

Outside on the sidewalk, the Cutlass summoned via the valet service, Sunny and Elisha waited patiently in the hot sun. Each of them faced away from the other, Elisha tapping her foot impatiently, and Sunny busying himself with folding the wad of cash that he carried around to tip valets and waiters with on Elvis' behalf. It was obvious from any vantage point that the two wished they were anywhere but together.

Elisha glanced over at Sunny for a brief moment, and looked disgusted by what she saw.

"Will you put that AWAY!" she whispered angrily. "I swear you like waving that around like candy!"

"Well, it is pretty cool that no matter how much I spend, there's always plenty to go around," Sunny replied without even looking up. "I would think that someone like you would appreciate that, if nothing else."

Elisha snorted. "Do you think that money is all that turns me on?" she asked condescendingly. "You know there's more to me than meets the eye."

"Oh, I'm very aware of what turns you on, little lady," Sunny smirked, as he continued to play with the bills in his hands. "And I'm also very aware of the parts of you that don't meet the eye."

Elisha whirled around to respond to the remark, but stopped short when she saw an older man dressed in what looked like old BDU's and a hat pulled low over his face, approaching Sunny. Before she could switch gears and get Sunny's attention, the man spoke.

"Do you have any of that to spare, m'boy?" he asked Sunny, looking directly at the bills in Sunny's hands. "I haven't eaten in a couple of days and I could really use some help getting a meal tonight."

Sunny didn't even look up before he stuffed his wad of cash deep into his pants pocket and replied to the old man.

"Get lost, old man!" he growled. "I don't got nothing you need!"

Elisha looked at him sharply, as the older man's shoulders slumped in response to Sunny's biting response. The man looked at Sunny's hand, where the wad of bills had been just moments before, and tried again.

"But sir, you have plenty of cash," he started. "Surely you have enough to buy a meal for a man who's down on his luck?"

"I said 'Get lost!'" Sunny replied tersely. "This cash isn't mine and I'm not at liberty to just hand it out to anyone who walks by and sees an opportunity!"

"What opportunity?" the man persisted. "I'm just talking about a meal. I haven't eaten anything decent in days. What would it hurt for you to buy an old vet a burger?"

"An old vet?" Sunny scoffed. "What makes you think I believe you're a vet? Your Salvation Army discards?"

"Son, you don't have to believe anything I share," the old man pulled himself up a little straighter. "But I know what I am and where I've been, and I don't deserve your disrespect. You will have to answer for your greedy ways" the old man scuffed and walked away. Shuffling a bit, but with his shoulders held a bit higher. Elisha slapped Sunny after the man walked past her, ticked off that he had treated the man so poorly.

"What?!" he barked.

"You were such a shit!" she accused. "What would it have hurt to give him 10 bucks for a decent meal?"

"It's not my money!" Sunny replied self-righteously. "And I don't know him from Adam! He could be a total con artist!"

"You're such a disaster!" Elisha shook her head in frustration. "I don't understand what Elvis sees in you."

"I'm just the driver, sweetie. He doesn't see anything in me but that," Sunny replied, pulling out a pack of cigarettes and preparing to light up. Just as he lit the first stick, Elvis appeared in the doorway of the Peabody.

"What's going on?" he asked, observing the ever-present tension between the two.

"Sunny totally stiffed a homeless man a minute ago," Elisha instantly reported. "He was such a creep about it, too!"

Elvis was silent for a moment before responding. "Where is he now?"

"How the hell do I know?" Sunny snapped back, feeling just a tinge of guilt under the stare of the older man.

"Sunny," Elvis began quietly. "I know you don't know that much about me, but that money in your pocket would serve that man far better than it will serve you."

Sunny fidgeted with his cigarette and watched Elvis with a guarded expression.

"You've never walked in that man's shoes," Elvis continued. "Or saw things through his eyes... or stood and watched with helpless hands, while the heart inside you dies."

The three of them were completely silent as poetic words from the past hung between them in the air. Elvis and Sunny locked eyes for the briefest of moments before Sunny dropped his and looked to the ground, dropping his cigarette and grinding it into the steaming pavement.

Just then, the Cutlass pulled up to the curb, and the valet jumped out to hand off the keys.

Elvis, without taking his eyes off Sunny, spoke first. "I'll drive this leg. Let's go."

Sunny and Elisha both moved silently into the car, Elisha in the back seat as usual, and Sunny in the right front seat. Elvis walked around to the driver's side door, whispered to the valet as he tipped the boy, and climbed into the car for the trip west. As they pulled out into the street from under the hotel's awning, they passed the old man in BDUs shuffling down Union Avenue toward 3rd Street. The man looked up as they trolled slowly by. Sunny avoided eye contact, but Elvis saluted him briefly as they drove past, and the old man tipped his ragged old Army cap in return.

"I feel so bad for that old guy," Elisha muttered. "All he wanted was a hot meal."

"He'll have that and more," replied Elvis with a wry smile. "It's all taken care of."

Elisha sat up straighter in the back seat with a confused expression flitting across her face. "Umm... what did you do?"

"The valet is arranging it for me," Elvis answered. "He'll be fine tonight."

Elisha smiled and sat back for the ride to the airport. Sunny slumped down in the front seat and concentrated on returning to Vegas.

CHAPTER TEN

The Las Vegas Hilton box office was humming with activity. The line for "Elvis Lives" tickets had kept them busy for several hours, ever since the announcement was made that the event would feature the "real Elvis." The attendants at the POS systems were barely able to take smoke breaks, and the phone operators in the back of the office were equally stretched for time, fielding all of the phone calls they were receiving.

It was insane—the activity this event was generating! After all, everyone knew that Elvis was dead. The funeral proceedings had been on TV for days and days, Priscilla and Lisa Marie had been in charge of his estate for four decades, and most of his entourage had scattered to the four corners of the Earth years ago. The attendants in the box office were confused and intrigued at the same time. What kind of gimmick was this anyway? Why would someone as established and respected as Clint Robertson plan an event that sounded as contrived and opportunistic as this one did?

Regardless of their questions, their job was to sell tickets, and this one had all the potential for a sell-out that all the other

Elvis-related events did. Even their established Elvis tribute artist, Trent Carlini, was curious as to the reason for this event preempting his regular Friday night gig, but it didn't preclude the fact that they had to keep up with the flow of ticket sales that had maxed out their office for over 24 hours.

The muted TV mounted in the corner on the wall above their heads was running the local cable news channel's headline news feed, and every so often the story of this new concert would float by. Having seen it numerous times by now, the box office staff didn't even look up anymore to wonder at the news that Elvis had returned to do a concert at his old stomping grounds. No one knew why, and everyone had a ton of questions about how a dead pop idol could suddenly reappear after forty years, but obviously those questions were not going to be answered anytime soon. All they could do was sell the tickets and hope that the mystery was revealed during the event itself.

The bottom line was they were going to make a killing on an event that had only been publicized for a couple of days, and everyone's end-of-year bonus was looking pretty damn good!

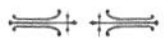

The three-winged tower of the Las Vegas Hilton rose impressively out of the desert, ringed by pool complexes and parking lots designed to entertain and contained the masses of guests that came and went on a daily basis. The monorail-inspired entranceway to the hotel was already packed with cabs and limos either dropping off or picking up their passengers with impeccable flair.

The dusty Mercedes rental car, drove slowly over the ramp toward the main entrance as it approached the crowd of people milling around at the several sets of turnstile doors that provided a formal barrier between the outside world and the grand lobby of the hotel. With the windows rolled up, the three occupants observed the landscape but did not stop the car as pulled slowly past the group who turned out to be primarily journalists looking for a story. Microphones and cameras were all evident as the reporters on the sidewalk took turns scanning the approaching vehicles and the hotel guests as they came and went, obviously searching for something in particular.

"I don't recommend that we stop here," Sunny cautioned, still in the passenger seat next to Elvis. "This looks like a problem for us. Where are we meeting Robertson?"

"I don't think we settled on a time and place when we talked,"

Elvis answered, driving carefully to avoid the pedestrians that were darting across the road in both directions. "I suggest we find a coffee shop somewhere and call him. I agree that we're asking for trouble if we get out here."

The car pulled out into the main roadway, avoiding direct contact with anything that moved, and moved back out into regular traffic. Searching for a suitable spot to stop for breakfast and a potential meeting proved to be a bit of a challenge, with the hotel located off the main strip. Heading into town, it wasn't long before they spied a rather unassuming shop that looked more like a home than a business. The Bluebird Coffee Shop seemed to be the perfect hole in the wall kind of place they needed for a travel break and to arrange a meeting with their so-far sight-unseen concert promoter. Pulling into the small parking lot, Elvis spoke first.

"Call Robertson and tell him to meet us here," he directed quietly. "Tell him we don't want to go to the hotel until we are sure everything is going according to plan."

Sunny nodded and picked up his cell phone, dialing Clint's number for only the second time. It didn't take long for the call to be picked up on the other end. Sunny waited for the greeting before launching into his terse but respectful message.

"Mr. Robertson. This is Sunny Carlisle, and we have arrived in Vegas," Sunny started. "No, you cannot talk with Elvis. He's driving and asked me to contact you to arrange a meeting at the Bluebird Coffee Shop.

We're there now, just pulling in. We'll get something to eat and wait for you to get here. What do you mean 'why do we want to meet here?' It's a coffee shop and we need some caffeine! About 30 minutes? Fine. See you then."

Sunny flipped his phone closed and put it back in his shirt pocket as Elvis shut the vehicle off and sat back for a moment in silent relief that the long trip was finally at an end. He stretched and dropped the keys in Sunny's lap before opening the car door and stepping out onto the pavement. Elisha woke up sleepily, and looked around as Sunny also climbed out of the car and stretched his legs. The small shop looked inviting to the three weary travelers, who all began envisioning the plate of food and mugs of steaming coffee they were about to enjoy.

Entering the building, Sunny and Elisha collapsed on the overstuffed chairs in one charming corner of the restaurant, leaving Elvis to approach the coffee bar by himself. Looking directly at the barista behind the counter, Elvis offered up his trademark grin and asked for a menu.

"We don't have a menu, sir," she answered politely, not appearing to be surprised that the King of Rock and Roll was engaging her in conversation. "Everything is either on display in the case or listed up on the boards," she explained, motioning behind her to the framed blackboards mounted on the wall, with every conceivable flavor and recipe that a decent coffee shop would offer listed with their prices. Elvis looked at the exhaustive list of possible selections and seemed more confused the more he read.

"Don't you have just regular old coffee?" he asked. "I have no idea what any of that other stuff is. What is a latte?"

The barista looked a little miffed. "A latte is a couple of shots of espresso with steamed milk and a shot of flavoring," she replied. "And yes, we have regular coffee. Do you want fair trade, organic, or local?"

Elvis looked even more confused. "Fair what? How about just some Maxwell House? Do you have that?"

At this point, the barista was getting annoyed. "What planet are you from? I have Green Valley and Las Vegas brewed. Those are your choices."

Elvis looked over at Sunny and Elisha, hoping for some help. Both had their eyes shut with legs stretched out in front of them. "Hey! What do you guys want for breakfast?!" he barked to get their attention. Both startled awake and stood up slowly, giving each other space as they made their way over to the counter.

Sunny looked up at the boards and in the case, scouting out his options, while Elisha stood patiently behind him waiting her turn. Looking up at the barista, Sunny gave her a tired smile and ordered a mocha cappuccino with two shots of espresso and a cinnamon croissant. Elisha stepped up to order a hazelnut latte and a fruit cup. Elvis stood there, no further ahead than when he approached the counter in the first place. Sunny looked at him curiously.

"I just want a cup of coffee that I can put some cream and sugar in," Elvis murmured quietly, not wanting to prompt any further frustration from the barista, who was waiting patiently for his order. "And I would love a fried egg on toast. Do they have those here?"

Sunny looked at the blackboard menus and shook his head. "Looks like the closest thing they have is an egg and bacon bagel breakfast sandwich," he answered, looking over at Elvis. Elvis shrugged in obvious indecision, and Sunny ordered one for him, along with an Americano with cream and sugar.

As the barista got busy making drinks and nuking the saran-wrapped bagel sandwich that had be pre-made in the wee hours of the morning and stored in the pastry case, the entourage moved over to a table at the back of the café to wait for their breakfast and their guest. Elisha excused herself to go look for the ladies room to freshen up, leaving Sunny and Elvis alone to wait for the food. Elvis ran a hand through his hair and then folded his hands on the table in front of him, closed his eyes and spent a moment or two in silent meditation before opening them again and looking directly at Sunny.

"What?" Sunny asked, suddenly feeling a touch of wariness, as if he needed to be on guard for what came next.

"When he gets here," Elvis started. "I expect that he will be confused as to who to deal with first."

Sunny didn't say a word.

"I don't expect you to negotiate this entire deal," Elvis continued, "but I do expect you to be my intermediary. I have plenty to think about without having to deal with the minutia of concert promotion. As long as he fills the place so I can speak to the people, everything else will fall into place."

Sunny wasn't sure what to say, but it was clear that Elvis expected him to stay on top of Robertson and the details of concert without knowing anything about concert promotion.

"Uhh… what exactly do you expect me to do, then?" he asked, a bit irritated that everything seemed to be planned on the run. "It's not like I've done this for years and a huge concert like this is the next logical progression in my career!"

"I have complete faith that when a decision needs to be made," Elvis answered, "That you will know what the right choice is."

"Well, I'm glad you have such faith in me," Sunny rolled his eyes. "I'm not so sure it's well-placed."

"You haven't let me down yet," Elvis answered with a grin.

"Yeah, but I haven't had to do anything except drive you around and make some phone calls," Sunny replied. "Anybody can do that shit!"

"Ah, but you have many skills that you don't even know you have," Elvis smiled. "You've been working gigs since you were 17. Just consider this a bit bigger than what you're used to, but still the same concept."

Sunny chuckled nervously. "A bit bigger? I'll say so! Kind of like comparing a rowboat to the Titanic, don't you think?"

Elvis sat back, still smiling. "Trust me. When the time comes, you'll know what to do."

"Is that more of that faith and promise stuff you believe in?" Sunny scoffed. "I understand the message, but I won't believe it until I see it."

"Just wait and see," Elvis replied. "You'll surprise yourself."

Elisha rejoined them at that point, sliding into the seat next to Elvis. Not making eye contact with Sunny, she shared a smile with Elvis, he put his arm around her and drew her to rest her head on his shoulder. Sunny again rolled his eyes, and watched them closely until the barista brought them their food and drinks. He still wasn't sure what had changed in their relationship.

They did seem closer, and yet they didn't seem intimate. He was sure he'd figure it out as time went on, but he didn't like the feeling that he was the odd man out in this triangle.

Just then, a tall, very distinguished gentleman in an expensive sports coat and Bergstrom-quality khaki pants entered the shop. Taking off his sunglasses, and looking around, he spotted the tired trio before they saw him. He stood for a moment, observing their silent breakfast and trying to get a good look at them before moving over to introduce himself.

Arriving at the end of their table before they even saw him, he surprised all of them when he spoke.

"I assume this is the Elvis contingent?" he asked in his professionally groomed voice. All three looked up immediately, and Elvis stood to offer him his hand in greeting.

"Yes, sir," Elvis started. "It's good to meet you. I am..."

"Elvis," Robertson finished for him, accepting the handshake cautiously. He was still scanning Elvis' face as he dropped the King's hand, and Elvis could sense that the stranger wasn't yet completely convinced that the real thing was sitting in a Las Vegas coffee shop.

"Why don't you join us," he offered, pointing to the seat next to Sunny. "I promise you he doesn't bite."

Clint looked at Sunny before taking the seat. "Mr. Carlisle, I assume?" Sunny offered his hand as well, following Elvis' lead and appearing to be magnanimous to the untrained eye.

"Good to meet you," Sunny said cautiously, glancing at Elvis and getting a nod of approval from him.

Clint Robertson sat slowly, smiling at Elisha and then turning his attention back to Elvis. Elvis waited for Clint to take the initiative, and Clint wasn't sure what to say, so the three of them sat there for a few moments, each waiting for someone to start the conversation. Elvis finally began.

"So, can you tell us how the plans are shaping up for tomorrow night's event?" Elvis asked.

"Well, we have a band that knows all the Elvis standards," Clint started. "We have a stage manager who is available tomorrow night that I think will be brilliant, and the ticket sales have been more than brisk since we made them available yesterday."

Elvis pondered all this. "What if I want to do some music that isn't considered 'standard'?" he asked.

"With all due respect, you can't pop up out of the blue and pull a concert together in 2 days and expect a band you've never worked with before to know music other than the standards,"

Clint answered rather matter-of-factly. "If you want to do something out of the ordinary, you might want to rehearse with them tonight or tomorrow and get them warmed up to the idea."

"Valid point," Elvis admitted. "There might be a gospel song or two I need to add to the program, and a rehearsal might be good regardless."

"I can set that up," Clint offered. "I have studio space available. It's small, but it would work to just get your feet wet.

I think they'd really appreciate the introduction so they know what they're doing before we get on stage."

"Sounds good. Set it up," Elvis instructed. "We need to find a way into the hotel and give my crew here a chance to catch up on some sleep. If you can help us do that, I can be available by this afternoon to work with the band."

Clint nodded, still studying the man across the table from him. The resemblance was uncanny, and he certainly had the mannerisms, from what Clint could remember. He had just been a kid when Elvis died, so it wasn't like he was an expert on Elvis' habits. Still, he didn't see anything that sent up any red flags. From all outward appearances, this seemed to be the real McCoy.

Clint cleared his throat and began to speak. "So, where…"

"Where have I been?" Elvis finished the question with a quick smile. "I can tell you have a lot of questions for me. I'm not sure I can answer any of them without you thinking I'm crazy. But, let's suffice it to say that sometimes you just have to have faith that things happen for a reason and we don't always have answers that fit into the nice, neat little boxes we create for our lives."

Clint broke into a slow grin as he listened to Elvis, and didn't skip a beat when Elvis finished. "Faith I have. Not necessarily in the same things you do, but the bottom line for me is, you look like the real thing, you talk like the real thing, so for all intents and purposes, you are the real thing. Let everyone else ask the questions. I'm just here to make some money and get you back out in the public eye."

Elvis' eyes darkened for just a moment before his smile flashed at Clint. "I trust you have my best interests at heart, sir, so I will also trust that you will represent me faithfully. Sunny here will be my point man from this point forward, and I expect you to discuss any matters of logistics with him while I am working on the creative side."

Clint glanced over at Sunny with a veiled look of cautious regard. "We've had our moments, but for the sake of pulling off this concert, I will work with whomever you tell me to as long as we can get all the work done before tomorrow night and I get paid my usual percentage. Do we need to discuss that?"

"You will be fairly compensated for your time," Elvis agreed. "I'm aware of industry rates, and if this event goes well, we will need your services for other events in the very near future."

Clint looked intrigued. "I'm comfortable with discussing those other events immediately following tomorrow night's event."

"Then it's settled," Elvis held out his hand. "Get us into the Hilton as soon as possible, and line up the band for an afternoon rehearsal, and we'll talk again tomorrow. Thank you."

"My pleasure," Clint replied, shaking Elvis' hand and standing up. "I'll call the hotel and book you a room.

"Please ask for Room 3000, the penthouse… if it's available," said, Elvis

"Absolutely," said Clint, turning to look at Sunny. "You have my number. Give me 30 minutes or so to get the room lined up, then pull around to the loading dock. If you call me when you leave here, I'll have a valet meet you there so you can enter the building without much notice."

Sunny nodded but said nothing.

Clint turned and left their table, only glancing back one brief time before leaving the coffee shop and getting into his Infinity IPL G coupe. Sunny and Elisha both looked at Elvis to try and gauge his reaction to the concert promoter, who had basically breezed in and out in less than 30 minutes.

"You comfortable with all this?" Sunny asked. "That was quick!"

"Yes, I have to be," answered Elvis. "We don't have time to not trust those who are helping us. Now, how do I eat this thing?" he asked, pointing to his bagel sandwich. "And what is this stuff that you call coffee?"

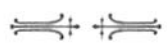

About 90 minutes later, the Cutlass headed back over the overpass toward the Hilton entrance. Sunny was driving this time, and Elvis sat in the back seat with a pair of dark sunglasses on, hoping to remain incognito for as long as possible. Elisha, also sporting a new pair of dark glasses, sat as far away from Sunny as humanly possible in the front seat.

The car crawled along in traffic as Sunny looked for the access road to the back of the enormous building. As they approached the front façade of the casino and convention center, they could see the busy crowd of reporters and cameramen still gathered on both sides of the main entrance. This time, however, there a couple of additional faces that hadn't been there earlier.

"Hey!" Sunny recognized a couple of the newcomers. "There's Andy and Barney! What are they doing here?"

Elvis lifted his shades and peered out of the back windows toward the crowd. "Not sure. I thought we lost them days ago."

"Lost who?" Elisha looked over at Sunny. "The cops?"

Sunny nodded as he kept his eye on them. The mercedes was forced to move at a crawl because of all the activity coming and going at the entrance to the hotel, and he was hoping to avoid notice until he could get past it.

"We had a bit of a problem after Elvis climbed into my car the other day," Sunny admitted. "But we kind of left them in the dust when this guy did his Speed Racer trick the first time."

"I don't know," Elisha sounded concerned. "I didn't sign on for anything including cops. This really isn't my style."

"It's not my style either," said Elvis from the back seat.

"Surely you're used to seeing this scene, " Sunny scoffed. "All the concert security and entourages..."

"But they were never after me," Elvis replied. "This is the first time I have felt pursued." He dropped his voice as if he was talking to himself. "Except for that time in Germany..."

"What was that?" Sunny looked in the rear view mirror to get a better look at Elvis behind him.

"Never mind," Elvis answered more loudly than was necessary. "I just meant that this development was not something I expected. I'm not sure what they want from us."

"They think you're an imposter trying to capitalize on Elvis' good name," Sunny replied. "And it's a slow crime week in Mayberry, so they don't have anything better to do!"

Elisha grinned in instant reaction to Sunny's statement before catching herself and looking out the window at the scene there. The two uniformed rural cops were attempting to question the people milling about in front of the hotel, looking very serious and professional, but somehow looking ridiculous at the same time. The people they were interviewing looked puzzled and irritated, and the bellhops looked frustrated that a black and white was sitting on their curb with its blues flashing. It was taking up valuable valet and loading space, and their toleration of the situation was ebbing quickly.

Elisha smiled at the scene, quickly realizing as Sunny had, that these wannabee cops were nothing to worry about in the long-term. Looking back over at Sunny, she shared her opinion.

"They're harmless," she chuckled. "If we just stay a step or two ahead of them, they'll tire of this pretty quickly."

Sunny shared a grin with her briefly before concentrating on the traffic once more. He had finally found the access road and was trying to navigate to it without attracting any attention.

Slipping onto the smaller, road to the delivery entrance, he drove toward the back of the building, where Clint Robertson's valet was supposed to be waiting for them with their pass to the top floor.

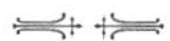

The door to Room 3000 opened to reveal opulence that neither Elisha nor Sunny were prepared for. If they thought the Peabody was special, they realized it paled in comparison to what lay before them now. Sunny dropped his suitcase and the laptop they had purchased on their way back to the hotel and began checking the place out, room by room. The doors off the main living area opened up to a solarium on the front of the suite that included a four-person hot tub and a bar built into the back wall. The outer doors of the solarium revealed a large balcony with luxurious outdoor seating and an incredible view of the city.

Elisha left her suitcase in the great room as well and went into the two bedrooms, each with a king-sized bed, chairs and fireplaces, and huge master baths. The closets were the size of nurseries, and the kitchen off the living room was designed for gourmet service. Finding herself back in the living room, Elisha just stood there staring at the luxury around her, as Sunny finished scouring the place for an extra bedroom.

"Where are we all gonna sleep?" he asked, as he came back into the main room. "Should we draw straws for the couch?"

Elisha glared at him, angry that he was trivializing the grandeur of the large apartment they had just discovered.

"Seriously?" she pushed his buttons. "I'm not sleeping out here on the couch. I'm the only lady, so I'm sure I'll get the second bedroom."

Sunny snorted. "I'm sure you're sure," he said, laughing. "But I'm sure that Elvis isn't going to make me sleep on the couch the whole week, either."

"We're not going to be here for a week," said a third voice from the doorway. Elvis entered the suite, carrying a garment bag packed full of clothing and pulling his rolling suitcase behind him.

Sunny and Elisha looked at each other briefly in surprise. Elvis tossed the garment bag over the back of the overstuffed sectional sofa and rolled his suitcase out of the way of the massive oak door before pushing it shut with his foot. Looking at Sunny and Elisha, he elaborated.

"Did you think that this event was the only one we'd be doing?" he asked with irritation. "Have you not listened to anything I've said in the last few days?"

Again Sunny and Elisha looked at each other, this time as if each one thought the other was withholding information.

Elvis sighed. "Did you think that when we moved from radio interviews and programs to concerts we were going to just stop with one? I still have 27 days to reach the world. I can't do it with one concert."

"Okay, okay," Sunny started. "I get it. We get it. But it sounds like we need to have a plan. And the first plan we need to make is where we're all going to sleep. After that, we can change the world!"

Elvis hesitated for a second, and then grinned at both of them. "Glad to see you have your priorities straight," he chuckled. "Each of you take a room and get settled. I'm not going to be here enough to worry about something as trivial as a bed."

Elisha moved toward him, stumbling up against her discarded bag as she went. "Where are you going to be? You're only practicing and performing for 2 days."

Elvis touched her shoulder and looked at her reassuringly. "Don't worry about me. We all have a job to do, and mine is a little different from yours."

"But what will we be doing here while you're out doing whatever you're doing?" she asked.

"I need you and Sunny to make sure everything goes smoothly tomorrow night and to work with Clint to plan the next several events," Elvis continued. "I have to reach as many people as possible in the next three weeks, and I can't do it without your help."

Sunny moved over to pick up the laptop in its still-sealed box. "Okay, do we know what we're supposed to do, or will it all be revealed in some divine message from above while you're out hitting the low notes with the band?" he asked.

Elvis glanced at the boxed computer with some wariness as he answered Sunny's hostility-laced question.

"I have already indicated to Clint where I want to focus next, and he has some ideas as well." The singer looked weary for the first time since they left Memphis. "I have my work cut out for me with getting this group of musicians ready for tomorrow night.

I will have to trust that you and the promoter can communicate well enough to figure out a tentative schedule for the next few weeks and get started with some planning."

"And what do you want me to do?" asked Elisha as Sunny began ripping into the computer box and muttering indistinguishable words under his breath.

"My dear," Elvis smiled at her. "I want you to go freshen up and then help Sunny in any way you can until I get back tonight. Then, we'll all go enjoy a good meal and relax. I will need some quality conversation with my two favorite people by then, I'm sure."

Elisha smiled back, and Elvis kissed her on the forehead.

"Will you two knock it off!" Sunny growled. "Or at least take it in another room!"

"You're just jealous!" Elisha retorted, turning away from Elvis, grabbing her suitcase, and heading into the smallest of the two bedrooms. "I'm going to take a shower and order some room service snacks."

"Yeah," Sunny muttered. "Jealous is what I am."

"You know, Sunny," Elvis walked over to the dining room table where Sunny was struggling with the laptop's packaging. "At some point, you should start looking past the immediate and view the world from a more positive perspective. Your negativity is preventing you from accepting a more faith-based life pattern."

"Mumbo jumbo, my man," Sunny replied. "You do your thing, and I'll do mine."

"You and I are closer in ideologies than you might think," Elvis continued. "You're just resisting the acceptance of what you know to be true. If you stop pushing it away so hard, you could embrace it and your life would be more whole."

Sunny looked up at Elvis, discontinuing the box dismantling for just a moment. "Like I said before, I don't try to second-guess what you're doing here, or how weird this all is, and I'd appreciate it if you would do the same for me."

Elvis was silent for a moment before replying. "Sunny, you know that my purpose in being here includes helping you accept a new world view."

"Yeah, well, I hope you're up for the challenge," Sunny replied, getting back to work on the computer. "Because I have no interest in being converted."

Elvis put his hand on Sunny's shoulder. "Well, three weeks is a long time. We'll see how it goes."

Elvis turned and walked through the double doors into the solarium. Sunny watched him go and then sat down at the table to install software.

"Who the hell does he think he is, dropping in from outer space and expecting me to just fall at his feet and turn all right-wing Christian on him," he thought to himself. "I must be a glutton for punishment, traveling the country at supersonic speed with a lying, scheming hooker and a religious zealot who thinks he's on a mission from God! Lord have mercy!"

He looked up and then around him, almost guiltily. "Too weird, too weird," he muttered and got back to work.

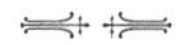

CHAPTER ELEVEN

Elisha looked at Elvis. "Are you nervous?" "A little, but nothing the king can't handle," he said, laughing lightly. "Elisha, can you excuse me for a second? I have to be alone"

Elisha, caught off guard a little by the request, responded in a quiet voice, "Sure, I'll be right outside."

She whisked herself to the door and glanced over her shoulder as she began to reach for the door knob. Elvis had already begun to pray. She quietly opened the door, eased out, and shut it gently. Elvis could hear the chanting of the crowd and the faint sound of a familiar voice in Wayne Newton. It was dawning on him that this was his first concert since returning, the gravity of the moment was heavy.

"Father, let this be a memorable show. Give me strength and allow me to be valiant. And, most of all, let this be You this time instead of me. Thank you for giving me this opportunity again Father, and may your will be done."

Raising his head slightly, he picked up the Bible lying next to him and opened to Matthew 21:21

"Assuredly, I say to you, if you have faith and do not doubt, you will not only do what was done to the fig tree, but also if you say to this mountain, be removed and be cast into the sea, it will be done. And whatever things you ask in prayer, believing, you will receive."

"I trust you Lord," he said softly, glancing at the mirror smiling.

The crowd chanted louder and louder as Wayne Newton finished his monologue on the return of the King. Behind the thrusting sound of "Thus Spake Zarathustra," Elvis walked to the edge of stage with his head down inhaling and exhaling deliberately murmuring to himself, "This is about you, Lord, not me. This is about you, Lord, not me."

"Thus Spake Zarathustra" faded into the intro of "CC Rider," as he entered the stage, feeling light like he was walking on air. "Something is with me this time, guiding me. I can feel it. This is nothing like I felt in the past," thinking to himself as he glanced over the crowd waving like he did in the past. "I feel like each step is predestined. I have purpose and meaning. This is the best feeling I have ever had."

Reaching for the microphone with purpose, he was deliberate with every move. He screeched out the lyrics to C.C. Rider.

The crowd went hysterical; it was the spirit in the concert hall that assured people that this was, indeed, the real Elvis. After the song, Elvis tossed his guitar to the side of the stage and grabbed the microphone.

"Thank you very much, ladies and gentlemen, and I would like to say, welcome to the Show. You're probably wondering where I have been," he laughs. "I've seen Jesus, and he has given me life to tell you there is hope in this world. Trust him as your savior today."

Elvis, with grace, the angels were in the concert hall marching like troops toward every restless heart. The energy was felt in every living soul. The hairs on the heads of thousands of people tingled with tantalizing flare. It was the spirit from this event that carried an unstoppable train through the hearts of everyone at the concert. Some of the concert-goers accepted it and some denied it. The choice was theirs, but one thing was for sure. There was no doubt the King was Alive again.

Immediately, the news spread over the nation as media hubs switched to a live feed of the Elvis concert. CNN called several Elvis experts to give analyses of Elvis and to determine his legitimacy. Jay Gordon said, "I think this has got to be Elvis. No one else can imitate Elvis like this. It's unreal, amazing."

Those words reverberated and resonated in the ears of millions of people who watched. "The King looks to be alive. This is a miracle"

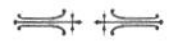

The Keystone cops waited anxiously outside the Hilton for Elvis and his entourage to exit. However, Sunny had a premonition before the show and scheduled to have a decoy limousine situated outside the Hilton to trick the Keystone cops. Elvis, Elisha, and Sunny were in stealth mode headed toward a solid gold 1964 Chevrolet Corvair owned by Sunny's cousin, Slick Earl the Pearl. His hair was greasy black and he sported a dated attire, a satin shirt with blue and gold stripes and beige bell bottom pants that was too long at the inseam with strings of material hanging from the bottom of the pants. A tooth pick in his mouth, a grin, and two golden teeth that sparkled when the sun light hit it just right, he was leaning against the car waiting for the clan of law-breakers seeking to escape the Keystone cops. Sunny greeted Cousin Earl with a hearty, brotherly hug.

"Thanks man, I'll owe you one," Said Sunny.

"You don't owe me anything. Oh, well, maybe an autograph from the King."

Earl turned his head and winked at Elvis.

"I got you covered, brother." Elvis responded.

Earl slammed on the accelerator and sped off.

"I see you and Sunny have the speed thing in common." Elisha said with a half -hearted smile.

Racing to the airport, Earl slammed on the breaks as the Corvair came to a streaking halt. Their bodies swayed forward from the movement of the car. Earl the Pearl jumped from the driver's side and reached to open the passenger side door for Elisha. His eyes widened as Elisha's right leg eased out the car. Earl offered his hand and Elisha lightly put her hand in his.

"My, my you're a very beautiful woman," said Earl.

Sunny glanced over at Elvis and laughed.

"Thank you kindly," said Elisha. She grimaced a little from his foul breath when he leaned in to kiss her cheek.

"Can I call you sometime?" asked Earl.

"You have to ask Sunny about that. I'm his girl." A slight grimace returned to her face

Earl smiled at Sunny. "Ah, Sunny you did ok this time didn't you?" Earl made a thumbs up gesture toward Sunny.

"Yeah, I guess you could say that." Sunny said, confused.

Elisha whispered to Elvis, "The things you have to say to get out of sticky situations."

The quick flight from Vegas to Memphis was welcomed by the clan of three. After arriving, they relished the stunning view of the surrounding Memphis skyscrapers, the plantation room of the Peabody Hotel.

"I'm raising a toast," offered Sunny. "A toast to a very successful Vegas trip. Elvis, you are the man."

The clinging of their glasses resonated from the rooftop and seemingly met the stars that twinkled a little brighter on this special night. The celebration lingered into the early morning.

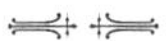

Elisha was awakened by a knock at the door. She momentarily forgot where she was. Then, it dawned on her that she was back in Memphis at the Peabody. Knock, Knock …

"Oh my God, who is it at the door?" She opened the door swiftly as the bellman stood emotionless with his hand out.

"A letter for you." He uttered.

"Thank You," said Elisha. She smiled at the bellman; the bellman refrained from smiling back as he walked off. She noticed the letter had Elvis' name on it. She instinctively looked around the room; curiosity began to get the best of her as she lifted the corner of the envelope to tear it open.

"Oh My God, what I'm I doing?"

She quickly put it on the counter in plain view so Elvis would see it when he got up. Still feeling a bit tired, she layed back down on the couch. Moments later, Elvis entered the living area of the immaculate suite. He noticed the letter and opened it, reading.

Welcome, my dearest friend and son in our Lord.

The peace of God will always be with you. I understand that God as sent you. However, I know nothing about how you were circumstanced. By the Grace of God, however, I think it shall be deemed that the two of us assemble to see that our voluntary intentions are the exact contrary to those of a soul that would offend God. No, my dear brother, you do not offend him at these painful times; your soul, on the contrary, is like Gold that boils in the crucible; it is purified and shines with an added luster. Never are you upheld in a more fatherly way by the hand of God, and, if you were able to see your state as it really is, far from being afflicted about it, you would return thanks to God of mercy for his ineffable gift.

I feel God has sent me to you, not in vain, but in an attempt to explain the chaotic mass of misery and weakness that is prevalent in your society.

There are some things left void in which the state that God has brought you and the knowledge you may gain to further your ministry. I can give you assurance which ought to satisfy you. In this assurance may you find comforting words.

Your method of prayer is good and will always be, as long as you continue it peacefully in entire abandonment, in a simple peacefulness, waiting a calmness that is quite resigned to the will of God. As each of us ought to follow his attractions in prayer and at other times, do not be afraid to keep yourself always in this great destitution which you will find within your soul. Remain therein without any formed thought, quite dull and insensible to all things. Love this state because, with regard to you, it is the gift of God and the beginning of all that is good. I have never come across any chosen souls whom God has made to pass through these dry deserts before arriving at the Promised Land, which is the terrestrial paradise of perfection.

I would like to cordially invite you to my Tabernacle located at 106 Popular Ave. at 6:00 pm

Yours Truly,

Zorzi

Clinton Robertson fell asleep in his black leather office chair, crumbles scattered on his shirt from the crackers he was eating earlier. The ring of the phone was almost deafening when it awoke him from his dream of the Elvis Concerts making him a multi-millionaire.

"Damn," he yelled.

The secretary in the lobby shook her head in disbelief.

"Sorry to wake you up, Mr. Robertson," said the secretary.

"You didn't wake me up, Brenda. I was just caught off guard again because I was reading over this proposal I got."

"Yeah, right" she thought to herself.

"Anyway, there is a man from a prison near Memphis, Tennessee, and he wants to talk to you; do you want to take the call?"

"What does he want?"

"He wants to know if Elvis can perform at his prison"

"Sure, I will take it," replied Clinton.

"Hello," answered Clinton.

"Mr. Robertson, I'm Chuck Ward, the Warden at the Federal Prison Camp outside of Memphis, Tennessee. I know your time is valuable, but I would like to ask you a quick question."

"By all means, Mr. Ward, ask."

"This prison hasn't had any excitement in a long time. I have been the Warden here since 1972, and I got the Job right out of High School. When I began my warden tenure at the prison, Elvis was pretty popular at the time, and whenever he performed locally, it would be telecast, and we could watch his concerts at the prison. It was a great way to keep the prisoners from going crazy. Well, anyway, I want you to know, I have been an Elvis fan since…"

"Excuse me, Mr. Ward, I hate to cut you short, but I've got an appointment in 2 min. can you get to the point?"

"Ahh, ok… well, would it be possible to have Elvis play at the Prison?"

"How much can you offer?" Clinton mumbled.

"Nothing. At the moment, our prison budget isn't large enough to pay you all I'm sure."

"How much? Just give me a figure." asked Clinton.

"Well, sir with all due respect, we can't offer you anything. I was just hoping you could perform free and, if you could, we will give 1 thousand dollars to the local Cancer association in your name, if you like."

"Forget it. We don't do freebies," Clinton hung up the phone.

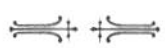

Elisha awoke once again by the sound of the door knob rattling. Sunny came barging through the door.

"Wake up, Dracula, the night is about to come. Where is Elvis?"

Elisha was still trying to get her head together, but she remembered the letter she left out for Elvis and quickly glanced toward the counter.

"The letter, it's gone."

"What letter?" replied Sunny.

"The letter I left on the counter for Elvis earlier."

"I don't see a letter," countered Sunny.

"Elvis," she raised her voice and looked in his room. "He's gone; he left without me hearing anything."

"Yeah, he can be a bit sneaky sometimes," proclaimed Sunny. "What did the letter say?"

"I don't know. I didn't read it."

"Why not?"

"Because it's none of my business, that's why not. I know you would have looked at it."

"Gosh, you know me quite well, don't you?" replied Sunny.

"Ah, you think! I know you too well, unfortunately."

Sunny laughed. "Let's go grab some grub. I'm hungry."

"You paying?" ask Elisha.

"I think you should pay for stealing my wallet," replied Sunny sarcastically. Elisha gave him a look like ice water.

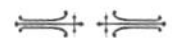

CHAPTER TWELVE

The bell tower seemingly touched the heavens as Elvis stood before it, mesmerized by the beauty of the church. He walked slowly across the sidewalk, which was lined by beautiful blue bachelor buttons nestled in the midst of the radiant black eyed susans. The assorted flora reminded him of some of the country roads he traveled as a young man. He continued toward the mammoth, reddish-brown, mahogany doors, his eyes fixed on black cross with an eye in a pyramid just above the entrance to the Cathedral. The symbol gave him an instant feeling of uneasiness. He opened the Majestic maroon doors cautiously. Taking a long, mesmerized look through the vestibule, he momentarily scrutinized the murals on the wall. One depicted a long, twisted branch descending upward toward a cloud. Inside the cloud was a keyhole. Beside the mural hung a picture of Jesus and Mary holding one another, embracing like lovers. On the opposite wall was a painting of a fierce dragon with fire coming out of its mouth. Situated alongside that was another picture of a furious Lion with venomous canine teeth. Reservations settled in on him, but he still felt the urge to press on.

Descending through corridor, a low light was cast over the wall of the foyer. The sanctuary appeared elevated and had a heavenly appearance to it. A beam of light cascaded down from the vaulted ceilings. Rich in architectural design, it reminded him of looking through a kaleidoscope.

The beam of light appeared to become a little brighter the closer he got to the pulpit; the pulpit was made of rich, genuine mahogany and maple with a white maple symbol applied to the surface. Two sculpted flames rose from the rich mahogany bases. The light from the ceiling appeared as a prism that cast tiny rainbow spectrums across the pulpit area. Situated above the pulpit was a silhouette of a man. Elvis presumed it was Zorzi. With the assurance of the Lord's protection, he walked closer to the silhouetted figure.

"Hello, are you Zorzi?" Elvis enquired.

"Yes," replied the figure.

The lights from the ceiling became brighter as it revealed a bearded man, tall and slender, with rounded shoulders.

He wore a white robe with a burgundy outline and long loose white pants that covered his feet. His hands were clasped together, and his eyes appeared of dark coal with a speckle of white in each eye. He reached out his hand and offered Elvis a hand shake. "It is a pleasure to meet you, Mr. Elvis."

Elvis extended his hand in friendly greeting. "You can just call me Elvis" he replied.

"May I call you Lion Man?" Zorzi questioned.

"Lion Man?" replied Elvis, his eyes narrowed, sizing him up.

"Yes, Lion Man," replied Zorzi.

"Or are you a pitiless sphinx from the desert?"

"Don't know what you mean, but I was sent back to earth from Jesus," said Elvis.

"Jesus, Lion Man? You have inspired a lot of people, and you come from the desert. You must be the second coming of Christ."

"That I am not. Jesus comes as the book of Revelation describes, not as a pitiless Sphinx, or Lion Man, in which you refer to it as. It sounds a little menacing to me."

"Please, excuse me for my reference of Lion Man. I do not mean any ill will toward you. I apologize," said Zorzi.

"Apology accepted," Elvis replied softly.

"So, you're a messenger from God?"

"Yes, I was sent back to earth to warn people that Jesus is coming soon," replied Elvis.

"Did God grant you with any powers?" probed Zorzi.

"Maybe the power to influence people toward accepting Christ," Elvis said.

"Indeed, that is a good cause, and perhaps you have the authority to provide food for your people as well?" questioned Zorzi.

"The manna is provided by God, if we have faith. Though, we should live by the Word of God," said Elvis.

"The mountains and the plains are the centerpieces of this earth. Perhaps, through our kingdom, this power may be granted to you. I would like to offer you a leader position in our Tabernacle; we need a charismatic individual such as yourself to lead our flock."

Elvis hesitated slightly to digest the offer from Zorzi. He raised his eyes from thought and looked toward the zealot. "The mountains of God's Kingdom are controlled only by him; I'm a messenger with one cause. My purpose is already determined. However, I thank you for the offer." Elvis answered.

"The guardian angels are among us, now, Elvis; let them reside in our hearts to lead us. My offer stands. Our kingdom is awaiting your wise choice." Zorzi said with a lofty voice. Zorzi handed Elvis a scroll. "Take this with you, my friend, and meditate on it tonight, and ask your God to lead you," Zorzi insisted.

Elvis handed the scroll back to Zorzi. "I'm already led, and my angel will protect me in my journey. He gives me wisdom to discern the truth, and the truth is not here." Elvis held his gaze for a couple seconds and turned his head from Zorzi, proceeding to walk back toward the corridor. Zorzi stared intensely after Elvis, but he continued up the aisle.

"The angels are not with you. You will be damned!" Zorzi boomed, his voice echoing through the Tabernacle. Elvis stopped, he turned toward the pews, and the light surrounding Zorzi became dark again. The silhouette faded, but his voice continued to reverberate in Elvis' ear.

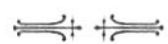

"So, what are you going to do? Are you going to stick it out to the end?" questioned Sunny.

"Yes Sunny, I'll say it again, I am. I think it's just amazing that this has happened," replied Elisha.

"So, you're getting all into this God stuff?" asked Sunny.

"Yes, IT has always been more than just GOD STUFF! to me. I grew up in London, England, and my mom was a devout Catholic, so I had no choice but to attend Catholic services on a regular basis. Our Mass was called the Divine Liturgy in England, and my mom would strike me with her belt if I refused to go. She would always tell me that I would go to hell if I didn't attend Mass every Sunday. My mom would also tell me that if the Lord can give you a whole week to live, you can at least spare one day out of every week of your life for him. She made me memorize the communal worship prayer." Elisha smiled and looked up at Sunny.

"My Jesus, I believe
That you are present in the Most Holy Sacrament.
I love you above all things,
And I desire to receive you into my soul.

Since I cannot at this moment receive
You sacramentally,
Come spiritually into my heart.
I embrace you as if you were already there
And unite myself wholly to you.
Never permit me to be separated from you."

Elisha finished her religious rite with the familiar sign of the cross hand gesture, but in a dramatic fashion signaling her careless regard for the Catholic faith.

"Quite impressive, I must say," Sunny smiled. "So what about your Dad? Where was he?"

"My dad was killed at war when I was 2 years old, so I don't remember him at all. That was one of the reasons my mom was so devoted to the religion is because my dad was a devout Catholic himself."

"What about your family,? Where are they?" Elisha ask.

"My dad was disabled during the Vietnam war. He's confined to a wheel chair. My mom left him for a rich lawyer when I was 12 years old. I guess that's one reason I don't respect women a lot because of the way my mom left my dad when he needed her the most. Being handicapped and confined to a wheel chair is tough enough, but being alone and confined to a wheel chair is even tougher. Ironically enough, he was a huge Elvis fan. I remember when I was a kid he would talk about Elvis all the time. He had pictures on the wall and all the memorabilia stuff like the gold albums and everything." Sunny let out a laugh. "Yeah he told me stories when he would go to his concerts and the women would get so horny from seeing Elvis that he would always get laid after the shows." Laughing again, Sunny concluded, "Yeah he is a cool old man."

"Well, now I see where you get your perverted ways," Elisha responded with a hardy laugh.

"Yeah, I guess I can blame my perverted ways on him."

Elvis returned to the Peabody, he was led to the Bible that was lying on the top of the lamp stand, by the window in the presidential suite; he turned to 1 John 4:1-6:

"Beloved, do not believe every spirit, but test the spirits, whether they are of God; because many false prophets have gone out into the world." Elvis bowed his head and prayed,

"Thank you, Father, for not allowing me to be misled, and for giving me the strength and the wisdom to deny a satanic influence. In your heavenly name, amen." Elvis raised his head and opened his eyes, and thought for a moment, "I wonder who this Zorzi guy really is?"

He made his way over to the table in the celebrity room, opened up the laptop, and punched in Zorzi Episcopal Church Memphis. Results returned "Zaira Zorzi, often called Zorzi by his associates, is an Italian-born bishop who now heads the First Episcopal Church in Memphis Tennessee. He was appointed head bishop in 1995 and oversees the dioceses. The synod meets twice a week, Saturday at 9am and Tuesday at 7pm. He was born in Frascati, Italy and was a devout Roman Catholic until age 19 when he met his wife of 20 years, Mrs. El-Borak Amar, born and raised in Qatar, Saudi Arabia. She later moved to Dubai in the United Arab Emirates, where she was hired in the Economic and Planning department of Foreign Trade. She later advanced to the minister position. She now heads the whole department and is considered one of the most powerful women in the world. And she is considered one of the key players in the proposed Transatlantic Trade and Investment Partnership agreement.

"Umm," Elvis murmured. Suddenly, he heard voices down the corridor. The voices became louder as the doorknob turned. Sunny and Elisha came through the door with their usual clatter of clashing tongues.

"Hey, Elvis, what have you been doing?" Sunny said in a loud, enthusiastic voice.

"I paid a visit to someone," Elvis said softly.

"Is that what the letter was about, Elvis?" Elisha asked.

"Yes."

"Who was it?" questioned Elisha.

"His name is Zorzi. He's a cult leader, and his church is located here in Memphis."

"How did it go?" asked Elisha. "He tried to entice me to join his cult," Elvis responded.

"Yeah, you're probably going to get a lot of offers to join cults," Sunny replied in a sarcastic tone. "The Mormons tried to get me into their cult one time."

"The worst cult of all are the Catholics," said Elisha with a dejected sound in her voice.

"The Catholics? What are you talking about? They're not a cult," demanded Sunny.

"Hey, guys, I hate to break up this discussion on cults, but have you heard anything from Clinton?" Elvis asked.

"Yeah, he said something about some stupid prison gig. I said no way," Sunny said hastily.

"What prison?" demanded Elvis.

"I don't know. Why does it matter?" Shouted Sunny.

"I want to know. Call Clinton and ask him what prison it was."

"Are you kidding me?" Sunny retorted.

"No, I'm not kidding" replied Elvis

"This is crazy; there is no money with a prison gig." Sunny demanded.

"I don't care. Call him."

"Ok, you're the boss." Sunny said reluctantly.

Clint Robertson was on his way to pick up two to go orders from Wendy's when his cell phone started ringing.

"Hello," said a raspy voice Robinson.

"Mr. Robinson, this is Sunny. I forgot to ask you earlier, where is the prison you were telling me about?"

"I don't know, some place called the Federal Prison Camp outside of Memphis. Why?"

"Elvis wants to know," replied Sunny reluctantly.

"Well, tell Elvis were not going to waste our time with a prison gig that doesn't pay anything."

"Yeah, I will. Thanks a lot,." Sunny hung up the phone. "It's no money in the prison gig," retorted Sunny.

"Where is it located?" asked Elvis.

"Someplace called Federal Prison Camp outside of Memphis."

"Umm," Elvis rubbed his chin. "Let's do the gig."

"Woah, now what a minute," snickered Sunny.

"Wait for what? Let's do the gig," Elvis replied.

Sunny shrugged his shoulders. "Come on, man., We need to think about this some more."

"Think about what?" replied Elvis.

"Think about the money for Christ sake," Sunny replied harshly.

"I don't care about the money," Elvis said with a stern voice.

"Well, you may have all the money in the world, but I don't, and I need to survive, and, as your manager I'm demanding we don't do the gig." Elvis reached in the inner sleeve of his black leather jacket and pulled out a clean, crisp one hundred dollar bill and placed it in Sunny's hand.

"We're doing the gig," said Elvis.

CHAPTER THIRTEEN

It was a cool, dark morning in Millington, Tennessee, outside of Memphis; the chain gangs were hammering away along the side of the road leading to the Federal Prison Camp.

"I can't believe it's this cold in early August," remarked Sunny.

"Yeah, I would think that every day is a dark and chilly day for these prisoners," replied Elisha.

"Who knows what goes on inside the mind of a criminal; this is kind of creepy if you ask me," Sunny remarked.

"Nobody is asking you." Elisha laughed.

Sunny gave her the look over. "Yeah, yeah, yeah," Sunny said, while simultaneously lighting a cigarette. Sunny pulled the convertible up to the prison gate. A guard came out to the greet them.

"Are you Elvis?" asked the security guard.

"Yeah, it's the king and his entourage," replied Sunny with a smirk.

"Wish I could see the show," said the security guard.

"What's your name?" asked Elvis.

"I'm Alexander Rigsbee."

"We'll make certain you get a video," Elvis said with a smile.

"Thanks. I'm a huge fan; my grandmother was too. I remember she would talk about you when I was a kid."

Sunny floors the convertible before the guard had a chance to say anything else, leaving behind him a large cloud of dust from the road.

"I'm sure the security guard really appreciated that," Elisha said, looking toward Sunny with a disgusted look on her face.

"Oh, well, he was a nerd any way," snickered Sunny.

"You're such a jerk, Sunny. You know that?" Elisha said in a hateful voice.

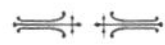

Zorzi was alone in his vast office pondering how to tell the world that Elvis is the Lion Man and the Anti-Christ, when a knock sounded at the door. "Come in," commanded Zorzi.

Alonzo entered the office. A recent seminary graduate from Mid-America Seminary, he stood tall and slim in his Arabic American frame.

"Dr. Zorzi, is there any way we can focus our attention on something other than the Elvis scenario?"

"Son, sit down for a moment," Zorzi requested calmly. "I'm a lot older than you, and I'm a little wiser. You will find out later that wisdom comes with age. I'm telling you from all my experience as an esteemed bishop that this man is the Anti-Christ. I think it is our duty to warn people that he is the Anti-Christ, to tell them he is trying to lure lost souls to hell and damnation."

"Are you sure, Mr. Zorzi?"

"Son, I am 100% sure. You see, I met with the man the other day. He refused to join us and help our cause, and he must be an imposter."

"Sir with all due respect, I have seen the man, and I do not believe he is the Anti-Christ."

"Son, you're still wet behind the ears, and you haven't developed your discerning spirit yet. Generally, that gift comes later in life, after you have gained invaluable experience and a couple of setbacks. Can you trust me when I tell you that he was sent here by Satan and not God as he claims?" Zorzi said in a gentle voice.

"Yes, sir, whatever you say." Alonzo lumbered back to the door with rounded shoulders, feeling as if he failed once again in confronting the questionable leader.

"Alonzo," said Zorzi.

Alonzo turned to face Zorzi once more, he exhaled.

"Yes?"

"Keep your head up. It's not the end of the world, or at least that's what we're trying to prevent." soothed Zorzi.

"Yes, sir." Alonzo walked away with a sulking.

Zorzi pondered a moment more. "Alonzo."

"Yes, Dr. Zorzi?"

"Can you call WMCTV and try to get me an interview with them?"

"Yes, Dr. Zorzi." Alonzo closed the door, and Zorzi looked away to peer through the window. Taking notice of a squirrel eating an acorn, a grin came over his face.

"Mr. Lion Man, I will expose you as the Anti-Christ." The squirrel finished eating his acorn and took a quick glance at Zorzi; his smile turned to a sudden grimace as an uneasy feeling came over him from making eye contact with the squirrel. He approached the blinds, waiting a minute, and then very reluctantly lifting one of the slats. The squirrel was still looking in the direction of the window. He let go of the shutter quickly. "Nonsense, it's only a squirrel."

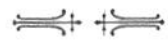

The long aisle leading to the back of the prison appeared to be squeaky clean, and the smell of ammonia was so strong it made Sunny's eyes water as it cleared the sinus pressure from his head.

"I think you guys put a hurting on these floors," exclaimed Sunny.

"Yes, we take pride in our fine establishment here. I'm sure you all will find this place to be immaculate."

Sunny looked over at Elisha with a smirk on his face, reacting to the wardens comment. Elisha elbowed sunny in his ribs.

"Ouch!"

The warden and Elvis turn their heads toward Sunny. "Is there a problem back there?" questioned the warden.

"No, sir, just had an instant pain come out of nowhere. Sunny looked at Elisha as she stared him down. Sunny gave her a half-grin, and Elisha looked away in disgust.

The warden continued, "We put a lot of time and effort into the upkeep of the prison, and it was voted the top prison in the southeast. We have fewer breakouts, and less disorderly conduct than any prison in the southeast."

"It is a pleasure to be here Mr. Ward." Elvis remarked.

The large cafeteria area had many tables and chairs lined up in rows resembling a concert hall. The prisoners were enjoying themselves waiting anxiously for the king. The voice over the intercom announced that Elvis was on the premises.

The light chatter turned into a loud celebration. The prisoners started jumping around with excitement, high fiving one another and dancing. For them, the party had begun.

Elvis greeted his crew with handshakes while Sunny and Elisha entered the stage behind him. "Hi, I'm Sunny. Are you all ready for the King?" the cafeteria turned into a circus. Prisoners jumped on tables, yelling to their hearts' delight. The security guards were at hand, armed and ready in case anyone tried to cause a fight or break out.

"Here is my side kick, the lovely Elisha."

Whistles from the cafeteria proclaimed approval, and prisoners shouted out "Hey baby, you looking good," some of the prisoners shouted. "Honey, can you see me after the show?" and a host of other, less appropriate, proclamations of attraction.

"She will be handing out Bibles for those of you who are interested."

"What is this? Church service or something?" Shouted one of the prisoners in the back.

"Yeah, you could say that." Sunny started to chuckle lightly at the comment. Elisha rolled her eyes and gave Sunny a half-witted grin.

"Ok, folks. Brace yourselves. The king lives." Sunny blurted out to the prisoners.

Sunny briskly walked off-stage and out of view with Elisha quickly following. The sound of "Thus Spake Zarathustra" began to boom through the amplifiers. The bass thundered and rattled the tables. The excitement rose. The fog machine behind the stage dispersed smoke on the stage, and Elvis entered through the cloud. He gestured toward the prisoners with a hearty wave, grabbed the microphone from the stand, and began with "Jailhouse Rock." The prisoners went crazy; the guards each had one finger on their triggers. The energy was vigorous and loud. The king was back once again. Sunny looked over at Elisha, sharing a laugh at the hysteria.

"This is unreal." Shouted Sunny.

"Yeah," Elisha yelled back at him. Momentarily, they enjoyed one another's company as if nothing had ever come between them.

Elvis concluded "Jailhouse Rock" and walked toward the center of the stage. He signaled the prisoners to calm down a little, and, after a few minutes, the place was quiet enough for Elvis to begin speaking.

"It's a pleasure to be here." The prisoners return to their frenzy, and Elvis once again signals for them to quiet down a little.

"Some of you may be wondering, 'Am I real? Is it the real Elvis?' I'm here to tell you, now, I'm real and alive. I want you to understand something," he raised his voice once again over the loud chanting of the prisoners, "If any of you have ever doubted the existence of God, you don't have to doubt anymore because I have seen the feet of Jesus."

The prisoners broke out into a deafening yell; exuberance was all around and the spirit was touching every heart in the cafeteria. Elvis concluded the concert by belting out "How Great Thou Art" with resonance and thunder. Some of the prisoners were moved to tears of joy as they reached toward the heavens with praises.

Sunny and Elisha started to hand out the Bibles. When most of the Bibles were dispersed, Elvis hummed the final few verses of the song before speaking softly through the microphone.

"You are all in here for a reason. Each of you made a mistake that cost you your freedom, but I'm here to tell you today that you are free, now, in Christ Jesus. I want to ask you if you are ready to confess your sins and your transgressions to Christ. Now is the time."

The prisoners lined up and Elvis began laying hands on some of the prisoners. Some were made unconscious by the Spirit of God, as Elvis prayed in the name of Jesus over them. Others walked off in tears, and there were a few that clung to

Elvis as if he was Jesus himself. Elvis quickly reminded them that Jesus is in heaven awaiting their confessions and their acceptance of Him as a personal savior. The scene was humbling, transcendental, and completely heavenly as the cafeteria was transformed from a rowdy concert hall to a sanctuary bringing souls to Christ.

A lump formed in Sunny's throat. He had never witnessed such a spectacle in his life. Emotion rose up in him, but he kept it in check. Sunny wasn't about to let anyone know how he was feeling. But, at a distance, Elisha eyed him and noticed the emotion written on his face. She was enthralled.

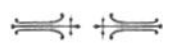

"I'll have another shot of bourbon, bartender, except make this one a double, please," Sunny said under his alcohol-breath. Alfred's was nearly empty except for a couple in the corner that was kissing on one another. Sunny glanced at the couple from time to time, turning his head quickly before they noticed eyes spying them. He adjusted his gaze toward the cigar in his hand as he thumped the cigar ashes in the ash tray. He glanced toward the ceiling each time he inhaled the cigar smoke. Every now and then, he would exhale through his nostrils, allowing the flavor to linger longer.

The T.V. in the corner of the bar was barely audible, but sunny was able to hear a strange word: "Zorzi." He glanced toward the screen before he took another draw.

"Would you mind turning that up a little bit?" Sunny asked the bartender.

"Reporting from Memphis, Tennessee, we are here live with the Reverend Bishop Zorzi from Zion Tabernacle. Reverend, you claimed to have talked with the risen Elvis personally?"

"Yes, I have. We met at my tabernacle, and he claims to be the Lion Man which is representative of the Anti-Christ," proclaimed Zorzi.

"Are you trying to tell us that the Anti-Christ is the risen Elvis?" replied the T.V. commentator.

"Yes. The risen Elvis is an imposter. I must warn everyone not to take this man seriously. He is a counterfeit. He claims to have come from heaven, but the scripture warns in Luke 21:8: "For many will come in my name, claiming 'I am he,' and, 'The time is near.' Do not follow them."

"There will be false prophets who claim to be like Jesus. He is the Anti-Christ, and I'm begging everyone to stay away from the man. He is very dangerous." Zorzi proclaimed his lies with gusto.

Sunny looked away from the T.V. and shook his head in bewilderment. "Really? Zorzi? What a freaking character." He chuckled lightly.

"Have you been keeping up with the story?" questioned the bartender.

"Yes, half heartily, I guess," Sunny mused.

"The Anti-Christ? Sounds like some bizarre stuff," claimed the bartender.

"Yeah, bizarre is a good word for it," Sunny whispered. He took another quick look at the couple in the corner as they were getting ready to leave. Sunny motioned for the bartender, "I'll have my tab." He laid a fifty on the table and followed the couple out the door.

"Do you all know Jesus?" Sunny said to the couple.

"Excuse me?" said the gentleman.

"Do you know Jesus Christ?"

"Excuse me, sir, but I think you may have had too much to drink," replied the uninterested gentleman. He and his lady-friend began to laugh as they walked away. Sunny stood haplessly in the middle of the sidewalk as the mist sprinkled his face lightly. He glanced at the green reflection from the traffic light on the wet street. He stood and watched it change to yellow, to red, and then back to green, yellow, and red. He was mesmerized by the changing reflection of the lights, and each time it turned a different color, he questioned the validity of Jesus.

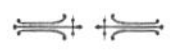

The sun was making its way over the horizon along the Mississippi river creating a bronze overtone across the scenic view of downtown Memphis. It was peaceful, and Elvis enjoyed the serenity of the moment before things started getting busy again. The bench on the path of the river was starting to feel uncomfortable after an hour or so. Magnetized by the silence, he reflected on times in his former life and on the history of Memphis. This area was the spot for the hustle and bustle of trade in historic Memphis. So many years Memphis flourished in Lumber and trade. And the assassination of Martin Luther King occurred here as well.

"Now is the time I need to make a more important historic memory than perhaps any of those in the past," he murmured to himself. "I want this historic moment to take place in Memphis, the city that I cherish above all cities, and it is Memphis that I consider home." He placed his head in his hands and began to pray.

"Lord, I know you want me to be a spectacle and a shining star for you. It is your will that I must do your will and not my own. Please give me a clear sign of what you want and how I should get there. This journey has to be done right to glorify you."

He lifted his head from his hands and, at that moment, a voice came from a distance. Turning toward the voice, a tall, slender gentleman walking toward him wearing a blue sports coat, khaki pants, dark glasses, and a brown hat.

"I'm sorry to invade your privacy, but you must be Elvis." He offered his hand. Elvis stood up to shake the stranger's hand.

"My name is Benjamin Neely. I heard about your prison gig, and I have a feel for what you may be trying to accomplish. I'm a spiritual man myself, and I realize it's important to put God's will above our own."

Elvis studied him for a few seconds. "It's a pleasure to meet you, Mr. Neely. You must be a sign from God because I just got done praying about our situation."

Handing over a business card, Benjamin encouraged Elvis. "Continue to pray, and when you feel the urge and want to know more, give me a call."

Elvis studied the card for a quick moment and placed it in his silver money clip. "Thank you, sir. Have a pleasant day."

Benjamin smiled and walked away.

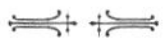

Elisha was applying eye liner when the phone started ringing. She put down her black eye pencil and walked over to the phone.

"Hello? Is the Lion Man available?"

"Is what available? Who is this?"

"This is your friend, Mr. Zorzi."

"Listen, jerk, I'm not your friend. You're a crazy person, so please leave us alone." She slammed down the phone. Elisha thought to herself, "Where is Elvis, anyway? No clue." She called down to the lobby. "Have you seen Elvis?"

"No ma'am, we haven't seen him."

Slamming the phone down once more, she returned to her bedroom mirror and began applying her eyeliner again. She stopped to study herself for a moment. "What am I doing?" Throwing down the eyeliner, she walked to the bathroom, wet a wash cloth, and began to rub the makeup from her face. "I've had enough of this trying to be somebody I'm not. It's gotten me nowhere, and I'm fed up. Lord, help me. I need a change. Please, help me."

Grabbing at her skirt, she ripped it off and slid into a pair of white jeans. Over her double D chest, Elisha pulled a bold green- and blue-patterned blouse with soft pleats. Getting on her knees to peer under her bed for some shoes, all she saw was heels. She hurried to the closet--heels, heels, heels, everywhere. No flats, no sandals, just heels, heels, and more heels.

"Forget it. I'll walk barefoot and buy me some regular shoes." She scribbled a quick note to Elvis saying, "Elvis, I'm bewildered and confused. I'm in need of some answers. It's time for a confession. I'll be at Saint Mary's Catholic Church if you need me. God Bless."

She placed the note near the Bible on the table by the window and glanced at the mirror one more time. Running her fingers through her long, curly, dark hair, she gave herself a kiss in the mirror, grabbed her purse, and hurried out the door.

Elisha walked briskly through the lobby, and the bell man at the front door glanced at her, his eyes venturing to her bare feet. Elisha took a quick glance at him. "What are you looking at? Haven't you ever seen a woman walk barefoot before?"

He blushed, eyes focused on the tight, white jeans hugging Elisha's bottom so elegantly. She twirled through the golden doors of the Peabody and wistfully pondered where she would go. Waving her arm in the air for a cab, it wasn't long until one pulled up to her at the curb. The passenger side window slid down and Elisha shouted, "Can you take me to a shoe store that doesn't sell heels, just a regular shoe store?"

"Yes, Ma'am."

She pulled the back door open and plopped in the back seat, exhaling and inhaling deeply.

"Are you ok, ma'am?" asked the cab driver.

"Yes, I need a pair of regular shoes; I don't believe I have ever owned a pair in my whole life."

"Really?" questioned the cab driver.

"Yes, really," snorts Elisha.

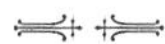

Sunny enthusiastically awaited a hot shower as he entered the front doors of the Peabody. The bell man greeted him with a smile, but Sunny returned only a half smile. Entering the elevator, the hot bath called his name. Still feeling the effects of the over-indulgence of alcohol, breath fumes lingering, even he was offended by the odor. Making his way to the luxurious confines of the presidential suite living room, he plopped down on the sofa, slid his shoes off, and began rubbing his tired feet. The phone rang an unwelcome interruption.

"Hello?"

"Sunny, this is Clint."

"Hey."

"So, you went through with it anyway?"

"It was Elvis' idea, and he's my boss, not you."

"I told you not to do it. We don't do free gigs."

"Well, apparently, Elvis was led by the Lord, and he wanted to do it, so just deal with it, man."

"I have to pay the Las Vegas Hilton, and you guys leave two days early and fly back to Memphis?" fumed Clint.

"Elvis didn't want to waste time with the keystone cops, so he decided to take an early trip back to Memphis."

Elvis entered the living room, and Sunny covered the receiver of the phone. "It's Clint. He's pissed about us doing the prison gig. What do you want me to say?"

"Tell him to cut a check for 10% of the Vegas show and make it out to Chuck Ward at Federal Prison Camp," explained Elvis.

"Are you sure, man? That will really send him off the deep end."

"Yes, I'm sure." Elvis turned and walked away. Sunny gazed in his direction trying to refocus on the conversation with Clint.

He took his hand off the receiver. "Elvis says write a check to Chuck Ward at Federal Prison Camp for 10% of the Vegas Show Money."

"Are you crazy?"

Elvis heard Clint yell from the executive king bathroom. He turned his head slightly and grinned. He walked back into the living room. Sunny placed his hand over the receiver again and looked at Elvis. "What do you want me to do?"

"I know. I heard him clear from the bathroom. Tell him he's fired and to wire us the money to Memphis National Bank."

Sunny started to laugh. "Have you lost your mind? We get our first gig and we're firing the promoter already? This is totally crazy. What are we going to do about getting concerts?" pleaded Sunny, staring intently.

"Don't worry about it. I have a backup plan."

Sunny shook his head in disbelief and took a deep breath.

"Elvis said your fired. Wire the Vegas show money to Memphis National Bank." Sunny grimaced again preparing himself for the onslaught of choice words. He pulled the phone away from his head and stared at it as the outpouring of obscene language filled the suite. Sunny slammed the phone down on the table.

"Whew. Wow, just fucking amazing, man. Please, tell me what the hell is going on?"

He turned to find himself talking to no one. Elvis had already made his way back to the bathroom, and Sunny noticed the steam escaping the bathroom and winding through to the celebrity suite parlor. "Great. Freaking great. I'm in the dark once again." He picked up his shoes and headed to the celebrity suite bedroom, the relief of a hot shower revisited his mind.

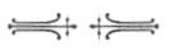

Elisha adored the black Paris Hilton Bonnie flats; she sat down and slid the shoe on her size seven foot with freshly manicured red toe nails. She put the other shoe on and paraded up and down the aisle. A saleswoman approached her, "How do they feel?"

"Umm, I don't know." She glanced in the mirror to see if the shoes went well with her white jeans. "I think they look good." She walked up the aisle again as the saleswoman noticed her nice figure. "I think I'll take these."

.

"Great. I'm glad you like them."

Elisha sat back down and propped her feet up on the shoe stool. The sales woman bent down and began to slide the shoes off Elisha's feet. The sales woman held Elisha's foot for a moment as she noticed the softness and fresh manicure.

"You have nice feet."

Elisha was taken a bit off guard by the comment

"Thank you," she replied, laughing slightly as the sales woman began to slide the other shoe off her foot. Elisha reached for her purse and noticed the saleswoman was still holding her foot, looking admirably at them. The saleswoman began massaging her foot slightly.

"I had no idea this was a massage parlor, too!" blurted Elisha.

The sales woman gently lowered her foot. "Oh, I'm sorry. I really like your feet. They are so soft and pretty."

Elisha was somewhat stunned about the comment and quickly reached for her purse.

"Oh, I will have to wear these out. I came in here barefoot. But, I'll put them back on myself. Thank you." She reached for the shoes and put them on her feet as she noticed the sales woman was still starring at her.

"Do you need a box for the shoes?"

"No, thank you, I'm fine." Elisha assured her.

"Follow me, and I will ring you up." The sales woman took her charge card and handed it back to her. She handed Elisha another card, too, and Elisha noticed the writing on the back.

"Call me anytime."

Elisha looked at her, stunned. Then handed the card back to her. "Thanks, but no thanks" A bit confused, she walked toward the door. She paused for a second and turned her head before leaving. The saleswoman was waving at her. Elisha hurried away. Once out the door, she paused for a second and thought to herself, "What was that all about?" She signaled for a cab, flopped in the back seat, and asked, "Can you take me to Saint Mary's Catholic Church?"

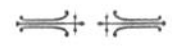

Zorzi sat plaintively by his desk pondering how to let the world know the truth about the imposter that had risen. He glanced down at his calendar pad and, looking at the date marked August 16, had a premonition that Elvis was going to plan something big for that day, perhaps even coerce all the gullible souls into following him to utter hell, similar to the Jim Jones cult years earlier.

"This man must be stopped!" He hit his fist hard on the solid oak desk and shook his hand violently trying to rid the pain. A knock on the door sounded.

"Sir Zorzi," murmured a voice outside the door.

"Yes, Alonzo, you can come in."

"Sir, Zorzi, I have found out some information about a man who claims he knows the risen Elvis personally and that he can help us get the Word out about the Elvis being an imposter."

"By all means, invite him in."

"Yes, sir." Alonzo walked out to the lobby, and escorted an older man into the confines of Zorzi's study. Zorzi rose from his seat and walked around his desk to greet the older man. He extended his hand.

"Hello, sir, and welcome to my study. How may I help you today?"

The older gentleman replied, "I have some important information about the risen Elvis."

"Well, by all means, have a seat and share your thoughts with me." The older man in the military jacket, his hat pulled low over his face, sat in the chair. His eyes roamed the room. He noticed the many different books ranging from the Bible to biographies of a host of legendary people from Winston Churchill to Raeford Faulkner. To the right of the book shelf, he noticed a picture of Zorzi when he was younger, his hair was darker, and his skin had a smoother tone and it was less ghostly.

"I saw your appearance on T.V. the other night, and I thought to myself that this may be a situation worth exploring. I have seen the risen Elvis, and, as a matter of fact, he gave me a sum of money early one morning about a couple of weeks ago. He may have felt sorry for me because I was lying on a park bench in Williams Park near Graceland."

Zorzi leaned in closer. "Are you a peasant?" Zorzi's eyes rolled upward to meet Alonzo's, and he lowered them back on the older gentleman.

"Sir, it was his demeanor, his kindness, his thoughtfulness. I have never had an individual touch me the way he touched me."

Zorzi's eyes once again met Alonzo's. He stood from his chair and planted his fist firmly against the oak table. "Alonzo, please escort this gentleman out of my office at once."

"But sir he told me that he…"

Alonzo was interrupted by the hostile Zorzi.

"At once," demanded Zorzi.

Alonzo nodded to the older gentleman as he rose from the comfortable leather seat. Zorzi's eyes stayed fixed on Alonzo as the two of them moved toward the door. Alonzo looked back at Zorzi to find his eyes still locked on him. Alonzo turned his head slowly and walked out.

"Damned," Zorzi yells, driving his fist once again into the oak table.

"Ouch!" He shook his hand vigorously, and strode around the room to try and shake it off. The secretary and Alonzo heard him scream in pain from the lobby area, but said nothing.

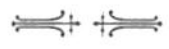

The cab pulled alongside Saint Mary's Cathedral on Poplar Avenue. The three red Romanist doors stood out, accentuating the monolithic cathedral. The grey sky complimented by the aesthetics of the massive edifice mirrored Elisha's sullen attitude. Somberly, she gave the cab driver a hundred dollar bill and exited the cab. The cab driver leaned his head toward the passenger side door. "Do you want me to wait for you?"

Elisha turned quickly as if the sudden remark startled her a bit. "No, I'm fine."

The cab driver reached for a business card; he held it out the window. "Well, if you need me to come back and pick you up, here's my number."

Elisha turned again to acknowledge the gesture and placed the card in her purse. "Thank you."

She refocused on the cathedral, walking slowly toward the rubicund door. Her emotions overcame her; she began to shake with cold chills. She felt like she was reliving an emotional trauma, the haunting memories of her troubled youth came crashing in on her. Sobbing, she reached for a handkerchief from her purse. Kneeling in a fetal position along the steps of the church, she began to pray. Suddenly, she felt something soft moving alongside her foot. She glanced down, and a black cat was brushing up against her side purring.

The cats soft sleek fur and the lush green eyes cut through to her soul. Mesmerized by the cat's beauty, she reached down and ran her hand through its silky fur. Looking up at the cathedral door, trying to keep her emotions in check, she glanced around to see if anyone was spying her. As she took another step closer to the door, she glanced around once more and pulled it open, cautiously making her way inside. The entrance to the corridor was grand; the artifacts were eminent, having a momentous appeal to them. Elisha ran her fingers over the deeply engraved relics hewn into the wooden oeuvre situated along the wall. Walking softly to the door of the sanctuary, she opened it cautiously. The light from the stained glass windows swallowed up the darkness of the corridor as her eyes veered upward toward the impressive vaulted ceilings.

The semicircular design was breathtaking as it sprung upward from the voussoir wall supporting it. The ring of the arch met at the highest point, a cascading design embellished the beauty of its radiating majesty and royalty.

The stained glass windows surrounded the walls meeting the pulpit and, hovered above it was a beautiful mural of Jesus Christ. Focusing her eyes on the mural, she walked closer to the pulpit. It appeared Jesus was looking down upon her. She became numb, as the silence and tranquility of the moment engulfed her.

She fell to her knees instantly from the weight of the numbness, her arms fell to her sides, and the palms of her hands faced outward as if she was preparing for something to rest in them. Her head hung low as her eyes began to water a tear ran down her cheek, followed by another, and another. Tears fell to the floor, a small dark spot formed on the bright auburn carpet. Her lips trembled, and her mouth became dry, as she uttered aloud the words of the sacred ritual prayer. The prayer embedded in her subconscious, formed from vain repetition as a child.

She was held captive in an inclusive environment protected from the outside world.

"Oh, most Holy Angel of God, appointed by God to be my guardian, I give you thanks for all the benefits you have ever bestowed on me in body and in soul. I praise and glorify you that you descended to assist me with such patient fidelity, and to defend me against all the assaults of my enemies. Blessed be the hour in which you assign me for my guardian, my defender and my patron. In acknowledgement and return for all your loving ministries to me, I offer you the fidelity, precious and noble heart of Jesus, and firmly propose to obey you henceforward, and most faithfully serve my God. Amen."

Quivering and shaking, a cold chill ran down her spine. The silence was deafening. She could feel her heart beating in her chest, "was it the presence of Jesus?" she thought to herself.

"I feel the spirit rising in my soul; something is coming closer and closer to me. It's moving, and breathing, but yet I feel calm. Is it Christ coming for me? Will he rescue me and save me from the deep darkness of my despicable life, a life of sin? My sins are confessed to you, Lord. Take me, Lord. Take me, now, Lord. Take me now. I'm ready to meet you. Make me your living sacrifice." Her breathing became heavier and more erratic. Her body felt warmer. The presence of Jesus hovered over her, and she could feel it.

It's coming closer and closer." Glancing over her shoulder, she saw someone standing behind her.

"Why are you crying, woman? Who are you looking for?"

"Elvis," uttered Elisha. She moved in closer to him. Elvis held her and gradually loosened his embrace.

"Don't cling to me," whispered Elvis.

"Where were you? You must have got my letter? Have you come to take me with you? I knew you would come for me." Elisha pleaded

"Jesus is with you and he will never leave you," replied Elvis. Smiling and trembling, she stared into his eyes. Leaning back into Elvis, she laid her head on his chest and wept.

"My time is measured. Try not to cling to me. I have to return to my father in heaven." Elvis spoke tenderly.

"I know, Elvis. I will cherish this time while you are with me."

"God does not hear vain prayer." Said Elvis.

Elisha gradually pulled away. "What do you mean?"

"Your prayer that you recite from memory, God does not hear that. It has to come from the heart."

"You heard me? You were here with me? How long have you been here?" questioned Elisha.

"It doesn't matter. Your prayer is a ritualistic prayer. It will not be heard. Prayers have to come from the heart to be heard. God does not hear vain, repetitive prayer. Speak from your heart and

He will listen. It is the confinement of religion that caused you to rebel against society and God. God is not about religion; he is about you being liberated by the sacrificial blood of Christ so that we will be free from sin. By dedicating your life to Christ, you will have no desire to sin. You can be tempted to sin, and that comes from Satan, but you will not continually live in sin if you know Christ as your savior," Elvis said with conviction.

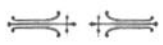

The squad car from precinct twenty-nine in downtown Memphis was sitting outside the Peabody. A chubby officer glanced over at the thin, hollowed face officer setting next to him.

"This Elvis character is staying here at the Peabody," declared Officer Dudley, the thin officer.

"If I was the real Elvis, I would have stayed at the heartbreak hotel." The chubby officer Bailey, started laughing at himself. Officer Dudley glanced over at him with a sly smile.

"Ha, ha, ha. Yeah, the APB is still out on the guy, but for some reason Sergeant Yalom doesn't take this too serious, said Dudley.

"I can't say that I blame him. If you think about it for a second, what difference does it make?" Officer Bailey Quipped.

"According to the zealous freak cult leader on T.V., he's the Anti-Christ." Officer Dudley inclined.

"The Anti-Christ? You're kidding me right?" said Bailey.

"No, I heard him on the news the other night talking about it. He said to beware of the risen Elvis, that he was sent by Satan," the chubby Dudley remarked.

"Sent by Satan…ah scary stuff, man." Officer Bailey started laughing at himself again.

Dudley looked over at Bailey, "This is serious business. I happen to believe in the Anti-Christ. My preacher talks about it all the time. We are living in the end times."

"We have always been living in the end times, ever since I can remember," said officer Bailey.

"Hey, check this out. Some guy looks like he is peddling something over there," remarked Dudley.

"Yeah I see him. I think I've seen that guy before. He's a pastor of some church around here," Bailey answered.

"Let's go and check this out." The two cops sluggishly walked over to the gentleman in question. "Good evening sir, how are you?" said Dudley.

"Oh, fine. Just here talking to some friends of mine," The black man with a frail body and a hearty smile gestured to the group.

"Friends of yours? I see," responded Dudley.

"Yes, I like coming to the Peabody it's a nice hotel," offered the pastor.

Officer Dudley looked at the frangible man. "Aren't you the pastor on the local channel here in town?"

"Yep, Pastor Earnest Halloway," he replied. "Yes, that's it. I thought I recognized you," Dudley said with a smile.

"Why are you out here?" Officer Dudley probed.

Reluctantly, the pastor put his hands in his pocket and pulled out the inner white seams. "No money."

"So you're begging for money?" asked Dudley.

"I'm asking for donations, yes," replied the pastor.

Officer Dudley reached for his wallet and handed the pastor a twenty dollar bill.

"Thank you and God will bless you," replied the pastor.

"I'm already blessed by being six feet above ground," Dudley said gleefully.

Bailey looked over at Dudley and laughed. "Can you loan me a few extra?"

"Ha, ha. You have a job," remarked Dudley.

"Ah, come on, man, don't be a fool the pastor didn't do anything to deserve that twenty" Quipped officer Bailey.

The sound of brakes squealing pierced the ears of the trio and they simultaneously looked over at the source of the squealing noise. A yellow cab came to a screeching halt along the curb of the Peabody. The back door opened and a gentleman standing about six foot tall exited the cab, sporting dark sun glasses, dark hair with long side burns, a multi-colored sport shirt with a luxurious prismatic design, and long bell bottom, lavender pinstripe pants.

"It's the Elvis guy," remarked Officer Bailey.

Elvis walked around the cab and opened the door for Elisha. Elisha, dressed down to the hilt, compared to her normal sexy attire, but hardly enough for the average testosterone male to get worked up in a frenzy over. Elisha placed her hand in Elvis' hand, and she stepped over the curb moving slightly to the side as Elvis closed the cab door behind her. Elvis embraced her arm and began to escort her past the trio of onlookers toward the golden front doors of the Peabody. At that time, Officer Dudley softly raised his hand in the air.

"Elvis?"

Elvis turned his head toward the officer.

"Can we ask you a couple of questions?"

Elvis lowered his arm slightly and turned toward the officer. Elisha reluctantly stepped to the side just a bit. Elvis glanced quickly at all three gentlemen, but held his stare a bit longer at the pastor. Then, his eyes veered toward the inquisitive officer.

"Sure." Replied Elvis.

"Are you aware that an APB is out on you?" questioned Dudley.

"I suspected it, but wasn't made aware of it," replied Elvis.

"We have the legal right to take you in, but it wouldn't serve us well to do that. But, I'm curious, are you the real Elvis?"

Elvis smiled and glanced at the three gentlemen. “Yes, it’s me. Are you all with the Shelby County Sheriff Department?”

“Yes,” replied Dudley.

“Does the name Roy Nixon ring a bell?” asked Elvis.

“Yes, there are several plaques with his name on them at the office.”

“Sheriff Nixon appointed me as a Special Deputy back in the day, got a real deputy badge and everything.” Elvis said with a grin.

Officer Dudley smiled and hesitated trying to think of what else to say.

Elvis questioned, “I see you guys carry 9mm now. Back in the day, the police carried .357’s. I had a special one made that I carried in a holster.”

Officer Dudley’s smile grew wider as he realized that the Elvis imposter was not an imposter and, if he was, it was the best impersonation job anyone could ever make.

“Elvis,” the pastor leaned in toward him as he was about to turn toward the golden doors again. “Can I ask you for a favor?” the pastor extended his hand slightly, but Officer Dudley lightly lowered it with his hand.

“Don’t solicit the king.” Said officer Dudley.

“It’s ok,” replied Elvis.

Elvis reached in his pocket and pulled out his silver money clip, and handed a hundred dollar bill to the pastor.

“Thank you, how did you know?” remarked the pastor.

“I have seen you on the local channel here asking for donations,” said Elvis.

“Yes, I’m about to lose my church to the owner cause we can’t make the rent.”

The king looked at the pastor. “With your permission, pastor, can I visit your church this Sunday?”

The pastor, with an surprised look, gazed at Elvis. "Certainly," the pastor's voice quivered slightly with nervousness. "Yes, you can," replied the pastor.

The pastor reached toward his back pocket and pulled out a card with the address of his church on it. "The service starts at 9:30. We'll be glad to have you there."

Elvis took the card and embraced the pastor. He shook the hand of the two officers and gestured toward Elisha. Then he turned toward the golden doors once more. As Elvis and Elisha entered the Peabody, a bright flash blinded them; a camera man took several quick shots before exiting the Peabody.

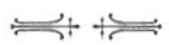

Zorzi gazed at the picture of Elvis and Elisha on the front page of the Memphis Daily News. "Damned," he shouted.

He reached over the desk and grabbed his letter opener, stabbing Elvis between the eyes. "Curse you, Lion Man. Curse you." Rising from behind his desk he shouted, "Alonzo!"

In less than a minute, Alonzo entered the office of the zealot.

"Get me an interview at once. Call every station in Tennessee if you have to," he commanded.

"But sir, you…" Alonzo was cut short of his reply.

"Now, now, now!" Zorzi shouted.

"Yes, sir." Alonzo lowered his head and walked toward the door with a dejected and somber look.

Amanda, the secretary in the lobby, looked at Alonzo. "Still on the Elvis kick, ah?"

"Yeah," Alonzo said softly, hoping the zealot would not hear him murmur. The secretary stood up from behind her desk, adjusted her black mini skirt that barely covered her heart shaped bottom, situated her blouse to show more cleavage, and began to walk toward the rattled Alonzo. She stood face to face with him as she moved seductively closer. Alonzo's eyes focused on her pink, quivering lips. She came closer and wrapped her thin arm around him, pulling him in toward her. Then, she planted a hot, passionate kiss on him. Alonzo went limp as a wet rag; her prowess in seduction was overwhelming, and he fell into submissiveness. She growled and scratched at his torso like a cat.

She shoved her victim up against the wall and gradually lifted her leg toward his groin. Moaning, she placed her hand gently behind his head, grabbing a handful of hair. She yanked his head back, her lips engaged his neck like a vampire, and she siphoned his blood to the surface of his skin. Then, she ripped open his shirt and pulled him toward her dangerous, waiting mouth. Alonzo's eyes focused once again on her alluring mouth. She whispered, "Go in there and tell Zorzi to back off the Elvis kick. Be a man and you can have me and do what you please to me tonight at my place." She released the tension as Alonzo fell gently against the wall. Desperately trying to readjust himself, he straightened out his shirt and pushed his glasses back up his nose.

"Ahem," he coughed.

She locked her eyes on Alonzo, pulled her skirt down over her exposed buttocks, and then she calmly strode toward the desk and softly sat down in the office chair. Glancing up toward the shaken Alonzo, she nodded her head toward Zorzi's office. She pulled out a mirror from her purse, reached for her lip stick, and moved it slowly along her lips, glancing toward Alonzo again. Moving her tongue over her freshly painted lips, she puckered them, gesturing a kiss, then she glanced back at the mirror to wipe away the excess lip stick with a tissue.

Alonzo, obviously unnerved, tried to collect himself by clearing his throat as he gingerly walked toward Zorzi's office door.

Raising his hand to knock, he glanced over his shoulder to look at the secretary. She was readjusting her blouse to cover her exposed cleavage; her eyes were fixed on her breasts as she fondled her erect nipples. Alonzo started breaking into a nervous sweat again; he turned to face the door and began to knock.

"Yes, Alonzo," replied the studious Zorzi as he was pondering the risen king.

Alonzo readied himself; clearing his throat again, he hurled his eyes in the direction of the seated Zorzi. "Sir, I have something very important to say to you."

Zorzi lifted his gaze toward the direction of the shaken Alonzo. "Sir, I've come to the conclusion that your attempt to thwart the Lion Man is futile and exhaustive. And, if we don't refocus our attention on something more productive, I'm no longer going to sacrifice my time toward this endeavor." His palms became sweaty, as the tension build up inside him.

Rising from his leather office chair, Zorzi walked toward the trembling Alonzo. With each step he took, Alonzo's eyes grew bigger and bigger as if anticipating him to manhandle him. Standing within inches of the rattled Alonzo, Zorzi stared him in the eyes. "You will obey me. You are my servant. I want you to leave my office now and schedule an interview with a local news station." Zorzi hesitated, and then he shouted, "Out!"

The secretary heard the shout from the lobby. She grinned slightly. Alonzo gathered the nerve to confront the zealous cult leader again. Shaking uncontrollably, his hands fluttering, he nervously replied, "I will no longer do anything you tell me to do." He held his stare for another second, turned slightly and began to move toward the door.

Zorzi shouted once again, "I'm warning you if you do not schedule my interview today you are no longer welcome in the sacred place." Alonzo stopped, closed his eyes, opened them again, and continued to walk toward the door. Each step felt like an eternity. He pulled the door open and took another step, closing the door quickly. Once in the foyer, he leaned heavily against the door. He started to hyperventilate, breathing rapidly. Alonzo slid down the door into a squat position.

The secretary glanced at the exhausted Alonzo; she rose slowly, like a wild animal stalking its victim, and with predatory instincts, she meticulously made her way toward the sunken, frail victim of an anxiety attack.

Walking closer, she stood directly over the sunken Alonzo. Alonzo's eyes peered upward toward the erect statue supported by long sleek luscious legs. His eyes moved upward, pacing over the pair of desirable thighs as they met the crease of her skirt. The secretary moved closer and Alonzo's eyes were still fixed upward toward her thighs. She was exposed before him. She raised her skirt slightly and placed her hand behind his head, pushing his head forcefully into her inner thighs and moving his head viciously in circles. She pulled Alonzo up by the hair as he let out a soft squelching sound of pain. Standing totally erect, she jerked Alonzo's head back once more and kissed him passionately. Stopping suddenly, she pulled away, and moved Alonzo toward the exit door, guiding him backwards until his back hit up against the door. She reaches behind him and placed her hand on the door, pushed it open, and shoved Alonzo through the door. He falls through the open door and onto the floor. She scorns, "You're worthless and weak." Slamming the door shut, adjusting her clothing once more, she smiled devilishly. Refocusing her attention back on Zorzi, she walked toward the door. She knocked softly.

"Yes," replied the zealot.

"May I come in?" asked Amanda in a seductive tone.

"Yes."

The secretary entered the confines of the office, but hesitated briefly.

"I'm sorry to disturb you, but I couldn't help but notice Alonzo's demeanor. He seemed so sullen and dejected."

"Yes, we had a bit of a disagreement you might say," replied Zorzi.

"Oh, my, I'm so sorry. I hope it wasn't serious," she feigned with devilish intentions.

"Actually, I don't think Alonzo will be with us anymore."

"Oh, my, what will we do without Alonzo?" she questioned.

"It will be ok, but can I ask you a favor?"

"Yes, of course," replied the mischievous secretary.

"Can you help me with my duties and take Alonzo's place?"

"Why, certainly, it would be my honor," she humbly replied.

"Thank you, and I will raise your pay accordingly."

She cleared her throat slightly. "Thank you, Sir Zorzi; a pay raise would be much appreciated."

Rising from his seated position behind the desk, Zorzi grabbed his money clip from his pocket, slid a hundred dollar bill from it, and handed it to the secretary. She humbly accepted the generous gesture.

"Thank you, you couldn't have timed it any better. I have to pay my rent tomorrow and I'm five hundred dollars short of my payment." She stood emotionless, bracing her hands together.

"Here you go. Hope this will help you." Zorzi gave her three hundred more dollars.

"Oh, you don't have to… But I really need it. Thank you so much." Amanda concentrated and refrained from smiling. She didn't want to give away her fake sense of meekness.

Zorzi gestured toward his hat and tilted it just a bit to acknowledge her response. "You're welcome my sweet lady. Can you start by setting up an interview with a T.V. station? I need to get the word out about the Elvis imposter."

"Yes, sir, Zorzi. I will work on it immediately," she replied.

"Good. Well, I'm leaving for today. I'll see you tomorrow." He reached for her hand and kissed it gently. "Night my dear."

CHAPTER FOURTEEN

Elvis and Elisha entered the Venetian room of the Peabody; it was lavish with golden accents and rich designs along the walls, the ceilings were highlighted with rich contours. The configuration more closely resembled a lavish ballroom with beautiful chandeliers producing a radiant light that cascaded throughout the room. Elvis and Elisha stood in the middle of the room admiring its beauty.

"I wonder if this is a taste of what heaven will be like," Elisha said, staring up at the beautiful chandelier hanging from the ceiling. Elvis glanced around the room,

"I don't know."

"Haven't you seen heaven?" Elisha questioned.

"No," replied Elvis.

"But I thought you said God sent you back here. You would have seen heaven..."

"The only things I saw were the feet of Jesus. Or, at least, that's all I remember," replied Elvis.

"So you haven't even seen heaven?" Elisha replied.

"The Bible describes three heavens and a New Jerusalem," Elvis explained.

"I'm familiar with the New Jerusalem. Doesn't it have streets of Gold?" probed Elisha.

Elvis reached for the ring on his left hand and gently slid it off, handing it to Elisha.

"Wow, it's so beautiful."

"It's a gold ring with black sapphire and a diamond; the New Jerusalem will resemble the ring, along with many other stones. I gave one just like it I gave to my uncle Vester."

Elisha marveled at it and handed it back to Elvis.

"It's yours to keep. Enjoy it."

"Oh! Elvis, I can't." pleaded Elisha.

"Please, keep it." Elvis persisted.

Elisha quickly glanced at Elvis; she smiled as a tear escaped the corner of her eye. "This will mean so much to me when you're gone. I will keep it forever until the day I die."

Elvis placed his index finger below Elisha's chin and lifted it gently, wiping the tear from her cheek. "There will be no more tears in heaven."

Elisha smiled and embraced.

"Ok, I hate to break up the love affair, but what's the next move since we don't have a promoter anymore?" Sunny barked as he entered the Venetian Room.

Elvis and Elisha quickly loosened their embrace and glanced toward the entrance of the room.

"How did you know we were in here," questioned Elisha with a hint of irritation in her voice.

"Ah. Premonition, my dear, premonition. This is the perfect atmosphere for romance," Sunny quipped with a sarcastic smile.

"We're not romancing, Sunny. We're talking about heaven," Elisha replied with bitterness.

"Heaven will have to wait. We got some more living to do and concerts to book." Sunny glanced at Elvis and gave him the look over. "So, my man, what is it? What do you have in mind?"

Elvis took a quick glance toward Sunny and reached in his back pocket to remove a business card. He gave it to Sunny. Sunny studied the card momentarily.

"Benjamin Neely, who is this Guy.?"

"He's a guy I met the other day," Elvis responded.

"Met the other day? Where?" ask Sunny.

"Met him along the river. Not far from here," Elvis said while gesturing toward the open window. "You can give him a call and tell him that we want him to be our promoter."

"What are this guy's credentials?" questioned Sunny sarcastically.

"I don't know," Elvis said in a reluctant voice.

Sunny began to laugh. "You don't know? You got to be kidding me, right."

Elvis walked toward the window to take a quick glance at the flickering city lights as they danced across the night sky, and he looked at the horizon beyond the "Old Bridge" of Memphis that crossed over the Mississippi River. The sky was orange from where the sun had settled in behind it.

"No, I don't know, but what I do know is he is a man that was sent to me by God." Sunny walked closer to the window, taking a glance as he leaned his shoulder into the window sill. "Nice horizon. Memphis is a spectacle at night." He said in a supple voice.

"Yes, it is," replied Elvis.

"So, tell me why you think he was sent from God." Sunny questioned with reservations. Elvis glanced at Sunny with a warm smile.

"Because I know."

Sunny looked down immediately, and he walked toward the center of the room looking at Elisha. "I'm sorry I bothered you two. You can finish your romancing, now." Sunny walked toward the entrance of the Venetian room as the clicking sound of his boots, along with the rattling of his wallet chain brushing against his side, followed him out the door.

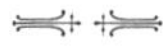

The rooftop view from the Metro 67 was the same as the view from the Venetian Room; the Mississippi River ran north and south as the sun set behind the "Old Bridge," the orange sky mingled with a hint of pastel as it covered the horizon. The voice echoing from the penthouse suite belonged to a lovely woman who filled in the short black mini-skirt nicely with a curvaceous figure. Her long, dark hair curled elegantly around her shoulders, and her fair complexion complimented the jet black mini-skirt well. Her coal black eyes had a white sparkle at the center. She peered out at the orange and pastel horizon that was rapidly fading to black.

"I received a little gift today," said the sultry woman in black.

"A gift?" questioned an ominous voice on the phone.

"Yes… one of my admirers," she laughed softly.

"Um, I know it was something beautiful, since you are a beautiful woman," replied the voice.

"Yes, I love to be desirable."

"So, tell me. What type of gift are you going to give me when you see me?" she probed.

"You'll have to wait and see," the anonymous voice replied.

"Well, my gift today was two thousand dollars. I'm sure you will give me a gift worth more than that," she purred.

"Yes, dear, that is petty compared to the gift I will have for you," remarked the voice.

"Oh, I can't wait to see you, dear. Tomorrow can't come soon enough," she said softly.

"This night will last forever without you," replied the voice "Ok, darling. Enjoy your night of anticipation. I'll see you tomorrow."

She hung up the phone, walked toward the kitchen, opened the refrigerator door, and reached for a bottle of Chateau Montelena Chardonnay. Taking two gulps from the bottle, she reached toward the Mahogany stemware rack and grabbed a Waterford clear white wine glass and filled it half way. She took a sip and placed a block of cheddar cheese on the counter. She sliced a small piece and ate a bite, followed by a sip of wine. She dials someone on her phone. It rings.

"Hello," replied the voice.

"Hello, Steve, this is Amanda Davidson. How are you?" she says in a soft, seductive voice.

"Amanda, my surprise, I haven't heard from you since I interviewed you after you won the Sunburst Model Search Pageant," replied Steve.

"I'm glad you remembered me. I've wanted to call you for a while now, but I keep having emergencies come up all the time," she purred into the phone with the sultry sound that normally accompanies her voice.

"How can I ever forget you? You're so beautiful and sexy." Steve said with an inspired cheer.

"Would you be interested in dinner sometime?"

Steve hesitated, "Sure, are you still in Nashville?"

"No, I'm currently in Memphis. I got a job offer down this way." She took another quick bite of cheese and a sip of wine.

"That sounds great. I hope you're doing well for yourself," replied Steve.

"Yes, I'm doing fine. What day is good for you?" she said

"Amanda, do you mind if I ask you a question?"

"No, I don't mind," she replied.

"Why are you asking me out for dinner out of the blue like this?"

"To be honest with you, I wanted to ask you out at the pageant, but I felt it would be inappropriate and may have cost you your job," she said with devilish whisper.

"Well, I'm flattered to say the least; I can drive down this Saturday. Would that be ok?"

She gazed at her glass of wine, twirled it around, and took another sip. "Oh, yes. Saturday is fine. I'm so excited. What time shall I expect you?" Amanda wet her lips as she questioned him.

"5pm should work for me," Steve said with an expectant voice.

"Fine. I will see you then. Have a safe drive down," she said seductively. She lowered her cell phone and placed it on the table taking another sip of wine and a bite of cheese. Glancing toward the computer with a sinful smile, she pulled up her website "privatelifeofasultryseductress.com" and clicked on the live cam button. The exhibitionist got up and walked toward her bedroom. Amanda opened the curtains, allowing only the sheer white liners to cover the window. She unbuttoned the top of her skirt, releasing it gracefully to the floor, imaging her internet viewers enjoying the view. She elegantly bent down to retrieve her silver bullet from the drawer of the night table and walked slowly toward the bathroom, running her hand slowly through her hair. Shaking her head passionately from side to side, enjoying the feeling of her hair moving freely, she reached into the shower and turned the faucet knob on, as the internet eyes lurked down on her from the ceiling. She stepped under the hot flowing water, moaning and howling, enjoying herself, as the sound echoed through the bathroom. Her knees buckled, and she slid down the side of the ceramic tile shower. Crawling along the slippery, wet floor of the shower onto the bathroom floor, her wet, sultry body still trembling, she made her way to the sink and positioned herself up against it, gradually lowering her buttocks into the sink. The water flowed quickly down the drain, and she moaned again. Her body trembling and shaking violently, she slid to the floor once more. Making her way toward the bed, she pulled her body on top of it, grabbed her knickknack and enjoyed one more.

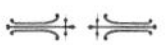

Automatic Slims was buzzing for a Thursday night and Sunny helped himself to a fine tasting Ashton Grand Habana. He got the tip nice and wet until he could taste the flavor. "Ah....the pleasures of a fine cigar," he said. He lit the end and inhaled until the smoke filled his mouth, then exhaled as the mist lingered in the air. He lowered it to tap a little ash off the end. Glancing around the bar, he noticed a few couples and some single people scattered here and there. There was a lady at the end of the bar that looked particularly attractive. Her red heels stood out against her pale, shapely legs. One leg was crossed over the other, which made her dress rise half way up her thigh. The red dress with white polka dots made her quite noticeable. Her hair was dark and wavy and curled at her shoulders. She glanced at Sunny and looked away. Sunny studied her for a couple minutes until she glanced over again. He smiled at her, but the girl didn't smile back. He stood up from the bar stool and walked casually over to the woman in red.

"Hello. Beautiful lady, how are you?" She glanced toward Sunny, studied him for a couple of seconds, and then glanced away.

"Excuse me; I'm trying to introduce myself to you. How are you?" He asked once more. The lady in red looked at him again and looked away.

"I'm with someone." The lady in red remarked. Sunny chuckled slightly.

"I have been checking you out for at least 20 minutes, and I haven't seen you with anyone," he implored.

"Do you really want to talk to me?" asked the lady.

"Sure, if you're willing."

"My fee starts at 100.00 bucks and goes up from there," she said plausibly.

"Woo…you look nice, but I'm not too sure if you look quite that nice." Sunny chuckled and walked away. He took his seat at the bar again. "Hey bartender can I have a whisky sour please?" He looked down at his cigar and noticed the ash had burned out. He put the cigar up to his mouth again and wet the end of it, then lit it. Inhaling deeply and then exhaling, a small sweet aroma lingered in the air. He pulled out his wallet and glanced through it finding the card that Elvis had given him. "Benjamin Neely?"

He scoffed to himself, grabbed his cell phone, and dialed the number on the card.

"Hello?

"Can I speak with a Benjamin Neely please?"

"This is he."

"Mr. Neely, I'm Sunny Carlyle, Elvis' agent. How are you?"

"I'm fine, thank you."

"Elvis said he met you the other day by the river, and he wanted me to give you a call."

"Yes sir. I approached Elvis and gave him my card. I believe I can help you all."

"Really? How so?" replied Sunny.

"My agency specializes in finding gigs for people that haven't been in the business for a while and are looking to make another go of it," said Neely.

"That sounds good. Can you meet me at the Peabody tomorrow morning at 9am?"

"Sure," said Neely.

"Good. See you then." Sunny put his cell back in his pocket and looked toward the lady in red again. He noticed the woman's dress was now a little higher up her thigh, and her blouse was unbuttoned exposing more cleavage. Sunny looked away and glanced at the bartender. "Hey, bartender."

"Yes?" answered the bartender.

"Do you know that girl in red at the end of the bar?" The bartender took a quick glance in her direction.

"Yeah man, she's just a local. She hangs out here on occasions, but not often; not enough rich guys hang out in here." The bartender quipped.

"Yeah, well would you happen to know her name by chance?"

"Yeah, her name is Amanda Davidson. She lives in that high rise, Metro 67 down the street."

"Thanks." Said Sunny. Sunny looked at her again; then he looked away. He took another draw of his cigar and placed it back in the ashtray. He stood up and walked back toward the woman in red. "Listen, I apologize about the comment I made a while ago." Sunny said with a low, unassuming voice. The woman continued to look straight ahead, and didn't reply. "Can I ask you a question?" The woman still didn't reply. "Do you know Elvis? Well, not the dead Elvis but the one that's alive?" Her head turned instantly toward Sunny.

"Do you know the Elvis that is alive?" replied the woman.

"Yes, you might say I do because I'm his manager." Amanda's eyes widened as she glimpsed back at Sunny. She looked away quickly trying not to be too obvious. "I was thinking maybe you can give me some of your time if I introduced you to Elvis." Amanda looked over at sunny, took his hand, and placed it on her thigh.

"Why don't you make yourself comfortable?" Sunny sat down.

"Don't mind if I do."

Early August heat was typical for Memphis, Tennessee, but what wasn't so typical was the excitement of a risen Elvis. Memphis was gaining attention as scores of people from around the nation started visiting once again with the hope of stumbling across the risen Elvis. Graceland was selling out every day. Hotels stayed booked, and local businesses were flourishing with tourists. It was becoming harder and harder for Elvis to remain anonymous. Elvis and Elisha barely made their way back to the lavish suite from the Venetian room.

Elvis glanced at Elisha. "Whew, it's been difficult getting around lately."

"Are we going to have to get security guards?" replied Elisha.

"We might be getting close to that time." Elvis grabbed his cell phone and called Sunny.

"Hello," answered Sunny.

"Did you call the promoter yet?" questioned Elvis.

"Done deal. He's meeting me tomorrow morning," Sunny said in an enthusiastic voice.

"You sound different, Sunny. Are you ok?" probed Elvis.

Sunny looked over at Amanda and squeezed her exposed thigh from the high slit in her dress.

"Yes, you could say I'm happy." Sunny smiled and winked at Amanda. Sunny covered the receiver end of the phone and leaned close to Amanda.

"I'm talking to Elvis." Winking at Amanda again, Sunny lowered his hand from the receiver. "Elvis, I met someone I would like you to meet."

"Let me guess. You met a very beautiful woman." Elvis looked over at Elisha and smiled. She could hear most of the conversation through the phone. She rolled her eyes in response to Elvis' comment.

"How did you guess?" responded Sunny.

"I don't think I needed to be a genius to figure that one out, Sunny," Elvis said with a sly grin.

"Elvis, I'll be up there in a minute.

I want to introduce you to her." Sunny clicked his cell phone off before Elvis had a chance to reply.

Elvis looked at his phone. "Swell."

"What?" asked Elisha.

"He's going to bring the girl over."

Laughing, Elisha added sarcastically, "Oh my, I'm sure we are going to be delighted."

Sunny looked at Amanda and caressed her exposed thigh again. He ran his hand slowly up her thigh and slid his hand under her tight, black dress. "You aren't wearing any panties, are you?"

Amanda shook her head. "I never wear panties," she replied.

"My kind of woman," Sunny remarked.

"So, are you going to let me meet the risen Elvis?" Amanda stared into Sunny's eyes seductively.

"Yes." Sunny signaled for the bartender. "Bartender, I'll have my tab," he blurted out with a prideful tone. The bartender slammed the receipt down on the table and looked at Sunny.

"Have fun, Buddy." The bartender waved the empty glass as a form of a good by gesture, smiled, and then looked away.

"I will." Sunny nodded to the bartender and layed down one hundred bucks. "Keep the change." He took Amanda by the hand. "After you, my dear." He followed Amanda, admiring her beautiful form contoured perfectly by her tight dress. With each step, her buttocks and her hips shifted pleasingly. Sunny looked back at the bartender and gave him the thumbs up. The bartender smiled and waved his bar towel a couple of times. "Wow, you have a sexy body," Sunny said with lust streaming out of him like a wild river.

The traffic moved swiftly, so Sunny took Amanda's hand and, at the first break, he led her across the street. They walked along the sidewalk under the red canopy that led to the Peabody. The guard was out front in his customary position.

"Hey, Sunny," the guard acknowledged. Sunny slid a twenty into the guard's pocket and winked at him. The guard studied Amanda's body approvingly then glanced back at Sunny and winked. The guard stepped in front of Sunny pulled the door open.

"Thank you, sir," Sunny said with cheer as he followed the sexy woman in black.

The music from the corner bar of the Peabody was clear as it resonated through the lobby and tickled Amanda's ears. She grabbed Sunny's hand and led him to the bar; making her way to the center of the floor, she started moving her hips swiftly to the music, gradually lifting her dress revealing her inner thighs. Sunny's lustful eyes studied the expanse of flesh.

Amanda pulled him close and ran her cheek up the side of Sunny's neck, nibbling on his ear. His excitement grew as he pulled Amanda closer to him and kissed her passionately. The two of them swayed to the rhythm of the music, moving in sync with one another, the bar patrons looking on, as Amanda and Sunny stole the show. The on-lookers let out shouts of approval. When the song finished, Amanda's luscious hair glazed the floor, her head hanging upside down, as she hung suspended in a dramatic dancing form. He yanked her back up with a swift, but graceful movement, and their lips locked once again. A couple in the corner started applauding the bold performance, and that lead to another applause and then another. The couple bowed together, hand in hand.

Amanda laughed and guided her hair back into place. "You're a good dancer." She said with a smile.

"You were awesome, you really know how to dance." Sunny said. He smiled and took her hand as he led her to the bar.

"What can I get you to drink, my dear?"

"I'll have a cosmopolitan. As her eyes remained steady and focused on Sunny.

"Whisky on the rocks," Sunny shouted.

"So, tell me about Elvis. Is he the real thing?" Amanda probed, still looking intently at Sunny.

"Absolutely," said Sunny, smiling; he took a strong sip of his whisky. Amanda, stirring her cosmopolitan with a licorice, placed her fingers in the drink and pulled out the lime, placing it in her mouth. She squeezed it softly with her lips, and the juice escaped the sides of her mouth down to her chin. Sunny was instantly mesmerized by her luscious red lips. Amanda moved her tongue slowly around her lips and wiped the lime juice from her chin with her finger, placing it in her mouth. She sucked her finger slowly as Sunny leaned in closer to her as he drooled with lustful desire.

"Are you going to take me upstairs to see Elvis?" said Amanda.

"After were done with this drink."

Amanda looked at Sunny with her seductive eyes, "I want to see him now," she said with a devilish grin.

Sunny placed a twenty on the table, picked up his drink, and took Amanda's hand. The pair walked out of the bar and ventured into the grand lobby. Sunny led her to the duck fountain and pulled out a coin from his pocket. "Close your eyes, and make a wish."

"Oh, I've played this game before." Amanda closed her eyes. "This guy must think he's Mr. Romeo or something," she thought sarcastically to herself. She kept her eyes closed long enough so that Sunny would think she is playing along.

"Ok, made my wish." She uttered.

Sunny kissed her again and passionately caressed her body with his probing hands. Exploring her curvaceous figure, he muttered, "Gosh you are a beautiful woman."

"I'm glad you think I'm beautiful." She smiled pretentiously. Meanwhile, Elvis and Elisha were in the presidential suite enjoying a re-run of "I Love Lucy." Elisha mocked Ricky Ricardo. "'Lucy, you got some 'splaining to do!'"

Elvis laughed. "Yeah, good ole' Ricky. I felt bad for him; Lucy drove him nuts."

Elisha laughed, "I don't think I missed an episode."

Elvis and Elisha turned quickly at the sound of the door. Sunny and his new companion walked gleefully into the spacious room.

Elvis looked at Elisha and whispered, "From what it sounds like, Sunny may have gotten lucky."

"Elvis, Elisha, can I introduce to you the lovely Miss Amanda?" Sunny held Amanda's hand aloft, and he bent over slightly to present her.

"I met her at Automatic Slims, and she is the most beautiful woman I have ever seen."

Elisha coughed loudly, placing her hand over her mouth and murmuring to herself "you pretentious little snot."

"You trying to say something Elisha?" Sunny questioned.

"Oh, no, not at all. Just clearing my throat." She laughed.

"What's so funny, Elisha?" Sunny demanded.

"Oh, nothing. Excuse me while I go in the other room. I'm having an allergy attack."

Amanda offered her hand to Elvis. "Pleasure to meet you, Mr. Elvis." Elvis extended his hand, and Amanda softly laid her hand in his.

"So, you're the real flesh and blood Elvis."

"Yes, I'm afraid so. It's me."

"Elvis, I know you don't know me well, but I was wondering if you could do me a favor."

Elvis glanced at Sunny. Sunny shrugged his shoulders.

"And what might that be, darling," Elvis hedged with a wry smile.

"I work for this T.V. station and would like to do a feature interview with you," she said.

Sunny looked at Amanda. "No wonder you're all into me. You just wanted to ask Elvis for an interview," Sunny said hastily.

Amanda looked over at Sunny and gently ran her fingers inside his shirt and started caressing his chest. "Oh dear, that's not it at all. I've enjoyed your company, and I can't wait to finish off this evening at my place."

Elvis rolled his eyes and turned his back immediately, as he gracefully walked to the kitchen.

"Oh, Elvis, I'm sorry," Amanda pleaded. She followed Elvis to the kitchen and slowly lowered herself onto a bar stool.

"I hope you didn't take it the wrong way. I was just asking if you could possibly do that. It would be an opportunity of a lifetime as a journalist, and I have been waiting for the longest time to catch a break, to further my career."

Elvis continued putting ice in his rocks glass; he filled it with water. "Sure. I will let you interview me," Elvis said hesitantly.

Amanda looked at Elvis and smiled. "Thank you, Elvis. I really do appreciate this. I will get back with you with a time," she said gleefully. Amanda walked around the kitchen bar and hugged Elvis.

Elvis held his glass of water up in the air to prevent Amanda from spilling it. He looked over at Sunny with grievance. Sunny walked toward Amanda and caressed her arm softly. Come on. I think we need to leave. Amanda blew Elvis a kiss. Elvis began to wave back, looked at his hand, and quickly lowered it to this side.

"Ah, Sunny can I talk with you a second before you leave?"

"Sure, man." Elvis gestured toward the back room. Sunny raised his index finger toward Amanda signaling to her for a moment alone with Elvis. Elvis eased the door shut behind them.

. "Sunny, something is up with this girl. I can't put a finger on it, but I'm afraid she's up to no good."

"Man, I should have known. Instead of being happy for me that I land a beautiful chick, you got to say something negative."

"I'm not saying anything negative. I'm trying to be a friend, and I'm concerned. That's all."

Sunny walked back toward the door, shaking his head.

"All I'm saying is to be careful. That's all," Elvis pleaded.

"Thanks, man. I will make certain to do that." Sunny closed the door hard behind him, leaving Elvis in the empty bedroom highlighted with the light of the moon. "God, give Sunny wisdom. Be with him tonight." He looked out at the moon intently.

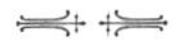

The deep red area rug meshed well with the rich, hardwood floors. The dark cherry wood coffee table made the plush design on the rug stand out. The living room was surrounded by a light tan microfiber couch and a dark bronze leather chair and love seat set. The huge bay windows were open with the blinds open; the curtains were tied to the side of the windows, leaving the whole living room in plain view to the outside world. Sunny stood in the middle of the area rug to take in the view.

"You want your whisky on the rocks," Amanda asked from the immaculate kitchen, which was highlighted with stainless steel appliances, black cabinets, and a center island with marble counter top.

"Yeah." Sunny walked closer to the black and white picture on the wall. Amanda handed Sunny his whisky. "This picture looks like downtown Memphis," Sunny asserted.

"It is. It was taken in 1945. "Old Memphis one" by Dave Berger. I love antique pictures."

Sunny took a sweeping survey of the apartment and looked at Amanda. "You have style, you know that?" a starry-eyed Sunny whispered.

Amanda grabbed Sunny by the shirt collar and pulled him toward her; she laid a lip lock on him, forcing her tongue down his throat.

Sunny broke away momentarily to say, "Wow, I love it baby," but she quickly grabbed him by the hand and pulled him toward the bedroom. She ripped open his shirt and buried her head in his chest, running her tongue up his neck. She jerked his head to the side and kissed him passionately below the jawbone. Sunny delighted in the passion as he responded to the heated fervor. Desire rose in him as thoughts of pure ecstasy raced through his mind. Her passionate breath touched his inner soul, radiating down toward his stomach. Suddenly, he felt nauseated. He grimaced with pain and ran to the bathroom, shutting the door behind him. Sunny falls to the floor violently, letting out a loud moan. Startled, Amanda reached immediately for her clothes, as she heard another loud groan. She paced back and forth, confused, bewildered and in shock.

Laying in his vomit on the bathroom floor, he glanced up at the ceiling. "what is wrong with me?." He uttered to himself.

He saw the shape of a cross over his eyes, acting like an imaginary shield of some sort. He shook and quivered fiercely. "What the hell is happening to me?" he uttered again. Amanda knocked on the door,

"Are you ok?"

"Yes, yes," Sunny responded with a desperately.

"Should I call 911?"

"No. Don't. I'm all right, really," Sunny responded as he grimaced once more. He reached for the top of the sink cabinet and pulled himself upright. His breathing became more relaxed, and his mind gradually came back into focus. He grabbed a towel and wiped the vomit from the floor. He got another towel and wiped the vomit from his clothes. He looked in the mirror, ran his fingers through his hair, and studied his face for a second to make sure nothing was on it. Glancing at the door knob, he took a deep breath, turned and opens it. "Amanda," he whispered. He looked around the room. It was Empty. "Amanda," he said a little louder. She was nowhere in sight. "Fuck. I can't believe this is happening. What in the hell is wrong with me?" Suddenly, a note on the granite kitchen counter caught his eye. He picked it up.

"I'm sorry I had to leave. Please lock the door behind you. I will get back with you soon. Thanks, Amanda."

"Shit!" he yelled out. Sunny tore up the letter, took a quick look around, and slammed the door behind him. "This is it. I've had enough of this crap. I can't believe this has happened to me. That son of bitch cursed me. He freaking cursed me." Sunny fumed aloud as he walked down the corridor, forcefully sticking his finger on the down button then entering the elevator. He leaned up against the wall with his hands in his pockets. A little girl and her mother were already on the elevator. The little girl looked up at Sunny. He glanced at her quickly, and then scanned over her face once again when he realized she was still looking at him.

"Hi," said the little girl.

"Leave that man alone, dear," said the mother.

Sunny remained quiet. The little girl smiled at him. He quickly looked away again. The elevator opened and the woman and the child exited; the little girl looked back at Sunny and waved. Sunny held his hand up and waved then lowered his hand quickly.

The elevator door closed. Sunny looked at himself in the elevator mirror and smiled. He noticed that his whole appearance changes when he smiles. Sunny realized he had never seen himself smiling before. He smiled again, retracted, smiled again, and retracted. Eventually, the elevator door opened. He quickly looked away from the mirror. He walked out of the elevator and entered the lobby area of the condominium. His eyes paced back and forth looking for Amanda. Walking through the lobby and out the front door, he whistled for a cab. A yellow cab pulled up to the curb, Sunny leaned in the window. "Can you take me to Automatic Slims, please?"

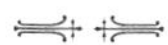

The morning dew was still lingering low to the ground as Sunny made his way back to the Peabody with the scent of alcohol on him. He wandered through the lobby area, and several bystanders noticed him walking aimlessly. A hotel clerk walked up to him

"Sir, can I help you? You look lost."

"Actually do you have a glass of water?" Sunny rasped. Sunny walked haggardly toward a table in the lobby where he plopped down in a chair. A clerk handed him the glass of water.

"Thank you," said Sunny. He gulped the water in one breath.

"Would you care to order any food this morning, Sunny?" asked the waiter.

"No, thank you. Just water, please."

"Sure," said the waiter. "If you see a guy come in that looks like he is looking for someone, can you point him to my table, please?" remarked Sunny.

"Sure. I will be right back with your water." Sunny looked to his right and gazed through the lobby window. His eyes started to focus a little more.

Coming more into view was a woman standing on the corner, smoking a cigarette; she took a draw, exhaled, threw the cigarette down on the curb, and crushed it with her red high heel. Sunny's eyes studied her a little more. "Red high heels? Is that Amanda?" he pondered to himself. "Holy crap, I think it is." He quickly stood up and turned toward the door, still focused on the lady at the corner.

"Excuse me," a voice called out. Turning sharply, he bumped into a rather tall gentleman with a blue sports coat and khaki pants, dark glasses and a amber hat.

Feeling a bit dazed from the incidental bump, he quickly turned his head to look out the window. "Damn, she's gone," he murmured softly to himself.

"Excuse me?" said the tall gentleman.

"Oh, I'm sorry. Never mind."

"I'm Benjamin Neely," the tall gentleman said as he offered his hand. Sunny shook his hand and gestured toward the chair for him to set down. The waiter returned to the table with the glass of water.

"Do you need anything, sir?" the waiter asked Benjamin.

"Just a water. Thank you."

"Sure," said the waiter.

Benjamin reached in his briefcase and handed Sunny the contract.

"You will find this is fair," suggested Neely.

Looking over the contract briefly, Sunny rubbed his eyes to try and see straight, in frustration he just signed it without bothering to read it and passed it back to Neely."You seem like a trustworthy guy to me," Sunny said with a flagging tone.

"You can take your time if you want to read it more thoroughly," offered Neely.

"Na, I know you and Elvis got the brotherhood thing going on," Sunny replied sarcastically.

"The brotherhood thing?" questioned Neely.

"Yeah, you know, you're both Christians. He wants 10% off the top to go to God," replied Sunny.

"Yeah it's in there. I thought he would want that," said Neely.

" So, where is the first gig?" Sunny slumbered.

"Hawaii. How does the Blue Hawaiian Bash sound to you?" asked Neely.

"I've never been to Hawaii, so it sounds good to me," Sunny said with a half smile, still trying to shake his hangover.

"Did you get any sleep last night?" probed Neely.

"None. Is it that obvious?" Neely laughed a little without answering.

"Can you give me a copy of that contract? asked Sunny.

"Sure. Here you go."

"Thanks. If you don't mind, I'm going to run up to the room and catch some R and R. I had a rough night," Sunny said sheepishly as he stood up from the table and extended his hand.

"You're welcome. I'll see you guys in Hawaii on the 5th," Benjamin said. He shook Sunny's hand and looked at his watch. "That's in seven days. That's going to be enough time for you all, right?" assured Neely.

"Sure, no problem." Sunny said, reluctantly.

"You sure? I can extend the date if you want."

"No. Actually, the sooner the better. Elvis is only here for 27 more days anyhow."

"Good. See you later."

"Later," replied Sunny.

"Kingdom House Church of God," Elvis said to Elisha. He read the name of the church from the card that Pastor Earnest Halloway gave him outside the Peabody days earlier. Pouring a fresh cup of coffee from the percolator and adding a little honey, the smell rekindled the feeling he had in his previous life at Graceland. "Nancy, the maid at Graceland, she always had a fresh cup of coffee for me. She was a dear lady." Elisha smiled.

"How long was she at Graceland?"

"She started in the late 60's and was there the day I died."

"The day you died?" echoed Elisha.

"Yes, until the day I died," Elvis responded.

"Do you know how eerie that sounds?" Elvis laughed.

"Yeah, I guess it does." Elvis looked down for a moment, pondering. I promised Pastor Halloway that I would come to his church tomorrow morning.

"Where is it?" asked Elisha.

"It's on the east side of Memphis, about thirty minutes from here.

"What's the name of it again? I'll look it up online"

"Kingdom House Church of God," repeated Elvis.

Elisha started typing the address in the search bar of her laptop. "Not much of a website. Just a picture of an old, white church in the middle of the woods." Elisha turned her laptop around toward Elvis so he could see the picture. A quirky smile spread across his face.

"It resembles the church I used to go to as a kid. I would walk to church every Sunday. The church wouldn't hold but so many people, maybe 45 or 50 people at the most."

"I guess that was in Tupelo Mississippi?" guessed Elisha.

"Yes, Tupelo. I would sing and play the guitar in that old church."

"What was the name of the church?"

"It was called East Tupelo First Assembly of God."

A loud thud was heard by both of them as they quickly glanced toward the apartment door. Sunny wobbled through the door, half asleep. He walked toward Elisha and Elvis. With a sudden burst of energy, Sunny gave Elvis a furious look

"What kind of curse did you put me under?"

"Curse?" Elvis asked.

"Yes, spell, curse, or whatever the hell it was."

Elvis didn't answer.

"Ok, be that way, then. Play it off like you don't know what I'm talking about, but you know what? You're full of shit, and I don't appreciate you doing that crap to me."

Elvis continued to look dumfounded.

"Just let me be, man. Do you realize I have never in my life turned down some nice snatch?"

"Snatch?" Elvis questioned.

"Yes, snatch."

"What is that?" Elvis replied.

"Google it. I'm outta here. Oh, by the way, quit praying for me. I don't need it. I'll help out with the gigs and be your front man until you're raptured to wherever the hell you came from, but in the meantime, lay off on the prayers." As soon as Sunny's burst of energy and fury had begun, it was over again.

He stumbled to the celebrity suite bedroom and slammed the door behind him. Within seconds of laying down, he was already asleep. A moment of silence came over Elisha and Elvis as they looked at each other speechless. Then Elvis cracked a smile, and the two of them started laughing.

Amanda positioned herself in the office chair and loosened the belt around her waist just a bit, as she felt a slight tummy roll beneath her polka dotted, red, silk dress. "Ugh! I hate this fat." She complained to herself. Zorzi came rushing into the office just before Amanda began to probe beneath her dress.

"Hello, Mr. Zorzi," she said warmly. Zorzi glanced quickly at Amanda and returned his focus toward his office door. He began to open the door, and Amanda quickly jumped up from her chair and started walking toward Zorzi he waited for the oncoming sound of her heels to come to a halt behind him.

"Mr. Zorzi, I have some excellent news." Zorzi turned slowly toward the enthusiastic and sexy voice; he allowed his eyes to drift over her body quickly, trying not to be too obvious.

"What might that be my dear?" He questioned.

"I got to meet THE Elvis."

"Really?" his voice trailing slowly.

"Yes," she giggled. "He actually hugged me, and he promised me that he would do an interview."

"Now, now, now. How did you manage that, my dear?" Amanda adjusted her skirt a little, and then readjusted her belt. She cleared her throat. "A little sex appeal goes along way," she mused.

Zorzi returned a half smile. "That's good, my dear, but you know I want to be featured in the interview, right?."

"Yes, I know, Mr. Zorzi, and I have a plan for that as well. I'm working on it, and I'm meeting Steve Finley from WSMV in Nashville."

"Great. Now give your boss a hug for doing good."

Amanda walked over to Zorzi and he put his arms around her waist, pulling her in gently toward him. Her scent aroused him as he moved closer. His hands wandered gently over her buttocks.

Amanda stepped back quickly. "Ta, ta, Mr. Zorzi. You can't be touching that. It's off limits."

Zorzi suddenly looked down.

"I'm sorry, dear. Return to your desk."

Amanda smiled and blew him a little kiss before walking away. As she left the room, she made sure to concentrate more sway in her hips and buttocks; she quickly glanced over her shoulder to see Zorzi mesmerized by her body. She smiled and winked at him.

"Just let me know if you need anything." Zorzi's eyes departed from her body and looked down again.

Amanda closed the door behind her and caught her breath. "Ah this is so creepy," she murmured to herself. Returning to her desk, loosening her belt again, she complained, "Ugh. I can't stand clothes. I would rather be naked all the time. Her phone rings.

"Hello, Steve."

"Amanda, how are you?"

"I'm fine dear, just calling to make sure you're coming down later today."

"Yes, I'll be leaving the office in about an hour."

"Great, I'll see you then." She uttered in a sexy voice.

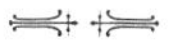

CHAPTER FIFTEEN

The morning sun beamed through the window of the celebrity suite bedroom directly onto the exposed head that peeked from the plush blankets and blue satin sheets. Sunny pulled the blanket over his head to block sun rays from his face. He drifted back to sleep, and then a subtle knock on the bedroom door woke him up again.

"Sunny," a voice sounded, "We have a gig this morning." He rolled over and covered his head with a pillow, trying block the sound of the voice. About 10 minutes later, another thump sounded at the door, followed by another thump. Sunny placed another pillow over his head. 10 minutes later, another thump sounded, followed by a voice.

"Sunny, we got a gig this morning." He rolled over, pulled the pillow from his head and looked at the clock on the night stand.

"Christ," he yelled out. "It's 7 am. Are you crazy? Leave me alone."

Elvis shook his head and walked back into the dining room to join Elisha.

"He's been sleeping a long time. I guess his little escapade with the lovely lady in red wore him out." He chuckled a bit to himself.

"Did you really put a curse on him the other night?" asked Elisha.

Elvis, caught off guard by the question, looked down at the steam rising from the fresh cup of coffee. He smiled then looked at Elisha. "Yes, I guess I did," He looked down at his coffee again and took another sip.

"Is that Godly?" Elisha probed. Elvis looked at Elisha and shrugged his shoulders. "I commanded the lust demon to leave him by praying a curse on him," he replied.

"I don't understand, how do you pray a curse on someone? Is that biblical? Probed Elisha. Elvis looked down at his coffee once more. Then looked up at Elisha.

"Have you heard of Elisha in the Bible?"

"Yes" she answered. "Elisha cursed a group of youth who mocked him, and two bears came out of the woods and mauled them to death. So, based on that same principle, I cursed the lust demon in Sunny to make him sick."

"Wow, you can really do that?"

"yes, but it requires a lot of faith and intense prayer."

"How come my prayers aren't answered like that?" she asked.

"It is God's will when he answers prayers. He doesn't answer prayers if it's not His will," he said humbly.

"But how come it's God's will that your prayers be answered and not mine?" said Elisha confused.

"God doesn't answer all of my prayers, only the ones that are in His will. He could have very easily allowed the lust demon to satisfy itself in Sunny. If my prayers happen to be in His will, He will answer them." Elvis chuckled a bit. "I guess I've been lucky a few times. I've counted my blessings since being given another chance. Before, I would take my blessings for granted, sometimes not even viewing them as blessings. But, they were blessings all along." He continued looking toward the window.

Elisha noticed a soft glow radiating around his face, she smiled and placed her hand on Elvis' hand. "Elvis, you've changed my life with your words."

He looked at Elisha and smiled. "I haven't changed your life Elisha; God has changed your life." He continued to smile at her, and he tightened his grip around Elisha's hand. "Elisha, God has used me as an instrument to change your heart." She began to shed a tear, followed by another

"Elvis, how can I live when you leave? I'm going to feel so empty," she wept. Placing his hand under Elisha's chin, he lifted her gaze to meet his.

"The Holy Spirit will be with you to comfort you and guide you; it will never leave you or forsake you." Elvis said warmly. She began to sob some more.

"You're quoting from the Bible, Elvis," She laughed a little. "This is like a dream. I can't believe this is happening. All of this..." She grabbed Elvis' hand, lifted it up toward her face, and kissed it gently. Tears rolled down her cheeks and onto his hand. "Elvis, Elvis... I can't..." she stuttered, placing his finger on her lips.

"Don't say it, Elisha. It will come to pass. Say only positive thoughts, comforting thoughts. Not thoughts of despair and loneliness. Be cheerful. The Holy Spirit is in you. You're happy, not sad."

Laughing a little, she wiped a tear from her eye. "That's easy for you to say." Laughing and sobbing at the same time, she grabbed a tissue and wiped her eyes again. "Why did this have to happen? Elvis, why? I'm too weak; I'm not strong enough for this type of emotion. Please, help me, Elvis." He leaned toward Elisha and wiped another tear from her eye with his finger. Squeezing her hand softly, he said,

"Elisha, look at me."

Her lips began to tremble, and her hands started to shake.

He pulled Elisha in toward his face, as his cheek touched her cheek. Moving his cheek softly against hers, he felt the moistness of her tears. Whispering in her ear, he comforted her. "Elisha, I love you, and God loves you." She turned her cheek in a little to try and have her lips meet Elvis' lips, but he pulled back slightly.

"Elisha, close your eyes." .

"Are you going to pray for me the way you did Sunny?" she chuckled wryly.

"Repeat after me, Elisha." She nodded in agreement.

"Heavenly father, I'm a sinner. I accept you, Lord, as my savior. The sacrifice of Jesus is my salvation. Thank you for giving me eternal life through your sacrificial blood. I love you, God, and I accept You as my savior in Jesus' name, Amen." Elisha repeated the prayer then leaned back in her chair and exhaled deeply with her eyes shut. Her body trembled softly, and she began to speak in tongues. Elvis repeated after her.

Woken by the murmuring, Sunny shifted his body upward and looked around, jumping out of bed and pressing his ear to the door.

"My God, what is going on in there?" He put on his pants and a shirt and opened the door softly. The voices got louder. He held his breath and grimaced slightly. Exhaling softly and then holding his breath again, Sunny took a couple more steps. He walked softly through the celebrity suite foyer, leaning in toward the wall, he gradually began to peek into the dining room. He spied Elvis and Elisha holding hands. Elisha was perched back in the chair with her face pointed toward the ceiling, and Elvis' looked in the same direction.

"What on earth are they saying?" Sunny thought to himself. "Oh, my God," he groaned as his heart started to race. Bracing his body up against the wall, he began to heave. A force pushed him down to the floor; he began crawl like a baby across the floor.

Sunny looked up. His eyes watered. Uncontrollably, Sunny panted, shivered, shook, his body temperature rising substantially.

"What is happening to me?" Making his way into the celebrity suite bathroom, he shut the door. Crawling toward the tub, he turned the water on all the way, shed his pants and shirt, crawled into the tub and splashed water on his face with furious strokes. Sunny attempted to cool himself down until the tub was full. Exhausted by the effort, he leaned against the tan tile, his eyes rolling back in his head.

"I don't know what's happening. Please, help me, Lord, please!" taken in a deep breath, and then holding his breath, he attempted to slow his heart rate. As he felt more relaxed, his eye lids became heavy. Sunny fell unconscious.

In his mind, clouds were surrounding him as his body lifted off like a spirit moving to another place. A light grew bright around him and his body cooled. He reached for a cherub, it was trying to say something to him. He couldn't make out what she was saying.

"What are you saying?" he asked. Sunny waited a moment for a reply. "It can't hear me. What are you saying?" He shouted louder still, "What are you saying?" Continuing without and answer, Sunny yelled, "What are you saying? Can you hear me?" Sunny rocked his head back and forth. He grumbled, "Quit shaking me. Stop. Stop."

"His shoulders are shaking." A voice uttered.

"Stop. Stop. I can't breathe. I can't breathe." He shouted.

In the dreamscape, the cherub slapped him. His eyes opened.

"Sunny! Sunny? Are you ok?" asked a voice. Elvis shook him again.

"Oh, my God." Sunny jerked up and grabbed Elvis by the shirt. "What are you doing to me? For Christ sake, what is going on?" Sunny's voice trailed…

Elvis put his hand on his forehead.

"You're hot, Sunny." Elvis helped Sunny to his feet, placing a robe around him. "I'm going to help you to the bed, Sunny." He walked him back to the bedroom and gently lowered him down in the bed. Elisha entered the room.

"Is he alright?"

"I don't know, but I have him on the bed, now." Elvis turned toward Elisha, "Can you get a hot towel?"

"Sure."

Elvis touched Sunny's forehead again.

"You're feeling a little less hot, now." Sunny eyed Elvis.

"What happened man?" He grabbed Elvis' hand and squeezed it.

"I don't know, Sunny," Elvis whispered.

"I mean, I saw you two praying and speaking some strange language or something, and then the next thing I know, I'm sick and then I get caught up in a dream of some sort," Sunny complains weakly.

"It's ok, Sunny, you're going to be ok." Elvis grinned and gave Sunny a firm shake on the shoulder. Elvis laughed softly. "Hey, buddy, you might have gotten baptized by the Holy Spirit."

Sunny leaned up quickly. "Man, what did I tell you about that mumbo jumbo? It's not for me, and now is not the time. I don't want to hear it," he demanded.

"Calm down, man." Elvis pleaded.

Elisha returned with a hot wash rag.

Elvis placed it on Sunny's forehead. "That's it." Elvis felt his forehead again.

"Rest here for a second. We'll be right back." Elvis nodded toward Elisha as the two of them walked back into the dining room.

"Elisha, I believe he was baptized in the Spirit." Elvis looked at Elisha intensely.

"Are you sure?" she asked.

"Yes, I think so." He took her hand and led her back into the parlor.

"Look, let's not talk about this anymore around Sunny; we will let him figure this out on his own. But what if he wasn't baptized in the spirit," she trailed.

"Let's not worry about it right now. Time will tell what happened." Elvis grinned.

He led Elisha back to the bedroom where Sunny had already fallen back to sleep.

"Why don't we just let him sleep?"

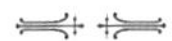

The Sunday morning light shined brightly across the room. Amanda was stretched across her king size bed. She yawned and started to roll over when her arm suddenly hit a body. She jerked her hand away quickly.

"Who, who the hell is this?" she blurted out. The body woke, but it didn't fully realize where it was at. After a long minute the silence broke. "Who the hell are you? repeated Amanda, directly.

"Who am I?" the body said.

Amanda rubbed her eyes hard to try and make them focus better. The unknown body laughed, "I am Steve, silly."

"Oh, my God. I am so sorry," Amanda said, her voice rising an octave with embarrassment. "Steve, please forgive me. I haven't woken up completely yet." He looked at her exposed chest.

"You have beautiful breasts."

Amanda rolled her eyes.

"Well, they're just breasts," She quipped.

Steve's choice of words instantly turned her off.

She immediately changed the subject.

"Steve." She leaned up against the head board.

"Yes?"

"I'm in a dilemma, and I was wondering if you could possibly help me out?"

Steve looked at her with a smile exposing his bleached white teeth.

"What do you mean help you out?" Steve suddenly started to get aroused, assuming that her problem may be of a sexual nature. He began to reach out for her breasts again Amanda gently guided his hand down off her breasts toward the bed. She laughed very softly. "Steve, can you help me by giving my boss some air time?"

"Air time? What exactly do you mean?"

"Well, it could possibly cost me my job if I can't get this interview."

"Baby, I would love to help you out. When do you need this interview?"

"As soon as you can," she murmured. Amanda looked the other way and focused her eyes momentarily on the "Waves" painting by Anthony Christian. She thought to herself, "I could be enjoying myself right now." Then, she turned softly back toward the sick, pathetic puppy dog of a man who was staring at her like he just had sex for the first time.

"Yes." She paused to clear her throat, and then continued. "Yes, my boss is an egotistical asshole from hell, and he is caught up in this make-believe fantasy that somehow the risen Elvis is the Anti-Christ."

Steve asked, "So why does he think he is the Anti-Christ?"

"Lord knows. He is a fervent zealot, crazed and possessed. In my opinion, he needs serious psychological help."

Steve laughed, but when he realized Amanda wasn't exaggerating, his smile immediately disappeared. "Do you think we'd be feeding his ego by giving him the interview?" asked Steve.

Amanda scoffed. "Do I think it would feed his Ego? Ah... Hell, yeah, but I don't give a shit because I want him to give me a raise." After noticing how terrible that sounded, she quickly added, "That I so desperately need."

Amanda lowered her head just a bit.

"Consider it done, baby." He began to kiss her again, but Amanda jumped up instantly.

"Excuse me for a second; I have to use the bathroom." She trotted toward the bathroom; she peered into the mirror to adjust her hair and apply a little make up, and then she lined her lips with dark red lipstick, puckered and gave herself a little kiss. "Thank you Steve, you wimpy-ass, pathetic, excuse of a man."

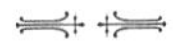

Elvis and Elisha were putting the finishing touches on their grooming. He smiled at himself in the mirror. Lowering the lid on the toilet, he sat down, bowed his head, and prayed.

"Lord, be with us today as we embark on this adventure. Lead us and allow your Holy Spirit to work through us, so that we may honor you. In Jesus' name. Amen." Raising his head, he stood up and walked toward the door. Elisha met him in the foyer.

"Are you ready?" she asked.

"Ready as I'll ever be."

"What about Sunny?"

Elvis looked toward the guest room. "Ah…we'll let him sleep. He's tired."

The two of them were headed out the door when Sunny's voice cut through the foyer. "Where are you guys going without me?"

Surprised, Elisha looked at Elvis.

"Yeah, that's right. Where are you two going without me? After all, we're on mission from God, right?" Sunny said, with a cocky smile.

Elvis smiled and reached toward Sunny, placing his hand on his shoulder, and gave him a quick embrace

"Glad to see that you feel better. It's time to chase that "Milky White Way." Elvis laughed.

"Ah, some of these days…Well, well, well…." Sunny hummed. Together as one, the three headed out the of the Celebrity suite door.

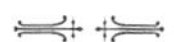

The long and winding rural road leading to the Kingdom House Church of God was barren, dusty with weeds growing sparingly along the side of the road, and sprinkled with wild yellow strawberries growing next to thorns and thistles. The surrounding area was desolate with the exception of a house or two scattered in the fields. Sunny's cutlass was transformed from yellow to beige as the dusty debris accumulated on the car. The pollen was thick, and the air was getting thinner by the minute as the sun rose higher in the hot August sky. The waves of heat seemed as if they came in bursts when the wind subsided, but Sunny was hell-bent on keeping the top down as Elisha battled to keep her hair in place.

"I'm going to look like a wretched witch by the time we get to this church," Elisha said grudgingly.

Sunny laughed, "It doesn't get any better than this on a beautiful summer day." Sunny looked in his side mirror and noticed a black boy on a bicycle peddling fast behind them. It seemed as if he was trying to catch up with the Cutlass. Sunny let his foot off the gas pedal gradually to allow the boy to catch up. Elisha turned her head to see what Sunny was eyeing, and she saw the boy slowly nearing the car. The boy smiled at the trio of travelers.

"You all going to da church?" The boy yelled over the road noise.

"Are you the Elvis people?"

Elisha smiled. "Yes we're the Elvis people." Elvis turned his head toward the boy and smiled.

"Follow me. I'll show you where to park," said the boy. Sunny let his foot off the gas again to give the boy a chance to get in front of the car.

The old, faded, white church was unassuming and rustic, and severely neglected. The round lancet window above the entrance acted as a bright star amidst a dark sky. It was bold against the faded white paint. The Cutlass came to a screeching halt, and the child let his bicycle fall on the ground as he went running inside the church.

Elisha couldn't help but think that the kid was comical, and she began to laugh. Sunny and Elvis turned toward Elisha.

"What are you laughing at?" Sunny said sarcastically.

"Oh, nothing just laughing at myself," replied Elisha. Sunny continued to stare.

"So what's the plan? Are we marching in there like the three wise men on a mission from God or something?" He chuckled to himself.

"No, as a matter of a fact, I you would like for you to go in first," replied Elvis.

"What, are you crazy? No way I'm I going in there alone. I'm not a religious person, and I wouldn't know what to say," Sunny said bitterly.

"It's no big deal. Just walk up to the preacher and tell him Elvis is here. That way, he can prepare the congregation," Elvis instructed. Sunny slowly made his way out of the car and uttered softly,

"How did I allow myself to get in this mess?" Elisha started laughing again. Sunny turned toward her with a stern look on his face. "What is so freaking funny? I do not find this amusing in the least. And, to be honest, with you, it's quite challenging to me." He looked at Elvis expecting a little sympathy from him, but, instead, he got no emotion whatsoever. Elvis just gestured with his finger to the church. Sunny turned and to walk toward the chapel doors.

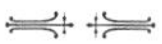

Benjamin Neely got on the phone and called Hank Rutherford at the Blaisdell Center in Downtown Honolulu.

"Hello," answered Rutherford.

"Hello, Hank, how are you?"

"Benji, how are you doing, stranger? I haven't heard from you in a while."

"Yeah, well I wanted to call and tell you some exciting news."

"And what might that be, my friend?" asked Hank.

"I'm representing the risen Elvis."

"What? The Elvis that played that big Wayne Newton Gig?"

"Yep, the same one," said Neely.

"How did you manage to get him signed up?" said Hank.

"God can work miracles," Neely said enthusiastically.

"Yes he can."

"Listen, I called to see if you can work with me on getting Elvis to play at your place."

"Sure, when do you want him to play?" asked Hank.

"Well, the sooner the better. He isn't going to be here long. Can you get me a spot in about a week?" asked Neely.

"Wow, that is short notice."

"Yeah, I know, and if you can't do it I'll understand."

"No, you don't have to worry about that. I appreciate you thinking about me first. This city would love to see the risen Elvis."

"Yeah, and Elvis loves Hawaii," responded Neely.

"Ok, then. Well, I'll start working on this immediately; I'll get the word out locally," Hank said cheerfully.

"Thanks, Hank, for working with me on a short notice."

"Not a problem. This will be the biggest excitement this area as had in a long time."

"Great. I'll talk to you later, then. Take care." Neely immediately called his promoter friend in Nashville.

"Hello?"

"Hey, Don."

"Benji, how are you?"

"I'm fine, thanks. How are you?"

"Can't complain. Can I ask you a question?"

"Sure. Go for it," replied Don.

"Is there any way possible you can help me promote the biggest event in the history of the United States and, quite possibly, the world?" asked Neely.

"Whoa, now, you wouldn't just want to blow me away one time would you?" Don laughed.

"Ok, brace yourself; I'm representing the risen Elvis!" Neely said enthusiastically.

"Congratulations! Wow, what a surprise. I thought Clint Robertson had him."

"Elvis fired him; he wouldn't take 10% off the top for God."

“That greedy bastard,” replied Don.

“Yeah, Greed doesn’t get you anywhere but to hell.”

“You got that right, buddy,” said Don. “Where do you want to have this spectacle?”

“None other than Memphis, Tennessee. I was thinking Tiger Stadium, the Liberty Bowl.”

“Um, ok. We might be able to pull that off; I’ve worked with them quite a bit down there,” replied Don.

“Ok, but I haven’t told you the challenging part yet,” warned Neely.

“And what might that be, my man?”

“This is going to be the final show for Elvis. Not only does this have to be the biggest show in the history of the world, but it has to be booked within about three weeks.”

“Woo, mighty Lord Moses! Ha, ha, Buddy, I like you and you’re my man, but that will take a miracle from God.” Don laughed.

“I feel confident that you can do it, Don.

“I don’t think it will be a problem. I think once we get the word out on this, there will be quite a few celebrities that would want to see the king live.”

“Yeah, you’re probably right. Well, listen. I’ll start working on this right away, and thanks for coming to me buddy. It will be a pleasure to be a part of history like this.”

“Take care, Don, and God bless you.”

“God bless you, too, Benji.” Neely immediately got on the phone and started calling the local newspapers, radio, and T.V. Stations.

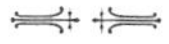

Sunny was greeted by the little boy on the bicycle as soon as he entered the church. The boy smiled from ear to ear.

“Are you going to sing, Mr. Elvis?”

"No, little man, I'm not Elvis. He's in the car." "Can you do me a favor, little man?"

"Yes," the little boy replied.

"Can you tell the pastor he has a very special guest here?"

"Sure," the little boy's face lit up with excitement. He immediately raced through the entrance of the nave; the doors swiveled back and forth as Sunny stared at them until they came to a complete stop.

Taking in a deep breath, he exhaled, and his heart picked up pace. Nervousness settled in a little. "Churches have always given me the creeps," he uttered to himself. His eyes probed around the foyer until they landed on a tawdry picture on the wall. On closer inspection, it was a picture of the pastor smiling, his teeth sparkling white and his eyes looked possessed. Situated in the distance was a cross with Jesus, and the words inscribed in the picture read, "On the road to Calvary."

Sunny quivered just a bit from the creepiness of it. He turned and stepped outside. He lit a cigarette, and breathed deeply, savoring the nicotine streaming down his throat and then exhaled through his nose.

"Ah, man I really don't know about all this. It's just too weird," he thought to himself as he watched Elvis and Elisha talking in the car. "What the hell am I doing? I need to be working and doing something constructive." At that moment, the little boy returned.

"You can come in, Mr." Sunny turned his head cautiously.

"Ok, we'll be in there in a minute."

The little boy went racing back inside. Sunny took another drag from his cigarette and held the smoke in his lungs as long as he could, then exhaled. He flicked the cigarette butt on the ground and crushed it beneath his black San Remo boots. He put his fingers to his mouth and let out a loud whistle. Elvis and Elisha turned their heads toward the sound. Sunny nodded his head to come on in.

Elvis swung the car door open and extended his hand toward Elisha to guide her out of the car. The two of them walked up the steps toward a disgruntled Sunny.

"What's wrong, buddy?" ask Elvis.

"Do you mind if I wait for you guys out here?" replied Sunny.

"What for?" asked Elvis.

"I don't know. I can't put a finger on it right now. I just need a couple minutes to clear my head."

"Ok," replied Elvis. Elisha gave Sunny a quizzical look as she walked past him. Sunny's eyes trailed Elisha as she and Elvis headed toward the tarnished mahogany front doors, a rusty iron cross protruding from each of them, as Elvis led Elisha through.

The faded brick aisle divided the pews in two halves. The pews were old and tarnished, lined with red cloth cushions. The walls were white with a small stained glass window on each side; they allowed just enough light to highlight the murky interior. The center aisle led straight to the sanctuary; the east sun coming through the large angelic stain glass window made the sanctuary appear a little brighter than the other side. The women were separated from the men, their section clearly marked "the amen corner". The men belonged on the other side with no particular label other than the usual picture of a sacred Jesus. The men and women were dressed formally, other than a few people scattered about. Quite visible were the perspiration stains on the backs of some people from the late morning summer heat. A few women were fanning themselves in desperate need of a little relief. The children scattered about in the congregation with restless eyes, amidst the adults in a kneeled prayer positions. Pastor Earnest diligently led the congregation in a steadfast prayer.

Sweat gradually permeated his pores. Elvis turned to Elisha and guided her to an empty chair. As he stood, he bowed his head and repeated the prayer in his mind. Elisha lowered her head and closed her eyes. After a minute, she opened her eyes and looked toward Elvis.

The trickling light coming through the small stained glass window on the south wall accentuated his figure and made it appear like an angel. A tear came to Elisha's eye as the surrealism of the situation engulfed her.

The more she stared at the transposing, angelic figure of Elvis, the gravity became heavier, and her emotions swirled. The tears flowed one after another. She lowered her head again and closed her eyes repeating the prayer from the pastor with sincerity. The voice of the pastor became louder and louder. Chanting began, and one or two people started speaking in tongues. Elisha prayed harder; the foreign voice rose up in her throat as it started to make itself audible. She began to tremble and shake. She fell to the ground. Elvis turned his head after hearing the thud. Kneeling beside her, he placed his hand on her forehead. A few curious heads in the congregation peered in the direction of where she lied. One gentleman got up and kneeled down beside Elvis.

"Is she all right?" ask the gentleman.

"Yes," replied Elvis, "She was just slain in the spirit is all."

The gentleman placed his hands on Elvis and Elisha. A foreign voice came to him. The intensity grew as another person from the front of the congregation fell to the floor. Then another and another. The Holy Ghost encompassed the whole sanctuary and moved through each individual, one after another speaking in tongues and getting slain in the spirit.

"All the angels in heaven are among us. The devotion of our congregation is being blessed by the holy angels above," yelled a boisterous pastor as the spirit lead him to stomp back and forth like a marching soldier. Each step he took was forced into the stone floor of the church.

Elvis looked up at the light from the rising east sun coming through the stain glass window of the sanctuary. “Lord you’re here. Your holy spirit is in this place.” Sweat covered his face, his eyes wide open, focused on the light. He trembled and shook, then glanced down at Elisha placed his hand on her forehead. “Elisha, Elisha…” Elvis called out.

.

Elisha opened her eyes. “Elvis, what’s happening?”

“You’re being slain in the spirit. You’re going to be fine,” Elvis assured her. Elisha continued to stare at Elvis, her eyes mesmerized and fixed on the angelic, kneeling statue that was Elvis.

Visions of her mom swirled in her mind; she was calling out to her.

“I’m home, dear, I’m home.” She closed her eyes and shook her head violently. “Mama… Mama, where are you?”

“I’m with God, dear. I’m home.” The voice trailed and vanished.

“Don’t leave me, Mama. Don’t leave me.” She started shaking more violently. Elvis held her firmly; the gentleman kneeling down beside Elvis held him more firmly as he and Elvis shook together. The congregation grew louder and louder.

It was calm outside as Sunny stood by a tree in the church yard. He heard the wind rustling through the tall pines. A pine cone fell to the ground each time the wind swayed the trees back and forth. He was enjoying another cigarette, his fifth one since they got to the church. In the distance, he heard the chanting from inside the church. He stared at the church and the two faded doors. Wondering what was going on, he shook his head in disbelief.

“What in earth are they doing? I don’t think I want to know.” He looked away and concentrated on the on the wind blowing through the pines, closing his eyes to take it all in. The whistling noise from the wind was relaxing as he enjoyed the serenity of the situation. He lowered his body to the ground and leaned up against the tree, a cigarette hanging haphazardly from his mouth.

"Why has all this got to be so weird? Why?" The cigarette bobbled up and down between his lips as he murmured to God.

The chanting and hollering subsided inside the church. It became deafly quiet. Elvis stood up from his kneeling position and looked at Pastor Earnest. The pastor grinned at Elvis and signaled him to come to the front. Elvis stood to the left side of the altar and waited on Pastor Earnest. The pastor waited until everyone returned to their original positions. Elisha gradually made herself sit erect on the floor, and then she stood up and returned to her chair.

"Ladies and gentlemen of the congregation, the Holy Spirit visited us today." A few hoots came from the congregation. The crowd started humming with light chatter when they noticed Elvis standing to the side. Elvis looked out over the congregation, and all eyes were on him instead of the preacher. Most people were smiling, but an occasional person stared at Elvis with speculation. Elvis smiled and nonchalantly waved.

"We have a visitor today, as you all may have already noticed." The chanting grew a little louder. "I asked Elvis if he could join us today, and he obliged. I'm glad to have met him the other day; I guess he is still flying under the media's radar." He looked over at Elvis. "How do you escape the media, anyway?" he wondered, laughing.

"It's not easy," Elvis replied. he grinned again at the congregation.

"Elvis, can you please fill us in on what is going on, exactly?"

Elvis walked up to the podium and hugged Pastor Earnest. "Thank you, Pastor." The congregation's volume rose ; Elvis waited a few minutes, and then asked everyone for a moment of silence. Elvis bowed his head. Silence filled the room once again. "The Holy Spirit visited us today..."

"Amen, Hallelujah," sounded the congregation.

Chuckling a little, Elvis continued. "I want to thank the Lord for giving me another chance here on earth, a chance to redeem myself and to glorify God."

"Woo," someone shouted form the back.

"It is a miracle from God that I'm standing here talking to you today."

Elvis loosened the collar of his black and white shirt; his cuffs were rolled up displaying a contrasting design.

Elisha stood in silence, admiring and clinging to every word Elvis said.

"You all might think this is a little strange, but I was actually at the feet of Jesus."

"Wahoo. Amen." Shouted several people. An assortment of other acknowledgments came from the congregation.

"I was lying there, begging for mercy. I thought I was going to hell. I didn't know what was going on, actually. All I knew at the time was that I needed to beg for forgiveness because I knew I had done a lot of things wrong in my life," Elvis said on a solemn note.

"Well, I was lying there, you see, covered in sweat, and I was trembling, shaking really badly."More praises rose from the congregation.

"I just knew something was wrong. I was nervous, but something down deep inside of me told me to ask for another chance, another chance at life here on earth. I heard this voice say, 'It is done,' and the next thing I know, I was transported down to earth in a beam of light out in the middle of nowhere. A desert in Nevada."

Some more screams and a holler come from the congregation. "The thing I need to tell you all is that Jesus will be back soon…"

Several people shouted in agreement. One lady started running up and down the aisle, screaming. She turned and started running for Elvis, but Pastor Earnest stopped her. She spun in circles yelling, "Hallelujah, praise God!" The pastor settled her down and helped her back toward her seat.

Elvis looked over at her and chuckled lightly. "That's the Holy Spirit working." Several other people started jumping. One woman screamed and another started shouting. Constant chatter developed. Several people resumed speaking in tongues. Elvis raised his voice, "But, I'm telling you by the blood of Jesus we are healed. Praise his Holy precious name. "Hallelujah!" The congregation erupted.

Sunny was still sitting by the tree enjoying the peace and quiet of the wind when he heard the church getting loud again. He looked down at his watch. "1:30. Man, it's taking them forever in there." He laid his head back against the tree. After a few minutes, he heard another sound coming from down the road. It sounded like a car. He didn't move. He just waited and pretended not to hear anything. The car came to a stop about fifty yards from the church. A man got out of the car; he reached in the back and pulled out a camera. "Media," Sunny uttered. "How did they find out about this?" Sunny stood up and started walking toward the photographer. "Hey," he blurted. "What are you doing?" He walked closer to the photographer. "What are you doing here?" he asked the photographer again.

"Is Elvis here?" asked the photographer.

"What business is it of yours?" said Sunny.

"Are you his manager?"

"You sure ask a lot of questions, don't ya?" replied Sunny.

"I'm sorry. I'm being rude. My name is Austin, I'm from the Daily News. Do you mind if I take just a couple of pics?"

Sunny gave the guy a quick look-over.

Sunny looked at his watch. "Ok, but make it quick. Just a couple shots or I'm going to come in there and get you," Sunny said with a stern look.

"Thank you," replied the photographer. The photographer walked toward the front doors of the church.

Sunny, glanced down at his watch again. "1:45. I'll give him 10 minutes." He hopped in his cutlass, eased the seat back, and propped his legs up on the door.

The congregation was jumping up and down, praising and worshipping, as Elvis belted out the lyrics to a gospel song in tune with the piano.

Elvis put the mic down and started going around the church, laying his hands on people to pray while the piano player continued to play.

A woman pleaded to Elvis, "Mr. Elvis, please pray for my boy. He has diabetes. Can you pray for him?"

Elvis took her hand and placed his other hand on her boy. "In the name of Jesus, I command this disease to flee and go to a dry place. In the name of Jesus, diabetes will flee, now. It no longer has residence here."

The woman came to tears. "Thank you, Mr. Elvis. Thank you."

"Your welcome," replied Elvis. "God loves you." One person after another came to Elvis and asked for prayers. He laid hands on as many people as he could. Elvis looked at Elisha. "Elisha, can you pray for some of these people? I have to talk a few minutes with the pastor."

"But, Elvis, I don't know if I can pray like this," pleaded Elisha.

"Just do the best you can. God will lead you."

Elisha smiled his words were comforting to her. Elvis winked at her and walked over to Pastor Earnest. “Pastor, I’m going to have to leave. If you need me for anything at all, here’s my phone number.”

Elvis placed a hand full of cash in the pastors hand.

“Oh, Mr. Elvis. Thank you, dear Lord.” He reached out and hugged Elvis.“God bless you, Mr. Elvis. God bless you.”

Elvis embraced him again and walked away from the sanctuary. He reached out for as many hands as he could, as everyone wanted to get one last glimpse of the king and touch him before he left. Elisha was trying to help him through the crowd as the congregation formed all around him like a swarm of bees. He and Elisha managed to get out the front doors of the church as the people filled in behind them; they all stopped at an invisible line to give him and Elisha some space to get in the car. Elvis gave Sunny a tap on the shoulder; Sunny jumped up and looked around, startled and bewildered from being asleep.

“You know better than to fall asleep behind the wheel,” joked Elvis. Elvis and Elisha jumped in the car and, after Sunny shook off the cob webs of sleep, he started the car, revved up the engine, and floored the accelerator in typical Sunny fashion.

Elisha waved her hands in front of her face to prevent breathing the dust from the dirt. “Do you really have to do that everywhere we go?” pleaded Elisha.

“What did you guys do in that place? You turned them into a mob,” Sunny barked.

The little boy from the church jumped on his bike and started racing behind them.

“Look. There’s that little boy again,” said Sunny. Elisha and Elvis turned to look behind them, and they both started laughing. The little boy was peddling his bike as hard as he could to try and keep up, but the cutlass and Sunny’s lead foot put more distance between them. The cutlass faded into the distance, the boy stopped and waved.

CHAPTER SIXTEEN

"THE RISEN ELVIS PERFORMS AT A LOCAL CHURCH," read the headlines of the Memphis Daily Press. The story was released on the AP wire and made the cover of USA Today. The photo of a praying Elvis kneeled over a man in a church. Zorzi scoffed at the headlines. A knock sounded at his office door. "Yes?"

Amanda entered the confines of the office, which happened to be less organized than normal. Scattered about were debris of newspaper clippings with beheaded pictures of individuals. Upon closer inspection, Amanda noticed that the individuals were pictures of Elvis. Her eyes widened, and thoughts that perhaps Zorzi was a sociopath rushed in her mind.

"I see that you have taken up a scrapbooking hobby, Mr. Zorzi," Amanda said in an unassuming voice. Zorzi's eyes rolled up from their fixed stare on the headline news to the shapely Amanda, who was adorned with a pearl necklace, a low-cut blouse, and half of her cleavage exposed. Zorzi's eyes returned to his media obsessions almost as quickly as they had zeroed in on her.

"No, my dear, just taking some samplings of the latest news."

"Well, I've got some great news, Mr. Zorzi. I have an interview lined up with Channel 5 in Memphis." Amanda jumped with excitement.

Zorzi quickly turned the other way. "Please, can you spare me the bunny hop routine?"

"Spare what, Mr. Zorzi?" asked Amanda.

"The Burlesque show," replied Zorzi.

Amanda quickly put her hands over her breasts. "Oh, these? I'm sorry."

"That's fine. Just spare me the extra movements. A man can only take but so much," replied a dejected Zorzi.

"I'm sorry, Mr. Zorzi." Amanda hesitated briefly. "Can you do the interview tomorrow?"

Zorzi looked down at his calendar. "Sure. What time?"

"I told them that 2pm would be good." Amanda grimaced a little, afraid that her initiative would be taken as conceit or assumption.

"Yes, that will work. Thank you, dear, for coming through. It's imperative that the world is warned about this Elvis imposter."

"Yes, Mr. Zorzi, for sure." Amanda turned toward the door; Zorzi cleared his throat.

"Here's a couple hundred dollars for the extra effort in getting an interview."

"Oh, Mr. Zorzi. You didn't have to do that, but it's good that you did. I do need to make a car payment. Thank you so much." Amanda leaned over to give Zorzi a hug. As Amanda began to loosen her hug Zorzi handed her five-hundred more dollars.

"Do you think I can take a swig from your juice box?"

"What?" Amanda said, confused.

Zorzi turned away to face the book shelf. "Can I take a tour of your Grand Canyon?"

Amanda thought for a second. "Are you asking me for sex, Mr. Zorzi?" she countered.

Zorzi nodded his head, still facing the book shelf with his arms crossed.

She looked down at the money and gave it back to Zorzi. "I'm afraid not, Mr. Zorzi. I work for you, and it might damage our working relationship." Zorzi pulled out another wad of cash, doubling the sum.

"How about now?" he uttered. Amanda hesitated briefly and handed the thousand back to Zorzi. "I'm so sorry, Mr. Zorzi. I just can't."

Zorzi looked briefly around the room, opened the bottom drawer of his console, and started turning the combination to the lock on the safe. Amanda's eyes grew very large as her heart started to race. "Mr. Zorzi, I can't. I just can't, and it doesn't matter about the money. I can't take any of it."

Zorzi kept turning the dial. It clicked, and the safe door popped open. Amanda exhaled, and she started pacing back and forth. Zorzi reached inside and pulled out a big stack of cash. He laid it on the desk. "This is ten thousand dollars. Will you take that?"

Amanda patted her forehead just a little to wipe off the perspiration. She paced back and forth again. "Mr. Zorzi, you're making this very hard on me." She suddenly stopped and exhaled deeply, and then she shut her eyes and took a deep breath. "How long?" she said nervously.

"Three hours," replied Zorzi. Amanda opened her eyes and lifted her hands up to her face. "That's too long. How about thirty minutes."

Zorzi answered, "2 hours."

Amanda countered, "one hour,"

Zorzi responded, "1 hour and a half, final offer."

"Ok." As she started to sob a little.

"Are you ok?" ask Zorzi.

"No, not really. I wish you could give me the ten thousand dollars without me having to do this."

Zorzi laughed. "I got to get something for my ten thousand dollars. It's a lot of money."

"When?" she uttered with frustration.

Zorzi stood still for a moment then walked around to the other side of his desk. He picked up the money and fanned it briefly, then placed the stack of dough in her hand. "Now," he said, as his voice cracked with a hint of nervousness.

"You think you can handle me?" She asked as she stuffed the money in her purse then immediately grabbed him by the shirt, ripped it open, pulled his hair back, and bit into his neck. Zorzi yelled in pain. She clawed him like a tiger, grabbed his hair again, and thrust his head onto her chest violently. "You want it, you got it," she yelled out as she proceeded with the barrage.

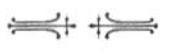

Elvis took another sip of his coffee as he peered over the contract Benjamin Neely had given Sunny. "This is a pretty simple contract; I like how you reminded him to deduct the 10% for God."

Sunny adjusted himself on the turquoise recliner as he was about to drift off. He shook his head trying to rid the urge to sleep. "Ah, well to be honest with you, Neely already had that in there," said Sunny.

Elvis looked over at Sunny with a smile. "Really?" Sunny looked down momentarily, "Yes, really. Coincidence, I know, right?"

"It just reconfirms that God is in on this deal," declared Elvis.

Sunny looked at his watch. "Elvis, can I ask you a favor?"

"What's that Sunny?"

"When we were at the church, I couldn't help but to think about my dad. I really would like to see him again. I think it's been over 5 years since I've seen him, but I just haven't had the extra money to go."

Elvis grinned and reached in his pocket. "Here, Sunny, take this and go see your dad."

Sunny looked down at the wad of cash. Enjoy yourself, and see your dad. That should be more than enough."

Sunny looked up at Elvis. "Where do you get all this money?"

"Just one of my heavenly perks," Elvis said with a smile.

Sunny shook his head. "You're amazing, man, simply amazing."

"Well, I better book the flight now so I can get back in time for the Blue Hawaiian Bash."

Elvis jumped up from his chair. "Yeah, you better. We'll need you for that, buddy. It's going to be a lot of fun. I love Hawaii."

"Yeah, I have never been to Hawaii."

Elvis reached out and patted Sunny on the leg. "Well, you're about to find out what it's like, my friend."

Sunny reached his hand out and grabbed Elvis' hand and pulled him close for a hug. "Thanks. I really appreciate it. This is a dream come true."

"You ain't seen nothing yet," said Elvis.

"What do you mean by that?" asked Sunny.

"You're going to find out soon enough. Just have faith." Sunny held a long look at Elvis and then turned away, unsure of what to say. "Well, I better book that flight." Sunny gave Elvis a pat on the back as he walked off into the celebrity suite bedroom.

Elvis went to the window and peered outside. The sun hovered over the Mississippi river, leaving yet another breathtaking view of downtown Memphis. "You ain't seen nothing yet," Elvis said to himself with a smile.

Sunny kept looking down at his watch and shaking his head; the flight to Long Island was delayed for another hour. He looked around briefly, and he noticed a little girl sitting on the floor trying to figure out a puzzle. The girl looked up at him and grinned. Sunny grinned back and looked away. He leaned his head back and shut his eyes. After a few minutes, he opened his eyes again and looked over at the little girl. He was mesmerized by her simplistic nature and desire to draw something. Sunny studied what she was drawing for a moment and realized that she was trying to draw a house.

"What are you drawing?" he asked.

The girl looked up at Sunny, "A house."

Sunny chuckled lightly. "Can I see it?" The little girl got up and walked toward Sunny to show him the drawing. "That's a pretty house."

"Thank you, mister," she said smiling. "Why don't you draw some trees around the house?"

The little girl looked at Sunny and smiled. "OK." She said, She ran back to her spot on the floor and drew the trees around the house. After she finished, she walked back over to Sunny and showed him the picture.

"Wow. That is beautiful. Why don't you draw some clouds in the sky, and a sun?" The girl ran back to her spot on the floor and set to work on the newest additions. She got back up and walked over to Sunny. "Here. How is this?" Sunny observed the drawing,

"Umm. Now, draw a family in front of the house holding hands."

The little girl smiled, and said "Ok." She ran back to her spot on the floor and drew the family. After a couple of minutes, she got up and walked back over to Sunny. "Here."

"Wow, that is a pretty family. Now, can you do one last thing?"

"Sure," she replied enthusiastically.

"Can you write on the bottom of the page 'God is Beautiful'?" The little girl started jumping up and down, and she darted back to her spot on the floor once more.

She quickly wrote it on the bottom of the paper, got up, and showed Sunny the paper. "Now, there you go. You have a complete picture, now." Sunny quickly looked around. "They're calling my plane. I got to go." He looked over at the girl,

"I see you later." The little girl ran up to her mother, and the woman smiled at Sunny.

Sunny looked at the woman while he grabbed his bags. "You've got an amazing little girl." He told the woman.

"You mean Allison, my daughter." replied the woman. The little girl smiled at Sunny.

"See you later, mister.," she said laughing.

Sunny reached toward his back pocket. "Do you live in Memphis?"

"Yes, I do," replied the woman.

"Well, I'm Sunny. Pleasure to meet you."

"I'm Susan. Pleasure to meet you, too."

Smiling, Sunny pulled out his card from his back pocket. "You can call me sometime if you'd like. Susan took his card and wrote her number on the back of it, and then handed it back to him. "I really liked how you were with my daughter," she complimented.

Sunny grabbed his luggage and looked at the little girl again. Susan laughed. He turned around and waved goodbye as he headed toward the plane corridor. He turned around once more before heading into the jet bridge. Susan and Allison were waving. He smiled and waved back. He noticed his steps were a little lighter as he headed toward the corridor.

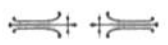

A hat pulled low over his face, and an inauspicious wardrobe that more resembled a hipster or a Justin Beiber look alike, than the king. Elvis snuck out of view of the paparazzi. He glanced down at the newspaper rack.

"ELVIS WILL PERFORM IN HAWAII," the headlines shouted. He glanced around, picked up the paper, tipped the older man a hundred. Before the old man had a chance to say anything, Elvis was gone. Once inside the safe confines of the presidential suite living room, he removed his glasses and studied the column under the glaring headlines.

"ELVIS WILL PERFORM IN HAWAII," Benjamin Neely the modern day "Colonel" Tom Parker. He laughed under his breath.

His cell phone rang. "Hello?"

"Mr. Elvis?"

He hesitated, flipped his phone over to check the caller ID, and sees "anonymous."

"Yes?" replied Elvis.

"This is Robert Sessions, Channel 5 Memphis."

"Yes, sir. How did you get my phone number?"

"A lovely lady by the name of Amanda Dickerson," replied Robert.

Elvis hesitated a second to recollect the lady in red that accompanied Sunny that evening. "Oh, yes," Elvis uttered with a regretful tone.

"Well, Elvis, I'm glad you recall her. She speaks highly of you. Can we interview you for a fifteen minute segment on our evening news special program that we feature once a month?" asked Robert.

"Well, sir, to be honest with you, I don't have the time. I have a Hawaii show I have to prepare for."

"I see, but the interview is only fifteen minutes, and Amanda made us aware that you promised her that you would make yourself available for an interview. Can you make it in tomorrow at 2pm?"

Elvis hesitated for a moment, shut his eyes. "Ok," he replied with dread.

"Great, Elvis. We will see you then." Elvis hung up the phone. After dropping in on the tail end of the conversation, Elisha asserted, "That sounded weird."

"Oh, you're right about that. Weird is an understatement. It was Channel 5 in Memphis; they want to interview me for fifteen minutes."

"Why did you sound so skeptical?" asked Elisha.

"It involves the woman that Sunny had over the other night, and there's just something about that woman I don't trust. She's up to no good. But, I did make the mistake of telling her I would do an interview."

"Can't you just back out of it and say no?" probed Elisha

"No, not really. I'm representing God, not myself," replied Elvis. Elisha gave him a friendly hug. "It'll be fine. Jesus will be with you," she said with a smile.

"Thank you, Elisha."

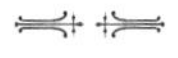

CHAPTER SEVENTEEN

Adjacent about one block west from where Sunny's dad lived at the Esplanade Residence for the Elderly in Manhattan was Riverside Park. The walking paths lined by beautiful lavender, black cherry trees and the deciduous conifer, Maidenhair Ginkgo Biloba, highlighted by a variety of other foliage created a rainbow landscape along the Hudson River. The nicotine, along with the fresh air invigorated, Sunny's senses as he leaned over the railing separating the park from the river. The New York City Skyline rested on the backdrop of the colored canopy as he marveled at the beauty of nature. It dawned on him that he had lived thirty-six years and hadn't taken the time out to enjoy the scenic view of the area where he grew up. Reminiscing about his high school years at Stuyvesant High a smirk came across his face when he recounted the time he won a bet from his buddy who wagered he couldn't run the five miles from the High School to Riverside Park.

"Man what I would do to have that kind of stamina again," he said, as he glanced down at the burning ash of his cigarette.

"I probably can't run a city block, now," he mused. He pulled out his Marlboro Lights from his shirt sleeve and glanced at it. "Twelve bucks for one pack of cigarettes. Damn, I'm freaking retarded. I'm a slave to this damn crap."

He took a quick glance around him and tossed the pack into the Hudson river. He watched the cigarettes as they floated on top of the water, bobbing up and down from the ripples. He turned around and focused his attention on a yellow-billed cuckoo perched on the bench. He was astonished by the simplicity of the bird, as if it didn't have a worry in the world. The bird took a quick glance at Sunny and then took off. His eyes studied it as it flew into a nearby Tulip Tree. "Damn, I've been living in bondage all these years, and I wasn't even aware of it. How could I be so stupid?"

He continued to walk down the tree-lined sidewalk of Riverside Park which twisted its way back toward west 74th street and West End Avenue. Entranced by pre-war architecture, he continued to walk until he stood in front of the Esplanade Manhattan. He looked up toward the seventh floor, about where his dad's room was located. "Man I can't believe it's been five years since I've seen Pop. That's freaking long," he marveled. He took a long stride forward, along with a deep breath, and entered the lobby area of the residence. Sunny was greeted by several silver-haired residences as he made his way to the elevator.

The elevator reached the ground floor, and he stepped inside. The doors shut, and it gradually made its way to the seventh floor. Departing the elevator, Sunny made his way toward room 707; he stood directly in front of the door, took another deep breath, and began to knock.

The door opened, and there stood Matthew Carlyle sporting the same ole leather jacket, adorned with a variety of Vietnam patches, he had had on when he last saw him. The familiar navy blue trousers flanked an old Vietnam shirt and hat. The once six-foot, lean, fighting machine now slouched, hump-backed, frail, and old. Though reliant on a wheel chair, Matthew Carlyle still had the fire inside he always had. Sunny reached out and hugged the old man. The old man grabbed Sunny's cheek with his hand and shook it. "You're still the same ole handsome lad you always were, haven't changed a bit."

"Thanks, Pop." The old man plopped back down in his wheel chair and rolled toward the living room.

"Have a seat, boy. Make yourself comfortable. What would you like to drink?"

"Water is fine, Pop."

"Ok, boy, you got it." The old man wheeled toward the kitchen.

Sunny quickly jumped up from his chair. "Hold on, Pop. Let me do that."

"You keep seated, boy. You're my guest, and I'm waiting on you. I can do for myself. This wheel chair is second nature to me, now."

"Ok," replied Sunny as he took his seat again. The old man rambled back into the living room with the glass of water and handed it to Sunny.

"Thanks, Pop."

"No problem, boy." He leaned over and placed his hand on Sunny's leg, shaking it firmly.

"It's so good to see ya, boy. Gosh you look good." The old man smiled in admiration. "How's life in Vegas? You still do the Elvis gigs?"

"Ha. Kind of, sort of, I guess," replied Sunny.

"What are you talking about, boy? You out of work?" said the old man. Sunny laughed under his breath a little. "I guess you might say I'm acting as a manager for a singer. It's a niche, I guess," Sunny replied haphazardly. The old man cheered.

"That sounds good. Who's the singer?"

Sunny cleared his throat a little bit, repositioned himself in the chair, and took a sip of water. He looked at his dad and noticed his intense gaze.

"You're still the same, Pop; you have that same passionate look in your eyes. Your health holding up pretty good, Pop?" asked Sunny.

"Just the normal dings of getting old his all; I visit the park every day in the morning for my exercise," replied, the old man.

"That's good. Any women in here to talk to, Pop?"

"I don't care about women anymore; I can't get it up anyhow, so why worry," The old man said with a hearty laugh. Sunny laughed along with him.

"Yeah, you're still the same pop I love." Sunny leaned over and patted him on the leg. Sunny settled back in the chair, still grinning.

"You never going to settle down are you, boy?"

"Na, probably not," he hesitated, "Unless something changes." He said it reluctantly.

"Changes?" The old man laughed. "I don't think you'll ever change, will ya? You'll always be Sunny, the wise-cracking, sharp-witted boy I raised." He laughed again. Sunny laughed, and then silence loomed for a moment.

"You never did answer my question a few minutes ago."

"What question?" asked Sunny knowingly.

"Who's the singer you're managing?"

Sunny looked around the room and spied a picture of Elvis on the book shelf. He stood up and walked toward the picture. He picked it up, looked at it for a second, and handed it to the old man.

"Yeah, the greatest singer of all time. There will never be another king," marveled the old man. "So, who are you managing, boy?"

"You're looking at him, Pop," Sunny said reluctantly.

The old man looked at Sunny confused. "What are you talking about?"

"I'm managing Elvis, Pop. The risen Elvis," Sunny replied.

"Are you talking about the Elvis they've been talking about on T.V.?

"Yep, that's him."

The old man laughed. "He is an impersonator."

Sunny glanced down at the floor for moment, and then looked at the old man. "He is not an imposter. I have seen him with my own eyes, and he came down from heaven."

"Are you experimenting with new drugs, boy? How many times have I told you to stay away from drugs?"

Sunny laughed, stood up, and gave his pop a pet on the shoulder. "Do you mind if I help myself to another class of water?"

The old man gave Sunny the quick look over. "Not at all."

"It sounds weird, I know, but it's the truth. He came down in a beam of light in the middle of a desert as I was driving out of Vegas." He poured himself another glass of water. Sunny walked back to his chair and plopped in it with the usual Sunny posture, legs outstretched back in a half-moon curve that conformed to the chair.

"I've been on an adventure with Mr. Pelvie for the last three weeks or so. We have a gig in Hawaii this Friday and then a final farewell concert. After that, he returns home."

The old man looked at Sunny with reservations. "And where is home?" Sunny took another swallow of water, cleared his throat, and utters, "Heaven."

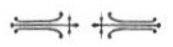

The crowd was huge outside of Channel 5. The taxi made its way toward the back of the building, and Elvis peered through the glass and lowered it cautiously making sure no one could see him. He looked over at Elisha.

"Let's make a go for it." He gave the cab driver a hundred and opened the car door swiftly, hurrying to the other side to take Elisha's hand and guides her from the car. The two of them darted inside as quickly as possible, and just before closing the door, Elvis noticed a tidal wave of people rushing toward the back door.

"Whew, just in time," breathed Elvis. He smiled as the T.V. coordinator greeted them.

"Hello, Elvis. I'm Mike Smith, the T.V. Coordinator."

Elvis gave him a firm hand shake.

"Glad you could make it, Can you guys follow me?"

Elisha and Elvis followed the gentleman toward a room with strobe lights, a back drop, and sound mics, along with three large production cameras.

A gentleman approached Elvis.

"Hello, Elvis, I'm Robert Sessions, the production manager. Thanks for coming out. We have about fifteen minutes before we go live. Can you make yourself comfortable here? Would you like to have something to drink?"

"Water is fine, thank you."

"And you, Ma'am?"

"Oh, yes, the same for me, thank you." Elisha took a seat next to Elvis. She looked at him with anticipation and excitement. Glancing around the stage area, she was amazed by all the camera gear and lighting. "Wow, I've never been on a T.V. show. This is exciting." She looked at Elvis and noticed and uneasy look coming over his face. "What's wrong, Elvis? You don't look comfortable."

"Something isn't right," murmured Elvis.

"What isn't right?" replied Elisha.

"There are three chairs here. Supposedly only one person is going to interview me."

"Maybe the third chair is for me," she grinned in her own admiration.

"I didn't tell them I was going to be with anyone," replied Elvis.

"Um, I don't know. I guess we'll find out in a second, won't we?"

The sound of the production manager's voice resonated from the back room. As his voice grew louder, Elvis' became more uncomforable. He could hear another voice that sounded eerily familiar. The production manager entered the stage area followed by a rather tall individual with rounded shoulders, long arms, and a grey suit with blue pants that didn't match. The producer showed the gentleman his seat and, as he turned his body to sit down, Elvis knew it was a set-up. The tall man with the out-of-vogue suit was none other than Zorzi. Elvis immediately rose from his seat and began walking toward the exit.

"Where are you going, Elvis?" asked Elisha. The production manager ran up to Elvis.

"Excuse me, Elvis. Where are you going?" Elvis turned to face the production manager. "You did not inform me that Zorzi was being interviewed with me," said Elvis as he kept walking.

"But, sir, this was a last minute change, and we didn't have time to make the adjustment," declared the production manager.

Elvis grabbed Elisha's hand. "I'm sorry, mister. I don't do business with shady people." Elvis headed toward the exit.

Suddenly, Zorzi shouted in the distance, "Where are you running to Lion Man? Are you scared of the truth? The truth is not in you, is it, Lion Man?"

Elvis stopped for a second. Elisha looked up at Elvis.

"Don't pay attention to him, Elvis; he's crazy. You would only be scooping to his level if you replied." Elvis looked down at Elisha. He tried hard not to look at Zorzi's as he moved closer to the door. Elvis grabbed Elisha's hand again and pushed the exit door open.

"Run you coward. Run." Zorzi's voice trailed behind Elvis as the door shut. Elvis immediately ran into a herd of people. As they all noticed him, the crowd moved in around him and Elisha. Everyone was pushing and shoving, trying to get closer to Elvis. Women were screaming, tugging on his clothes, and Elisha was trying to protect him, but the force of the crowd broke her away from Elvis.

Elvis shouted out, "Back away, now." A big, burly guy pushed Elvis hard to the ground.

"You're not telling me to back off, you imposter," the big guy shouted. The force of the crowd pulled Elisha further away from Elvis like the under tow of the ocean. Zorzi made his way through the crowd; he immediately noticed Elisha was separated from Elvis. The big burly guy kicked Elvis in the side. Elvis rolled over in pain.

"You're worthless and weak, you imposter. Where is your Jesus now?"

The crowd formed around Elvis and the big guy. Elvis tried to get up, but the big guy hit him across the jaw as hard as he could. Elvis fell to the ground once more. Visions of Jesus came to Elvis as he bent over on the ground.

"Oh Lord, please forgive me. Let me do your will. Give me another chance." The repeated words of his plea to Jesus resonated in his mind. With another kick in the side by the big guy, Elvis groaned with pain.

"You're worthless and weak. You're not a man of God," the big guy shouted. Amanda drove the car around to pick up Zorzi as he grabbed Elisha and wrestled her toward the car. Elisha kicked Zorzi in the shins.

"Ah, you bitch! Damn you!" Elisha fell to the ground, the pavement ripping into her leg; blood started streaming down her leg. She got up again and started running toward the crowd of people. Not a soul noticed her as all the attention was on Elvis. Zorzi ran quickly toward Elisha before she got to the crowd, and he pulled her arm hard toward him. Elisha's ankle turned from her high heels. She yelled and fell to the ground.

Zorzi grabbed her other arm, dragging her across the pavement. Her dress ripped apart from the asphalt.

Amanda grabbed Elisha's legs as the two of them hoisted her to the car. Elisha's screams were drowned out by the roar of the crowd. Elisha shook violently, kicking and screaming trying to get Amanda and Zorzi off of her. Amanda managed to open the back door then Zorzi shoved Elisha hard into the back seat. She continued to kick. Her heel struck Amanda in the face. She hollered and punched Elisha hard in the face. "Take that bitch." Amanda hit her again, feeling a rush come over as her adrenaline kicked in. She beat Elisha profusely, her fingernails like tiny knives raking across Elisha's face. Elisha cried out as Zorzi forced the back door shut. It slammed against Elisha's leg, and she yelled out again in pain. The blood from Amanda's finger nails ran into Elisha's eyes. Elisha sobbed, still continuing to kick and jab at Amanda. Zorzi reached for the glove box of the car and pulled out a syringe. He jammed it in Elisha's arm and forced the serum into her.

Elisha yelled, "You evil, satanic bastard." She spit in his face. "You two will pay for this dearly." Zorzi hurried into the driver's side of the car, and stomped on the gas, causing the tires from the black Cadillac to burn as a cloud formed just outside the crowd of people.

The big burly guy delivered a final blow to Elvis. His knees buckled beneath him, and he tumbled to the ground. His head hit the pavement, knocking him unconscious. Several people ran up to Elvis to check on him. "He's out cold. Someone call an ambulance," shouted a bystander.

"A real man? He didn't even defend himself. What a weak, pathetic bastard. He's not the real Elvis," the big guy shouted to the crowd. Several girls came up to the big guy asking for his name. One girl brushed against him suggestively as she told him what a hero he was. They walked away from the scene laughing and talking to one another. The crowd dissipated as sirens neared. A handful of people were left standing around the fallen Elvis when the police arrived, followed by an ambulance. The EMTs quickly attended to Elvis and lifted him up into the rescue squad. The police collected reports from the bystanders.

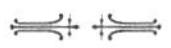

The sun rose along the Manhattan skyline, leaving an orange, transparent light that made the old man's apartment seem like the inside of a marmalade jar. The morning light hit Sunny in the face; he took a glance and then rolled over quickly to block the light. A moment later, he heard the T.V. come on. He turned over on the couch and noticed his dad in the recliner with the remote pointed toward the T.V.

"Pop, what are you doing up so early?"

"I'm up early every morning boy".

"Can't you read or something and turn the T.V. off?" Sunny quipped.

"Ah, quit being a grouch, boy, and get up. Rise and shine," replied the old man. Sunny took the pillow and covered his head to avoid hearing the noise. He started to drift off again, and then the name Elvis found its way through his drowsiness. The next word he heard was police. He turned around quickly to catch a glimpse of the T.V., wiping his eyes a few times to try to bring them into focus.

"Action news five scheduled interview with Elvis, turns into a mob scene as hundreds of people gather around to witness a fight between Elvis and an anonymous individual." The voice trailed on about an incident in Memphis.

"What the hell is going on?" Sunny barked.

"I don't know, sounds like some kind of riot or something," said, the old man. Sunny quickly started looking for his cell phone. "Where is my phone?" Sunny jumped up off the sofa, he lifted up the pillow, nothing. He continued to search. "Where in heaven is my cell phone?" He checked his luggage, nothing. Then, he happened to glance out on the patio and saw it lying on the table near the apartment bay window. He quickly called Elvis.

"Damn, no answer." He tried Elisha's number. "Damn, no answer." Sunny grabbed the remote and started flipping through the channels trying to find out about Elvis. "Ah, here we go."

"This is Matt Stevens reporting live from channel five Memphis. Elvis was last seen here at Channel Five news for a scheduled interview and, according to several eye witnesses, Elvis started a fight with one of the fans that was waiting outside to view the king."

"Elvis wouldn't do that," defended Sunny.

"Elvis was knocked unconscious during the fight; he was transported to Methodist Memorial Hospital. We are told he is in stable condition. This is Matt Stevens reporting to you live from Channel Five Memphis. Back to you, Charlie."

"I go for a freaking day and look what happens, panda freaking monium, unbelievable.

CHAPTER EIGHTEEN

The room was dark and candles were circled around her. She couldn't see anything but the flames burning. The chanting, it was constant. Elisha tried to move, but she couldn't. Her arms and legs were tied. She felt naked; the cold air drifted through her. She heard breathing amidst the chants around her. She twisted and pulled as hard as she could, but could not get loose.

"Oh, my God, where am I?" she said to herself. She felt a hand on her body, and then another hand. A third and what felt like many more moved up and down her body. One moved along her legs, another around her waist, her feet, and yet another on her inner thigh. She tried to shut her legs, but she couldn't. Fingers began to enter her.

"No!" She screamed at the top of her lungs, but the hands kept moving.

"No!" She screamed and yelled, squirming as hard as she could to prevent the intrusion. And then, a member was completely in her. She began to sob as her loud screams turned into faint murmurs. Then, finally, her body became limp, and she lay lifeless. She became numb; there were several more, maybe three or four inside her at different times. There was a female, too. She felt breasts up against her, moving up and down her body. Elisha felt men come on her one after another, and she felt the moistness against her face as woman rubbed across her harshly. She couldn't breathe. It was smothering her. It ran into her mouth as she tried hard not to swallow, but then she felt more wetness. She had no choice but to breath and, with each breath, there was more. She cried again. It seemed like it lasted forever and wouldn't stop. The stench made her sick to her stomach. The room filled with constant moans as more and more spilled onto her. She cried. All she could do was lie there in agony.

⸻

Elvis was awakened by a nurse; she looked at him and smiled.

"How are you feeling?" she asked. Elvis turned slightly to adjust himself in the bed. "Ouch." He instantly lowered his hand back to his side.

"Be careful," said the nurse. "You have a broken rib."

"A fractured rib?"

"Yes, and you received a severe blow to the head." Elvis instantly felt the pain in the back of his head as he moved to sit up. The nurse gently pushed him back toward the bed.

"Relax," she said smiling, You got beat up rather bad. That guy didn't like you to much, did he?" she asked.

"No, it all happened so fast; I can't remember most of it," replied Elvis. Elvis closed his eyes and started to pray. The nurse looked at him while his eyes were shut. "Father, thank you for protecting me. Thank you, Lord, for always being with me." Elvis opens his eyes again.

"You're a Christian?" The nurse asked.

"Yes," he replied

"How long have you been a Christian?"

"Most of my life. He has always been there for me." The nurse put her hand on his wrist to check his blood pressure. "150 over 110. You're running a little high," she said.

"Thank God that was the worst of it."

"It doesn't seem to me that God was there for you; If He was, you wouldn't have got beat up so bad." Elvis rolled his eyes toward the nurse.

"I'll pray for you. What's your name?" The nurse grinned at Elvis and adjusted his pillow behind his head.

"I'm Nancy. I don't need any prayers, but thanks anyway. You rest up, ok?" The nurse pulled the sheet up a little higher. Then, she walked out of the room.

"Amazing." Elvis shook his head again. "If only they knew." He looked around for his phone--nowhere in sight. He reached for the little red button on the side of the bed. The nurse came back in the room, Smiling.

"What seems to be the problem?"

"I can't seem to find my phone. Do you know where it might be?"

We have your personal belongings in a box for you; you can get it when you check out," she explained.

"Can you get my phone from the box? It's an urgent call. I have to let my friend know where I am."

"Ok, I'll see what I can do." She turned and headed out the door. Elvis leaned his head back and waited for the nurse to return.

"Elvis, here's your phone. Is there anything else you need?"

"No, dear, I'm fine. Thank you very much." The nurse smiled and left again. Elvis immediately called Elisha. No answer.

Sergeant Yalom at precinct twenty-nine was asleep in his office chair, a half-eaten Twinkie laying on his desk, along with an assortment of cluttered paperwork, a half empty coffee cup, and a cigar that was only a half inch long. The ring from the telephone startled him. He haphazardly answered.

"Sergeant Yalom, this is Deputy Arnold." The Sergeant rolled his eyes in irritation.

"Yeah, Deputy, what is it this time?"

"It looks like the Elvis character that you keep defending as a righteous man has had another outbreak of injustice. It seems as if he started the altercations outside of the T.V. Station."

"Look, Deputy, I'm telling you for the last time. Butt out of my business. I fully understand what's going on here, and I don't need you to babysit me."

"Sergeant Yalom, is it not so typical of a Metro Jew to turn a blind eye to an obvious obstruction of justice?" the deputy said hastily.

"Keep your discriminatory comments to yourself, Deputy. You're just showing your own ignorance." The Sergeant slammed the phone down.

"For Christ sake. Why can't people keep their noses out of other people's business?" he murmured to himself. The bubbly secretary entered the office with a de facto document from the dispatcher's office. She elegantly passed it to the sergeant.

He winked at her. "Thanks, Adam."

"You're welcome, Sergeant." She winked and turned away. The sergeant studied her shapely figure for a second as she exited his room. He reaffixed his attention on the telegram.

Dispatchers Docket

Document Title: Assault report

Victim: Richard Sherman

Assaulter: Elvis

Date Received: August 01, 2019

This is an official warrant issued to said Assaulter, Elvis

The Accuser, Richard Sherman

Sergeant Yalom tossed the letter to the side, picked up his hat from the desk, and gingerly walked out the door.

⟹ ⟸

The room resembled a cave, dank, dark, and silent with the exception of a glimmer of light that precipitated down on Elisha's sullen face. She trembled nervously; her hands shook uncontrollably; her eyes felt heavy from the drugs they had injected into her. The stench was foul and rotten. She heaved as she peered down at her nude body. It was soiled with dried-up crust on her skin. She grimaced with horror, heaving again. She shook her head and rolled her eyes underneath her eyelids. They felt heavy, burdened, and sad. She was confused and angry.

"My God," she whispered out loud.

Glancing up at the ceiling, staring her straight in the face was a mural of a red dragon. The dragon's teeth were razor sharp and had what seemed like blood stains on the tips of the two canine teeth. The spiny tongue was vividly detailed as if it was going to jump off the ceiling and terrorize her. She gasped in horror and shut her eyes as tight as she could. When Elisha opened them, she turned her gaze away from the dragon mural, but failed to escape the frightening scenery. On the left wall was another mural, a wild oxen, which had horns protruding from the image of its face.

"My God, what has happened to me? Why did you allow this to happen to me, God?" "Why, Lord, Why?" she sobbed.

A spirit suddenly appeared to her. She visualized two eagles with extremely large wingspans descending upon her. She grabbed the sheet covering the bed and ripped it off violently and wrapped it around her nude body. As she tied the sheets together in a knot just above her breasts, a wave of strength came over her. She glanced toward the window and noticed it was a ground level window. Realizing she could use the ground as leverage to pull her body all the way through the window. "It should be big enough to get through if I can just break the window. I've got to find something in here that's hard enough." She Whispered softly. All she could see in the gloomy basement room were mushrooms of sheet-covered furniture. She felt her way through them, probing for anything hard and small enough to break the window. There was nothing she could use. She fell to her knees and began to cry. The darkness closed in around her, and a voice called,

"It is over; your life has no value. It's the end. Give up." The voice resonated. She called the voice out immediately. She knew instantly it was the voice of Satan.

She gradually raised her body from the fetal position and leaned against the bed. She grabbed the bed post and pulled it to leverage her body. Suddenly, there was a loud crack. She fell down as her head struck the floor violently. Everything went black.

Sunny reached in his jacket for a pack of smokes. Thanks again for the breakfast pop… What?" he said. He rifled through the other pocket. Nothing. "What the hell is going on? I don't have any smokes."

The old man gave him a startled look. "What's wrong, boy?" he murmured. Sunny closed his eyes in anguish. He suddenly realized. The river. He threw them in the river.

"Pop, do you have a smoke?" he asked desperately. The old man laughed,

"Boy, you know I haven't smoked in years. I'd be six foot under by now if I hadn't given those things up." He grinned.

"How did you give them up, Pop? This is driving me nuts; I'm having a panic attack." The old man looked at Sunny and made a gesture for him to sit in the green, worn, leather chair nestled in the corner of the living room. From a glance, one would think that a wise man made residence of it for many hours. Sunny made himself comfortable. A light grin came over his face as he looked up at his dad. The old man strolled over to the lamp stand opposite of the chair and picked up a book and then gave it to Sunny.

"There you go," he mumbled.

"What, it's the Bible, Pop." The old man made himself comfortable in the other green recliner that wasn't as worn as the one Sunny was sitting in. With an intense expression, the old man looked at Sunny.

"What, Pop? What are you looking at me like that for?" Sunny half-grinned. The old man continued to hold his stare. Sunny glanced down at the Bible, and his hands gently ran across the ruffled cover, a worn strip of brown ran down the spine of the book, the right corner was ripped off, and the pages rippled like they were water damaged. Sunny opened it and, in the inside cover, there was an inscription, "Matthew B. Carlyle Class of 1955."

"It was a graduation present given to me by my granddad. I've never let it go; it has been with me all these years." Sunny glanced through the pages with amazement. It seemed as if the Bible was held together by a mystical force. It was desiccated and worn to the point that it seemed like it would crumble and blow away.

"Turn to James 4:7," said the old man.

"What does it say, Pop?"

"Just read for yourself."

"'Therefore submit to God. Resist the devil and he will flee from you." Sunny quoted. The old man looked at Sunny earnestly and said, "Any form of addiction is Satan trying to attack you. Your body is the holy temple of God. Satan wants to destroy it any way he can." Sunny closed his eyes and inhaled deeply, then forced out a thrust of air. "You know, Pop, you must have grown more spiritual since the last time I saw you because you have never mentioned anything about God after I became an adult."

The old man continued to stare intently at Sunny, and then he glanced over at the picture on the lamp stand. Sunny followed his gaze toward the picture.

"You still keep Mom's picture out, Pop? Isn't that torture?" Sunny inquired.

The old man continued staring at the picture, and then glanced back at Sunny.

"I've only had it out the last couple of years. I couldn't bear to look at it before because it made me feel lonelier." He coughed to clear his throat. "But one day, after a long prayer, something told me to put it out. Now, every time I look at the picture, it reminds me I'm not alone." Sunny hesitated a moment and looked out the sliding glass door. An orange glow illuminated the late afternoon sky, painting a picture of serenity amidst the busy streets of Manhattan.

"I don't understand, Pop. Why would it make you feel that way?" Sunny questioned.

"Because if she hadn't have left me, I probably never would have gotten to know God."

The impact of the old man's words resonated in Sunny's mind. The apartment became deafly quiet. They were both lost for words. The orange hue of the setting sun cascaded through the sliding glass doors, creating a prism of light in the living room. Sunny gazed at the light as it glittered and twinkled among the dust particles floating in the air. After a couple of moments, Sunny stood up from the worn recliner and walked over to place his hand on his father's shoulder.

"Lord, continue to be with Pop and fill his heart with your everlasting grace and love."

"Thank you, Son. I'm glad you said that. It's good to see that you're allowing God to work in your life."

"Well, Pop, all this is new to me, and I'm still trying to figure it out, but your revelation about Mom and this whole ordeal with Elvis has really got me thinking, I must admit," Sunny said whimsically. He grabbed his jacket and headed toward the door. "I love you, Pop."

"I love you too, Son. Take care of yourself and come back to see your old man soon."

"I will, Pop, and thank you for your words of wisdom." He headed out the door and down the corridor. Sunny pressed the elevator button and glanced back at the old man standing at the door.

"I love you, Pop." Sunny smiled and disappeared into the elevator as the doors shut behind him.

The old man continued to stare at the elevator, a light smile washing over his face as he turned and strolled back inside. The orange prism of light was still lingering in the living room. The old man glanced at the recliner, turned, and lowered himself gracefully in it. With a quick look at the Bible and photo on the lamp stand, he drifted off to sleep.

A light knock at the hospital room door startled the praying Elvis. Elvis turned his head toward the door.

"Hello, how are you?" Sergeant Yalom stepped inside and extended his hand toward Elvis.

"I'm fine. And your name, officer?"

"I'm sergeant Yalom from the twenty-ninth district in Memphis.

"What brings you in today, Sergeant Yalom?" inquired Elvis.

"Well, first of all, I just want to say it's an honor to finally meet you. I've heard a lot about you since you reintroduced yourself to society."

Elvis laughed. "Reintroduced myself?"

"Well, born again or something of that nature," he laughed slightly.

"It's ok, I understand." Elvis said with a lighthearted laugh. "Have a seat, Sergeant." Elvis pointed toward the chair as he leaned up in the hospital bed.

"Can I ask you a question?"

"Fire away, Sergeant."

"Are you some kind of teacher who has come from God?

Elvis hesitated for a moment and looked around the room. "Well, first off, I am born again. Unless a person is born again, he cannot see the kingdom of God," Elvis answered.

"How can you Christians say you're born again? I don't understand that."

"Sergeant Yalom, it's not being born again of the flesh, but being born again from the spirit. Jesus was crucified to atone for our sins; he was the perfect sacrificial Lamb of God.

Through his atonement, we have been washed clean of our sins and born again through the spirit of God," Elvis said with a smile.

"Ok, so I have to accept Christ in order to be born again?"

"Yes Sergeant, you have to accept Christ. Make no bones about it," said Elvis.

"I believe you speak the truth, but I'm afraid I have to be the bearer of bad news." "I know what it is, Sergeant; someone has filed an assault charge against me," replied Elvis.

"Can you tell me exactly what happened?" The sergeant asked.

"I was leaving the T.V. station trying to get through the crowd in the rear of the building. This man comes out of nowhere and shoved me to the ground. The next thing I know, he was relentlessly beating me while I was lying on the ground. I tried to get back up, and he hit me repeatedly. Every time I managed to regain my feet, I fell to the ground again, and the next thing I know, I'm being carried to the hospital." The sergeant glanced out the window momentarily, with a blank stare on his face.

"People love the darkness more than they do the light because their deeds are evil. Everyone that does evil deeds hates the light. Therefore, they come to you in the dark so their deeds are not exposed. The accuser came to you in the dark, but believe him if you wish," Elvis said, maintaining his calm demeanor.

Silence fell over the hospital room for a moment; the sergeant glanced around the room. "Born again, ah? So, can you help me? There is some kind of void in my life; I don't know what it is," Yalom uttered softly.

"Do you want to accept Christ as your savior right now?" asked Elvis. The sergeant glances around the room again.

"Yes, I want to accept him right now. I'm ready for a change."

Elvis slowly eased down from the bed, holding his side to brace himself from the pain, and bowed down to one knee.

"Can I have your hand, Sergeant?" Elvis extended his hand toward the sergeant. The sergeant, taken off guard a little, reluctantly offered his hand to Elvis. "Sergeant, I want you to recite this prayer after me, and think about the words you're saying. This will allow the Holy Spirit to come into your heart.

Close your eyes and repeat after me. God, I know that Jesus is your son and he died for my sins. And he was raised from the dead.

The nurse entered the room and was taken off guard by the spectacle. She gasped and quickly turned back down the hall.

The nurse quickly pointed toward Elvis' room and covered her mouth, the other nurse quickly ran down the hall and slightly peered into the room. She quickly returned to the nurses' station. The nurses gathered around in a circle chatting about what they witnessed.

"I have sinned, and I ask Jesus to come into my heart right now and forgive me of all my sins. I accept you, Jesus, as my Lord and savior. Lord, thank you for your forgiveness, eternal life, and hope. In Jesus' name, Amen." The Sergeant repeated the prayer leaned back in his chair and exhaled deeply, his eyes still shut. He breathed deeply again slow and deliberate. Then, suddenly, he opened his eyes and a smile came over his face. He laughed.

"Oh, my. Wow. That was invigorating." He bowed his head and leaned back up to face Elvis.

"Thank you. Thank you very much." He wiped at his eyes. "I had no idea it was going to be that intense. I feel better like something was lifted off my shoulders."

"Yes, Sergeant, that's because the yoke was broken. It was broken off of you. You're no longer bound by sin and the burden it carries. You're free to live your life with purpose, direction, and conviction. In Jesus' name. You will carry out his testimony and live for him from this day forward. You are a new man in Christ. Congratulations," Elvis said with a hardy smile.

Elvis reached and gave the sergeant a hug and then an enthusiastic hand shake. He placed his hand on the sergeant's shoulder and jostled him a bit. "Congratulations, again, Sergeant. You did it, you did it, and praise God!" Elvis said with joy and passion. "Look, if you ever need me for anything at all, give me a call. Here's my number. I want to warn you that the enemy, the devil, is going to try to steal this joy from you. You have to work hard at sustaining this joy, and read your Bible daily. You can start in Romans and then go from there. And remember to meditate on the scriptures so it will sink into your heart and mind. Do you think you can do that for me?"

"Yes, I can do that. Thank you very much." Said Yalom. A smile came across the sergeant's face. He walked toward the door feeling lighter. He tipped his hat toward Elvis. "Carry on your ministry, Elvis, carry on," said the sergeant as he headed out the door and down the hall.

The nurses were congregating by the station as all their eyes focused on the transformed sergeant. The sergeant smiled at the nurses and tipped his hat. "You all have a fine day and may God be with you ladies." The nurses looked at each other in amazement, and they were bewildered over the sergeant's new attitude. The chatter continued from the nurses as the sergeant neared the elevator doors.

Elisha awoke with her head throbbing in pain. She leaned forward. Her vision blurred; she closed her eyes, and then opened them again. Her vision was still blurry. "Ah, me... what happened?" She noticed the broken foot board piece. It was shaped like a sword with a pointed edge and a round, hard end. She picked it up. After a few minutes of staring at it trying to remember exactly how it got there, it suddenly dawned on her. "Oh, Lord, a weapon, a weapon!" She glanced at the window intensely.

She turned the make shift sword around and grabbed the center of it with both hands so that the round hard end was facing away from her. She took a deep breath, raised her arms above her head, holding onto the make shift sword, and ran as hard as she could toward the window. The sword thrust through the glass, her body slammed into the wall from the momentum. She fell back on the floor as glass scattered all around her. She rested on the floor momentarily, noticing the makeshift sword sitting in the window frame. She braced herself to get up, and then suddenly, she heard footsteps. "Oh, my God, someone heard me."

She ran toward the window and jumped up toward the broken frame with jagged edges. She felt the edges of the glass ripping through the bed sheets she had wrapped around her body, piercing and tearing her skin. "Ah." She shrieked with pain. The door creaked open. She turned her head; it was Amanda. "Oh, my God, not her again," she murmured to herself. Amanda rushed toward Elisha's legs and started pulling them. "No you don't. Not this time, bitch," shouted Elisha.

Elisha grabbed a chunk of dirt from the ground trying desperately to get some kind of hold on something firm. She started reaching for a small shrub to the side of the window.

She felt her body being pulled back inside. She kicked her legs as fast as she could. She broke one leg free from Amanda's grip and then kicked her in the head as hard as she could. Amanda fell backwards onto the floor.

"You fucking bitch. I'm going to fuck you up now," shouted Amanda.

Elisha was able to nudge her body a little more through the window, just far enough to reach the shrub outside the window. She got one hand on it, and as she attempted to grab it with the other hand, Amanda seized Elisha's legs and pulled her back through the window. They both fell to the floor. Amanda quickly lunged toward her. Elisha instinctively reached behind her for anything large enough to attack with she grabbed a large piece of shattered glass lying on the floor.

“I’m going to fuck you up, bitch,” Amanda yelled as her long fingernails came in toward Elisha’s face,

“Not this time, you evil cunt,” Elisha yelled. She rammed the broken piece of glass in Amanda’s eye.

Amanda yelled and fell backwards toward the floor, clutching her face. Elisha immediately gave her a swift kick to the temple and Amanda rolled the other way. The pain from the kick shot through Elisha’s foot and as she limped toward the window. She thrust her body up once more toward the broken window.

Amanda pulled the glass from her eye. “Oh my God, I’m going to be blind. I can’t see.” She felt her eyeball partly hanging out of her eye socket; she began to sob and then looked up at Elisha trying to get through the window again. Elisha grabbed the shrub with one hand and then quickly reached her other hand toward it and began to pull herself through the window. Suddenly she felt Amanda’s hands pulling her legs. Her body slid back inside again. “No, please. God, help me.” She pleaded.

The makeshift sword was lying on the ground just in front of her. She let go of the shrub and reached for it.

She gripped the sword as hard as she could from the blunt end. Amanda tugged with all the strength she had, and the two of them fell back onto the floor once again. Elisha, holding the make shift sword quickly rose to her feet before Amanda had a chance to get up.

“You die, bitch.” Elisha launched the pointed end of the makeshift sword right through Amanda’s chest. “You evil, satanic bitch! You die, you die,” she screamed as blood spewed from her mouth, Elisha body started trembling as she spoke. Blood started coming out of Amanda’s mouth, her right eyeball hanging from her eye socket. Elisha’s stomach turned. She looked away; she couldn’t bear to watch. “Oh, my God, I just killed someone.” She glanced at Amanda’s lifeless body on the floor and began to sob.

Leaning up against the wall, she buried her head in her hands and cried. Elisha, once again heard the sound of footsteps racing toward the room.

"Oh, no." She quickly jumped up toward the window again, with the little strength she had left. She grabbed the shrub with both hands. The door creaked open, Zorzi gasped with horror as he noticed Amanda's grotesque body lying in a pool of blood. Elisha pulled has hard as she could and her body fell forward on the ground. Zorzi quickly looked up toward the window and noticed Elisha trying to escape. He ran toward the window and grabbed her legs, and pulled them forcibly toward him. "Oh no, not again." Elisha blurted in agony. She started kicking her legs vigorously, as Zorzi lost his grip; he grabbed the sheet covering her body and yanked it fiercely as he fell down toward the floor. Elisha lay on the ground, free at last, but not a stitch of clothing on her. She quickly got up and started running toward the street. Pedestrians walked by startled as she ran naked with terror down the middle of the road. A man noticed her and ran up to her. He tore the shirt off his body and immediately wrapped it around Elisha. She trembled in his arms, as another pedestrian called the police.

Amanda's broken bloody body was lying on the floor. Zorzi could do nothing but stare at her in shock and sob. "You are so beautiful. I'm so sorry you had to die." He fell down toward her body and laid his head on her chest. He heard a faint thump. "Oh, my God. You're still alive!" He promptly called 911.

The flight back to Memphis had a layover in Atlanta. Sunny was still trying to call Elvis and Elisha with no luck of reaching either one of them. "Damn, I wish I knew what the hell was going on." He murmured to himself.

"Hi, bartender. How are you?"

"Fine, sir, how can I help you?" the bartender replied.

"I'll have Jim Beam straight up. "Ah, Just what I needed." He habitually reached for his jacket pocket for a cigarette. "Damn, I forgot I'm trying to quit. Shit!"

The bartender approached him. "What's wrong? You sound a little frustrated over here."

"Yeah, that's an understatement, man."

"I'm sorry; can I offer you something to eat maybe that will help you feel better?"

"No, man, but thanks. I can manage." He reached inside his jacket and pulled out a little Bible. "I've got this to get me through." He shook the Bible and put it down on the bar.

The bartender glanced up at him and smiled. "That's nice." He continued to wipe down the bar.

"Hey, bartender."

"Yeah?"

"Do you have a T.V. in here?"

"Yeah, it's up in the corner, there."

"Can you turn it on for a second? I just want to check the news."

"Sure." The bartender reached for the remote and pointed it toward the T.V. "You say you want news?"

"Yeah."

He turned it to CNN.

"This is Bobby. He is in love with Billy, and they celebrated their union in N.Y. City, now legally married. Friends and family were there for the wedding along with a special visit from Michael Sam and Oprah Winfrey," the reporter from CNN announced.

"Good grief. Not this shit. Give me a break." He gulped down the rest of his whisky and tossed a ten on the counter. Sunny sprayed a mint shot in his mouth and tucked his Bible away in his jacket. "Thanks, bartender. I'm out of here."

"We have a breaking story in Memphis, Tennessee. There seems to have been an altercation at a local church. One person stabbed and a woman running nude from a chapel."

Sunny quickly turned toward the T.V. The bartender gestured to turn off the T.V.

"No. Wait a minute. Can you leave that on a second?" shouted Sunny.

"The altercation happened earlier this evening as pedestrians and onlookers stood in shock when they saw a naked woman covered in blood running from the cathedral. We have a witness here that saw her." said the reporter.

"Yes, it was horrifying to say the least. I was walking my dog as I normally do this time of the day and then, out from nowhere, this nude woman comes running down the street screaming with her arms in the air. Then, a gentleman came up to her and offered her his shirt and wrapped it around the lady in distress. Horrifying. Absolutely horrifying," said the pedestrian.

"The naked woman is reported to be Elisha Matthews, thirty-two years old. Another woman was found stabbed, and she was immediately rushed to the hospital. She is said to be in critical condition. Her name has not been released. Back to you, Charlie."

"Oh, my God. What the hell is going on? I leave for a couple of days and total mayhem lets loose…Un fucking believable," Sunny declared outwardly.

"Can you watch your language, sir?"

"Oh, yeah, I'm sorry, bartender, but I know that woman. I got to get the hell out of here."

Sunny ran toward the waiting area and paced back and forth as he desperately tried to contact Elisha and Elvis. No luck. Feeling helpless, he fell back in a chair, put his shades on, and fell quickly to sleep.

Moments later, the phone rang. Sunny nearly jumped out of his skin. His cell phone fell on the floor, and it began to swirl around from the vibration. Quickly picking it up, he yelped, "Hello?"

"Sunny, have you heard anything at all from Elvis? I have been trying to call him for two days," said a concerned Benjamin Neely.

"No, I've been doing the same thing. Have you seen the news?" asked Sunny.

"Yes, I've seen it. That's why I've been trying to get in touch with you guys; we have a show in two days."

"Benji, in all honesty I don't see that happening. You're going to have to postpone it or something," Sunny admitted.

Neely exhaled. "I believe you may be right. I'll see what I can do and let you guys know if I'm able to get another date."

"Ok, Benji, sounds good, and if I get a hold of Elvis I will let you know."

"Thanks, talk to you later," said Neely.

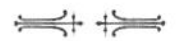

The only sound in the hospital room was the faint sound of the heart rate monitor. Elvis stood at the door, perplexed and confused. "What happened to her?" he murmured. He anxiously wanted to know, but didn't want to disturb her yet. Suddenly, he felt a hand on his shoulder. He turned his head, and Sunny stood there with a bewildered look.

"What is going on?" demanded Sunny.

"I wish I knew the answer to that one."

"I go off for a few days, and the El Crappo hits the fan."

"Yeah, you would think that wouldn't you," Elvis laughed.

"I guess you're not going to do the Hawaii concert."

"Not until I find out what happened to Elisha."

"What happened to you?" questioned Sunny.

"Long story," Elvis quipped.

"You were involved in some type of brawl at the T.V. station," Sunny asserted.

"Yeah, it was a mob outside of the station, and some guy just started beating on me for no reason," explained Elvis.

"Did you make him mad or something?"

"I guess I did, but the whole moral of the story is that we never should have done the interview anyway. Something kept telling me not to do it, but I did it anyway."

"Was that the voice of God?" asked Sunny.

"You know what, it probably was, and if that's the case, I got what I deserved. Just wish I knew exactly what happened to Elisha."

"We'll find out soon enough."

A police officer was at the nurses' station asking questions. Then, one of the nurses pointed toward Elvis and Sunny. The officer walked toward them.

"Hello, how are you two doing? I'm officer Patrick, Memphis police. Do either one of you gentlemen know Amanda Davidson?"

Elvis instantly turned toward Sunny.

"Brunette, about 5'7"?" asked Sunny.

"Yes." Replied the officer.

"Yes, I know her."

"Well she is in intensive care, critical but stable condition. Apparently there was an altercation between she and Elisha Matthews."

"What caused the altercation, Officer?" asked Sunny.

"I don't know. That's why I'm asking you. Where were you yesterday between the hours of 6pm and 12am?" asked the officer.

"I was flying back from New York; I went to see my Dad."

"Elvis, I knew you were here all along, and this altercation between the two ladies happened about a day after your altercation at the T.V. station. I find that very ironic to say the least, and perhaps more than a coincident," said the officer.

"Well, I'm sorry we can't help you any more than that, Officer," said Elvis.

"Thank you, gentlemen." The officer proceeded down the hall.

"Amanda Davidson. Umm… looks like your lady was up to no good after all. I think someone told you that, but you didn't want to believe it," Elvis said in a joking way.

"Yeah, yeah, yeah, whatever. I know. So I used bad judgment; what can I say?"

"I wouldn't let the eye candy draw you in so often, chum." "Ha, who are you kidding, Romeo? Your eyes ruled you back in the day."

"Yeah that was then…" Elvis trailed.

"Well, that don't have anything to do with it. You're still you."

"Christ can change us all."

"Actions speak louder than words."

"And what do you think I'm doing now? You don't see me in Hollywood chasing broads, do you?" replied Elvis.

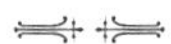

The police were in full sleuth-mode gathered outside the Zion Tabernacle. Squad cars, media, pedestrians. Zorzi was being escorted to a police car. Several officers were at the scene probing for evidence and asking questions. Forensics were gathering the evidence from the scene of the stabbing. The window where Elisha escaped was covered in Elisha's blood, and forensics had a cotton swab to gather DNA from the pointed glass. Off in the distance, a patrol car was parked at the corner.

"Well, well, well, looks like the Anti-Christ accuser is being called in for questioning?" Officer Dudley remarked acidulously.

"This whole scenario, with the Anti-Christ and Elvis, is totally nuts. Sounds like something straight out of a sci-fi movie or something." His sidekick, Officer Bailey, bristled.

"Sci-Fi my ass, more like straight out of the Bible," replied Dudley.

"Ok, please don't start in on your Bible thumping antics again," Bailey scoffed.

"Can't you see things for what they really are? I mean, the end times are right here in front of us, and all you can do is say it's make believe or something," Dudley argued.

"Ok, already. Let's not get into this discussion. Obviously we have a difference of opinion on this matter, ok. I'm more practically minded and you're more delusional," Bailey attacked

"Ok, buddy, you keep on with that attitude and see where it gets you," Dudley replied.

"Hey, look over there. Looks like the pastor guy we saw at the Peabody that day," remarked Officer Bailey.

"Yes, pastor Halloway. It's him. Let's find out what he's doing out here." The police car eased in a little closer to the pastor. The pastor took a quick look toward the police car and started walking away.

"Umm, a little suspicious don't you think?" remarked Bailey.

"Don't jump to conclusions. A lot of people feel uneasy about the police," assured Dudley. The officers gradually got out of the car. "Pastor Halloway," Dudley hollered. The pastor turned toward the officers. Dudley and Bailey walked a little closer.

"Good to see you again, officers," greeted the pastor.

"What brings you out this way today?" probed Dudley.

"I heard about the incident on the news and decided I would see what's going on."

"Who was that you were talking to a second ago?" asked Bailey.

"Oh, that's just Nathan. I see him from time to time," replied the pastor.

"You seem to be a bit uneasy," Dudley pointed out.

"Oh, no. I'm fine, but thanks for asking, officers. Nice seeing you two again, Have a good day." The pastor walked briskly away.

"Umm, very peculiar if you ask me, muttered Bailey.

"Yeah, but we can't jump to conclusions," reminded Dudley.

"Let's just keep an eye on him. I think it may be more than a coincidence that a religious leader is at the scene of a crime that took place at another church," proposed Bailey.

"Come on, let's go. I've had enough of this place. Enough drama going on around here to last a lifetime." The two officers sauntered back to the patrol car.

⟹ ⟸

Fuzzy and unclear, two figures standing by the door came gradually into focus. The two figures had concerned looks on their faces, but that is all she could make out. They walked cautiously closer. She closed her eyes.

"Am I dreaming? Where am I?" she thinks. Opening her eyes once more, a hand reached toward her. The hand was warm. She squeezed it, not wanting to let go. She closed her eyes again, and began to sob. Her soft brown eyes looked up at Elvis.

"Why?" she moaned.

Elvis squeezed her hand tighter. "God is with you."

"I know, but why? I didn't do anything to deserve this," Elisha pleaded.

Sunny leaned against the door frame. "Sunny," Elisha croaked.

He moved in closer behind Elvis.

"I love the two of you so much." Elisha reached for Sunny, and he moved in over her and hugged her gently.

"I'm sorry," Sunny said, despondently.

"Can you talk about what happened?" questioned Elvis.

Elisha peered through the open window. The light from the sun pierced her eyes, and she squinted and turned her head quickly away, her eyes watering more from the sudden light. Tears poured down her face. Elvis handed her a tissue. She wiped the tears from her face, her hands shaking nervously. Elisha could not reign in the body-wracking sobs. Elvis turned toward Sunny and placed his arm around his shoulder.

"Let's step out here in the hallway for a second," said Elvis.

"She's in bad shape," observed Sunny.

"Yeah, let's give her a little more time."

"Hey, look. I'm going to let you be alone with Elisha. I think she will open up more without me being here."

"Ok," replied Elvis.

"I just want to let you know that Neely called asking about the Hawaii concert."

"Tell him we'll do the show. Just need a little more time to find out exactly what happened to Elisha."

"Ok, I'll tell him." Sunny leaned in and gave Elvis a hug.

Sunny walked away, the clicking sound of his boots fading and becoming less audible as he disappeared from view. Elvis turned gently toward the open door of the hospital room. The light of the sun shone a little brighter than before as it radiated through the window. Elvis squinted as he kneeled down beside her bed. Elisha peered up at him, searching his eyes for some explanation of her plight. He reached out and grabbed her hand; it was still wet from the tears. Squeezing her hand tightly, Elvis gazed into her hollowed eyes. They appeared frightened, empty. He closed his eyes and began to pray. "Lord, your spirit is with us; your light will expose the evil and destroy it. She was violated. Come now to restore her, Lord. Mend her heart, repair her, and make her whole with your loving spirit and grace. In Jesus' name."

She opened her eyes, and more tears streamed down her face. "Oh, Elvis, I'm so glad you're here. I'm so glad to still be alive. It was horrible beyond explanation."

"Just relax and concentrate on your breathing. Soft and slow." He placed one hand on her forehead and held her hand softly with the other. "Elisha, can you close your eyes? Concentrate on your breathing. In and out, in and out." Her pulse slowed.

"Elvis, the day we were at the T.V. station, Zorzi and Amanda forced me into a vehicle. Zorzi injected something in my arm, and I lost consciousness shortly after that. I can't remember how I got to that place, but the place where they held me was horrifying. I was lying on a bed, tied down by ropes.

I was naked and there were at least 3 or 4 people in the room; it was hard to tell, it was dark. It could have been more. I was raped, Elvis. All of them raped me." Elisha wept with abandon.

"It's ok. It's over, now. You're here with me, Elisha."

"Oh, Elvis, thank you for being here. I don't know what I would do without you." Elisha still couldn't stop crying, despite the growing comfort she felt. "There was a woman, too..."

"A woman?"

"Yes. I think it was Amanda. She forced herself on me as well."

"My God," said Elvis.

"Where was God? Why did this happen to me?"

"I don't know, Elisha; we won't understand all the horrors in life until after we die."

"But you should know. You have died," Elisha said bitterly.

"Yeah, but like I told you before, I have only seen the feet of Jesus. Not God. The only words I heard from Jesus were, 'It is done,' after I begged him for mercy. I knew I did something wrong, and I knew I was about to be judged."

"You knew? How did you know?"

"I just knew. I can't explain it. I felt as if I was a bag of dirty rags lying before him. It was horrible."

"Weren't you saved?" exclaimed Elisha

"Yes, but I still felt ashamed for some reason. All I know is that I didn't want to be judged because I knew I would go to hell."

"You wouldn't have gone to hell, Elvis. If you were there with Jesus you wouldn't have gone to hell. The people that go to hell will never see Jesus because they go straight to the white throne judgment."

"You're right, Elisha. That's what I meant to say. But it's still a judgment for Christians.

All I'm trying to say is, you know as much as I do. We won't know the reason why evil exists until after we face God." Elvis paused a moment, considering.

Elisha turned her head and sobbed.

"Elvis…" her voice trailed. "I killed Amanda." Elisha burst into loud wails of guilt and fresh memories. Grabbing her hand and squeezing hard, Elvis said, "Elisha, hold on. Amanda is not dead."

"What are you talking about? She's not dead? I watched her die before my eyes; blood was coming out of her mouth!"

"I don't know, Elisha; it's only what the cop told me. She's in intensive care right now, critical but stable condition."

"How can it be? I stabbed her in the heart. I know I did," said Elisha fiercely.

"Calm down, Elisha. You can't get yourself too worked up. You have to relax."

"Relax? Are you kidding me? How can I relax knowing that this evil, satanic woman is still alive? She wants to kill me!" Elisha's emotions vacillated between fury and remorse, not wanting to be a murderer, but also wanting her horrible captor to suffer as she had. Elvis reached out for her hand and held it softly.

"Father in heaven, I pray for the blood of Jesus to protect Elisha right now. Protect her from harm. Your blood is all-powerful and mighty, and we claim it now for protection in the name of Jesus. You're protected by the blood of Jesus, Elisha. We just ask God for protection. You have nothing to fear."

"Thank you, Elvis." She leaned toward Elvis to embrace him.

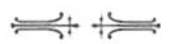

Sunny's wry smile grew larger when he learned from Benji about the new booking date for the Hawaii concert. Nextel offered one-hundred thousand upfront as part of the advertising for the show.

"Get on the phone now and contact Elvis. We have to do this show," demanded a persistent Benji.

"Will do, buddy."

"Elvis, we have an upfront cash offer to do the Hawaii show, not to mention the money we're going to make on the concert ticket sales," Sunny said with urgency.

"What's the date?"

"August third," replied Sunny.

"Ok. Elisha is still in distress, so we might have to do the trip without her," Elvis said in a sullen voice.

Elvis placed the phone down gently and walked back into the room. Elisha had drifted back to sleep. He kneeled down once more.

"Lord, heal Elisha, now. Give her peace and understanding. Don't take your holy spirit from her. Let her understand that evil is not from you, but from man. We were all born into sin by the transgressions of Adam."

He kissed Elisha softly on her forehead and calmly left the room.

"Mr. Elvis, Amanda Davidson has requested to see you in Room 144," said a nurse.

"Amanda Davidson?" echoed Elvis.

"Yes. She said she knew you."

"Yes, I met her once before. Thank you for letting me know."

The nurse smiled and walked away.

Amanda laid in the bed with a breathing apparatus attached to her mouth, her eyes shut, and a holter monitor with wires running over her chest like a spider web.

"You must be Elvis."

Elvis, startled a bit, turned sharply toward the voice that broke the mesmerizing sound of the holter monitor.

"Yes, sir." Replied Elvis

"Do you know the patient?" asked the doctor.

"No, not really. Just an acquaintance is all. Your nurse just told me she was in here."

"She had a severe stab wound just below her heart. We had to do a Pericardiocentesis, which helped draw blood from her pericardial space. She experienced penetrating cardiac trauma, and it is a miracle that she's alive. Most people would have died," explained the doctor

"I see," replied Elvis.

"Speaking of miracles, I think I'm looking at another miracle right now." A light grin came over the doctor's face.

"Yes, you might say that, Doc." Said Elvis with a smirk on his face.

The doctor gave Elvis a light tap on the shoulder as he exited the room.

Looking at her intensely, her breathing very relaxed and the holter monitor reading a steady beat of 45 beats per minute, Elvis leaned in and placed his hand on her head to say a silent prayer.

Her eyes opened suddenly. Elvis was taken off guard slightly but remained calm.

Amanda's coal-dark eyes studied Elvis momentarily. Then, she used her eyes to point to the table next to the bed. Elvis looked at the table and saw a glass of water. He picked it up and handed it to her, but she shook her head back and forth indicating a no. He put the glass back down. He noticed some tissues and picked them up and handed it to her. She shook her head back and forth indicating no again. He looked at the table again a saw a pen, so he handed her the pen and placed it in her hand. Amanda leaned in toward the dinner tray and scribbled on a napkin, "Elisha will pay."

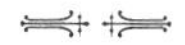

CHAPTER NINETEEN

Precinct twenty-nine had its usual riff raff of detectives, officers, and clerk people pacing back and forth. The fax machine was spinning off its daily agenda as Ada Adamczak was parading around in an extremely revealing mini skirt. Officer Bailey walked by and offered his usual flirting gestures toward her, but she quickly dismissed them the way she did all the heavy bombardment of daily sexual conations from the sexually deprived officers who all seemed to have a one track mind.

In the back corner of the office facility, Zorzi sat, confident, in the interrogation room as the sergeant questioned him.

"Like I told you all before, I'm not telling you a thing without my lawyer," persisted Zorzi.

"Mr. Zorzi, you're only making this more difficult for yourself by not complying," said the irritated Detective Smith. Commander Blake put his arm around the irritated detective.

"It's no use. He knows what his rights are," said the commander.

"Ok, well I don't want to let him go," griped Smith.

"We have to. We have nothing on him," instructed the commander.

"Ok, ok." Detective Smith walked over to the proud Zorzi. "We're going to let you go, but I'm telling you right now, keep away from the Elvis character. That goes for you and your accomplice, Miss Davidson."

Zorzi eased out of the chair and nodded toward the detective. "Good day, gentlemen."

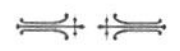

"We need to book this flight now; the concert is in two days," said Sunny.

"Ok, let's do it," replied Elvis.

"What about Elisha?"

"I don't know. It could be a last minute thing."

"You still didn't have any luck getting information out of her?" questioned Sunny.

"Sunny, Elisha was gang raped," remarked Elvis flatly.

"Oh, my God, you have got to be kidding me."

"No, I'm not kidding."

"I've got to talk to her before we leave. How did it happen?" prodded Sunny.

"Zorzi and Amanda nabbed her at the radio station after the show we were supposed to do," replied Elvis.

"I'm going in there right now."

Elvis grabbed Sunny by the arm. "Sunny, can you wait?" "She hasn't even told me the full story yet, so let's hold off."

"Ok, but let's start packing, now, for Hawaii. We're doing this gig come hell and high water. I can live off this concert money long after you're gone."

"Ok, wise guy, let's not get greedy," teased Elvis.

"It's not being greedy…"

Their conversation trailed off through the usual sarcastic banter that seemed to fuel their relationship and their packing efforts.

⟜ ⟝

"Aloha from Hawaii," spewed over the headlines and all eyes were centered on Honolulu. CNN was set up outside the Neal S. Blaisdell Center. Cory Grinder was checking himself out in a mirror making last minute adjustments before they were set to go live.

"Ready, set, live," yelled the crew director. Cory quickly turned toward the camera.

"Ladies and Gentlemen I'm standing outside the Neal S. Blaisdell Center, named after our mayor and originally called the Honolulu International center, where Elvis first performed on January 14, 1973. To my left, you can see the bronze statue of the king of rock 'n' roll." The reporter glanced at his watch. "In exactly twenty-four hours, Elvis will return. I hear this time will be different, but he is just as anticipated as he ever was."

An excited young lady walked up to the commentator. "And what's you're your name young lady?"

"I'm Lisa and I'm so excited to be here I can't stand it. I saw him in Vegas and decided from that point I wanted to see him again."

"You're so young, Lisa. Do you know much about Elvis?"

"Yes, I grew up with parents that absolutely loved Elvis, and my grandparents loved him as well. I was forced to watch his movies and see some of his concerts."

Cory laughed lightly. "You were forced to watch his movies and concerts?"

"Yes, I had no choice but to like Elvis, or I would be disowned by my family."

Cory laughed again. "Ok, Lisa, well I hope you enjoy the show. Back to you, Charlie."

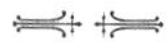

The somber faces were focused on the furious cult leader. His words were like fire spewing from his mouth as he paced back and forth in the assembly room.

"Condemnation to our enemy! He has caused great harm. We gather here today to offer prayers and condolences to our secretary, Amanda Dickerson. She needs our thoughts and continual prayers. The lion man has caused great damage. We must gather and come together as one. Through adversity we will become stronger. We pray today that God will give us the strength to defeat the enemy."

The congregation lightly scattered throughout the room. Their faces were hollow, their eyes misty, and their brains numb. Ready to receive marching orders from the cult leader, a sense of urgency fell on them.

"Matthew Mercendell, proceed forward, please. I will place you in charge of our scouting division. You will scout the evil one and let us know of his whereabouts. We will strategically attack the enemy when he least expects it. Can you with due diligence proceed with this command?"

"Yes, sir, Zorzi. Most certainly I will proceed, and it will be an honor to uphold the righteousness that we have," replied a sullen but steady Mercendell.

"Our cohorts are few, but God is on our side. We are his people that must thrust forward and carry on the duties of this most high establishment that our Great Lord has bestowed upon us. In his name, we carry on like Christian warriors."

"Bridgette, I would like for you to be my personal secretary while Amanda is healing. Your job is to uplift my presence before men and to amplify anything that I might see deemed important. Bridgette will you accept this responsibility in good standing with our society and the people of our good Lord?"

"Yes, sir, Zorzi. I will accept this responsibility with good cause and responsibility," said the only woman in the assembly room.

"Good. Let's all come together as one and pray to our Lord for continued favor."

⸻

The trip was tiring. Elisha was heavy on Elvis'mind. The shaking of the plane from the turbine engines reminded him of his tumultuous past life. He was concerned for Elisha. He started to feel uneasy about leaving her behind.

"Mr. Elvis, would you care for a coke?" offered the stewardess.

"No, Ma'am."

The stewardess walked away, and then turned her head to smile at him. She gave him a wink.

He laughed and then thought to himself, "In my former life, I would have returned the wink and flirted with her." He chuckled at the thought. He felt a light tap on his shoulder.

"Hey, man, only 3 more hours, and we're in Hawaii," Sunny said joyfully. "I've never been to Hawaii. Can't wait to finally see it."

"It's beautiful, very scenic. Peaceful," replied Elvis.

"Peaceful. That will certainly be a welcome change" said Sunny.

The plane suddenly swayed left, then right. Sunny fell in Elvis' lap; the stewardess lost her balance and fell in the aisle as the tray full of drinks spilled all over her. The corridor lights blinked on and off rapidly. The other people on the plane were rocking back and forth. A voice on the intercom broke in.

"We have hit some violent wind. Stay calm, stay calm."

"That easy for you to say," shouted Sunny. "We're losing altitude fast. I can feel it," shouted Sunny.

"Stay calm," the intercom voice said once again. The terror-stricken faces of the people on board were wide-eyed and desperately holding onto each other, or anything sturdy, to keep from tumbling and falling over top of each other.

"We're going to die," Sunny shouted.

Elvis closed his eyes. "I rebuke that in the name of Jesus. Lord, Jesus, it's not our time. In your name, Lord, calm the winds and straighten the plane." The plane continued to rock.

Elvis put his hands together and pressed his head firmly against his hands. "Lord, I know you hear my prayers. This mission is not over yet. Straighten the plane out, calm the winds in the name of Jesus." The plane rocked and hurled, wildly as it descended rapidly.

The intercom voice broke in again. "Fasten your belts, and place the breathing apparatus on."

"Is this it Elvis? Are we going to die?" said Sunny fearfully. Sunny grabbed his safety belt and breathing apparatus, then desperately looked over at Elvis.

Elvis was praying. Sunny grabbed Elvis and held on to him tightly. He could feel Elvis pleading to God.

"Lord, Jesus, it's not our time; I know it's not our time. Please, in your precious name, straighten the plane," Sunny prayed still clutching Elvis.

His heart was about to explode from the sudden decline in altitude. Sunny placed his hand over his heart. "Jesus, straighten the plane! Please, Lord, it's not our time. We still have thousands and thousands of more souls to touch." Pleaded Sunny. Elvis peered over at Sunny, and thought to himself. "He is certainly drawing closer to God with that fervent prayer."

Suddenly, the plain veered upward. The force drove Sunny back into the seat. His heart felt as if it was going to fall out of his chest. "Oh, my God," he yelled.

Elvis looked over at Sunny and immediately held his hand. “It’s ok,” he assured Sunny.

Sunny desperately tried to catch his breath. “What in the name of Jesus was that all that about?”

“I don’t know,” replied Elvis, “But we’re fine now.”

“Are you sure?” replied Sunny.

“I’m sure.” Said Elvis

CHAPTER TWENTY

The sound of the footsteps was barely audible. Elisha turned her head slightly and saw a shadow moving in toward her. "It's here. The angel was right." She thought to herself. The footsteps came closer. She grimaced and squeezed the sheets. Something sharp pressed against her. A voice whispered in her ear, "Die, bitch." The knife entered her belly; she felt the blood rushing from the incision. She reached for a glass next to the table and shattered it across the intruder's head. The intruder fell backwards, leaving the knife in her belly. Elisha pulled it out of her belly and yelled with excruciating pain. She held the knife firmly and lunged toward the intruder. The light from the hall exposed Amanda's face, a patch over her eye. Elisha raised the knife in the air and violently thrust it into Amanda's heart. Sickening déjà vu passed over her, except this time was different. She twisted the knife continually until she was sure Amanda's heart was torn to shreds. Blood gushed out onto the floor. When she was done, she fell back and covered the slit in her belly. Suddenly, she reached for the red button by the side of the bed. Moments later, a nurse entered the blood-filled room. She turned on the lights and looked in horror at the two women lying on the floor covered in blood. Screaming at the top of her lungs, she turned and ran down the hall yelling for help. The doctor ran to her as she fell in his arms. The other nurses ran toward the room, and they all looked on in horror. The nurse at the substation yelled, "Emergency, emergency. Ninth floor." The emergency personnel carried both women toward the operating rooms.

The following morning, a Chaplin told the reporter from the Memphis news that they could not save Amanda. Elisha was in stable, but critical condition from the knife wound.

"WMPG reports that Amanda Dickerson has died from yet another stab wound to the heart. Elisha Matthews was involved in the fatal attack. Now, one has to wonder why these two women were in the same hospital together. The hospital is being investigated now. The governor's office is seeking answers as to why the local authorities decided to have the two women placed in the same hospital.

This was a very poor decision on behalf of Sergeant Yalom; he should have had the two victims in separate buildings." The lead commenter touted.

"Yes I agree," relied the reporter.

"Back to you, Samantha."

The crowd outside the Hilton Hawaiian Village in Honolulu was enormous as Elvis peered out the ninth floor window. Enjoying the view and reminiscing about the movies he made on the beach below, he stood in amazement at the miracle of God allowing him this opportunity once more. He pinched himself to see if he was dreaming. "I'm not dreaming; this is real. Thank you, Lord, for this opportunity. Jesus is with me." Suddenly, he bowed down and began to weep. "Lord, let me seize this opportunity to honor you. Give me the strength to carry on and be a living example of your glory."

"Elvis, Elvis," the silent prayer was broken up by the desperate pleas of Sunny.

"What is it?" Elvis asked.

"It's Elisha. She was attacked by Amanda again."

"Is she ok?"

"She's in stable, but critical, condition." Still on his knees, Elvis shook his head. "I shouldn't have left. Something was telling me to stay, but I didn't stay." He hung his head and wept.

"It's ok. It's ok. You didn't know," Sunny whispered.

"It's hard. The voices... are they my own or God's?" Elvis murmured.

"What do you mean?" replied Sunny

"I'm confused sometimes. I know I'm on a calling from God. I'm fearful my own conscience will intervene."

"It hasn't, Elvis. This show must go on. Thousands and thousands of people need to hear this from you," Sunny encouraged.

"I don't know. I have to fly back. I can't do the show." Elvis walked away.

"Elvis, no! I insist we must continue."

Elvis continued to walk toward the door. Sunny ran to the door to block Elvis.

"You're not going back." Sunny said firmly. Sunny stood securely in front of the king holding his ground.

Elvis gave Sunny an intense stare. "Sunny move, Please."

"No!" Sunny said firmly.

Elvis grabbed Sunny by the collar and shoved him out of the way. Sunny fell to the ground.

"My God, what in the hell?" Sunny shouted

Elvis immediately opened the door and headed down the corridor.

"Wait…" Sunny yelled.

Sunny ran to Elvis again and launched his body at the king, wrestling him to the ground.

They rolled and tried to pin the other on the ground. Sunny had a firm position on top of the king, and Elvis put his hands together and hit Sunny in the chest. Sunny fell back from the power of the thrust. His heart felt like it was going to explode. He started hyperventilating. Desperately trying to catch his breath, Sunny fell to the floor and Elvis disappeared.

He gathered himself momentarily, took a deep breath, and darted toward the elevator. He pushed the down button frantically, knowing that it wouldn't come any sooner. Glancing at the floor indicator light it gradually changed from 9 to 8…it was staying on 8, not budging. He looked at his watch. "Damn, this isn't going to work." He quickly turned toward the stairs; his feet and legs felt heavy, his heart seemingly bursting from his chest. Suddenly, a pain in his heart forced him to the floor, hands clutching at his chest.

"Am I having a heart attack?"

Looking up toward the stairway door, floor number six was clearly marked above. Crawling on the floor, Sunny realized he couldn't go on.

"Damn, what is wrong with me? I know….. I'm going to call Elisha….I've got to get Elisha." No answer. "Damn, I'll try the hospital."

"Hello, Baptist Memorial Hospital."

"This is an emergency. I'm Sunny Carlisle, and I have to talk to Elisha Matthews."

"Hold on please," replied the operator

"Hello, suite thirty-one traumatic unit."

"Yes. Hello, this is Sunny Carlisle. Can I speak with Elisha Matthews, please?" Sunny pleaded.

"She can't talk at the moment. She is still in critical condition."

"Please. I have to talk to her. It's a matter of life and death."

"Hold on..." The nurse placed Sunny on hold.

"Hello. This is Dr. Evans."

"Dr., this is Sunny Carlisle. I have to talk to Elisha Matthews. Can you please check and see if she is able to talk for a second? This is an emergency."

"Mr. Carlisle, I can't right now, but the minute we transport her to recovery I will have her call you."

"If she is conscious can you please tell her to call me?" entreated Sunny

"I will see what I can do." Replied the doctor.

"But I need something..." A sudden dial tone sounded in Sunny's ear. "Shit. The bastard hung up on me. Great. I'll call Neely."

"Hello?" answered Neely.

"Benji, Elvis is trying to go back to Memphis."

"What?" Neely reciprocated.

"Yeah, he's headed toward the airport, and he and I just had a fight."

"What is going on?" Neely demanded, partially concerned, mostly furious.

"Elisha got attacked again, and Elvis wants to cancel the show and go back to Memphis to see her."

"Oh, my God. This is devastating. My reputation and good name is on the line. I'll call him right now and try to talk him into staying." Neely quickly hung up and called Elvis. No answer. "Damn." Neely shouted.

Zorzi's roving eyes stilled as horror resonated through the phone wire. "Amanda Dickerson is dead." He replied, to the voice on the other end. Calmly placing the phone down, he turned and walked toward the open window. "My God in heaven, you have betrayed me," he whispered. "I will handle this myself." Sliding the drawer back, he revealed a .357 handgun. There comes a time when you have to take matters in your own hands." He squeezed the handle on the handgun, opened the chamber, and slowly, deliberately placed 5 bullets in the revolver. "Lion Man, you will be stopped." His churlish eyes gazed out the window. He hit the window with his fist "Damn, you took her away. I wanted her. Eventually, she would've been mine. I am the supreme. Do you hear me? I am the supreme! …He shouted. Since you refused my offer you will die, you will not bring glory to a God that never talks, to a God that doesn't stand by your side, to a God that doesn't care. You and your God will be damned."

The Neal S. Blaisdell Center stood in the background as the reporter looked back at the crowd waiting to get in.

"We are only 2 hours from this historic event. Excitement is in the air. A beautiful, absolutely gorgeous night. Tonight, the king will appear in concert. Wow, I can't believe this, Barbara."

"How long has the crowd been outside the arena?" asked Barbara from the news studio in Honolulu.

"Barbara, this crowd is getting larger and larger by the minute and, if you turn the camera… Thanks, Chris… above, you will notice a plane that keeps circling the arena with a banner that reads, "Welcome back to Hawaii, Elvis!"

Laughing, Barbara tried again. "Wow, that is amazing. So when did the line start forming outside the arena, John?"

"Oh, I'm sorry I got off track a little. Barbara, people camped out last night to be the first in line today. So, we have some dedicated Elvis fans out here today in Honolulu."

"Yes, I would say you guys do," replied Barbara.

"I feel the energy, Barbara. This is amazing and, again, the statue." John pointed toward the statue. "Chris, can you pan in on Elvis' hand here? See here, ladies and gentlemen, you'll notice the ring on Elvis' hand. This is the same gem ring he wore the night he performed here. And this statue was erected in 2007. The suit he is wearing is the official American Eagle suit that he wore in concert that night, which was the first concert broadcast via satellite worldwide. So, Hawaii and Elvis set a record that year, and the two of them are about to set another remarkable record tonight, about 2 hours from now. As custom has it, fans placed floral lei around the Elvis statue. I will place mine here. Back to you, Barbara."

"Thank you, John. Wow, that statue looks very realistic. Amazing. Well, that raps things up here at WHON Honolulu Hawaii. We will see you later after the show."

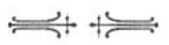

The cab pulled up next to terminal A at the Honolulu International Airport. Elvis reached in his pocket and pulled out two-hundred dollars.

"Keep the change." He said as he handed the cab driver the tip.

"Elvis, you are a good disguise. Nobody will notice you," said the cab driver with a smile.

"Thank you, Earnest. Thank you very much. God bless you."

"God bless you, Elvis," replied Earnest.

He tipped his hat and turned toward the terminal.

Elvis walked up to the ticket counter. "Can I get a one way ticket to Memphis?"

"Sure. Let me see if I have anything available. Umm, it looks like the next flight isn't until 5:20."

"That's fine."

"Ok, let me see your identification, please."

Elvis looked through his wallet and pulled out his passport.

"Thank you," The agent looked up and gave Elvis a long, hard stare. "Ha, ha, you have the same name as Elvis, and you look just like him. Can you take your glasses and hat off, please?"

Elvis reluctantly removed his hat and glasses.

"Oh, my God, you are Elvis!" replied the ticket agent.

"Shh! Can you be quiet? I need to get out of here without making a scene."

"I can't believe you're really Elvis."

Elvis reluctantly grinned at the agent.

"Ok, Mr. Elvis. I'm sorry. It's not every day that you see someone that has been brought back to life. So, if you can excuse my gawking, I would be very thankful."

"No problem. No problem at all, sir." Replied Elvis.

"Ok, I got you a seat on Flight 111 headed to Memphis, departing at 5:20. The ticket is eight-hundred fifty even.

"Here you go."

"This is too much. I only need eight fifty." The agent handed Elvis back the difference in change.

"No, you keep the change." Insisted Elvis

"Are you sure?" replied the agent.

"Positive. God Bless You." Elvis confirmed.

"Oh, thank you, Mr. Elvis. You just made my day. Well, actually my whole week and month." He laughed profusely.

"Can you do me a favor?" asked Elvis. "Can you give ten percent of it to God?"

"You mean give it to a charity or Church?" replied the agent

"Yes. That's the only thing I ask."

"Yes, no problem, Mr. Elvis. Consider it done." Replied the agent.

"Thank you, and you can just call me Elvis. But, if you could wait until after I depart to tell anybody that you saw me, I'd appreciate it."

"No problem, Elvis." The agent grinned warmly.

Elvis tipped his hat and walked away. Elvis walked toward the security checkpoint. Causally, he placed his bag on the belt, walked forward, and raised his hands to be searched. The officer scanned him from head to toe.

"Ok, you can lower your arms, now." The security guard studied Elvis. "You look familiar." Elvis didn't reply.

"Ok, you're clear. Have a good flight."

"Thank you very much," replied Elvis.

"Hey, wait a minute," said the security guard. "Say that again."

"What?" replied Elvis.

"Oh, never mind. I thought you sounded like someone I know. Have a good flight."

Elvis tipped his hat toward the guard and proceeded through.

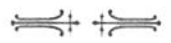

"Can you go a little faster?" asked Sunny.

"I don't think so, buddy," grumbled the cab driver with a cigar stub stuck in his mouth and a body stench that lingered in the cab, giving Sunny the dry heaves.

"It would be nice to get there before he catches a plane." Pleaded Sunny.

"Where is he flying to?" asked the cab driver.

"Memphis." Sunny retorded.

"Why Memphis?"

"Because he's Elvis, that's why," snarled Sunny.

"Are you guys the same Elvis gang that has been in the news?"

"Yeah." Sunny replied trying to hold in his frustration.

"I thought Elvis was scheduled to perform tonight."

Sunny exhaled loudly as his patience was wearing thin from the barrage of questioning.

"He is. That's why I'm in a hurry to get to the airport to try and keep him from flying back to Memphis," argued Sunny.

"Let me get this straight. He is here in Hawaii, scheduled to do a gig tonight," the cab driver glanced at his watch, "but he is flying to Memphis two hours before he's scheduled to perform?"

Sunny exhaled even louder than before…."You got it."

"So what's in Memphis that's keeping him from doing the show tonight?"

"A woman, look man I don't want to be rude but can you just get me to the airport I'm not up for all the questioning." Demanded Sunny

"I'm sorry, I was just curious is all, since it's the King were talking about here."

"It's ok, buddy. Just get me there as quick as you can"

"You got it!" The cab driver stomped the gas and Sunny was thrown back in his seat.

"That's what I'm talkin' about, buddy." Sunny glanced at his watch again, grimaced and shook his head.

Sunny's body careened forward when the taxi halted at terminal A.

"Here's two-hundred. Can you wait here? I might need you to race us back to the coliseum."

"Sure thing, bud. Good luck," said the cab driver chewing on his cigar stub.

Darting through the airport terminal, Sunny rushed to the ticket desk. "When is the next flight to Memphis?" he asked a check in clerk.

"Hold on just a second, and I'll check for you. Umm, looks like at 5:20."

"What flight number is it? This is an emergency. I have to get to the plane before it departs."

"It's flight 111, gate 28 but the ticket will be eight hundred and fifty sir."

"what?" roared Sunny.

"Yes sir, you have to purchase a ticket before continuing." Replied the agent tactfully.

Looking at his watch once again, Sunny exhaled loudly … "Damn, I can't believe this crap," he urgently gave the agent the money.

"Here you go sir; if you hurry you can make the flight." Said the agent Sunny rushed toward gate 28.

"Damn. Just my luck the line is long as hell. Umm, what can I do now?" Panicky he looked around. "Got it!" He pulled out a crisp hundred and darted to the front of the line. "Excuse me, sir, would you be willing to let me in front of you? This is an emergency." He handed the crisp new bill to the gentleman.

"Sure, no problem, dude." Replied Gentleman.

"Thanks," replied Sunny.

"No luggage?" probed the officer.

"No, sir, I have to catch up with someone before his plane departs. So I'm in a big hurry."

"Ok, I need you to step to the side, please," demanded the officer.

Sunny reluctantly moved to the side.

The officer gestured toward the guy Sunny gave the money to and he moved forward.

"Hey, wait a minute. What are you doing? He said I could go before him," shouted Sunny.

The officer ignored him and continued to check the other guy.

"Damn, what a freaking jerk," he murmured to himself.

After money-man got through, Sunny moved back into place.

"Hold on. I didn't tell you to move back in line."

"Man, what is your problem?" squelched Sunny angrily.

"I don't have a problem. You're the one with the problem, dude. Go to the back of the line and wait your turn," demanded the guard.

"Man, this isn't right. You would've let me through if I hadn't have said I'm in a hurry."

"I need you to keep your mouth shut and move to the back of the line."

"Sir, please, this is an emergency. I have to get to this flight before it departs at 5:20."

"That's not my problem, bud." The officer gestured for the next person to move forward.

Sunny pulled out his wallet and got another crisp, new Benjamin. "Can you take this, please? This is an emergency," pleaded Sunny.

"Sorry. There's nothing I can do. Get to the back of the line."

Pacing back and forth he pulled out his wallet again.

"Look, man, here's another hundred. Can you *please* let me through?"

"Five-hundred," propositioned the guard.

"What? Are you kidding me?" Pacing back and forth again, Sunny wrestled with his choice. "Damn. I can't believe this jerk." Breathing deeply, he pulled out his last three-hundred bucks. "Here. That's all I have."

The guard took the money and counted the bills slowly to himself, then gestured for Sunny to move forward.

"Damn snake," Sunny griped under his breath. He quickly ran through the corridor toward gate twenty-eight. "Please, Lord, let me get there in time." He peeked at his watch again.

Sunny noticed Elvis with his head in his hands. The camouflage look he was wearing was familiar. It was the same get-up wore to the cemetery to visit his mother--the beard, mustache and, most noticeably, the glasses with dark rims and big lenses. Sunny questioned how a grown man could really go out in public like that.

Doubts aside, Sunny eased onto the bar stool next to him trying not to disturb his meditative state. "Ok, I've got to be cool about this. How can I do this without pissing him off?" Sunny said to himself. Sunny sat two chairs down from Elvis. "Excuse me, bartender?" he murmured.

"Yes, how can I help you?" "Can you tell my buddy at the end of the bar that Sunny needs to talk with him and it's urgent?"

"Why can't you tell him?" bristled the bartender.

"We just had a fight, and I mean a literal fight. You know, the physical kind." The bartender glanced over at Elvis. He cleared his voice. "Hello, sir…"

"Yes?" Elvis murmured without looking up.

"Someone is here to see you."

Elvis remained in the same position.

"Who is it?" inquired Elvis

The bartender walked back down to Sunny. "What's your name?" the bartender whispered.

"Sunny."

"It's Sunny," the bartender relayed to Elvis.

Elvis quickly glanced over at Sunny. "Oh, no." He got up and started walking away.

"Hold on," shouted Sunny.

"Look, I have made up my mind. I'm going to Memphis."

"Elvis, we have to do this show. It's got to go on." Sunny begged.

Elvis looked at Sunny with a harsh stare.

"For once I want to do the right thing. Just once. In my previous life, I was always busy doing this and doing that. I was thinking about me all the time. Whatever satisfied me is what I wanted to do. I didn't make the sacrifices I needed to make. Now that God has given me a second chance, I don't want to do what I did before. I've got to do it right this time. I have got to sacrifice myself for others instead of just pleasing myself all the time. You understand?" replied Elvis.

"I understand all that but we're already here, now, so we might as well do the show. There are people out in the audience that will need to hear what you have to say about Christ. They are lost souls, and the words you have to say just might help someone. It just might keep someone from killing themselves. Plus, what you're doing now? Abandoning this responsibility to go see Elisha, no matter how good your intentions are, is still you being selfish, doing what you want and when without regard to the impact it has on others. How is that sacrificing yourself?" beseeched Sunny.

"Since when have you cared about other peoples' feelings? Or cared about the saving grace of Jesus?" urged Elvis.

"People change, and I feel there is someone that needs to hear your message tonight."

"Who is that someone?" asked Elvis.

"I don't know." Implored Sunny.

"Is it you?" asked Elvis.

"Ha ha…you're funny, man." Smirked Sunny.

"No, I'm serious. Is it you?" replied Elvis passionately.

"Yeah, it's me." Sunny's phone rang. "Give me a second." Sunny walked away from Elvis and signaled to him that he'd be back in a second.

"Elisha?"

"Sunny, where is Elvis?" probed Elisha

"He's here with me. Are you ok?"

"By the grace of God, I'm alive. The doctor told me you needed me to call right away. What's wrong?" ask Elisha.

"Look, Elisha. We're in Hawaii. Elvis is scheduled to do a show in about an hour and a half. But we have a huge problem."

"What is it?"

"When I told him what happened to you, he said he didn't want to do the show, and now we are standing here at the airport, and he is waiting for a flight to Memphis. Is there any way you can try to talk him into staying? It's imperative that he does the show tonight. Neely's reputation is at stake, and I feel deep in my heart there is someone that needs to hear his message tonight."

"Let me talk to him, right now," demanded Elisha.

"Ok, hold on," replied Sunny. He turned and noticed Elvis was gone. "Holy crap. Hold on, Elisha I've got to find Elvis. He disappeared." He ran up to the ticket booth at gate twenty-eight. "Have you seen Elvis?"

"Who?" replied the ticket person.

"Elvis." Shouted Sunny.

The ticket person looked at Sunny quizzically.

"Ah, I mean a guy about six feet tall, beard, with glasses and a hat."

"Yes, sir, he has already boarded the plane," said the ticket person.

"Oh, my God, I've got to talk to him before the plane departs." Sunny rushed toward the open door leading to the plane. Security grabbed him by the collar.

"Hold on. Where do you think you're going?" shouted one of the guards.

"I need to get on the plane. It's an emergency. Here is my ticket"

"If you don't chill out, we're going to call the police." Roared the security guy.

"Look, here's my ticket already...geez," implored Sunny. He wrestled his arm loose and grabbed his phone. "Ok, ok, already. Chill out for a second, will you?" Sunny jerked his other arm free and took several steps away. "Elisha, hold on a second, Elvis is on the plane. Elisha...you there... Hello?"

His cell phone sounded, and Elisha's name appeared on the caller ID. "Elisha?" Elvis answered.

"Elvis, are you ok?"

"The question is, are you ok?"

"Yes, I'm fine. Thank God He was there for me."

"Yes, and He will always be there for you, and I'm sorry I left you alone. If I would have been there by your side, Amanda would not have done harm to you," said Elvis.

"Elvis, why aren't you doing the show?"

"I need to be there with you."

"Elvis, I forgot to tell you that I had a visitor come by and see me."

"I know you did. It was Amanda," replied Elvis.

"No, I'm talking about a heavenly visitor."

"A heavenly visitor?"

"Yes," confirmed Elisha.

"Who was it?"

"It was a messenger, an angel of God."

"An angel?" replied Elvis.

"Yes. It appeared as a man in white linen, and he had a golden belt around his waist. His eyes were like flaming torches, his arms and legs were like bronze, and his voice was like the sound of thunder. He was glowing and mostly white."

"What did he say?" "That the enemy would try to kill you and me. Amanda tried to kill me with a knife; my life was spared.

When she entered my room, I knew she was going to try and kill me. I suspected Amanda, and it was her."

"I guess I'm next?" said Elvis.

"Yes, that's what I'm thinking," replied Elisha.

"Who will it be?"

"I don't know, but it will happen between now and your rapture back into heaven."

"Zorzi," said Elvis.

"Possibly, yes." "When and where?"

"It doesn't matter, Elvis. You will survive it whenever he or she tries to kill you. That's why you should stay."

"Why does it make a difference if I stay?" asked Elvis.

"People need to hear your message; didn't Jesus tell you to spread the message of Christ? You can't spread the message of Christ being at my bedside. I'm fine. You live for Christ. Don't let your flesh control you like it did before. It has no control over you. You live by the spirit, now. Do God's will and perform tonight. Not only perform, but give the most powerful and graceful concert you have ever done. Win souls to Christ tonight. It is why you are here. God gave you this chance of life again to give him glory. Now, go give him glory," Elisha ordered with confidence and conviction.

Elvis hesitated. He placed his hand around the crucifix hanging from his neck and closed his hand to make a fist around it. He became transfixed.

When he opened his hand, a light burned inside him, and Elisha's plea resonated in his mind. "It isn't about me; it's about Christ," Elvis said in a loud whisper.

"Christ, be with Elvis," Elisha's voice broke with emotion.

"Thank you, Elisha, for your words of wisdom. I will see you after the show."

"Yeah! Amen! And God be the glory," Sunny said loudly. As he saw Elvis exiting the plane.

"Come on. Follow me. We have a concert to do," Elvis shouted, as Sunny gave him solid embrace.

Sunny ran ahead of Elvis to make way. "Hail to the king. Here we come!" He shouted as he ran down the corridor. People turned and looked at him like he was crazy. "Make way for the king," he shouted again.

The cab driver was still waiting outside the terminal; Sunny leaned in through the passenger window. "I'm back, and guess who's with me," he said with a big grin on his face.

The driver turned his head and saw Elvis shed his beard and glasses. "Damn, it really is Elvis."

"Can you get us there in thirty minutes?" ask Sunny

"You betcha." The cab driver smashed the accelerator and left a trail of white smoke in front of the terminal.

Sunny quickly called Neely. "We're on our way."

"Thank God in heaven." Neely exhaled, only then realizing he'd been holding his breath all afternoon. "Tell the cab driver to come to the back of the arena," instructed Neely.

"Will do." Sunny looked back at Elvis. He had his eyes shut, and his lips were moving in silent prayer.

"Do you have an extra cigar?" Sunny asked the cab driver.

"Yes, they're in the glove box."

"Do you mind?" ask Sunny

"Not at all. Help yourself." Replied the cab driver

"Don't mind if I do. This is cause for a celebration." Sunny wet the end of the cigar, bit a piece off, and spit it on the car floor. He pulled out his cigarette lighter, lit up the stogie, inhaled deeply, and let out the sweet smell of smoke which swirled around in the car and then out the window.

"Ah, that tastes good. I haven't had one of these in a long while. Satisfaction, baby, satisfaction." Sunny reveled in the tobacco fix, looking over at the cab driver, who was staring intensely at the road, weaving in and out of traffic with the caution lights flashing.

The cab came to a screeching halt behind the arena.

They all exited the cab and entered the arena. The arena was already at deafening decibels as they made their way down the hall. Neely stood at the corner of the stage with a smile.

"Glad to see you again, Elvis."

"Glad to see you, too." Elvis looked at him with focus, a fiery, intense smile signaling his renewed determination.

"This is it, brother." Sunny helped him with his jumpsuit as he zipped it up. He tucked in a couple of scarves under the suit to cover his chest. "Knock 'em dead, kid." Exclaimed Sunny

Elvis walked up the stairs leading to the stage. The rhinestones on his jumpsuit twinkled, as the spot light shined on Elvis entering the stage. The concert goers were all standing; their deafening cheers reverberated throughout the arena. The sound pierced his ears and electrified his soul. The spirit guided him as he reached for the microphone and looked over the large crowd.

"Electrifying, spectacular. This is like heaven will be," he whispered to himself. Standing there, taking it all in. "Amazing God, simply amazing. I want to thank each and every one of you for coming out tonight. I had a couple of obstacles to overcome on the way here, but I made it by the grace of God. This has been an unbelievable journey.

God has given me a second chance, and I want to share the message of hope and inspiration with you. I love Hawaii." The cheers erupted the applause was thunderous. "Hawaii! God loves Hawaii," Elvis shouted.

"He touched me, He touched me," Elvis lead the band into the gospel hymn that stunned the crowd. Finishing the first set, Sunny ran out on stage to hand Elvis a water. "Ladies and gentlemen, I want to introduce you to a man that has come a long way with God." Looking at Sunny with a wide grin, Elvis pulled him in close for a hug. "This man right here has been with me the whole way, sticking by my side. This has been a remarkable journey together, and I want to share this journey with each of you." Sunny smiled at the king and walked off the stage.

"This is about you and your life. Have you thought about where you're going to be one-hundred years from now? Do you know? With Christ, there won't be a doubt about where you're going to be. You're going to be in heaven with God. WITH THE LORD JESUS!" Elvis shouted to the crowd. Elvis turned toward the band and gave the signal for "How Great Thou Art."

The crowd gave way to the song, swaying back and forth with the melody in everyone's heart. Sunny hurried back to the side of the stage to grab a stack of Bibles, and then he handed them out one by one along the front row running beside the stage.

"You all are absolutely beautiful, each and every one of you." Elvis shut his eyes and began to hum. "I want you all to repeat after me. Lord."

The crowd followed with a thunderous reply. "Lord."

Sunny stood in awe as he looked over the crowd, and it seemed as if every person in the crowd had their eyes shut, with the exception of some people who seemed like they were caught off guard by the religious overtones and he noticed some people walking briskly towards the exits.

"Amazing," he uttered to himself.

"Lord," Elvis said again. The crowd repeated it again. "Lord, I accept you today."

The crowd chanted their echo through the rest of Elvis' prayer.

Chills reverberated up and down Sunny's spine. Sunny turned and ran offstage. In the dressing room, he quickly kneeled down. "Lord Jesus, be my savior today. I know this is real beyond a shadow of a doubt. Take me, Lord. I'm yours. Please, forgive my sins,

Lord; I give my life to you. Today." Letting out a cry, looking up to heaven, an angel of light appeared before him.

"Do not be afraid. I will be with you today and forever." The thunderous voice resonated from the towering angel. It gave off a shining white glow, and its skin shined a bright gold, the transparent glow quickly vanishing.

"Oh, my God..." Rising quickly, he hurried toward the door. He hesitated and looked back once more to see if the angel would reappear. Waiting momentarily, then quickly opening the door, Sunny ran toward the stage. The kneeling Elvis was on the stage, the crowd in complete silence.

"I've never seen anything like this." Sunny looked over at Neely, and he had his eyes shut, too. Sunny took in the crowd, and the angel appeared again, hovering over the crowd. Except, this time, it appeared larger, with six wings and two wings covering his face and two covering his feet. The train of its robe seemingly filled the whole arena. And with two, he flew.

"Holy, holy, holy, this whole place is full of his glory." Sunny chanted.

A loud clap came across the concert speakers. Elvis jumped up and every eye in the arena fixed its attention on the sparkling suit that twinkled under the concert lights. The piano played a soft melody, and an organ blended in to create a tune so beautiful it made everyone sing glory to The Highest. Everyone was transfigured into light and, instantly, every soul was examined. A light from above continued to radiate down on the crowd. The soft melody turned into "Sprach Zarathustra" and then proceeded into "CC rider". He paraded around the stage and kneeled down to high five all the people on the front row. Pulling a boy up on stage, he placed his hands on the boy's head and said a silent prayer. The boy jumped up and down and hopped off stage. Elvis handed him a scarf. He circled back around to make another run of high fives before exiting the stage and waving to the exuberant concert-goers.

Sunny grinned at the king as he trotted down the stairs and ran toward the dressing room. Sunny ran in behind him and locked the door. The two of them held hands and began to pray. "I didn't think it was going to be like this, but something told me tonight was going to be huge, and it was," said Sunny.

"The night is only the beginning. It's only the beginning." Elvis trailed. They lowered their heads once more to pray.

"This was an amazing spectacle here tonight. What was it like inside there tonight?" investigated the news reporter.

"It was nothing like I have ever seen in my life. I'm not a religious guy or anything, but this was unreal. Jesus is real; he is coming back for sure."

"What makes you so certain of this?" replied the reporter

"I just know. I think everybody in that place tonight knew there was something else in there, a higher power. There's no way a human would have that capability to control that many people without some type of supernatural being helping. It had to be God"

"Thanks for being with us," said the reporter. "Here, let's ask another person how it was. Hi. How are you?"

"I'm fine." "What's your name?"

"Samantha."

"Samantha, what did you think of the show tonight?" "I liked it up to the point where he started acting weird. I didn't understand why he started to pray, and it was really creepy, so I just left." shared Samantha.

"That's strange. We just talked to someone that said it was the most awesome thing he'd ever experienced."

"Well to each his own, I guess. Everyone is different, but it wasn't great for me." The girl shrugged her shoulders and walked away.

"Looks like we're getting some mixed reviews about the show tonight. Back to you, Bridgette."

A small crowd gathered outside the Elvis Statue to pay homage to the king with a candlelight vigil. Some of them held their cigarette lighters. The crowds of people were silent as several news crews walked up to them to ask questions. The praying crowd was oblivious to the reporters. There were several protesters outside in the streets shouting, "The king is a religious nut," and "The king has lost his mind." The chants grew louder as the protesters started taunting the seekers.

One of the protesters kicked a praying man across the face. Another praying person jumped up to confront the abuser. A fight broke out between the two of them, and a small crowd formed a ring around the two fighters. The riot police charged the crowd and began to club everyone involved, not paying any mind to who started it. Blood spilled in the streets. As spectators gathered to view the violence, the news crew was in full force covering all the action.

The limo with Elvis and Sunny safely inside drove past the riots.

"What in the world is happening?" Elvis felt a pang of shame course through him that such an event would break out so soon after the momentous spiritual experience they had just experienced.

A police car pulled in behind the Limo. "Oh geez, what is this?" Sunny piqued.

"Looks like we're getting pulled," replied Elvis.

"For what?" Sunny smirked

"I don't know." Replied Elvis

The officer got out of his patrol car and walked alongside the limo with one hand on his holstered gun. He leaned in toward the driver's side window keeping the rest of his body out of plain view. "May I see your license and registration, please?"

The limo driver handed the license and registration to the police officer.

"Who is in the limo with you?" ask the officer

"Elvis and his manager, sir." Replied the limo driver

"Can you please tell them to step out of the car?" demanded the officer.

"What for, Officer? They haven't done anything."

"Shut up and just do what I tell you." Demanded the officer

The limo driver looked at the officer and shook his head in disbelief. He looked back over his right shoulder and watched as the window separating the driver section from the rest of the limo lowered.

"Hey, guys, the officer wants the two of you to step out of the car."

"What ? You got to be kidding me," fumed Sunny.

"Just do what he says and this will be over in a minute," assured Elvis.

The two of them stepped out of the limo, Elvis following Sunny.

"Can I see your identification, the both of you?" the officer glanced at the identifications.

"Are you Elvis?" The officer asked.

"Yes." Replied Elvis

"Are you Sunny Carlyle?" ask the officer

"Yes. And what's the problem?" said Sunny caustically.

Elvis raised his arm and nudged Sunny. "Shh, be quiet!" At that moment, the officer grabbed Elvis' arm and twisted it behind his back and shoved him hard against the outside of the limo.

"What the fuck are you doing, asshole," Sunny blurted out and grabbed the officer. The other officer quickly grabbed

Sunny's arm and twisted it behind him, shoving his head onto the window. The officer immediately called for back-up and then reached for his gun. He pointed it toward Sunny's head.

"Hey! Hold on, asshole," Sunny yelled.

"Hands behind your head, or I'm shooting you," yelled the officer. The officer slapped the cuffs on Sunny, then turned toward Elvis and instructed him to do the same thing.

"Raise your arms high so I can see them." Elvis nudged his arm up a little. "Higher, asshole, so I can see them." He raised his arms up higher. The officer grabbed him by the arm and violently twisted it toward Elvis' back, and then he grabbed the back of Elvis' head and pushed it onto the window of the limo as hard as he could. Elvis hollered. Blood started running down his face. The officer grabbed Elvis' other arm and slapped on the cuffs.

"You two are under arrest for resisting arrest and assaulting a police officer. That's going to carry a lot of time, you know." As the officer rattled off their rights, the limo driver was in the seat recording the incident on his phone.

He immediately called Neely. No less than a minute later, the whole entourage of police cars pulled up to the scene. Officers jumped out of their squad cars and hurried to assist the officers.

"I've got these trouble-makers, Anderson. Send them to jail where they belong."

"Can you tell the limo driver to get out of the car?" demanded the officer to another.

"Sure"

"What's your name, boy?" the officer shouted in Sunny's ear.

"I don't appreciate you yelling in my ear," retorted Sunny.

"Ok, so I guess you rather for me to beat the shit out of you then, asshole." The officer punched Sunny in the kidneys.

"Ahh, shit! You fucking asshole." Sunny shouted.

"Shut the fuck up asshole," the officer hit Sunny in the face.

Sunny leaned over as blood started spewing from his mouth.

"You're not an officer of the law; you're a fucking thug asshole is what you are," Sunny jibed.

"What did you call me, boy?" barked the officer. The officer hit sunny in the stomach, and Sunny bowed over again in pain.

"You're going to pay for this, creep." Sunny moaned.

"Pay for what? You're the one breaking the law. I have a whole list of charges against you, boy." Replied the officer.

"Leave him alone," said Elvis.

The officer grabbed Elvis by the hair and pulled his head back. "I suggest you shut up, Elvis Punk. You hear me?" shouted the officer.

"He's not the real Elvis. He's a punk-ass imitation of the king is all. A cheap impersonator," another officer laughed.

Officer Anderson started walking toward the limo driver's door.

The limo driver laid the phone down in an inauspicious place to continue recording. Officer Anderson tapped on the driver's side window.

"Get out of the car, please." he demanded, the "please" just a meaningless knock-off of civility.

"Is this your car, son?" ask the officer.

"No, sir, it belongs to Hong Sui Limo Service." "Well, you might want to call your boss because were impounding the vehicle and taking your clients to jail."

"Ok." Replied the limo driver.

The officer walked back toward Sunny and Elvis.

"Did you know the two of you are fugitives from the law?" "What are you talking about?" Sunny demanded answers.

"There is an APB out on the two of you from the Reno Nevada police," said the officer.

"Oh brother, Andy and Barney." Sunny rolled his eyes and looked over at Elvis.

"Are you aware of this?" asked the officer again.

"Yeah, kind of, I guess." Remarked Sunny

"You guess?" exclaimed the officer.

"Never mind," said Sunny.

"You two are acting very strange. Take these two thugs in boys and book 'em," shouted the officer."

"Yes, sir," replied another officer.

An officer grabbed Elvis and pushed him forward toward the patrol car, and then another officer grabbed Sunny and pushed him along.

Sunny looked back at Elvis and rolled his eyes. They were both shaking their heads.

"Keep your head straight, punk," yelled an officer.

As they got to the patrol car, the officer pushed Sunny's head violently into the car, and then the other officer grabbed Elvis and shoved him into the car behind Sunny.

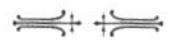

She awoke from a deep sleep and started to shake violently. Cold sweat poured from her face. Shivering, she searched deep in her soul for an answer. She reached for her phone and tried to call Elvis again, yet again no answer.

"Something is wrong, I just know it." She grimaced hard when she turned her body away from the hospital bed. As she bent over the side of the bed, she reached for her abdomen then She fell to the floor. She looked down and noticed the blood seeping through the bandage placed securely over the knife wound.

"Damn." She murmured softly with pain

"Miss Matthews, what are you doing?" said the nurse as she bent down to help Elisha stand up. "You really shouldn't be out of your bed; you are far from being healed."

"I'm sorry, but I don't know how much longer I can stay here," Elisha said while she was holding her side.

"We can't let you leave like this, Miss Matthews; this type of wound takes months to heal."

"Months?" echoed Elisha.

Yes, months. You need plenty of rest." Erecting her upper body against the head board, she began to weep a little.

"What's wrong?" asked the nurse.

"I can't believe this has happened to me. I mean, everything happened so fast, and for the worst. We were happy together, and I was looking forward to finishing the concerts with him."

"The concerts?" ask the nurse.

"Yes, Elvis has at least a couple more concerts before he has to go back to heaven." Answered Elisha

"Heaven?" replied the nurse with a skeptical look on her face.

Elisha looked at the nurse. "Oh, never mind."

"No, please, tell me."

"I don't know. Something tells me you're not going to understand.

You'll probably think I'm crazy."

"No, I promise I won't think you're crazy." I'm not like some of the other nurses around here.

"Thank you. You're so sweet."

"Please, tell me," the nurse entreated again.

Clearing her throat a little, Elisha moved her hand from her abdomen to the side of the bed and reached for the nurse's hand. "Never in my life have I been through such a roller coaster of emotions."

The nurse reached for a tissue to wipe Elisha's tears away. "It's ok, baby. You're going to be fine," assured the nurse.

Elisha reached for some tissues as well and began to wipe her own eyes.

"This is so crazy. Everything that has happened, it just seems so surreal like it's not even real. It's like a dream. And I keep expecting to wake up anytime."

"I understand. I have been through similar things myself, and it doesn't seem real sometimes what we have to go through."

"Can I ask you a question?" ventured Elisha.

"Sure." Responded the Nurse

"Do you believe in God?" probed Elisha

"I suppose I do. I don't know. Why?" countered the nurse.

"I was raised a catholic, but I never really felt God until these last three weeks or so."

"How can you feel God when you just said you have never been through so much pain before in your life?" asked the nurse.

"I have felt joy and pain, but mostly joy. Although, I must admit I'm still confused, and I wonder why all this has happened to me and why." Said Elisha.

"I still don't understand how you can feel God in the midst of pain." The nurse speculated.

Elisha continued, "A lot of people confuse joy and happiness with knowing God. Just because you know God doesn't mean life is like a bed of roses. As a matter of a fact, it seems as if the more you know him and feel him, the enemy comes at you harder."

"The enemy? Are you referring to?" ask the nurse

"Satan the Devil." Replied Elisha.

"I don't believe in Satan," replied the nurse.

"It's your prerogative, I guess, but I can assure you that Satan is real," said Elisha.

"How can you be so sure?"

"Because Jesus said Satan was real." Elisha said with a stern look.

"Ok, well…if you need me for anything just call, ok?

"Did the name 'Jesus' scare you?" asked Elisha.

"No, not at all. I just can't talk about this right now. I'm working," the nurse replied and hurried out of the room.

"Geez, I don't understand why so many people are scared of the name 'Jesus.'" She picked up the phone to dial Elvis again. Still, no answer. She tried Sunny--no answer.

Frustrated, she reached for the remote and clicked on the T.V.

"Ah, the same ol' crap. CNN…TBS…the normal news stuff."

"We are standing live outside the Neal S. Blaisdell Center; several riots broke out shortly after the Elvis concert. The police have arrested numerous individuals, and they have also taken into custody Elvis. Yes, you heard me right. Elvis was arrested shortly after the concert tonight. The charges range from assault to resisting arrest. The police have also taken into custody Elvis' manager, Sunny Carlyle. As you can see, the crowds have subsided quite a bit from earlier this evening. Back to you, Leslie."

"I've got to figure out a way to leave here and soon." Elisha reached for her phone and immediately started to dial Neely.

"Great, no answer. What in the hell is going on? This is driving me nuts." The phone rings.

"Hello?" answered Elisha

"Elisha, this is Benji how are you doing?"

"Neely thank God you called, I'm worried about what the hell is going on,"

"Yes, all this is crazy.. I just heard the news myself; I will find out how much the bail is and try to get Elvis and Sunny out as soon as I can."

"How did they get arrested? I know damn well Elvis didn't do what the media is saying he did." Elisha said, frustrated.

"I don't believe it either, not for a second, but you know how the media is…" Neely trailed.

"It's got to be some kind of mistake," replied Elisha.

"Yes, I'm thinking the same thing, too. Don't you worry, sweet heart. I'm going to get to the bottom of this, and we'll have Elvis and Sunny out in no time. Don't you worry about a thing. You get plenty of rest, ok?"

"Ok. Thanks for calling me back, Benji," Elisha said softly.

"No problem. We will talk a little later, ok?"

"Ok."

CHAPTER TWENTY ONE

The burning inferno was lying beneath his feet. It rose higher and higher. The bottom of his feet felt constant, sharp pains. He saw arms of people rising beneath the constant inferno. There was no relief in sight. The sulfur ascended to his knees, which buckled, leaving him to fall head-first into the inferno. Excruciating pain scored through him as his skin melted off his body, and his bones were exposed. He reached toward his face and no longer felt his flesh, but felt his eyes without eyelids. His mouth moved, but uttered no sound. It consumed him. As he raised his arms up, he realized there was no heaven, nothing but fire all around him burning.

"I can't breathe. I feel like I'm suffocating. Lord, help me. There is no Lord, not here. Not where I am right now. How did I get here? Please, help." Sunny pleaded.

At last, water; it cooled the fire, his skin reappeared, and Sunny's eyelids returned. "I'm free at last. Thank you, Lord." Sunny replied.

Suddenly, an arm from the fire reached for Sunny's ankle; it pulled him back into the inferno.

"Lord, no, not again. Please, no," Sunny yelled out in desperation. He felt the heat again, flesh melting from his bones once more. As the heat intensified, Sunny wailed, "My breath is going. It's leaving me again. I'm dying. No, no, not again; Lord, please help me." The inferno rose to his waist.

Sunny reached up and touched his skeletal head, bones hot and without flesh. His eyeballs fell from his skull. He couldn't see anything, but Sunny could feel the constant burning. "It's getting hotter and hotter. Help me, Lord," he cried once more. With despair, he realized there was no Lord anymore. His screams and prayers fell on deaf ears. "I'm helpless to the inferno. It's consuming me."

Every breath he took felt like a thousand needles in his throat. Suddenly, the screams of many voices filtered in from afar. The screams gradually got louder. He looked up and saw a body coming down from a red sky highlighted by dark shadows.

The shadows moved across the red sky, and it formed a face. Eyes appeared on the face, and then a mouth appeared. From the mouth fell another body into the fire. The body screamed and yelled as it fell through the air and landed in the pit. A persons arm came out of the inferno and reached for Sunny's head; the force of the arm drives his head under the inferno. The screaming sounds became muted. Deafness engulfed him.

"I can't see or hear. There's just the pain of the heat burning my bones. My flesh is gone!. My bones are disintegrating!" There was nothing left of his body, yet he still felt pain. "How can this be possible?" he questioned. "Where are you, God? Where are you? Why, why, why?"

Instantly, cold water splashed across his face.

"I can see!" he shouted.

A fist hit his face, and the force from it drove his head against the wall. Blood from his forehead stained the wall. He turned toward the person; he was dressed as a police officer.

"What the fuck is your problem?" Sunny scorned.

"Keep your screams down, boy," yelled the officer.

"What? What are you talking about? Is this a dream, or what?"

"You shut up or you will rot in this jail boy," yelled the officer again.

"My flesh is back. I can talk again!" The four green brick walls stared at him. "Damn!" he shouted, suddenly realizing he was in jail. "Hey," Sunny yelled.

"What is it this time, boy?" shouted the officer

"Where is Elvis?" ask Sunny.

"Don't you worry about that. He's in safe keeping." The officer retaliated.

"Please, can I talk to him?" ask Sunny.

"You're not talking to anyone, and the best thing you can do is shut up. Do you hear me?" He walked away as the keys to the jail cell jingled on his hip.

Sunny clung to the green bars. "Shit. I can't believe this. Lord, please get me out of here." He sat on the hard floor, resting against the wall. "Oh, God that was horrifying. That dream had to have been hell. Please, get me out of here, Lord."

Not a minute later, Sunny heard footsteps coming down the hall. The keys rattled once again.

"You have a visitor," uttered the man in uniform.

"Who is it?" Sunny blurted out instantly.

The officer shrugged lamely. "Somebody made your bail. Follow me."

"Oh, God, thank you. Thank you very much." Sunny pleaded.

Following the uniformed officer and feeling free once again, Sunny recognized the light at the end of the tunnel. To the left stood Elvis, standing behind the green bars.

"Hey, buddy," said Sunny.

"Hey," replied Elvis.

The officer unlocked Elvis' cell. Elvis looked over at Sunny with weary eyes. "What a night," he mumbled.

"Yeah, tell me about it. I was in Hell all night," replied Sunny.

The clinging of the keys sounded on the officer's hip again as they continued down the jail corridor.

A woman dressed in a green uniform stood behind the fiber-glass window. She slid their personal belongings in a steel tray through a small rectangle. Sunny and Elvis gathered their stuff. They followed the officer through the doors and into the lobby.

Wearing his usual hat, khaki pants, and a blue sports jacket, Neely was seated and leaning forward with his palms facing together in a praying position. He quickly got up from his chair.

"Neely, thank God," exhaled Sunny giving him a gigantic hug. Elvis leaned in to embrace Neely, too.

"Long night. Thank you very much. God bless your soul" Elvis said calmly.

"Come on. You guys can tell me about this over coffee. I haven't completely woken up yet," suggested Neely.

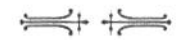

Zorzi scoffed as he watched the morning news. "Why do I find this not surprising? The imposter is always getting in trouble." The phone rang.

"Hello," blurted Zorzi.

"Sir, Zorzi, I have some excellent news," said a raspy Matthew.

"And what might your good news be, elder Matthew?"

"Elvis is in jail."

"I know. It's all over the T.V." said Zorzi in an agitated voice.

"I'm sorry, sir. I was unaware that you had seen the news."

"Yes, brother. I do keep up with the world around me," Zorzi retorted.

"We will have our chance with Lion Man. He will return to Memphis. You can return home, my good servant, you have done well" Zorzi said with an assuring voice.

Matthew placed his phone back in his pocket and turned an ear to the voice that sounded behind him.

"Do you have a light?" asked a man wearing a military jacket with a hat pulled low over his face.

"No, sir." Replied Matthew

The man tipped his hat and walked off slowly. He looked back at Matthew as he walked away.

Matthew gazed at him, puzzled.

His eyes instantly spied Elvis and company walking into a breakfast diner. He walked in behind them and gradually eased his way into the booth behind the trio. He quickly raised his menu to obscure his view and called Zorzi again. "Sir Zorzi, I'm at a diner, and I see Elvis along with his manager and another guy."

"Good, elder…" his voice trailed.

"They're talking about returning to Memphis and then having a final concert in Memphis at Tiger Stadium."

"I'm sure we're going to find out about that soon anyway. Keep an ear open for anything else they may be doing that won't be exposed to the media. We want to catch them off guard."

"Will do, Sir Zorzi. I'll keep you posted."

"Good, my faithful servant."

Matthew gracefully slid his phone back in his pocket and continued to spy.

"We just about have everything in place for the final concert. All I need is the ok from the Memphis mayor." Said, Neely.

"Today is the ninth, so we have to have this thing finalized no later than tomorrow because we need at least four or five days to get the field ready and have everyone prepared for the show."

"This is record-breaking speed for concert promotion," quipped Elvis.

"Here are your flight tickets back to Memphis.

You two are leaving at 2pm. You'll get back in Memphis around 3am. Make sure you get plenty of rest tonight, and I'll see the two of you on Tuesday morning at the blue plate café. 11am."

"Got it, and thanks again for everything, Benji. Oh, can you do me a favor?" replied Elvis.

"What is that?"

"Can you arrange to have twenty-four harp players and a white robe for everyone that attends the concert?" Elvis asked nonchalantly.

Neely gave Elvis a puzzled look. "What is the reason for the harp players and the white robes?"

Elvis smiled wryly, "Revelation 5:8 and 6:11."

Neely returned a smile to Elvis, "I know exactly what you mean."

Sunny, wearing a confused look on his face, chimed in. "What are you guys talking about? Have you got some kind of secret language going on between the two of you?"

"No Sunny it's not a secret language it's the 24 elders seated before the Lamb of God which is Jesus Christ as he prepares to reveal the judgment upon the earth. This takes place in heaven during the tribulation period." Elvis explained.

Matthew, who was still lurking at the table behind them, watched their every move. Elvis reached for his gold money clip and pulled out a hundred dollar bill and placed it on the table. The trio exited the diner as the inconspicuous Matthew trailed behind. The waitress returned to the table to find the hundred dollars.

"Oh, my!" She instantly ran out the diner and walked up to Elvis.

"Thank you, Elvis." She leaped up and gave him a hug.

"Are you saved?" asked Elvis.

"Yes, I'm saved. I love Jesus."

"Good" replied Elvis

The waitress jumped up and down with excitement and gave Elvis another hug. "Thank you, Elvis, thank you."

"Tell everyone you know the Good News and that Jesus is coming soon, ok?"

"I sure will," she said excitedly.

The trio meandered on down the street in a wistful mood.

A young man proceeded down the hall of the hospital. He turned to the nurse at the station. "Can you please tell me where I can find Elisha Matthews?"

"She's in room 367,"replied the nurse.

"Thank you very much." He tipped his hat and proceeded toward the room. The door to Elisha's room was open. He stood in the doorway and knocked on the door lightly.

"Yes," said Elisha in a light voice.

"Miss. Matthews, can I come in?"

"Yes, you may."

The lanky young gentleman, dressed in a grey suit and red tie, entered the room. He walked slowly, with reservation, deliberately concentrating with every step.

Elisha observed the young man and noticed he was a bit nervous. Her eyes widened with concern. Her first thought was that maybe Zorzi was up to no good. She studied his hands closely making sure he didn't have a weapon.

"You can have a seat." She gestured toward the chair next to the bed. The man took his hat off as he sat in the chair. Running his fingers through his hair, trying to make it look presentable, he stalled. "Please excuse my appearance, Ma'am," he issued softly.

"It's ok," replied Elisha.

Silence fell over the room as the man continued to stare at the floor.

"Did Zorzi send you here?" questioned Elisha.

The man looked up instantly, "Zorzi..."

Elisha noticed he seemed a bit uneasy after she mentioned his name.

"No ma'am I came of my own accord. However, I do know about Zorzi. He is evil. I feel like I should warn you."

"Ha, ha... you're a little too late for the warning. I found out he was evil some time ago."

The man lowered his head again. "I'm sorry." He mumbled the apology as if his pride had been destroyed by his failure to come sooner.

"No, you don't have to be sorry. It's better late than never, and it's the thought that counts." Elisha tried to repair him with a cheerful voice.

"I think you're a beautiful woman. I've seen you on T.V.

"Please don't try to flatter me, I'm not in the mood for that at the moment I have been through a lot." Replied Elisha resentfully.

"I'm sorry I didn't mean for it to sound like cheap flattery." Alonzo responded quickly.

"Why did you come to visit me? I don't know you, and your acting very strange. Are you sure Zorzi didn't send you?"

"No! He didn't send me, but I used to be a member of his tabernacle. I was his assistant, before I got replaced by Amanda."

Elisha turned her head quickly toward the young man. "Amanda!" she shrieked loudly.

"Yes, I was replaced by Amanda, and I know what happened between the two of you. I would like to help you and Elvis if I can."

"What is your name?" asked Elisha.

"Oh, I'm sorry. My name is Alonzo."

"Well, Alonzo, it's a pleasure meeting you."

"It's a pleasure meeting you, too."

"How long were you with Zorzi?"

"A couple of semesters. I was interning at school."

"What's your major?" ask Elisha

"Religion." Replied Alonzo

"Oh, I guess I should have known that," Elisha laughed.

"Yeah, I want to be a pastor of a church someday," replied Alonzo.

"Do you have a denomination?"

"I grew up in Saudi Arabia, so, therefore, Islam was my religion."

"I grew up Catholic," added Elisha.

"I'm familiar with Catholicism. It's the world's largest denomination." Said Alonzo.

"Yes, I know, and it's amazing to me how someone can feel so alone in that religion."

"Why is that?" asked Alonzo.

"I was kind of forced into the religion by my mom. I really didn't know Jesus personally. I just followed along and participated in all the rituals and the rites blindly because my mother made me." Elisha retorted.

"Yeah, that's why I don't believe in the Islam religion because it was forced on me, and when I heard the gospel of Jesus, I knew in my heart it was right. Jesus preached against organized religion, the Pharisees, for example, but also the Sadducees. This made perfectly good sense to me, so it was a no-brainer. Yes, I wasted so many years away on that religion. I could have been building a relationship with God all along, but instead I was lost in a cold, spiritless religion. When are you scheduled to get out of the hospital?" Alonzo asked.

"They want to keep me in here another week, but I'm not staying that long. I feel like I'm well enough now. I still have a pain in my abdomen from the knife, but the pain medicine is helping me deal with it." Elisha's phone rang, cutting off her train of thought.

"Hello?" answered Elisha.

"Elisha."

"Elvis," replied Elisha enthusiastically.

"We're leaving Honolulu at 2pm, should be there around 3am."

"I'll be so happy to see you. I miss you so much." Said Elisha

"I miss you, too. How are you feeling?" Elvis countered.

"I'm much better. I feel like I can leave, but I think they want to keep me here longer. Hey, guess who's with me right now?"

"Who?" ask Elvis.

"A Zorzi defector." Replied Elisha.

"Be careful; it could be a trick," replied Elvis.

"It's not a trick. His name is Alonzo, and he was interning with Zorzi before Amanda took over. He has told me all about the corruption and misdeeds."

"That's good. I'm glad he was able to get away from that evil cult." Remarked Elvis.

"He wants to help us out, Elvis." Said Elisha

"That's good. Our final concert is in Memphis on August sixteenth."

"You're having a final show here in Memphis?" acknowledged Elisha.

"Yes. Neely booked it. We're just waiting on approval from the Memphis mayor." Countered Elvis.

"That's great. I'll tell Alonzo right now. He's still here. I feel God is going to come through big for us, and I feel that this nightmare is finally over."

"It is over. We still have to go through trials and tribulations, but if you keep the faith and don't give up, everything works out in the end." Said Elvis.

"Yes it does." Echoed Elisha.

"Take care, and God bless you. Tell Alonzo I said 'hi and welcome aboard.' Give him Benji's number. He can fill him in on everything he needs." Elvis ordered.

"Ok, see ya later, Elvis."

⁂

Elvis placed his head back on the airplane seat and closed his heavy eyelids. The constant roar of the airplane engine sent him off into a deep sleep. Sunny looked over at the sleeping king and laughed to himself. "Am I dreaming? Is all this for real?" The words kept trailing in his mind as he leaned his head back and joined his slumbering row-mate. A few moments later, a soft voice became audible.

"Excuse me, but would you like a drink?"

Sunny looked up at the hostess and a light smile came over him. He noticed her beautiful brown hair with a hint of auburn highlights.

"Don't mind if I do. A whiskey over rocks and a glass of water will do."

The hostess reached for a glass, put a couple cubes of ice in it, and calmly poured the whisky over them. She handed the drink to Sunny. As she began pouring the water, Sunny blurted in his usual, not so suave, tone,

"What's your name? Princess?"

The girl laughed. "Princess?"

"Yes, Princess," replied Sunny.

"Why do you think my name is Princess?"

"Just a wild guess since you look like a Princess."

The young lady smiled and laughed again.

Sunny reached for his pants pocket.

"Here, take this and call me. I'll have a free ticket for you in Memphis for our final concert."

The young lady looked at his card.

"You have a name and a phone number written on the back." She handed the card back to Sunny.

Sunny glanced down at the card.

"Oh I'm sorry I didn't realize someone else's number was on it, try this one."

"Are you Elvis' manager?" she asked

"Yes, and I'll get you in free. Plus, you can hang out after the show with Elvis and me..."He quickly glanced at the sleeping king. "Ah, well... maybe just me."

The young stewardess placed the card in her pocket. "Ok, thank you," she said softly.

"You're welcome." Sunny took a quick sip of his whisky, he quickly flipped over the card the stewardess had handed back to him. "Susan, yeah, the girl at the airport with the kid when I was leaving for New York. I remember." He quickly typed the number in his cell phone, placed a book over his face and then eased his head back again. After a moment, the same voice interrupted his brief state of sleep readings.

"Excuse me. I'm sorry, but can I ask you a question?"

Sunny quickly opened his eyes and leaned up. "Sure."

"I'm trying to finish school.

"That's great," mused Sunny.

"What year are you in?"

"I'm a junior, but I'm really struggling."

"Struggling?" questioned Sunny.

The stewardess instantly became bashful. "Oh, I'm sorry. Oh, never mind. I shouldn't have woken you," she uttered nervously.

"I will call you, for sure," she said.

"Ok. I promise you'll enjoy the show," Sunny smiled. Sunny quickly remembered a little Bible sitting in his bag. He reached for it. "Excuse me," he blurted to get her attention again.

"Yes?" she replied

"Here. Take this." Said Sunny.

"Oh, thank you, but I have a Bible at home." She replied

"You can take this one for the road, if you want to."

"Ok," she smiled at Sunny and put the Bible in her pocket.

The papers spewed out of the copying machine one after another.

LAST ELVIS CONCERT AT THE LIBERTY BOWL

A picture of the King wearing his Tiger orange and black jump suit embraced the uncanny glossy brochure.

"How do they look?" asked Neely.

"They look great," replied Alonzo.

"Great. Place them around town and we'll sell the first five hundred tickets this way before the press release."

"Make sure you get a name and address on each ticket purchase. I'm giving you ten percent of the ticket sales."

"ten percent" he replied. He quickly added up his commission in his head.

"You're going to pay me five thousand dollars?" Alonzo said in a nervous voice.

"You got it, kid. Let's see how good you are at marketing." Benji laughed.

Alonzo's heart started beating through his chest.. "Consider them all sold," replied Alonzo.

"Great. I love a man with confidence," said Neely.

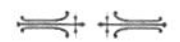

CHAPTER TWENTY TWO

Elvis once again found himself sitting on the wrought iron bench facing the meditation garden. It was early evening and he still felt a bit woozy from the long flight from Hawaii. Elvis knew deep down this would probably be his last chance to see his family's gravesite before returning home. Once again in the bosom of his beloved south, where everything started, it would ultimately end. He knew this time would be his final farewell, at least from the earthly perspective. His eternal existence in a heavenly body awaited him.

"Jesus said I'm saved by his blood. My eternal salvation rest with him. He promised me that, and I'm at peace with it.."

He gazed at his mother's tombstone. Inscribed was the Star of David,

"Not mine but Thy will be done,"

Kneeling down, he looked up toward the blue masked sky, highlighted with a sprinkling of white studded stars.

"My Lord and Savior was a Jew and I'm proud to be part of that heritage." He murmured in a soft voice. "I'm returning home, Mother, once and for all."

Tears of joy streamed down his face as he glanced down at his Chai necklace lying in the palm of his hand. He closed his hand around the necklace and held it up toward his head.

"Lord, Jesus, I'll be home soon in your presence. Please allow me to cherish every last moment here on earth. I pray that I take nothing for granted. I'm with you always in flesh and spirit. In your precious, holy name I say these things. Amen."

Suddenly, he heard a muffled sound. He turned his head quickly, his eyes instantly gazing down the barrel of a revolver.

"Lion man, you have met your fate. I curse you and your Lord." Instantly, a bright white light flashed over them.

Elvis instantaneously covered his eyes. A shot went off. The piercing sound resonated in his ears as he fell back toward the ground. The light instantly vanished. Lying on the ground, Elvis vigorously rubbed his eyes trying to see through the glaring white light that left him blind, the night sky gradually came into focus.

The stars glistened once again. A white feather lingered in the sky, falling gracefully in the sky. His eyes followed the path of the feather until it rested next to the body lying on the ground. Gasping, Elvis rushed toward the body.

"Zorzi." He reached out toward his throat to feel for a pulse. "Nothing."

He immediately frisked the body for the gun, but found nothing. Glancing around nervously, he noticed the gun lying nearby. He seized it.

"A .357 revolver," he uttered softly. Suddenly, another light hit him squarely in the eyes.

"Freeze! Drop the weapon now." He instantly dropped the gun.

"Place your hands behind your head. Slowly!" He felt cuffs locking around his wrists.

"You're under arrest." Said an officer

"For what?" Elvis replied.

"Did you not notice there is a dead body in front of you?" replied the officer.

"I know. It's Zorzi, Officer. He just tried to kill me." Replied Elvis

"Then how come he is the one dead?" Retorted the officer.

"I don't know. I….."

"Hold on a second," a second officer interrupted.

"He has the right to remain silent, Officer Bently," clamored officer Dudley.

"Hi, Elvis. We meet again."

"Yes, it seems that way. Unfortunate circumstances this time, however," replied Elvis.

"Yes they are. Do you wish to remain silent for now?" said Officer Dudley.

"I have nothing to hide. He tried to shoot me with the revolver, and a bright light appeared in the sky and blinded me. The next thing I know he was laying on the ground. I picked up the weapon out of curiosity is all," Elvis said calmly.

"I believe you, Elvis, but we have to take you in for questioning. It's a formality. You understand, don't you?" asked Dudley.

"Yes, I guess so." Elvis said softly. Dudley nodded toward the arresting officer. "Don't ask him any more questions, ok? Not until we get him down to the precinct."

"Yes sir," replied Bentley. The officer ushered Elvis toward the patrol car where he placed his hand over Elvis' head to lower him gently into the back seat.

The old man picked up the morning paper with the glaring headlines, "**Man Murdered at Graceland, Elvis is Suspect**." He reached in his ragged military jacket to pull out a coin and handed it to the newspaper boy.

"It's free. Don't worry about it." Said the newspaper boy.

"Thank you," the old man murmured. He walked off slowly with his head down, glancing at the paper. The boy studied him for a few minutes.

"Hey, sir." He ran up to the old man. "Hey, sir. I don't mean to bother you, but I see you around here a lot. What's your name?"

The old man turned his head slowly, the lower part of his face visible. The wrinkles were deep; his lips were very dry and chapped. He lifted his head and, underneath the hat visor, his blue eyes piercing through. He reached in his pocket and pulled out a piece of paper. Handing it to the newspaper boy, the child studied it momentarily.

John 14:1-3: "Let not your heart be troubled: ye believe in God, believe also in me. In my father's house are many mansions: if it were not so I would have told you. I go to prepare a place for you. And if I go prepare a place for you, I will come again, and receive you unto myself; that where I am, there ye may be also."

After he read the verse, the boy looked up. "What? Where did he go?"

He ran down to the corner and searched both directions--no old man in sight. He ran to the valet guy in front of the hotel. "Excuse me. Did you see an old man in a military jacket?"

"No." replied the valet guy.

"Weird," he murmured to himself. As he turned away from the valet guy and started walking in the other direction.

He picked up his cell phone and typed, "John 14: 1-3 what does it mean?"

The search result answered, "In the above verses, God promises that he is coming back for us. At the appointed time. True believers will be with him forever. This promise will soon be fulfilled as well."

He put the phone back in his pocket and ran toward the first person he saw.

"God is coming back," he yelled.

The person pulled away instantly. "Have you lost your mind kid?"

His heart raced as he hurried to another person. "God is coming back." He said it with a lowered voice, but still got the same response.

"What seems to be troubling you, kid?" He turned on his heels toward the voice.

A relatively tall, slender young man in sleek clothes was holding a flyer in his hand. He handed a flyer to the boy.

"**ELVIS LAST CONCERT AT LIBERTY BOWL**," the boy read aloud.

"I'm pre-selling tickets. You can get them for one-hundred bucks each now. After tomorrow, they'll be sold by the promoter for one fifty."

"I don't have a hundred bucks. Do you work for Elvis?" replied the kid.

"Yes," replied Alonzo.

"What happened at Graceland? Did he kill that guy?"

"No. More than likely that guy was trying to kill him. He was my former boss. His name was Zorzi."

"Why would he want to kill Elvis?"

"He was just sick in the mind. How many papers have you sold?" asked Alonzo.

"I don't know. Maybe a dozen," he replied.

"I can check back later. Maybe you'll sell enough to cover the ticket?" asked Alonzo.

"Yeah, I doubt it. I've never sold that many before," said the kid.

"There's a first time for everything," Alonzo smiled.

"Will you save me a ticket in case I do?" ask the boy.

"Sure, how long are you here for?"

"'Til eight tonight."

"Ok, I'll check back with you then." Replied Alonzo

"Ok."

"Oh no! Not again," Neely said over the phone.

"Yes, I'm afraid so," said Elvis.

"So, what was it this time?" probed Neely

"Zorzi. I knew it was going to happen. He tried to kill me while I was at Graceland."

"At Graceland?" replied Neely.

"Yes," said Elvis.

"How much is the bond?" questioned Neely

"Fifty thousand." Uttered Elvis

"That's crazy. They're just trying to hustle us for money is all. You won't even be here for the hearing," argued Neely.

"Exactly." Acknowledged Elvis

"Go to the safe deposit box at the Peabody. It's in there. Sunny has the key."

"Ok, I'll call Sunny, and we'll get you out as quick as we can." Echoed Neely.

"Ok, thank you. God bless you," said Elvis.

"God bless you too, Elvis."

Elvis lowered the phone on the hook. The clerk looked at him.

"I'm sorry you have to go through this." The clerk said softly.

"It's ok. I knew it was going to happen. Just the enemy coming for me is all."

"The enemy?" asked the clerk.

"Yes, the enemy," replied Elvis.

"What enemy?"

"Satan." Elvis responded.

"Satan?" The woman laughed.

"It's not a joking matter," retorted Elvis.

"You think Satan is real?" the clerk said in a sarcastic tone.

"Do you have a Bible in here?" inquired Elvis

The clerk looked around the room. "Nope. 'Fraid not."

"Do you have one at home?" quizzed Elvis

"Nope, I have never felt the need to own one." Replied the clerk.

"Bring a Bible tomorrow, and I will show you Satan is real."

"Aren't you going to get someone to bail you out?" replied the clerk.

"Yes, but I'll return tomorrow and show you." Said Elvis.

The woman glanced down and murmured, "You don't have to do all that for me."

"What's your name?"

"Elsie."

"I will see you again tomorrow, Elsie." Elvis turned away slowly, and the officer escorted him through the door to the jail corridor. The officer turned his head toward Elsie with a derisive smile. Elsie nodded her head.

The noon day sun blinded Sunny when he turned toward the ringing phone.

"Urgh... what time is it?" He rubbed his eyes awkwardly. "Damn, 12:30 already?" Sunny reluctantly answered the phone. "What?" he snapped.

"Hey, Sunny. It's Neely."

"Oh, sorry about the rudeness. I just woke up." Sunny calmed.

"Look, have you heard what happened yet?"

"No" replied Sunny.

"Elvis. He's been arrested again." Proclaimed Neely

"What? Are you kidding me?"

"No, It's true. He's in jail as we speak."

"Oh, my God, I can't believe this! What happened this time?"

"A man was shot at Graceland. Supposedly it was Zorzi, and they are saying Elvis shot him."

"They are full of shit. Oops, I'm sorry… full of crap, I mean. Elvis wouldn't kill anybody, even Zorzi," responded Sunny.

"Yeah, I know that, and you know that, but the cops and the public would like to believe anything." Neely declared.

"And the tabloids, throw them in the mix as well," fumed Sunny.

"Have they had the bond hearing yet?" ask Sunny.

"Yes, the judge said fifty k."

"That is ridiculous." Sunny huffed. "The court just wants his money, and they know he is not going to be here to appear in court."

"Don't be so sure of that," said Neely.

"What do you mean?" Sunny inquested.

"I would be willing to bet they don't believe this story about Elvis."

"Yeah, you're probably right. Nobody in their right mind would."

"You believe it," Neely laughed.

"Yeah. You're right, but the only reason I believe it is because I saw him come down from heaven or the sky or wherever he came from. I know it was supernatural."

"I take that back," said Neely.

"Take back what?"

"The comment about the judge not believing. I don't know what's in his heart; only God knows."

"If he believes, then why did he set bail so high?"

"Because he wants to profit off of it," replied Neely.

"Exactly, and that's exactly what I said."

"You will know a man's heart by the fruit he bears," declared Neely.

"You took the words right out of my mouth, brother."

"Listen, I'll be back in Memphis in a couple of days. Can you get the money out of the safe and pay the bail?"

"Sure, I'm headed there right now. It's no sense in him staying in jail longer than he has to."

"Ok. God bless you, and I'll see you all in a couple of days."

"Bye."

Sunny went immediately to the safe, kneeled, and carefully dialed in the combination. With a click, the door popped open. As if the room had an echo, another click sounded from behind him. He turned quickly to find himself staring down the barrel of a .357 revolver.

"Hand me the Money." The intruder demanded.

"Who are you?" demanded Sunny.

"None of your business. Just give me the money. All of it."

"You're with Zorzi, aren't you?" Sunny pressed, mixing courage with stupidity.

"Oh, wow. You're good at putting two and two together, aren't you, Sherlock?" The intruder scuffed.

"Zorzi is dead. Elvis shot him last night," Sunny snapped.

"Don't be so sure of that, wise guy."

Sunny at him intensely.

"Hand me all the money, now, or I'll blow your brains all over the wall…Sherlock!"

Sunny slowly turned his head toward the safe.

"Put it in this bag." The intruder tossed the bag down beside Sunny.

"I want it all." The intruder pressed.

Sunny stuffed all the money in the bag.

"Ok, keep your hands up and walk away. Slowly!"

"Ok, doc, no problem." Sunny brusqued.

"Say your prayers to your Lord Jesus because you're about to meet him." He slowly pulled back the hammer of the .357.

Sunny grimaced as a loud bang echoed through the room, and the intruder fell to the floor.

"What the hell..!" Sunny wailed. "Elisha what the…!"

Sunny confused by her sudden entry, he stepped over the bleeding man as if he was an inconveniently placed footstool to greet her.

"Where did you come from? I thought you were still at the hospital." Sunny grilled sharply.

"I was at the hospital, but when I saw that Elvis was back in jail again, my first instinct was to come to where the money is so I could bail him out." Elisha said, trying to catch her breath, while holding her side from the knife wound.

"Thank God you came when you did." Sunny reached out and gave Elisha a firm hug. "Relax its ok." Sunny trailed, trying to calm her down.

"What is it with this tender-heartedness stuff, anyway? You can't be showing emotion. Remember Mr. Tough Guy?" she laughed nervously.

Sunny grinned. "We better call the cops."

"Already have," Elisha blurted. She raised her cell phone in the air.

"I heard voices in here, and it didn't sound right, so I called the cops before I even walked in."

Sunny peered out the window and, sure enough, a flood of blue and red lights surrounded the entrance to the Peabody. "I didn't know you carried a gun." He questioned.

"After everything I been through ...are you kidding me," Elisha boasted. "I bought a gun right after I left the hospital."

"The old Elisha is back, and I should have known when it comes to money you would be here," Sunny laughed.

"Ha, ha," Elisha mocked.

CHAPTER TWENTY THREE

The hill leading alongside the panache palace winded and circled to a small graveyard that was situated on top of it. The followers, assembly members, and a priest gathered before his resting place. The lasting prayers for their fallen leader lay on the casket as it was gently lowered into the ground. Onlookers stood at a distance, and photographers with super-zoomed lenses got a few pictures in for the press. Zorzi's widow stood in silence, with a black shroud over her face.

"Zorzi's widow is here?" A curious onlooker whispered to Alonzo.

"No one knew, but she flew in from Dubai. He replied

"So you know her personally?" asked the onlooker.

"Yes. I interned with Zorzi briefly while attending seminary"

"Shh." A mourner glanced over at Alonzo pointedly. Alonzo immediately stood erect and fixed his face forward as if he weren't talking.

"My friends, we are gathered here today to rest the soul of an astounding individual. A man that led his church to great heights and beyond. A man whom many loved and followed." A note was handed to the priest by the widow. The crumbled piece of paper barely resembled a note, but the priest managed to view the short paragraph that was written on it. The unsettling wrestling of the paper drew a couple hums and yawns from the followers and mourners. A slanted eye stared at the widow, amazed at her audacity to intervene in the ceremony.

The priest cleared his throat a bit and uttered, "my dear friends, the widow would like for me to read a few words. 'Upon my resting, the billowing wind that sprays across your face at the service reminds us of our decency and our power, the power of His majesty which lies within us and, therefore, never dies.

We are of one accord in spirit, and forever I shall remain on the mantle of the great one. You're reading this as my remains are lowered into the ground, but I arise in spirit to battle the Lion that was held captive until the final days. The followers are a chosen few that will help corral the lion, for it will be put to rest. And at last it was. In the precious name of the one who made me, I must return. Thank you all for honoring me.

The love that left me has finally returned. She is my widow, a woman of many years, but she was the one I decided to marry. She thronged me with security and safety, by which my ministry was aided. If not for her, there would be no recourse. Don't pity yourselves with the lonely, lost feelings, but enrich your hearts with the everlasting soul of a lion-tamer that rescued you all from the pits of hell. Yours truly, Zorzi.'"

The priest cleared his throat once again and peered quickly over the panning eyes of the followers and mourners. Not a tear fell. The black shroud hid the face of the widow, but beneath it was a frown. She never understood the man she married, but reviling divorce, she would be forever married. Her late husband had told her to never marry a man on a mission because the years would be lonely. He had been right. Now, she knew that she could marry again upon his death.

The preacher returned to the original eulogy. "The lasting memory of our chosen leader was as a lion tamer. He knew the ferocity of the lion. He painted the vision as clear as the sky. The pictures that hang on the wall at the cathedral are donned in fine ornament. We protected them with prayers. The lasting memory, a soul that won't sleep, it passes by like a swift, cool, summer breeze. A keeper and a long friend who held the flame high at gates end. To the hour we have come, and lay to rest the one who is buried in our hearts. We will miss you, and we cherish the love you gave and the passion you shared. Rest in peace."

The priest put away the eulogy and opened the Bible. He read 1 Kings 8:12-13. "Then King Solomon spoke: 'The Lord said He would dwell in the dark cloud. I have surely built you an exalted house. And a place for you to dwell in forever.'"

"May we bow our heads in prayer; Lord, we humble our grieving souls to you today. Our friend and your confidant has passed to be with you forever. May our hearts go on in this time of sorrow, and may you lift our souls and bring us to a bright and shiny light that enriches us. In the name of our great and mighty Lord, amen."

The crowd slowly disassembled, and the onlookers from afar were gone but one. A tall, slim onlooker stood and watched as the widow made her way around the crest. She came closer in view. She was within feet of him. He hesitated, and then took in a deep breath.

"Mrs. Amar." She stopped suddenly and turned toward the onlooker. "Do you remember me? I'm Alonzo, your keeper of the garden."

She hesitated and slowly lifted her shroud. She responded in Arabic, "My son. Why in God's name," She clasped her small hands together and leaned forward, then receded a bit.

"It's ok, Mrs. Amar. You can hug me."

"I have wiped the tears from my eyes many times, young man. You're a little older, now, but still a young lad." She replied in Arabic.

"I'm glad your doing better, the divorce and the hard feelings must have been hard on you" replied Alonzo.

"It's ok, now. Time heals and life goes on. I didn't blame it on God. I love him dearly. Still." She replied in a sullen voice.

Alonzo smiled and hugged her again softly.

"You follow that Jesus?" She asked in Arabic

"Yes, I do," replied Alonzo.

"Oh, don't be foolish. It's never too late to better yourself." She responded in Arabic.

Alonzo turned his head momentarily, and ignored her accusation.

"I must go to my car; would you care to escort me?" she asked in Arabic.

Alonzo exhaled deeply. "No I don't mind."

"Can you be honest with me?" she asked in Arabic.

"Yes," replied Alonzo.

"Did it scar you?" she asked in Arabic

"No, I realize You and Zorzi had your differences, but do you know the truth now?" delved Alonzo.

"The truth.. How do you mean?" she asked in Arabic.

"Do you know Jesus?" Alonzo questioned.

"Certainly not. Muhammad is the true messenger of our God." she trailed in Arabic.

Alonzo stood speechless staring at her. She closed her door to the long limousine and slowly lowered the veil back over her face.

"You are weak, and you will not deny Allah." She trailed with a bitter tone in her Arabic voice. Alonzo pondered over her departing words and stood in silence as the limousine disappeared along the trail descending down the hillside.

⸻

Sunny and Elisha were interrogated profusely as the officer peered at the sheet of paper lying on his desk. "It says here that you all had a few run-ins with Zorzi. I can't understand for the life of me why he would think you would do harm to society. It sounds like he viewed you all as a threat."

"Officer, in all due respect, the man was crazy," Sunny responded hastily.

"Yes, I think that is apparent, but we have to go through the formalities here. After all, there was a dead man in your hotel room."

Sunny looked over at Elisha. "Elisha saved my life," he murmured softly and then winked at her.

Elisha turned back toward the interrogator.

"Ok, I'll let you guys go. I believe every word you're saying, but please, be careful and stay away from anyone that may resemble a follower of Zorzi because I'm sure he still has more followers out there that are brainwashed."

"Thank you, officer. We really appreciate you believing us," said Sunny.

"You're welcome." Replied the officer.

"Officer, can I ask you another question?" interjected Sunny.

"Sure." He replied.

"Is there any way you can drop the bail money for Elvis? You know as well as I do he is not a threat to society." Sunny pleaded.

"Well, I can put in a request to the prosecutor, but it may take a while. Things like that don't happen fast, so if you want

Elvis out of jail, your best is to pay the money. If Elvis returns to heaven, the court may give you the fifty k back anyway."

Sunny glanced down at his watch for a moment. "Yeah, I guess you're right." Sunny stood up from the table and offered a hand shake to the detective. The two of them shook hands, and Sunny and Elisha walked out of the interrogation room.

They strode down to the clerk's office to offer the bond money. Sunny handed over the cash reluctantly.

Elisha shook her head in disbelief. "You still can't get over the love of money, can you?" she snarled.

"What are you talking about?" replied Sunny.

"I know it really hurt you to give up that money. I could see the torture on your face. And it wasn't even your money. It belongs to Elvis."

"Well, it's only normal to feel that way. It was a huge hunk of change," Sunny retorted.

"You're going to have to get over your love of money to really experience God's love," Elisha responded.

"Ok, you done preaching to me, Elisha?" He turned to the desk attendant. "We need to get Elvis." He muttered back at Elisha.

"He'll be here in a minute; I'm calling for his release now." The clerk ordered. Sunny and Elisha took a seat in the lobby just outside the clerk's office. Several minutes later, Elvis walked through the door. Elisha immediately walked up to Elvis. "Oh, God, I missed you," she shouted.

Elvis looked down on Elisha with a weary smile. "I'm glad to see you all too." Elvis winked at Sunny, then he turned toward Elisha.

"I didn't expect to see you out of the hospital this soon."

"I had to sing myself out of the hospital, I was to concerned about you and Sunny." Trailed Elisha.

"Well, it looks like we have some work to do, don't we?" said Elvis.

"Yeah, Neely said the final show is in the books, slated for August sixteenth." Said Sunny.

"Great. We have a whopping four days left to prepare for the concert," replied Elvis.

"It's so hard to believe it's come down to this, only four days," added Elisha.

"Well, don't hold your breath. A lot can happen in four days," Elvis laughed.

"Amen to that, brother," said Sunny.

"Speaking of which, follow me," said Elvis.

The trio headed out the door and walked toward the booking area of the jailhouse.

"Where are you headed?" demanded Sunny

"You'll find out soon enough." Replied Elvis

"Mr. Suspense," chuckled Sunny.

Elvis entered the booking area and strode up to Elsie, who was behind the petition that separated the office from the common area. She had her head buried in a stack of papers, her eyes roving over them intensely. Elvis put his hand to his mouth and faked a cough.

Elsie maintained focus. Her nose was only an inch or so from the papers. She was obviously far-sighted. Elvis cleared his throat. It echoed through the green, brick office. Still, there was no reaction from Elsie. He leaned in toward the hole in the fiberglass partition. "Excuse me, Elsie," he prodded.

"Haaa," Elsie blurted. She jerked her head up quickly and placed her right hand over her heart. "Oh, my God, Jesus,"

"Good to know you know Jesus," Elvis grinned.

Elsie adjusted her blouse, took a look at the small make up mirror perched behind two books out of view, and rose, pulling her skirt down below her knees. Clearing her throat. "Elvis, you're back."

"I told you I'd come back," Elvis said buoyantly.

Elsie, appearing a little nervous, held her hands behind her back.

"Did you bring your Bible?" asked the probing Elvis.

"No, I don't think I did," she answered nervously, looking around the room trying to spy a Bible somewhere.

Elvis grinned. "Follow me."

"I can't leave, Elvis. This is my job. I'm sorry."

"Can you step out here for a second?" he asked.

Hesitating, Elsie slowly made her way around the desk and cautiously opened the side door leading to the lobby area where the trio stood.

"Where did you grow up?" Elvis challenged.

"What?" she challenged.

"Where did you grow up? Let's just sit down for a minute." Elvis gestured toward the chairs and the long bench situated in the lobby. Skeptical, everyone took a seat. Elisha and Sunny were dumbfounded, not sure what to say or do.

"So, let's start this over. Where did you grow up?" Elvis asked again.

"Umm, well I grew up right here. I've been here all my life," Elsie replied.

"All your life." Elvis reiterated.

"Yes, my mom was a big fan of yours." She chuckled lightly.

"How old are you?" asked Elvis.

"You know you're not supposed to ask a woman that. Shame on you," Elsie said in a joking manner.

"Did you grow up in a religion or anything?"

"No, not really. We went to church from time to time, but never really got into it as a family."

"Have you ever thought about eternity?" examined Elvis

"No, really I don't give it a lot of thought."

"Are you the least bit curious about what will happen to you when you die?" asked Elvis.

"I guess from time to time I might wonder about it, when I see a pastor on T.V. or something," she murmured.

"Well, how about if I told you right now there really is a God, and I kneeled before Jesus?"

Elsie took it in, but didn't reply.

"Well?" pushed Elvis.

"I don't know. I don't want to insult you. I really don't know," replied Elsie.

"Don't worry about it. You won't insult me. I promise. Just tell me how you feel and don't hold anything back."

Elsie inhaled deeply then exhaled and looked around the room. She felt nervous and uncomfortable. "Ok, to be honest with you, I think it's all a bunch of hog wash," she spilled. She lowered her head and became embarrassed about her abrupt, brash comment.

Elvis inched closer to Elsie. "Be honest with me. Is there anything in your life that needs changing? Are you happy with your life?" he probed.

Elsie looked down immediately, Elvis' intense stare pierced her soul, and she began to weep. Elsie's body fell forward into Elvis' arms; she became limp and continued to cry. Elvis gracefully placed his arm on her back. Elisha moved forward and put her hand on the woman's back as well. Sunny sat patiently waiting for it to play out; he had a hunch about what was going to come next. He got a little nervous and walked toward the door. He shuffled through his pockets for a smoke.

Elisha and Elvis started praying over the woman. Elsie's body started trembling nervously as Sunny looked on. Wrestling with his unsettledness, he walked outside for a breath of fresh air. A car door slammed as two police officers started walking toward the entrance.

One of the officers reached for the entrance door and, as he was about to open the door, Sunny leaned his arm forward against the door handle.

"Can you guys wait a few minutes before you go in there?" asked Sunny.

The two officers glanced at one another suspiciously, and then turned toward Sunny.

"Why? What's going on?" one officer questioned as his hand slowly moved closer to his hand gun in his holster.

"Oh, nothing to be alarmed about. It's just a prayer."

"Just a prayer? Then why do you look so nervous?" rebutted the officer.

One officer nodded toward the other officer as they both placed their hands on their hand guns.

"No, seriously guys, they really are…" Sunny couldn't finish his sentence before the two officers pulled the door open, and one officer stepped inside while the other officer went in behind him.

They pulled their guns out immediately when they saw Elisha and Elvis hovering over a stretched out Elsie.

"Freeze!" the two officers yelled simultaneously.

Elvis and Elisha oblivious to the command as they remained hovered over Elsie speaking in tongues. The two officers yelled again, but to no avail. The prayer duo was still hovered around the laid-out Elsie. One of the officers took a sudden leap forward, stretching his arm forward to try and pull Elvis away. Then, suddenly, a bright light came bursting through the window and knocked both officers to the floor. Elsie stood up as the light consumed her body. She spoke in tongues as the trio stood together and the light engulfed them. Suddenly, they fell to the ground all at once. Sunny heard the loud thump and cautiously opened the door. He stood in awe as he saw everyone laid out on the floor. He cautiously walked toward Elvis, turning his head frequently to check on the cops. Sunny leaned down to shake Elvis. “Wake up, wake up,” he repeated.

With no response, Sunny looked around the room and saw the guns lying on the floor, so he took both guns and slid them underneath the bench out of sight. He turned and inched his way back toward Elvis and Elisha. Squatting over Elisha he placed his hand on her and shook her. Nothing. They were still out. “Damn. What in the hell is going on?”

He leaned over Elvis again to listen for a breath. Sunny lifted his right hand and proceeded to slap Elvis. His hand made a loud smacking sound, and Elvis’ head turned to the left as his face reddened a little from the slap. “Wake up!” Sunny shouted as he slapped him again across the face.

Elvis made a faint sound and murmured and unintelligible word.

“Elvis.” Sunny shouted again. He quickly looked around the room and saw a cup of water on Elsie’s desk. He reached for the door knob to the clerk’s office, but it wouldn’t open. He walked back over to Elvis and shook him violently, not knowing what else to do. “Wake up!” he pleaded once more.

Elvis made another sound, as his eyes began to open.

“Come on man, come on. We’ve got to get out of here.” Sunny leaned in and helped Elvis to his feet.

Elvis turned his head side to side trying to shake off the cob webs. Fully waking up, he instantly looked over at Elisha and then Elsie.

“Come on we got to get these two woken up before those cops wake up,” demanded Sunny.

Elvis turned quickly and noticed two cops lying on the floor.

“How did they get here?” asked Elvis.

“I’ll tell you about it in a few minutes, after we get these two out of here.” Sunny leaned in and pulled up Elisha, bracing her against his body. He walked slowly toward the door. Elvis maneuvered Elsie toward the door in the same manner. Sunny leaned against the door while holding Elisha to allow Elvis to get through with Elsie. Elvis and Sunny lowered them against the wall outside.

"Maybe some fresh air will help them wake up." Sunny shook Elisha. She made a little sound as Sunny shook her harder. Elisha opened her eyes slowly.

"What happened," she blurted out.

"I don't know, exactly. You two were knocked down by something," Sunny continued to help Elisha to her feet as she started to regain consciousness. Elvis was trying to do the same thing for Elsie as she eventually started regaining her consciousness as well.

"Hold on. I'm going to run and get the car. I'll be right back." Sunny blurted out.

Sunny ran as quickly as he could to the olds, jerked open the door, flopped inside, turned the ignition switch, and slammed down on the accelerator. The rear wheels turned as a cloud of white smoke from the burned rubber rose toward the late afternoon sky. He pulled the car up next to them and guided everyone in. Just as they were pulling off, Sunny glanced in his rear view mirror and saw the two cops coming through the door.

"Wow. We got out just in the nick of time."

Elvis looked over at Sunny. "They're going to think we kidnapped Elsie."

"Ha, you're right. I didn't even think about that. What do we do?"

Elvis turned toward Elsie. "Elsie, how are you feeling?"

"I'm fine. I don't know exactly what happened, but I feel liberated and at peace. Something happened to me, but I'm not quite sure what it was."

"You were slain in the spirit, Elsie," replied Elvis.

"What is that?"

"Slain in the spirit is when you lose consciousness and faint because the holy spirit moved over you and consumed you."

"Are you kidding me? Wow I thought I would never experience anything like that. I have seen it on T.V., but always thought it was fake and a put on."

"Do you still think it's a put on?" asked Elvis.

"No. It was real. I could feel it." She replied

"You accepted Jesus Christ as your savior, and then the Holy Spirit came over you."

Elsie stared intensely at Elvis. "I'm a believer; there is no question."

Elvis held her hand gently to assure her; he smiled and looked over at Sunny.

"Here, turn down this alley," shouted Elvis. Sunny quickly turned the Cutlass into the alley, next to the old Orpheum theatre.

"Oh, Lord, here we go again," Sunny said in an exasperated voice.

Elvis turned toward Elsie. He grabbed her hand once more. "Elsie, you were just slain in the spirit, and you are now a new person in Christ. Here's what I want you to do. Take this card and do what it says, we have to let you off here because they are going to come to the Peabody looking for you. Do you mind walking back to your car?"

"No, I don't mind," replied Elsie. She gave Elvis a hug.

"Thank you for saving me," she said softly.

The sirens got louder as Elsie walked from the shadow of the alley to the light shining on the corner of Main and Beale Street. She stood in silence. As she turned, another police car went roaring by her, and then she stood still for a moment, closed her eyes, and said a quick prayer. "Please, get me back to my car safely."

She looked both ways before crossing the street. The late afternoon light grew dim. As she began to get short-winded; she noticed a park bench about a fifty feet away. She started to feel light headed, dizzy, and her vision became blurred. She fell, and her head struck the ground hard, knocking her unconscious. Moments later, a hand with fingerless gloves reached for her unconscious body. The hands grasped her underneath her armpits and pulled her to the park bench. The hands gently lowered her body in a lying position on the bench; he stood for a moment, wiped the tear from his eye, and began to walk away. As he was walking away he heard a faint moan. He turned quickly and noticed the woman regaining consciousness. He looked around to see if anyone else was near, then he proceeded to walk slowly back toward the woman.

Elsie caught her breath as she tried leaning up right against the back support of the bench.

The man stood a couple of feet from her. “Are you ok?” he asked.

Elsie slowly turned toward the man and gasped a little from fright.

“Yes, yes. Where am I?” she replied.

The man remained standing a couple of feet from her, trying not to frighten her. “Ma’am, you passed out on the street a moment ago, and I helped you up to the park bench.”

Elsie, still dazed and confused, started to search for her purse and adjusted her wrinkled shirt, trying desperately to make sense out of what was happening. Elsie looked back up at the man. A hat was pulled low over his face.

She couldn’t see his eyes. The military jacket he had on looked old and ragged, and she thought immediately that he must be a bum. She searched frantically for her purse, but then suddenly realized she left it in her car.

“Do you need help?” asked the ragged man.

"No, I'm fine. Thank you." she replied.

"Ok, God bless you," the man replied. He began to walk away.

Elsie looked around in and noticed the man drifting quickly out of sight.

"Excuse me," she raised her voice trying to get his attention.

He didn't hear her plea as he continued walking.

She rose quickly from the bench and began to walk briskly toward the ragged man. "Excuse me?" She raised her voice a little more, though the man still didn't hear her. She started walking faster, almost in a light jog. Elsie got within a couple of feet from the man. "Excuse me!" She pleaded even louder than before. He turned his head. She noticed and slowed down slightly to catch her breath. Gulping for a breath of air, she ventured, "I'm sorry, but can you walk me to my car, please?"

"Sure." Replied the man.

They walked along the dimly lit street; the shadows from the street lights gave Elsie an uneasy feeling. The man remained silent as he walked next to her. The familiar lights of the Memphis police department were beginning to come into view. The ragged man took Elsie's hand; she was startled, but remained calm. They crossed the street, hand in hand as he escorted her across the street.

"This is my car; I'm fine, now, and thank you very much for your help."

He let go of her hand softly. "You're welcome. My pleasure," he replied.

"Oh, wait, hold on a minute," Elsie said. She quickly opened her car and grabbed her purse. "Here, take this," she insisted. The ragged man looked down as she slid a one-hundred dollar bill into his military jacket pocket.

He quickly reached in his pocket to pull it out. "Are you sure, Ma'am?"

"Yes, please take it" replied Elsie.

The ragged man placed it back in his pocket and tilted his hat just a little bit. Elsie caught a glimpse of his ice blue eyes.

"Who are you?" she asked.

The ragged man reached into his pocket and pulled out a card.

"Elsie quickly looked down at the card; it read Psalm 91:11: "For he will command his angels concerning you to guard you in all your ways."

She looked back up quickly and he was gone.

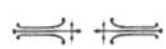

The police made it to the Peabody hotel before the trio arrived. Sunny drove the olds by the valet attendants. The three of them cautiously got out of the car, and the attendant gestured to Elvis as he gleefully got in the car. The car rounded the corner out of sight, and the other valet attendant opened the entrance door to the Peabody lobby for the trio to go inside.

Four police officers were standing in the lobby of the Peabody surrounded by several Peabody workers and the manager. The manager noticed Elvis and proceeded to walk up to him.

"Hello, Elvis. Looks like you attracted a few friends. They said they need to ask you a couple of questions," said the manager.

"Yes, I'll be more than happy to," he said with a smile.

"Hi, Elvis," said Officer Bailey.

"Hello, what can I do for you gentlemen?"

"Do you know Elsie Summers?"

"Yes, you mean Elsie at your station?" replied Elvis.

"Yes."

"Is she with you?" asked the officer.

"No, she isn't." said Elvis

"Officer Stanley and Burdock said they saw you praying over her in the lobby, and they were blinded by some kind of light.

And, when they came to, you all were leaving with Elsie. So, we have a suspicion of kidnapping, and we have a search warrant to search your room and your car," Officer Bailey explained with empathy.

"Ok, that's fine with me," replied Elvis.

The officers and the trio headed up to the suite. The officers entered with caution. Sunny looked over at Elvis and rolled his eyes. A light smirk came across his face. The police looked through the presidential suite living room, and then they made their way to the dining room, bathroom, and gradually back to the door.

"Dispatcher to Officer Bailey," a voice sounded over a white noise-filled walky-talky device clipped to his uniform. Officer Bailey pushed down the little red button on the radio. "Yes, Officer Bailey to dispatch." He replied.

"Elsie Summers has reported back to headquarters," the reply sounded over the static.

Elvis looked over at Elisha and Sunny; a light grin came over their faces.

"Well, it looks like she's made it back to the station," Officer Bailey said reluctantly.

"I'm glad she made it back ok," Sunny retorted.

"Sorry for the inconvenience," replied Officer Bailey.

"Not a problem, Officer," replied Elvis.

The officers exited the suite in single file. Officer Bailey turned toward Elvis upon exiting. "Elvis, I wish you all the best, and I hope your final show is a success. Just try to be careful, and keep the drama to a minimum," uttered the Officer with a sheepish grin.

"I'll try my best." replied Elvis.

Elvis reached in his jacket and pulled out a wad of cash. "Can you be my escort on concert night?" He slid it in the officer's pocket.

"It would be my honor. Thank you, Elvis," replied Officer Bailey.

"I would like to have at least two police cars escort me. Is that ok?"

"Yes, that will be fine. I'll schedule it in at the station."

Officer Bailey couldn't let go of his broad smile as he walked out of the suite and closed the door behind him.

⟹ ⟸

"Thank you," replied Alonzo as he stuffed the one-hundred twenty dollars in his pocket. The delighted purchaser trotted off. Alonzo looked down at his sales sheet and scratched off the last sale. "Hell. Yes!" he shouted loudly, and then looked around to see if anyone heard him. Chuckling to himself, he immediately pulled his cell phone from his pocket and began to call Neely.

"Hello," said Neely.

"I just sold the last concert ticket," said an enthusiastic Alonzo.

"Congratulations," replied Neely. Neely looked down at his watch and realized what time it was.

"I'll get back with you, Alonzo. I've got to get going."

"Ok," replied Alonzo.

Neely immediately called his manager, John. "John, great news," Neely shouted over the phone. "We sold the first hundred tickets of the show. Schedule the press release for ten tomorrow morning at the Memphis Convention Center."

"Got it," answered John.

"Order extra apparel. Elvis will probably do two or three outfit changes, and we need stage hands and extra security to boot." The call waiting started beeping on Neely's phone. "Hold on."

"Sunny, I'm on the line with John."

"That's fine; I'll catch up with you later. We got Elvis out, and the cops are off our tail."

"That's great. I'm glad to hear that. We have the press release scheduled for tomorrow morning. Start scheduling public appearances about the concert," instructed Neely.

"Right on," said Sunny.

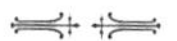

CHAPTER TWENTY FOUR

"A peanut butter and banana sandwich would fit the bill," replied Elvis.

"Your favorite, my man," replied Sunny.

"Yes, it was, and I haven't had one since I came back."

"Well, let me have the honors," replied Sunny.

"Don't forget to fry it, and add a little butter."

"I got it, buddy."

The T.V. suddenly became louder as it rattled off the news.

"Local preacher at the Kingdom House Church of God was arrested today for selling drugs to an undercover police officer. Pastor Earnest Holloway has been senior pastor at the Kingdom House Church of God for twenty years. Pastor Holloway is a member of the Memphis fellowship of local pastors, often contributing his time for the need of the less fortunate people in the inner-city Memphis area. We will go live to Burt outside precinct twenty -nine police headquarters in downtown Memphis."

"Yes, Cindy, I'm standing here outside of precinct twenty-nine Memphis police department, were Pastor Holloway was just arrested for trying to sell drugs to a local undercover police officer. Elvis was seen at Pastor Hallway's church about 3 weeks ago, contributing to a local service of prayer, and performing a couple of gospel songs for the congregation. We will keep you abreast of the latest news coming from this unfortunate situation.

"Back to you, Cindy."

"Thank you, Burt."

Elvis jumped up from the comfort of the couch. "We have got to get Earnest out of jail."

"I think if I hear about anybody else being in jail, I will puke," shouted Sunny.

"It was just on the news. Pastor Halloway has been arrested for drug trafficking."

"You're kidding me, right?"

"Serious as a heart attack. Grab some money out of the safe. We are going to bail him out."

"Do we really have time to involve ourselves with that man? We have to promote this final concert," protested Sunny.

"We can't lose sight of what we are ultimately here for."

"Whatever you say, boss man. Here's your peanut butter and banana sandwich." Replied Sunny.

"Thank you....Umm, not bad." Said, Elvis.

"I've got the stash. Let's bolt." Said Sunny.

Elisha stumbled out of the bedroom wearing one heel. "Has anyone seen my other heel?"

"Elisha, can you give Solange a call at the radio station and ask if we can have a promo show?" Elvis entreated.

Elisha stood in the middle of the floor emotionless as Elvis and Sunny walked briskly out of the door. Watching the door shut behind them, she exhaled with disbelief. "Thanks for letting me know... uhh, what's going on?" she whispered to herself.

Plopping down on the couch, she turned and peered through the open window. She spotted a plane with a banner flying through the sky. It read “Elvis’ last concert, Tiger Stadium August 16th 2019. Tickets on sale now call 800-865-7822.”

“It’s not long now,” she whispered softly. Sliding off her heel, massaging her foot briefly, and reaching for her little black book, a marker held in place almost in the middle of the book, she glanced through the notes she took a while ago.

She read, “A miracle has happened in my life. My former self is gone. I’m new, I’m reborn. I finally know what it’s like to have the love of God in my heart. Elvis lead me through the most powerful transforming prayer I have ever experienced. I had no idea that a conversion of this magnitude could take place in my life. I have about another three weeks with this extraordinary human being. I will pray continually that this spirit stays with me and never leaves me. I am changed, and I want this feeling to last for the rest of my life. Life is precious, gentle, and I will never take my life for granted again.

Lord I thank you for this miracle that has happened in my life.”

She closed the black book and her eyes. Feeling a tear coming down her face, she smiled. “God, I love you.”

A moment escaped her, as she remembered the whole point in opening the black book was to call Solange.

The fax spun out of control once again in the office of Sergeant Yalom as Miss Adamczak stood like a statue waiting to retrieve the latest information coming in from the wire. Her cell phone was glued to her left ear. Her mini-skirt was a vibrant red with black dots that stood haphazardly on the satin material outlining her figure. And, as always, every head rubber-necked as she passed. Without taking a glance at the fax, she placed it on the nearby table and walked gingerly toward Sergeant Yalom's desk.

Once again, his eyes were shut, his body slumped over in the office chair, crumbs on his shirt, and the sound of Mozart resonating from his head phones. The door squeaked. He opened one eye and immediately raised his body to attention. "Hello, my lovely Miss Adam."

She walked toward his desk and leaned over toward him, placing her ample chest in Sergeant Yalom's view.

"You're looking good today, Miss Adam."

"Can I ask you a favor, Sergeant?" she said softly.

"Yes you may, dear, anytime." Replied the sergeant.

"This has been a long day, like every day. I have to have the hardest job in the world. My feet are tired, and I have a horrible headache."

"I can give you a foot massage if you like," said the Sergeant with a timid grin. Miss Adam, smiled, "I'm sure you're like that wouldn't you."

"Say no more, my lovely, beautiful queen. You can have the rest of the day off."

She stood erect as she pulled her blouse up a little to cover her cleavage.

"Actually I was going to ask you for a raise," she murmured.

"I'll see what I can do darling." He replied.

She smiled and winked at him, turned slowly, and walked out the door.

"Sergeant." The secretary from the front office shouted over the intercom.

"Yes, Margaret?"

"Elvis wants to bail out the preacher man."

"What?" he replied violently.

"Yeah. Can you come down here and talk to him?"

He slammed the phone down. "Damn." He left his office piqued.

⸻

Elvis grinned at Elsie, and she rose from behind her desk to greet him and Sunny. "I didn't expect to see you back so soon. Do you miss this place?" she laughed.

"Well, not exactly. I came here to bail out Pastor Halloway," replied Elvis.

"Is he a friend of yours?" asked Elsie.

"Yes, you might say that. Have you found a church yet?" asked Elvis.

"No, but what you did was not in vain because I have been in the presence of the Lord ever since that day." Replied Elsie.

"That's great."

At that moment, Sergeant Yalom stormed through the door, his eyes hollowed and bloodshot, bags hanging under his eyes, and enough grease in his hair to oil down the geezer. "What on earth is going on here?" he shouted.

Elvis extended his hand to offer a hand shake, but the sergeant didn't reciprocate the gesture.

"Elvis, you just left the jail cell and, now, you're back less than forty-eight hours later. Would you mind telling me what is going on?" he said sharply.

"Sergeant, I apologize if this is an inconvenience for you, but Pastor Halloway is a friend of mine, and I…"

"Are you mixed up in drugs, too?" questioned the sergeant.

"No, sir, I can assure you I'm not," replied Elvis.

"Yeah, that's what they all say. What are you planning on doing once he is released?"

"I'd like to have a talk with him and make sure he is right with God."

"Well, he was caught selling drugs to an undercover officer, so he can't be but so right with God."

Elvis gave a wry smile. "Sergeant, I know how you feel, and I'm on your side, believe me."

"Elvis you have a way with words, but I don't want you doing your religious stuff around here anymore. We have to have these officers on duty to fight real crime, and when we get false alerts from you and your cohorts, it only ties up our force."

"Yes, and like I said, I do apologize."

"I will let you have this guy, but you have to promise me to stay away from the police station after this."

"It's a promise, Sergeant." Elvis grinned at the sergeant and gave him a pat on the back. Sunny looked on.

Pastor Halloway was given up to Elvis and Sunny, and the three of them drove off.

Passing the Peabody, Sunny drove up to Automatic Slims. He parked under the sign, which had horizontal green and blue lines passing behind the words.

"The usual," Sunny barked to the bartender.

"I'm going to have a few drinks; you guys can sit over there and talk business." He gestured toward the corner.

"Sorry to disappoint you, Elvis."

"Don't be sorry. I know how easy it is for Satan to deceive us."

"I was caught in the middle of a financial tailspin, and there was no way out," murmured the pastor.

"Well, I probably don't have to tell you, but Jesus will always provide a way out."

"Yes, he will, and I believe he will in this situation, too. I just have to have faith."

"I trust you have the faith, and I believe in you."

"Even now?" replied the pastor

A taciturn moment came over them as they each looked at each other intently. The pastor appeared a bit nervous. He reached for his pocket and pulled out a crumpled piece of paper. Elvis eyed it as the pastor slid it across the table. Looking up at the pastor, he began to unravel the paper. Elvis looked down at the crumbled paper. It read, the text from Psalm 91.

"Where did you get this?" ask Elvis.

"An old man in a military jacket gave it to me about 3 weeks ago."

"Was it before or after I came out there?"

"I thought he was a messenger telling me about you," the pastor said with a staunch look on his face.

"I think I've seen this guy, I'm not sure.

But I have to be honest with you. After that day you came by, I've been through hell." The pastor confessed.

"How is that?" said Elvis.

"I don't know. It's like this evil spirit came over me and consumed me. The temptation was so strong I couldn't resist."

"I know all too well about those, and I know exactly what you're talking about. It seems like when I lived before, whenever I would do something good, a strong temptation would come over me and a voice kept telling me that I couldn't measure up, that I would always fall short."

"Yes, that's it. I had the same voice. the pastor said fervently.

"That was the voice of Satan. We both gave in, but it just goes to show that the Lord still had his hand on us."

"Undeservingly so," replied the pastor reluctantly.

"God knew our future. He knew we would be here together, now, talking about this. Everything happens in divine order."

"Yes, it does," said the pastor.

"We know the truth, now. It's the enemy that lies to us when we reach a level of holiness. He wants to undo what God did."

"I know there was a time in my life that nothing mattered to me, and I didn't see things as good and evil. But, when God revealed his word to me, I could recognize the difference between good and evil. And to be honest with you, it has been a struggle," confessed the pastor.

I think it's important from this moment on to understand the ways of Satan and be able to know when he is trying to deceive us."

"I understand, now. Loud and clear," affirmed the pastor.

"Would you like to stay with us until the concert?" inquired Elvis.

"We need an extra hand."

The pastor looked down at the table and then looked back up at Elvis. "It would be an honor."

Elvis reached out for the pastor's hand. "Lord, I want to thank you for intervening in our lives and bringing the two of us together at such a crucial time. From this moment on, I command your angels to guard over Pastor Halloway. In the name of Jesus, I bind the evil spirit that tempted the pastor and I command it to go to a dry place. Right now, in the name of Jesus."

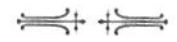

Sunny found himself gazing at the wrinkled business card that was folded in his wallet. Embossed was the name Susan McDonald on the right corner, followed by, "7th Grade Math Teacher. Memphis Middle School. 7005 South Grace St., Memphis, Tennessee." Fighting the urge to light up a cigarette he yapped "Bartender can I have another?"

The bartender grabbed another glass from the freezer, poured the whiskey, and slid the glass to Sunny. Sunny simultaneously grabbed it and downed it in a flash. With his added shot of courage, he dialed the number on the card.

"Hello, Susan."

"Yes," replied a voice.

"Is this Susan?" asked Sunny.

"Yes it is."

"Hello, Susan. This is Sunny from the airport a couple of weeks ago."

"I thought I would never hear from you again," said Susan.

"It's been a busy couple of weeks and, believe me, that is an extreme understatement. My daughter talks about you, still."

"Really?" replied Sunny.

"Yes, she does. You made quiet and impact on her. You have a knack for communicating with children, don't you?"

"Well, I guess so, probably because I'm a big kid inside," he chuckled lightly. "Have you heard anything at all about the risen Elvis?" asked Sunny.

"Yes! How could I not hear about that?" "Why do you ask?" probed Susan.

"Well, I happen to be Elvis' Manager," Sunny said humbly.

"You're kidding me." replied Susan.

"Nope. I'm afraid I'm not kidding." Sunny laughed, still somewhat amazed himself at his situation.

"How in the world did you land that job?"

"Well, it literally came from above," Sunny answered sardonically.

"What do you mean?"

"It's a long story. Can I tell you about it over a drink?"

"Sure," replied Susan.

"Are you familiar with Automatic Slims?"

"Yes, I go there occasionally," she replied.

"I'm sitting in here now, as a matter of a fact.

"That's ironic I'm not too far from there."

"Really? Well, why don't you just come on by and join me?"

"Ok, I would love to," she replied.

"I'll be sitting at the bar."

"Great. See you shortly."

In a dark room, there stood a person, visible only in a silhouette, with arms stretched toward the heavens. "Allahu Akbar," was uttered by the standing figure. Gradually, the person's hands lowered and folded over its chest.

"In the name of Allah, the Gracious, the Merciful. All praise belongs to Allah, Lord of all the worlds, The Gracious, the Merciful, and Master of the Day of Judgment. You alone do we worship, and Thee alone do we implore for help. Guide me in the right path —the path of those on whom Thou hast bestowed *Thy* blessings, not incurred *Thy* displeasure, and those who hath not gone astray. And your Lord says, 'Call upon me; I will respond to you.' Indeed, those who disdain my worship will enter Hell rendered contemptible."

The silhouette appeared, as he descended down a hall leading to a light in a distance. There, beyond the light, stood another man robed in a black garment. He placed the black garment over his head. "My sacrifices are to you my Lord Allah. the dark robed man uttered in Arabic." The light at the end of the hall faded into the black. There was nothing, blackness, profound blackness.

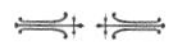

CHAPTER TWENTY FIVE

The intense August heat bore down on Elvis as he sat on a bench near the Mississippi river. He desperately inhaled to catch his breath in the thick murky humidity. He knew deep in his heart that this was the time, the time for reckoning, the time for intense worship. He glanced down at the Chai cross bracelet in his hand and closed his hand in a fist. He had seen his Lord and Savior. He knew that this wasn't all there was to this second life. He knew there was more, in the heavens, in another galaxy. He was there for only a moment, but long enough to take a glimpse of the seated Jesus. Elvis mused to himself, "How often have people been given this opportunity? Rare, indeed. Others may have been given another chance at life, but their identity was never revealed, or else the history books would have told us so."

This mission was drawing to a close. His gut was wrenched from the inside like a bad case of food poisoning. He leaned forward on the bench, the same bench he had sat on many times before. Things had been revealed to him from this bench in the past. Neely made himself known from the bench. Revelations had become crystal clear from this bench. It was a time for meditation and reflection. "Lord, I feel the presence of your spirit inside of me. I know you have a calling on me, and I know I'm here for a purpose. There is one thing I need to do. Please reveal it to me, show me. I am trapped in the flesh once again. But, unlike before, your spirit controls me and directs me. I'm depending on you, Lord. Please let me be obedient to your voice."

Perspiration dripped from his forehead. Elvis' intense prayer always made him perspire, but this time was more feverish. His insides twisted and turned. He held his abdomen, leaning over and grimacing in pain.

"Why am I in pain?" he said out loud, not thinking if anyone was around to see him. He completely zoned in on the pain, oblivious to his surroundings. The beating of his heart pulsated from his head to his feet. His hands trembled; his fingertips grew clammy from sweat. He looked out at the Mississippi river; the cascading lavender and orange blanket wrapped around the horizon. An angel of light appeared before him. It was transparent, having the appearance of a man, and he heard a man's voice between the two banks of the Mississippi river. The light was blinding, so he shielded his eyes. It appeared closer. A voice resonated from the light.

"Understand. This vision is the sign of the end. The evil one shall be revealed before your return." It sounded like many rivers, as it echoed in his ears.

The voice faded out and, suddenly, the light was gone, yet he held his stare at the burned orange sky. Appearing amidst it was a sparkling star. It looked different from any star he had ever seen.

Falling to his knees, he shouted, "My Lord." His head brushed the ground. He felt the presence of someone. He opened his eyes, his vision blurry and murky, and wasn't able to make out what was standing before him. It looked as if it was a pair of feet. He leaned back, and it came more into focus. The feet bore resemblance to a pair of feet he had seen before. His eyes focused, and he gazed upward regarding a garment of faded black and very loose fitting. He searched further upward, noticing the bottom part of a pale orange shirt. The figure's hands rested at its sides, palms open. A drop of blood from above fell on the open hand. Elvis looked up quickly, and he immediately was blinded by a white light.

He jumped back in fear and he fell over the bench, rubbing his eyes, as he thought for a second he might be hallucinating. Elvis immediately tried to get to his feet, but he could not see, and a spell of vertigo fell on him.

He desperately grabbed at his shirt to straighten it out, trying to get his composure back.

"Look at you, Elvis. You don't know what to say or do, now do you? You're confused. But listen to me carefully. Take a deep breath, relax. You have proven to me that the God you worship will protect you, and since you have died once, you will not die again. Have no fear."

"Are you an angel or messenger from God?" murmured Elvis.

"My God sent me to you. I'm the angel, Gabriel. I know you love God with all of your heart and soul, and that you shall not worship any God other than the God of Israel. The enemy will reveal itself shortly." The angelic voice resonated.

"Who is the enemy?" he murmured, trying desperately to return to his feet.

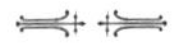

The final piece of the puzzle was needed to make the biggest trade deal in the history of the world. With eleven countries around the globe already in, there were several more countries that needed to join in order for it to go into effect. The cabinet was adjourned with world leaders and its diplomats scratching their heads for a solution to complete the trade.

An ominous voice shouted out from a distance, "Would you allow me a moment, Mr. Secretary?" The room became deafly quiet. Each representative looked at each other.

"Please come forth and address the assembly," uttered the secretary.

"It has come to my knowledge that countries that are not currently in the Trans Pacific Partnership TPP have something to lose, a lot to lose as a matter of fact. Saudi Arabia and United Arab Emirates, for one, but there are more, including the U.S. Through my negotiations with the international corporation and development and the studies through the socio-economic programs and research agencies. With corporation from the European Union, we would like to propose an agreement whereby the hub of all trade would be located in the Global City, New York and London being the two major hubs. We need the consent of these two major distribution points to facilitate the deal. The countries with the highest GNP have the most to lose, therefore, our plan would make certain that all trade hubs and the World City is through these countries. If that may be the case, Mr. Secretary the TTP will become globalized. "

"Thank you for your enlightened proposal to the assembly. And, excuse me for asking, but what might your name be, Sir?"

"Zaira Zorzi."

Susan stood in the doorway and studied the man at the bar, he was wearing jeans, a white shirt, and black cowboy boots. He dangled a unlit cigarette in his left hand and gently caressed the rim of the rocks glass with the other. Upon further inspection, she could see that it was Sunny. She gradually made her way to him.

"Hello," she said softly.

Sunny looked to his left immediately and a quick smile came to his face. "Hi, how are you?" he asked. He stood up and offered her a hug.

She made herself comfortable, adjusted her shirt, and crossed her legs. Sunny glanced down at Susan's red heels. He nonchalantly looked upward toward her thighs and cleared the lump in his throat with a brisk swig of water. He tried swallowing without making a gulping sound. "You look very beautiful," he said in a raspy voice.

"Thank you." Susan instinctively pulled down her skirt a little in fear she could be exposing herself.

"How have you been doing since I last saw you?" he asked.

"I've been fine. Just working."

"You teach, right?"

"Yes," she replied.

"How long have you been doing that?"

"10 years."

"You teach in Memphis?"

"Just outside of Memphis, in Germantown." She replied.

Sunny found his eyes drifting down toward Susan's thighs. He quickly looked back up in fearing she noticed. He tried desperately to push the lustful thoughts out of his mind. "Would you like to have a drink?"

"Yes, don't mind if I do… I'll have a Cabernet," Susan said with a smile.

"Ok."

Sunny leaned in toward the bar. "Bartender, a glass of cabernet."

The bartender shouted, "Right up."

"Where's your daughter?" asked Sunny.

"She's with her dad for three straight days. I'm all alone."

Sunny swallowed hard once again, then looked away briefly. He turned back to her, trying desperately to regain his thought pattern and fight off the lustful thoughts racing through his mind. "I'm sure you won't have a problem." Sunny took another quick glance at her thighs. He quickly gulped down the rest of his drink. "Bartender, I'll have another." He barked.

Smiling at his obvious squirming she asked, "Am I making you nervous?"

"Oh, no, not at all. No… just trying to get down that last drink. I want to get plenty hydrated for the heat outside."

"Yes, it's hot outside, and it's hot in here as well." She placed her hand on her skirt and quickly fanned it up and down. Sunny wiped the perspiration from his brow and nervously picked up his drink.

Susan took a long, gentle sip from her wine glass and placed her glass on the bar.

"You said you were going to finish telling me about your managing this new Elvis character." Sunny instantly became more relaxed as he pushed his drink to the side. Clearing his throat once again,

"Well like I said it's a long story, it would probably take me several hours to explain it all to you."

Susan looked at her watch, "I have several hours to spare," she smiled.

⸺

The mid-afternoon sun glared through the window of the presidential suite, creating an intense heat on Elisha while she was lying down on the sofa. She awoke from her sleep, rubbed her eyes, and looked over at the clock on the table. "Oh, Lord, its 4:15. I've got to call Solange. She quickly grabbed her black book and dialed the number frantically.

"Hello?"

"Can I speak with Solange?" asked Elisha.

"Who is this?"

"It's Elisha. I'm with Elvis."

"Oh, yes, how could I forget? The trio that has found fame," Girl Friday retorted sarcastically.

"Ah, yes, I guess you could say that," Elisha said reluctantly.

"What can I do for you guys?"

"Well, Elvis wants to know if we could appear on your show one last time before his final concert."

"Hold on a second. I'll ask Solange."

Elisha looked around the room and peered out the window. From a distance, she noticed the figure of a man bent forward, struggling to walk. She hesitated momentarily and then took another glance. "It looks like Elvis," she whispered to herself.

Girl Friday came back on the line. "Yes, Solange said it was fine."

"Thanks. What time does he have available?" asked Elisha. She looked down again; she noticed the figure walking toward the hotel. "That has got to be Elvis."

"11 am tomorrow."

"Thanks. We'll see you then." Elisha dropped the phone and ran toward the door. She hurried toward the elevator and pushed the down button repeatedly.

"C'mon," she huffed, slamming her foot down on the carpeted floor. The elevator door opened gradually. It was almost full as she inched her way in. She felt someone pressing in behind her, and, suddenly, a hand grasped at her buttocks. She turned quickly and saw a tall man with mirror shades and a wicked grin. She grimaced with shock as the man appeared ugly and very strange to her. She quickly turned away and closed her eyes. She started counting in her head. The door finally opened. She took a quick step forward out of the elevator, and ran toward the lobby. Elvis walked through the front door.

"Elvis," she yelled. She quickly looked around and waved away the onlookers. Quickly, she removed her blouse to cover his face, hoping no one would notice, but more eyes noticed her lace bra barely covering her breasts. She quickly escorted Elvis to the side while shrugging off a few lustful stares.

She wiped his forehead with her hand and drew him in toward her bare breasts. Elvis' eyes instinctively glanced at her uncovered chest; he quickly removed the blouse from his head and handed it back to Elisha.

"Here. You're half naked, Elisha. Please put this back on." He chuckled softly.

"What happened?" she asked as she quickly reached for a pair of shades from her purse and placed them on Elvis' face.

Elvis looked at Elisha intently. "I don't know, exactly. I don't know whether I was hallucinating or whether it really happened."

"What happened?

"I think I saw an angel," Elvis said unconfidently.

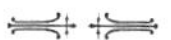

Alonzo stood over the dingy green kitchen counter, a permanent fixture among the antiquated cabinets and the fragmental tile job, another empty promise from the landlord remodeling the archaic apartments.

"Ten thousand dollars," he said out loud peering down at a check written to him from Neely. He jumped up and down. "Yes, yes, yes!" Alonzo opened the refrigerator and pulled out his favorite wine, a vintage Vitiano 2012 Rosato, poured a glass half full, and raised a toast. "Cheers to me." He took a gulp and let out another loud cheer. Just as he was about to pour another glass, the phone rang. After one ring, he picked it up. "Hello, it's a beautiful day and God is great," he said with a robust cheer. Dead silence was on the other end of the phone. "Hello?" Still, silence. "Umm..." As he was about to hang up the phone he heard a voice.

"Alfonso." Arabic voice sounded.

He placed the receiver next to his head. "Yes." He uttered.

"Is this Alfonso?" said the Arabic voice again.

"Yes, it is. How can I help you?" Alonzo trailed.

"Alfonso, it is I, El-Borak Amar."

"What?" He followed his surprise with a big gulp of wine.

"I need your help," replied Amar, in Arabic

"What kind of help?" Alonzo shot back.

"I have a million dollars for you." She said.

"A million dollars! Holy cow, my God."

"I need you to come at once."

"I can't; I have a job that I must complete." He said reluctantly.

"Your job will not pay you what I'm offering. I need an answer by tomorrow morning. You will hear about it on your news." She mused.

"I can't. I'm serving the right God. I'm happy where I'm at." Alonzo's anger boiled away at his previous celebratory mood.

"Tomorrow morning, I will call you back. Have your answer for me."

When she was finished growling her demands, a dial tone rang in his ear. He pounded the phone on the counter. Alonzo immediately turned on the T.V. He scrolled through the channels.

"This takes forever, geez." Upon seeing some startling events, he immediately raced to his laptop and searched the breaking news.

The anchor man from CNN news discussed international business.

"A major trade deal is being worked out with Australia, along with Canada, Mexico, and recently, China. This trade deal would allow the U.S. Pharmaceutical companies to use European money to fund major, sweeping changes that would create substantial job growth here in the United States.

Behind this deal is an independent council that derived from Memphis, Tennessee, by an individual named Zaira Zorzi, otherwise known in the Memphis area as Zorzi. Zorzi was killed recently when involved in a skirmish with the newly claimed to fame "Risen Elvis." It is uncertain at this point what political connections this group out of Memphis has or plans to gain with the U.S. Government. But, it is clear that the deceased Zorzi has a link to the United Arab Emirates, and resources tell us that the possible funding for this deal is 'Unlimited.' In large degrees, this spells out a very bright future for the United States. Amidst the civil unrest in our society against the progressive and feminists groups that are gaining power, but not without resistance from conservative groups and tea partiers, this emergence has sparked political interest, and a member of this group, Matthew Spleen, is publically stating that Zorzi is alive and well. Brenda, how can this be? Is it a mere rumor at this point? We are uncertain at this time, but certainly we will keep our viewers aware of what is going on. Back to you, Brenda."

"Oh, my God," Alonzo blurted out. "What in the hell is going on?" He rushed toward the phone and called Neely.

"Hello?"

"Neely, this is Alonzo. Have you heard the news?"

"The news? What happened?"

"Please, tell me what you're talking about, Alonzo," Neely rushed.

"Zorzi, my former leader… I think he is still alive," Alonzo uttered in desperation.

"How do you mean, still alive?"

"First chance you get, please turn on the news. It's the main story right now. And I think Zorzi's ex-wife is behind it. He has unlimited amounts of money, and something tells me he will try and thwart our effort to promote this concert."

"Calm down, calm down. We have already sold enough tickets; it's too late for him to do anything now," Neely comforted.

"I hope you're right. However, I just got offered a million dollars by Zorzi's ex-wife."

"What?" stuttered a shocked Neely.

"Yes, a cool million dollars."

"A million to do what?" he questioned.

"A million to revert back to Islam," Alonzo responded.

⁂

The evening sun made its way down, transmitting a fluorescent sea of apricot across a pastoral Mississippi river. Sunny gazed at the Memphis Queen 2 river boat, and then looked back at Susan. "Well, it's been a pleasurable day today, and thank you for your time."

Susan, mesmerized by the sea of tangerine, looked softly back at Sunny. "It was my pleasure as well." The two of them rose simultaneously and stretched in unison. Sunny habitually reached for his cigarette box rolled up in his white cotton shirt sleeve only to find one cigarette left.

"Damn," he murmured.

"What," Susan laughed.

"I'm down to my last smoke."

"Are you trying to quit?" she asked.

"Yes, I'm trying to. I've come a long ways, though. I started out the day with only three cigarettes in the pack, so I'm weaning myself off little by little." He chuckled softly, reached for his lighter and lit his last one. Closing his eyes, he inhaled deeply, then exhaled and lowered the cigarette to his side. "I started out cold turkey, but my body couldn't take the withdrawal symptoms."

"So you consider yourself a mechanical smoker?" she asked.

"A mechanical smoker? What is that?" he said with a clueless stare.

"It's when you pretend that you're smoking, but you're really not."

"Yeah, I've been doing that a lot lately trying to quit. I remember Robert Blake doing it when he would appear on the tonight show with Johnny Carson. I loved Beretta. He was my man."

"Ha ha, I used to watch that show a lot. I loved Joan Rivers when she was the guest host."

"Comedy was my gig, once," replied Sunny.

"How do you mean?"

"I started doing improve before I got into doing Elvis impersonating."

"Really?"

Laughing, Susan reached for her sunglasses in her purse. "You are a fascinating character I must admit."

"It's a big joke without even saying a word," he smiled.

Sunny walked her to her car, opened the door, his eyes studying her long legs, and her red heels as she lowered herself gently in the car seat, her skirt rising up her thigh slightly. He quickly moved his eyes toward her face and leaned into the driver's side window. "I'd like to see you again soon, and I'll have the tickets for you."

She looked up at Sunny and lowered her glasses. "Sounds like a plan." Then she blew him a kiss. The driver's side window eased up. He gazed at his reflection in the window and smiled as his eyes followed her car out the parking space. A text came across his cell phone.

"Call me immediately."

⸻

A light grin came over Elvis' face when Elisha told him about her conversation with Solange. "Is he looking forward to seeing us again?" Elvis asked.

"I don't know. The conversation was brief because I was trying to see if it was you out in the street when I was looking down from the room. When I realized it was you, I hung up and raced to the lobby."

"Thank you for being so concerned. I really appreciate it." The telephone rang.

"Hello, Neely."

"Hi, Elvis. Something very strange is going on. Alonzo said he was contacted by Zorzi's widow, and she offered him a million dollars to come back to Saudi Arabia."

"What's so weird about that other than the million dollars?" replied Elvis.

"I asked the same question. From the way it sounds, a major trade deal is about to happen between the U.S. and Australia. It involves other countries as well, but they say the source of political interests is coming from the group Zorzi use to lead."

"How can that be?" replied Elvis

"I don't know because Zorzi is dead." cited Neely.

"I'm beginning to wonder whether he really died or not. It sounds to me like he is somehow behind this. It's really bizarre." Trailed Elvis.

"Yes I know and it sounds like Zorzi's ex-wife is behind this and that's the reason she is trying to entice Alonzo to come back to Saudi Arabia.

"But, anyway, we have a concert in two more days. It's coming down to the wire, Elvis."

"Yes, I'm aware of that, and we must focus on the task at hand."

"I've ordered a shipment of Bibles; we have a guest list a mile long. Celebrities want to meet you in person, and they are willing to pay top dollar. Would you be opposed to meeting several of them?"

"Not really, but I would have to meet them before the show because we will only have until midnight to get back to the beam in Nevada."

"I'm going to arrange a private jet take you to Nevada. The contributions from celebrities should cover that expense."

"The show will start at 3pm. There will be two hours of a headliner, then you are coming on at 5pm. You will perform for two hours, so the show will end at 7pm. How does that sound?"

"It sounds fine to me, as long as I get to the beam on time."

"Oh, you'll get there with time to spare. We will have a Gulfstream G-500 with speeds exceeding 650 mph. We got you covered, Elvis. I booked you with the band tomorrow afternoon at 5pm for a rehearsal. They will be waiting for you on the stage at Tiger Stadium the Liberty Bowl."

"Ok, Neely. Thanks

"Your welcome,"

"Neely, can we meet after my rehearsals, all of us?" requested Elvis.

"Yes, that's fine. Where would you like to meet?"

"Marlowes."

"Ok, have a blessed day and call me if you need anything."

"Ok, God bless," replied Elvis.

The following morning was still and deafly quiet as Elvis gazed over the picturesque sky. He thought about the quiet before the storm with each sip of his coffee. He pulled the chair out from under the table and reached for the Bible. Opening it to a random page, his eyes instantly fell upon Revelation 22:6-7.

"Then he said, 'These words are faithful and true,' And the Lord God of the holy prophets sent His angel to show His servants the things which must shortly take place. Behold, I am coming quickly! Blessed is he who keeps the words of the prophecy of this book." He closed his eyes and meditated on what he just read. He instantly felt a hand on his shoulder; he imagined it being the hand of Jesus. Elisha took a seat next to his. Elvis didn't react; he kept his head lowered. Elisha took a quick look at the beautiful morning sky, and then closed her eyes. There, spirits came together as one; they could read each other's thoughts and prayers. Opening his eyes and lifting his head up slowly, the light of the morning sun almost blinded him. He felt the heat radiating through his shirt. Leaning toward Elisha, he opened his Bible to Revelation 1:3. "Blessed is he who reads and those who hear the words of this prophecy, and keep those things which are written in it; for the time is near."

"Study this book while I'm gone. It will prepare you for what is coming."

Elisha looked softly at Elvis. "I can't believe this is all coming to an end." A tear came to her eyes.

Elvis gently wiped the tear away with his hand. "There will be no more tears in heaven."

She exhaled quickly and wrapped her arms around him, sobbing.

Elvis felt the responsibility of relaying God's Word resting heavy on his shoulders. "Don't worry. The Holy Spirit will be with you always. It will never leave you or forsake you."

"Thank you so much for your kind words," she uttered as more tears streamed down her face.

He placed his hand softly under Elisha's chin and guided her head upward. She gazed at him, and then he tenderly directed her gaze toward the sky. "Jesus told us to look up because his redemption draws near."

Elisha smiled passively. "I wish I had the insight and the strength that you do."

"Don't fear because God will give you this: he will give you strength and insight. Just ask for it, and you will receive it."

She smiled again.

"There are so many things I want to ask you. I will forget most of them, some people do not know anything outside themselves, so they could never understand anything the Bible says." Proclaimed Elisha

"Don't worry about other people, concentrate on your own salvation, but help others understand the truth, just sow God Word to people and let God handle the rest. It's similar to gardening, you plant the seed and if its fertile ground, the seed will grow into a plant. Jesus said this in Mark 4:26.

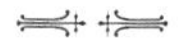

CHAPTER TWENTY SIX

Startled by the ringing of the phone, Alonzo snapped to attention. "Damn, I overslept." He glanced down at his phone, it displayed unknown caller. "could it be Mrs. Amar?" he uttered to himself. Exhaling deeply, he answered the phone.

"Hello?"

"Alfonzo?" and Arabic voice sounded.

"Yes…" he replied.

"Have you decided?" said Mrs. Amar in Arabic

"My faith is in Jesus Christ. I can't accept the offer."

"Why?" speaking in Arabic

"Because, I just told you, my faith is in Christ."

"Alfonzo… Why are you so nervous? Just come here at once. I will pay you the million once you get here." Mrs. Amar speaking in Arabic.

"Ok, let me get this straight. You're going to pay me a million just to come there."

"Yes." Replied Mrs. Amar in Arabic.

"But why do I need to come there? Can you just wire me the money?"

"No, you must come here and get it." Replied Mrs. Amar in Arabic

"But what are you going to have me do?"

Please, Alfonzo. Why don't you just fly out here and we will talk about it. I promise you won't have to compromise your faith. So, will you accept the money?" Mrs. Amar pleads in Arabic.

Alonzo inhaled deeply. "No."

"That's a grave choice, my dear Alfonzo." Replied Mrs. Amar in Arabic.

He slammed the phone down and cracked the glass screen. "Oh man, my brand new iPhone 7…"

He grew nervous in fear of El-Borak and what she may do. He ran to the bathroom, wiped his face, brushed his teeth quickly. Tempting voices shouted in his head. "You could have a new car, a new place to live, date beautiful women…"

"God, get these voices out of my head." He shouted out loud.

A sense of urgency rose up within him. He quickly grabbed a little gel and combed it through his hair. He sprayed deodorant on him haphazardly, grabbed his Ivey cap, and promptly headed out the door. Marching through the corridor with a mission and a look of determination, he grabbed at his back pocket to make sure his business cards and wallet were in place. Walking briskly to the elevator, he pushed the down arrow desperately. Spying a man toward the end of the corridor, he rapidly walked toward him. The man casually looked up at him, sensed something wrong, then immediately entered his room.

"Damn." Alonzo clinched his fist.

The elevator door opened; he took a giant step inside. As the door closed, he concentrated on not staring at the woman standing beside him. He sensed her beauty, and her perfume smelled familiar.

"Excuse me, ma'am, do you have the time?" She looked over and noticed a watch on his arm.

"Does your watch not tell time?" she asked.

"Oh, I'm sorry. I forgot I have it on. I'm very sorry." His voice trembled. He quickly looked down, reached for his back pocket, and pulled out a card.

"Can I ask you a question?"

The woman very cautiously looked over at him, and then quickly looked away without uttering a word.

A lump settled in his throat. Alonzo swallowed hard as he began to perspire. "Do you know Christ as you Lord and Savior?" he blurted out toward the Lady. His eyes locked in on her, concentrating on her face. He made sure not to look away. Complete silence filled the elevator. He closed his eyes, concentrating.

The elevator door opened with a tension-breaking ding. The woman quickly exited, staring straight ahead like a race horse with blinders. Inhaling deeply, then exhaling, he followed her out, and then quickly looked around the lobby area. Thankful no one was around, he leaned his head into the wall. Frustration settled in on him.

"Damn." Alonzo quickly looked around to see if anyone heard him. Gathering himself again, he briskly marched out of the condominium lobby into the streets and then walked up to the first person he saw.

"Help me." He grabbed the pedestrian.

"Get off me, jerk." Yelled the pedestrian.

Alonzo honed in on another pedestrian. "The end is coming, the end is coming." He grabbed another pedestrian. He continued walking down the street, crazed; trying to talk to everyone he laid eyes on.

Suddenly, a loud squealing noise streaked across the road. His head turned toward the noise. A door to a long limousine opened and someone jumped out and grabbed him and forced him in the limousine. He heard dark, hollowed voices. Something smothered his face and he lost consciousness.

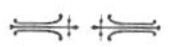

The urge for a smoke arose in him. He desperately searched his pocket. He stumbled on a cigarette, alone, bent, torn, but still together. "Hey, lady," he blurted. The lady turned as Sunny approached her.

"Got a light?" he asked.

She smiled. "Who are you?" She looked cautiously at him.

"Sunny," he introduced himself, gasping for a breath.

"Why are you here on the streets again?" the woman probed.

"Who, me?" sunny remarked.

"Yeah, you." Said the woman as she giggled.

"Have you heard about the Elvis gig Tuesday night?" Sunny asked.

She gasped, "You mean the concert? Of course I have."

"are you going?" ask Sunny

"not sure why you ask?" replied the woman.

"do you know Christ as your savior?"

The lady turned and walked away. "Hey, what about the light?" he shouted out. Confused, he looked down and saw a piece of paper rustling with the wind gliding it across the concrete. He bent over to pick it up, opened it, and read Colossians 2:17. "Which are a shadow of things to come, but the substance is of Christ."

He looked around for the woman thinking she may have dropped it. Then, he glanced forward and began an onward march toward a place he could take refuge away from the public eye. His head fell into his open hands; he cried. "My whole life has been a lie up to this point. Lord, I rest in you. I accept you as my Lord and My Savior, and my life is worthless without you. I need you. Give me a clear vision of the future. What is it you want me to do?" At that time, a vision came to him. An evil king was reborn and was working in the political system. Before him was a vision of a woman on a scarlet beast having seven heads and ten horns, holding a golden cup. And, then, a great beast appeared, and let out a loud roar.

The vision instantly disappeared. His eyes burned. He tried to open them, but the glare was too intense. He held them shut for a few more minutes, then gradually opened them again.

"What does all this mean?" he whispered.

After gaining his consciousness, he heard his phone ringing.

"Hello?"

"Elvis, I need to talk to you, now." His heart pounded.

"How ironic. I was about to call you."

"Really. I saw a vision. It happened all at once. Instantly I was mesmerized by it; the vision was clear. It was about a king, this..."

Elvis gasped and interrupted. "Hold on a second, before you continue, let's meet for coffee at the Arcade. 9am, sharp."

"ok," sunny replied his heart still racing.

⸻

The neon green light of the Arcade stood out amidst the low cloud that hovered over the corner of Main Street and Patterson. Sunny glanced down at his watch. "Eight. Great,

I have an hour. I'll just get a paper." He anxiously pulled six quarters from his pocket and slid it into the newspaper machine outside the door. He grabbed a copy and tucked it under his arm.

"Hey, Karen, how are you?" ask Sunny

"I'm fine, thank you. Coffee?" the waitress answered.

Sunny smiled. "Yes, coffee." He strode to his usual baby blue booth adjacent to the two Elvis pictures on the tropical peach colored wall. Along with an Elvis signature plaque, were pictures of the Zepatos family. Sunny spread the newspaper out on the table. In bold print across the top of the paper, the headline read "**Trade deal worked out, with Global implications. New one world currency introduced.** The inside trade deal was finished in an all-night session with congress and global elites in Australia, Canada, Malaysia, Mexico, New Zealand, Peru, Vietnam and Japan."

Sunny read on in amazement. Below the major headline, Elvis concert got some publicity as well. **"The risen Elvis in concert tomorrow tonight at Liberty Bowl Stadium."**

Amazing, the coming of the end, so it appears." He murmurs.

The waitress approached. "The usual, Sunny?

"Yes, but why the gloomy look?" ask Sunny.

"My boyfriend dumped me last night."

Sunny gave her the look over. "How about you and I get together... Oh, I mean, I'm sorry to hear about that."

The waitress expressed a puzzled look.

"What were you going to say?" remarked the waitress

He hesitated for a moment. "Nothing. I truly am sorry. Hey, cheer up, girl. Too many guys out there to be bummed out on one, you know that," Sunny quipped.

"I've always liked you, Sunny. You're positive and upbeat. I wish I could be that way..." Her melancholy sucked the air out of the space between them.

"Hey, look, sit down for a second. You're a beautiful girl, you know that. And, my former self would go out with you in a heartbeat, but something changed me, you know."

"What changed you?" she asked.

"It's really a long story, but all in a nut shell, I found out that God is real."

The waitress slowly moved herself upward and away from the table. "I don't think I want to hear this, Sunny," she said dejectedly.

"No, wait a minute. Hold on. It's not what you think it is. Can you please sit back down for a second?"

The waitress reluctantly eased herself back in the booth. The sullen look on her face dulled the sparkle that was usually in her eyes.

"Look at me. You've seen me come in and out of here on a regular basis for a while. Be honest with me. In your wildest dreams would you ever had thought for a moment that I was a God type person or a religious person?"

The waitress looked down. Sunny turned her head once more toward him. "Be honest with me," he trailed.

"No." she said in a low tone.

He leaned back against the booth seat. "See? Told you." Leaning in closer to the waitress, he whispered, "I didn't think in my wildest dreams that I would be anywhere near the Godly type, or believe in all the religious flowery language that only gay people believe. And you know what? My subconscious still bothers me, but these last forty days, and my experiences with Elvis, have changed my whole mind about all this God stuff. It makes complete sense to me now." He pointed toward the headlines on the paper. "See this crap?" The waitress looked down at it.

Sunny continued, "All this garbage is prophesized in the Bible, you know that?"

The waitress stared at the paper. "Hey, Karen, can you wait on these people over here?" shouted the manager. She looked up at Sunny; a half grin came over her face. She sat up from the table and made her way to the other table. Sunny twirled his unlit cigarette around his finger like a baton. Then, he placed it in his mouth and inhaled. The scent of tobacco temporarily pacified his nicotine covets.

He happened to glance up as a man walked through the entrance of the Arcade, a hat pulled low over his face, and wearing a military jacket. He was unshaven and heavy set. The stranger walked up to the bar and took a seat. Not bothering to open a menu, he stared at his closed hand.

Sunny, bewildered, thought for a moment. "I've seen that guy somewhere." His stare intensified as he scrutinized the mysterious diner.

Suddenly, from nowhere, a voice sounded.

"Hey, how long have you been here?"

Sunny startled, jerking back in his seat. "Man, where in the hell did you guys come from?" Elvis lowered himself into the booth, and Elisha followed in behind him. "You guys scared the crap out of me. Jesus!" Sunny raised his cigarette up and was about to place it between his lips, when he peered over Elisha's shoulder to spy the mysterious man once again.

"What?" Elisha looked around trying to see what Sunny saw.

"Where the hell did he go?" Sunny blurted out.

"Who?" Elisha murmured.

"The man. He was sitting right up there." Sunny hurled himself toward the bar. "where did he go" he said out loud. Every head in the diner turned toward Sunny. Totally oblivious to the attention directed toward him, he trotted outside and looked around in every direction. Raising his arms in frustration he darted back inside the diner.

The waitress turned toward Sunny. "Hey, Sunny the guy you're looking for left you this note." Sunny walked over to the waitress and snatched it from her hand then opened it, he read it to himself.

"Elvis, we have talked to each other often, even as you lay in bed in the dark silence of your room. I came to you as a spirit while you were in the flesh. I am ashamed. My destiny was not like you, my brother. We were separated at birth. You lived, but I died, yet I remain alive, living in tents, poor, lost. I represent the condemned nation that awaits the judgment of God, for I was the one sacrificed. 'A ram caught in the thicket by his horns.' It is you that lived, not I. However, I'm alive in spirit, and you have not seen me yet, but others around you have. Brother, I love you. Serve God well. He waits for your return. I must suffer with the ones that are left here, but my soul is saved by grace. You will see me shortly in the New Jerusalem, which I have caught a glimpse of. It's glorious, beautiful, and we shall live together forever in heaven here on earth. Jesse"

Mesmerized, and in a state of stupor, Sunny walked gingerly toward Elvis and Elisha.

"What's it with all the commotion?" Elisha inquired.

Oblivious to her comment, he handed the note to Elvis. "I think this is for you."

Elvis lowered his Versace sunglasses, and then glanced at Sunny. He gradually looked toward the letter.

A moment of silence overtook the table. It seemed like eternity to Elisha, who was desperately eager to know the contents of the letter.

"This is about my twin brother. How did you get this letter? Who left it?" questioned Elvis.

"He was sitting at the bar a moment ago when you walked in, but I have seen him before. He has shown himself on several occasions."

Elisha snatched the letter from Elvis' hand and started reading it.

"What did he look like?" asked Elvis.

"He looked lowly and withdrawn. He was wearing a military jacket..."

"In August?" Elisha interrupted.

"Yes, a military jacket, and when I saw him before, he was wearing a military jacket, too. He also had a hat on that was pulled low over his face. I think he had a beard. Not a long one, but just a scruffy beard."

"Hey wait a minute. I've seen that guy, too," Elisha added.

"When did you see him?" asked Sunny.

"Remember that time when a bum came up to you and asked for money? That had to have been him."

"No, way..." "I don't understand why he didn't reveal himself to me. I'm here right now" pleaded Elvis.

"Well, like he said, he could only be seen by some people, not everybody," Sunny interjected.

"But I'm not just anybody. I'm his brother," Elvis commented sharply.

"He said he would see you shortly in heaven," challenged Sunny.

Elvis lowered his head, placing his hand around his eyes. Elisha leaned toward him and embraced him warmly. Elvis put his hand in hers. Elvis suddenly raised his head up, "wait a minute.. It may have been Jesse lying on a park bench that time I went to my gravesite at Graceland." Elisha looked over at Elvis, "When was this?"

"Oh... this was shortly after Sunny and I got to Memphis."

Sunny looked toward Karen and smiled at her. The waitress walked over to their table. "Do you guys need anything?" Karen asked.

"We're fine, thanks," said, Elisha.

Sunny looked over at Elisha as if she cut him off, but he shook it off. "Hey, Karen," he raised his voice. She turned and walked back toward the table. "Can you think about what I said?"

"Yes, I will," she said.

"In the meantime, here's a ticket to the Elvis concert."

She glanced down at the ticket, and noticed a folded 100 dollar bill on the backside of the ticket.

"Oh, wow! Thanks!" She quickly stuffed it in her pocket. She looked over at Elvis. "I can't wait to see your show, Mr. Elvis."

Elvis looked up at her and smiled. "You're welcome. Give God a chance. I promise your life will be different." The waitress smiled again and walked off.

"So, Sunny tell me more about this vision," said Elvis.

"Yeah, that's right." Sunny let out a light chuckle. "I can't believe I almost forgot about that. Thanks for reminding me. Yeah, you know, I found a piece of paper, I thought this lady dropped it, but the lady just disappeared into thin air. Shortly after that, a vision came to me. It was a woman on some type of beast with seven heads and ten horns. She was holding a golden cup. Then, I heard a roar. It sounded so real it scared the daylights out of me. That's when I snapped out of it and immediately called you. Now, we're here."

"I believe that was an angel that spoke to you. It's a prophetic message concerning the final days. The prophecy is in Revelation chapter 17," Elvis said while taking another swig of his coffee.

"You mean to tell me that vision I saw was in the Bible?" asked Sunny, incredulous.

"Yes, it's in Revelation. I'll show it to you right here." Elvis reached in his pocket and pulled out a miniature New Testament Bible. Thumbing through the pages, he marked a place in it and handed it to Sunny.

"It's verse 3 on that page." Elvis pointed toward the page.

Sunny read the passage. "This is amazing stuff. It's like a dream. How do I know I'm not dreaming?"

Elisha quickly reached over and pinched him.

"Ouch! What is wrong with you?" demanded Sunny.

Elisha laughed. "You're not dreaming."

Sunny squinted at her. Elisha grabbed the miniature Bible from Sunny. "Hey, what are you doing?" Sunny interjected.

"Sorry, I have to see this for myself. We never studied Revelation in the Catholic Church."

"Geez, I wonder why?" She quickly looked back at Sunny. "And what do you mean by that remark?"

"Think about it. Most Catholics don't know diddly squat about the Bible. They're just brain numb robots that obey the priest."

Elisha shook her head and kept reading. "This is pretty amazing stuff. So, who is this harlot woman?"

"The Bible doesn't say, but she represents a nation that has fallen into an abyss of sin, and she is consumed with fire," said Elvis.

"So the whole nation is burned?" Sunny blurted out.

"Yes. Originally it was burned, but later the Medes conquered Babylon," replied Elvis.

"Ok, then, so this harlot represents another Babylon?" asked Sunny.

"Yes, it's called the Mystery Babylon; she is the mother of all Harlots," Elvis said with a smirk.

"So, let me get this straight... there will be yet be another Babylon that will be destroyed?" Sunny lamented.

"Yes, and the Mystery Babylon is a nation in power today," replied Elvis.

A moment of silence fell over the table.

Breaking the silence, Sunny blurted, "Who is that nation?"

The trio became reluctant to speak. They gazed at one another for a long moment. The silence resounded.

CHAPTER TWENTY SEVEN

Neely stood in the middle of the Liberty Bowl football field and gazed at the stage being erected. His heart skipped a beat as he realized this was going to be the biggest, most important concert he had ever produced. He glanced down at his phone once again as it continued ringing.

"This phone has been ringing all morning, and I'm not answering all these calls. I don't have the time," Neely said to one of the stage hands.

"It may be important," said the stage hand.

"I doubt it; it's probably just another vendor that wants to be at the concert."

The stage hand shrugged as he mentioned a couple more things that needed to be done to the stage.

"Ok, thanks for the suggestions," remarked Neely as the stage hand walked away. Neely was once again gazed at the magnificent stage. It was majestic highlighted in pink and lavender. He glanced over at the stage hand talking on his cell phone. Then, out of curiosity he quickly glanced down at his own phone to see who the last caller was. "Alonzo?" He immediately dialed the number.

The call connected, but no one said anything. Neely waited a moment and then said, "Hello?"

"Cancel the concert or your helper, Alonzo, will die," an anonymous voice demanded.

"Who is this?"

"I'm a friend telling you that you must not have the concert if you want your friend to live."

"Where are you?" Neely demanded.

"All you need to know is that your friend will die if you have the concert."

The dial tone sounded in Neely's ear, and he immediately called the police. "Yes, I need the police now, but I have to keep this undercover. Who can I talk to?" ask Neely.

"I'll have you speak with Sergeant Yalom." Said the operator.

"Ok." Replied Neely.

"Sergeant Yalom. Can I help you?"

"Sergeant Yalom, this is Benji Neely, Elvis' concert promoter."

"Yes, Mr. Neely, how can I help you?"

"Someone just called and threatened to kill one of my concert helpers. He said that he will kill him if I continue with the concert."

"Did the number come up on your caller ID?"

"Yes,"

"What did the voice sound like?" ask the sergeant.

"He had Arab accent, his English was broken up, and he didn't speak it clearly."

"Ok, we will run a check on this line and find out where the call was made from. I'll get back with you as soon as we find something out."

"Ok, thanks." Replied Neely.

Neely put his cell phone back in his pocket and exhaled deeply.

He lowered his head and stood still for a moment saying a silent prayer.

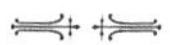

The light at the end of the descending hall exposed a dark silhouette of a man swaying back and forth. He spoke Arabic, but Alonzo could not understand what he was saying. Masking tape across his mouth, his hands tied. All he could do was sway minimally. He closed his eyes, and then suddenly a voice sounded.

"You traitor, you deny Muhammad," accused the man in Arabic.

Alonzo looked up; he could only see the eyes of the perpetrator. His head was wrapped in a dark turban, his robe solid black. The silver rigged end of a bayonet was placed under Alonzo's chin. The weapon moved slowly, methodologically, along his neck.

"Your Jesus will not protect you. Your prayers are futile, and your God is weak. Muhammad is the only prophet of God." The Arabic voice dripped with hatred. The assailant ripped the tape from Alonzo's mouth. He shrieked with pain. The kidnapper placed the bayonet beneath Alonzo's chin again.

"Render the prayer of Muhammad now, or you die." The Arabic voice commanded. Alonzo lowered his head. He felt the pressure of the bayonet against his skin.

"Say it now," the Arabic voice commanded

He took a ragged breath. The bayonet pierced his skin, and blood trickled down his neck. "I bear witness that Muhammad is the prophet of God," Alonzo uttered. Gasping for a breath, his body became limp. Suddenly, a loud thump sounded as the assailant fell to the floor. Another thump sounded; a substance burst out of the other assailant's head as he fell to the ground. Alonzo came to and looked toward the light down the hall. The silhouetted figure's head fell from his body. He saw blood spurting up from the figure as it fell to the floor. He gasped in horror. "Oh, my Lord," he said to himself. Suddenly, a hand grabbed him and pulled him up straight up.

"You're safe," someone assured. Another pair of hands untied his arms, and yet another pair untied his legs. The mysterious men dressed in black pulled his body up and guided him down a dark hall. He could see a ray of light coming from between a pair of doors. One of the mysterious men pushed the set of doors open. He quickly covered his eyes from the blinding sun. The heat came over him like a wave. Blinded by the sun, he couldn't see.

He felt a hand on his shoulder. "You're fine now, my friend."

Alonzo saw a man in black rip a black mask from his head and stuffed it in his pocket. The man stood there in complete silence, and then the silence was interrupted by a voice over a walkie-talkie.

"We have apprehended the victim. Clear unit from the area immediately."

The light was still intense, but everything gradually came more into focus. The man dressed in black disappeared almost as quickly as he had appeared. Alonzo looked straight ahead as a police officer started walking toward him.

"Are you ok?" said the officer.

"I'm not sure; I'm confused. What in the world just happened?"

I'm sergeant Yalom from the Memphis police department. We just dispatched a local seal unit to take care of the perpetrators that were holding you captive for ransom."

"Ransom?" Alonzo murmured.

"Yes, they were holding you for ransom, trying to black mail your boss into not having the Elvis concert. Do you have any idea who these people are, and were you affiliated with them in any way?" questioned Yalom.

"No, but I was just offered a million dollars from El-Borak Amar in Saudi Arabia."

"Who is she?" responded Yalom.

"She is the widow of Zorzi, and she was extremely upset that I converted to Christianity."

"You were once a Muslim?" asked the sergeant.

"Yes. I guess she sent these people to try and kill me."

"Sounds like this was an Islamic terrorist group, a small group I might add, but I'm sure there are more in the area. Would you mind going to the precinct to answer a few questions? We have to investigate this thoroughly to make certain this terrorist group doesn't bring any harm to the area."

"No, I don't mind at all," replied Alonzo.

"Lieutenant Johnston, can you escort Alonzo to the precinct?"

"Yes, Sir."

The sergeant called Neely.

"Hello," said Neely.

"Mr. Neely, your helper, Alonzo, is safe now, and we just have to take him in for a few questions is all."

"Wow, that was quick," Neely replied.

"Yes, once we knew were the call was made from we just dispatched a local seal unit to apprehend the victim, and they took care of the terrorists quickly and efficiently."

"Thanks." Replied Neely.

"We will have to beef up security for the concert. We believe there are more Islamic terrorists in the area that might not want this concert to take place."

"Thank you for the extra protection. We sure appreciate all your help."

"Good luck to you guys, and I hope you have a great show."

"Thanks."

"The final concert tomorrow will be momentous and glorious. We have special plans for the people that attend, and we promise it will be the best show they will ever see."

"Elvis, you first appeared on this show on July 9th. At that time, I have to be honest with you, I thought it was all a Hoax, but you have proven me wrong. When I heard your testimony, and when I heard you sing, that convinced me that you were the real Elvis," said Solange.

"Thanks, Solange, I appreciate that. At that time, I was running on pure faith. I had no idea what we were doing was going work. But, I trusted God, and now look. We're on the verge of having the biggest concert in the history of the world," replied Elvis.

"How has all this changed your perspective on your life today? And is this short life today better than the forty-two years in your first life?"

This life is by far better simply because my life is not my own. God is in total control over everything I do. And I like having the creator of the universe as my pilot. This life will have a glorious ending because I get raptured into heaven. In the first life, I died a humiliating death on a toilet. I was shot up with drugs to get me by, but in my life today, I have the most powerful drug in the world, and it's all natural. It's God's love. God's love is the best drug any human being can take, and it has no harmful side effects."

"Well said, Elvis. I have to admit, you have moved me with your story, and I'm glad you decided to ask me if you could come back on the show."

"Solange, without you, I probably wouldn't be in this position. God used you as an instrument to have all this take place. Without you allowing us to be on your show, we never would have gotten the Word out," praised Elvis.

"Thank you, Elvis. You have helped our ratings being on the show twice. We have been able to command more advertising dollars, and we have gained more sponsors. Changing gears, now, I'd like to talk about your friends. So, basically, you've had two sidekicks with you the whole way. Would you like to introduce them to our listeners?"

"Yes, it's my pleasure; sitting to my right, here, is Sunny Carlyle. He is the first person that saw me. I have never seen a man more terrified before in my life." Elvis Laughed. "The look on Sunny's face when he first saw me..." He continued laughing looking over at Sunny.

"Where did he see you?" asked Solange.

"Out in the desert about fifty miles east of Vegas, off the old highway 66, and, ironically enough, this was the same place a spiritual awakening happened to me in my first life."

"Really?" inquired Solange

"Yes, I was with my personal hair stylist at the time. He was mentoring me on God and the spiritual world. I looked up in the clouds that evening and saw the face of Joseph Stalin, and then shortly after that, I saw the face of Jesus. The experience was astonishing, and it made an impression on me that lasted throughout my life."

"That is very interesting. So it seems God had a plan to have you descend and arise in the same place where you saw that vision," replied Solange.

"Yes, and the more I think about that, the more I realize now that Stalin represented my first life, living in the flesh and of the world, and the image of Jesus represents this life and what I have become through Jesus."

"Well, that makes sense to me," replied Solange. "Can you introduce this beautiful woman sitting to your left?"

"Sure. This is the lovely Elisha." Elvis smiled and winked at her. "We ran across her when we first got to Memphis from the desert in Nevada. She and Sunny had a little skirmish. I had to help them settle," Elvis said laughing under his breath.

"A skirmish is putting it mildly," Sunny butted in. Elisha gave him a hard look.

"Oh, sounds like you guys had a little misunderstanding before," replied Solange.

"Ah, that is a severe understatement as well," Elisha interjected.

They all laughed together as Solange looked at his notes.

"Ok, Elvis. You told me at the beginning of the show that you were not going to sing a song, but instead say something to our listeners."

"Yes, that is correct. For those of you attending the concert tomorrow, you will have a chance to hear me sing for the last time here on earth. But for those who believe I will be singing with our Lord for eternity, we will be singing together in a heavenly choir, all in one accord, and I can't wait. I love this life God as granted me, both my first life and this life I'm living now. The end times are near. Jesus told us this in Matthew 24. May I?" Elvis raised his Bible.

"Sure," replied Solange.

"These are the Words of Jesus shortly after Jesus prophesized about the destroying of the Temple on the Mount of Olives, where Jesus ascended to heaven. Opposite the Mount of Olives was a majestic temple that King Herod built. This temple was destroyed by the Romans, thus fulfilling the prophecies of Jesus when he said in Matthew 24:2 'Do you not see all these things? Assuredly, I say to you, not one stone shall be left here upon another, that shall not be thrown down.' The disciples came to him in private and asked him when will these things come to pass, and what would be the sign of His coming, and of the end of the age." Elvis continued, "And this is what Jesus said to them, I quote from Matthew 24:4, 'And Jesus answered and said to them: 'Take heed that no one deceives you. For many will come in my name, saying, 'I am the Christ,' and will deceive many. And you will hear of wars and rumors of wars. See that you are not troubled; for all these things must come to pass, but the end is not yet. For nation will rise against nation, and kingdom against kingdom. And there will famines, pestilences, and earthquakes in various places. All these are the beginning of sorrows. Then they will deliver you up to tribulation and kill you, and you will be hated by all nations for my name's sake. And then many will be offended, will betray one another, and will hate one another. Then many false prophets will rise up and deceive many. And because lawlessness will abound, the love of many will grow cold. But he who endures to the end will be saved. And this gospel of the kingdom will be preached in the entire world as a witness to all the nations, and then the end will come.'"

A collective silence came over the studio. Solange exhaled deeply. The sound of his breath scratched through the small microphone pinned to the lapel of his polo shirt.

"Excuse me, but I feel like we must have a moment of silence," Elvis suggested.

Elvis extended his hand out to Sunny, and they all clasped hands and formed a circle. After a long moment of silence, Girl Friday quickly walked from her desk to the studio. She peered through the studio window. She suddenly gasped. She couldn't believe what she saw. She knocked on the glass several times attempting to get Solange's attention. But to no avail. She tried to open the studio door, but it was locked. She walked back up front, sat behind her desk, and rigidly waited the silence out.

Several calls came in over the radio. No answer. Girl Friday glared at the clock. A whole three minutes had gone by. Nervousness overcame her, and she squirmed in her seat. "Don't they realize that their on the air?" she uttered to herself. Another minute went by, still with complete silence. She got up from her desk, ran to the studio, and began to pound on the studio window.

Elvis slowly raised his head, looking straight forward, and didn't acknowledge Girl Friday.

"God bless all those who come in silence before him," Elvis said. Solange raised his head, followed by Elisha and Sunny. Solange looked around the studio as if he couldn't remember where he was. He was lost in a temporary moment of stupor.

Elvis extended his hand and placed it on Solange's shoulder. "Are you ok?" he asked.

"Umm, Yes. I'm fine. I don't know what happened."

Elvis gripped his hand firmly. "Do you want to accept Christ as your personal savior?"

Solange stared at him blankly. "Yes," he eventually replied. They all held hands once again as Elvis lead him in the sinner's prayer.

Solange leaned back in his chair, taken away by the prayer he had just made. His eyes shut, and then they suddenly opened, a big smile came across his face.

"Thank you, Lord," he shouted.

Elisha, Sunny, and Elvis applauded.

"Oh my…" Solange rubbed his eyes. "Are we live?" he looked up quickly at the On Air sign, and it was still on red. "Oh Lord I forgot to go off air during our prayer." He said reluctantly.

"It was a pleasure to have you on the show again, Elvis, and I'm glad you had a chance to tell people your testimony. Hopefully some of our listeners had a chance to accept the Lord, also. We will be back in a moment, after you hear a word or two from our sponsors." He clicked the off switch.

Solange clasped his hands together and embraced Elvis. "Thanks again. That was quite an experience. Needless to say, I'm sure some of the sponsors are going to be peeved."

Elvis looked in the direction of Girl Friday standing outside the studio window. "Looks like your sponsors are not going to be the only ones that are peeved." Elvis chuckled softly as Solange quickly turned toward the window, realizing that Girl Friday was peeved, he unlocked the studio door. Girl Friday dashed through the door.

"Do you realize you were live for almost 4 minutes with no sound what so ever!" she blurted out in frustration. "I was trying to get your attention. Aren't you worried about losing listeners?"

Solange rolled his eyes. "Lord help me."

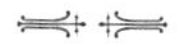

CHAPTER TWENTY EIGHT

Elisha wearing a polka dot black and white dress and a big, white, elastic belt wrapped tightly around her waist, accentuating her figure eight curves. Stood beside a big pig statue situated by the front entrance of Marlowe's Restaurant. Every head turned in her direction as Sunny clicked away with the camera, directing her to stand in different poses by the pink pig and a pink Cadillac that was also in front of the restaurant. Elvis stood to the side trying to be discreet with his black and gold Versace sun glasses and a 100% silk Nat Nash black shirt complimented by relaxed-fit silk pleated khakis. Elvis tipped his head slightly to each patron that walked into the restaurant. Most guest turned their head slightly toward him as they passed by, and some patrons gawked as if they had seen him before, trying desperately to figure out who he was. Finally, after standing there for a few minutes, a lovely woman in her 60s turned and walked back toward him.

"Are you Elvis?" Elvis looked at her and smiled, and put his finger to his mouth as if indicating to be quiet. The woman smiled back at him and walked inside. Elvis whistled toward the wanna-be fashion photographer. Sunny turned instantly.

"You think you're going to shoot for Vogue magazine or something?" shouted Elvis.

"Hey, you never know. After having you on my resume, I might be able to get a lot of jobs." Sunny chuckled.

Pastor Halloway exited the cab and waved his hand toward Elvis.

"Thanks for inviting me out," said Halloway, embracing Elvis with a warm hug.

"Nice to see you again, pastor," said Elvis. A couple of minutes passed before Alonzo walked up to Elvis.

"Mr. Elvis, thank you for your invitation to the communion."

Elvis smiled and embraced Alonzo. "I heard God rescued you from the hands of Satan," asked Elvis.

"Yes, Sir, he did," replied Alonzo.

Moments later Neely arrived, and then Solange. Sunny and Elisha followed Neely.

"I love to have my pictures taken." She pinched Elvis on his cheek, as he held the door open for her. He laughed and followed her into the restaurant. Sunny walked up to the host.

"Reservations for Carlyle." Elisha walked over to the life-sized cardboard statue of Elvis wearing his gold suit. "Oh my, standing next to the king is a dream," she laughed.

"Follow me," said the hostess. The hostess led them to a secluded banquet room separated from the main restaurant. They each took a seat by the long table. Sunny sat down and tried to be as formal as possible, tucking his sweat-stained shirt under his belt and then neatly laying his cloth napkin on his lap.

After taking a quick look at Sunny's table etiquette, Elisha snipped,

"Since when are you so conscious of table manners?"

Sunny looked at his watch. "I have a guest that I invited to join us," he said definitively.

"Oh my, a lady friend. Imagine that," Elisha said in a patronizing tone.

Sunny smiled. "She isn't your normal broad." His phone rang, Sunny excused himself from the table.

"Did you know that Sunny was going to invite someone to join us today?"

"Not a clue," Elvis mumbled.

"This may not have been the idle place to have our final dinner Elvis," Elisha said softly.

"Why do you say that?"

"I don't know. I guess I was thinking it would have been best to have it in private." She murmured.

"Well, it's quiet back here. I think it will work fine." Elvis winked.

Elisha smiled, and glanced back at the chatter from up front. Sunny came walking through the door with his new friend.

"Elvis, and guests, I would like to introduce you to Susan."

Elvis stood up and nodded toward Susan, then extended his hand.

He took her fingers gently and kissed her hand.

Her face turned a bit feverish. "Oh, my. You look just like the real Elvis."

She blushed as she took a deep breath. Sunny pulled a chair out as Susan sat down. Susan tried hard to keep from being too obvious, but she couldn't stop staring at Elvis.

"Welcome to my favorite barbeque place. They have the best ribs in Memphis," Elvis said proudly. Elvis stood up at the table, "I want to thank you all for being there when I needed you. I couldn't have done this without you."

"Ditto," Sunny replied.

"Elisha, my beautiful Elisha...." Elvis trailed.

"And our new friend, Susan. Pastor Halloway, Alonzo, and our producer, production manager, Benji. Thank you all for taking the time out to be with us tonight. As you all are well aware, tonight is the final night I'll be here with you, in this life, anyway, but all of us will see one another in heaven, so this is only the beginning of a lifelong friendship together." Elvis hesitated for a moment, and then gradually lowered himself back onto the chair. "Susan," he said softly. Susan quickly turned her head toward Elvis.

"Do you know Jesus as your Lord and Savior?"

Susan turned her head toward Sunny with a quizzical look. Sunny returned a quick smile to her. She turned her head back toward Elvis. "I can't answer that," she said.

Elvis took a quick look around. "If you don't mind, may I ask you why?"

"It's just personal to me, and I don't feel comfortable talking about it with a table full of strangers."

"Have you heard the good news of God's grace?" replied Elvis.

"Yes, I grew up in church, and I know all about God," Susan said with a hint of retaliation in her voice.

Sunny sensed her uneasiness and looked over at Elvis. He signaled him to tone it down a little.

Elvis lowered his head and began to pray. The waitress walked in the banquet room and saw everyone with their heads down. She immediately turned back and walked back toward the door.

"If there is anyone without love in his heart, God is not there. If you have ever experienced love, God is there. God is Love. Amen."

Elvis calmly arranged his dinner utensils.

Sunny; Elisha glared at Elvis with a blank stare on their face.

The waitress took a quick peek through the door and noticed they were not praying, so she proceeded back to the table. "Have you all decided yet?" she asked.

"Yes, we will have a loaf of bread for all of us, and 6 glasses of wine."

"And what would you like to order?" the waitress asked, looking squarely at Elisha.

"Excuse me!" Elvis interrupted. "I made the order for all of us."

"All you want to order is a loaf of bread?" she asked, confused.

"Yes, and 6 glasses of wine."

Moments later a waiter showed up with the order.

"What happened to our waitress?" Sunny blurted out.

"Oh, she had to tend to another table. I'm sorry," the waiter replied.

"No, you're not sorry. She is the one that's sorry," Sunny reviled. Elisha gave Sunny the evil stare down.

Sunny leaned in close to Susan and whispered. "I guess she figured she wasn't going to make much tip money, so she pawned us off to the new guy."

The loaf of bread was placed near Elvis, and each guest was given a glass of wine.

"Would you like to accept Jesus Christ as your Lord and Savior right now, Susan?" Elvis asked.

"I'm not in a position to do that at this time, thank you." Susan responded.

Susan stood up, slid her chair up under the table, and politely headed toward the banquet room door.

Sunny looked over at Elvis with his classic "WTF" look, and then stood to follow Susan to the door. "Susan, wait." He blurted out.

She continued walking toward the front door. Sunny reached out and grabbed her right arm and gently pulled her toward him. "Hold on a second."

"You don't have to follow me. You can take your communion with your fake friends," demanded Susan.

"Wait a minute, Susan. You don't understand," said Sunny.

"I understand completely. I understand that your friends are a bunch of religious, stuck-up assholes is what I understand, and you led me into a trap." Susan turned and started walking toward the door again. She took several steps as Sunny grabbed at her arm again.

"Please, let me explain," he pleaded.

"There is no explaining to do. Just forget that you ever met me."

She turned and walked through the door, toward the parking lot. Sunny hesitated, walking slowly after her. As he began to cross the threshold, a man pushed him out of his way.

"Look where you're going, asshole," a tall, miserly looking man with mirror sunglasses, baggy jeans, and a black t-shirt blurted out.

Sunny gasped in horror from the monstrousness looking man. The man walked toward his car, and then turned toward Sunny, shooting him the bird and laughing loudly as he continued walking toward his car. Sunny refocused his attention toward Susan. She slammed the car door shut, backed up, and sped away. Following behind her was the monstrous-looking man in a black corvette, the license plate read, 'SonsofGod' Sunny stood there in shock as people tried to pass by him.

"Excuse me, sir, but can you stand out of the way of traffic please," the hostess pleaded.

"I'm sorry." Sunny backed up a couple of steps and continued gazing down the street as Susan's car disappeared into the twilight. The black corvette still following her. Sunny turned and gradually made his way back to the banquet room. He walked over to his chair and eased back in it contemplating what just happened. Silence fell upon the table again. All eyes looked toward Sunny. As soon as he looked up, everyone looked away at once. Everyone except Elisha, who continued to give Sunny the stare-down. Sunny looked at Elisha and widened his eyes. "What? Why are you staring at me?" said Sunny, raising his hands in the air.

Elvis sliced the bread, placed it on a plate, and slid it to each person at the table. Elvis held the bread up. "Thank you, Father, for the Gift of your son. By the stripes that fell on his back, my body is healed, from the crown of my head to the very soles of my feet. Every cell, every organ, every function of my body is healed, restored, and renewed in Jesus' name, I believe and I receive." Elvis gave the gesture for all to partake in eating the bread. He then reached for the cup and held it up. "Lord, Jesus, thank you for your precious sacrificial blood. Your sin-free, disease-free life is in your blood. And your shed blood has removed every sin from my life. Through Your blood, I am forgiven of all my sins past, present, and future, and made completely righteous. Today, I celebrate and partake of the inheritances of the righteous, which are preservation, healing, wholeness and provision. Thank you, Lord Jesus, for loving me and sacrificing your life for me so that by having faith in you my sins will be forgiven. Amen." He then drank the wine.

Elvis' final supper meeting dwindled down to Sunny, Elisha, Neely and Alonzo. Solange and Earnest Halloway left shortly after the communion. The four of them stood outside of Marlowe's underneath the blue canopy. Sunny fidgeted restlessly, pacing and murmuring to himself about the unexpected departure of Susan.

Elvis nodded toward Sunny. "Why are you still thinking about that girl?"

"I don't know. It was just something weird about what happened."

"What do you mean?" asked Elvis.

Sunny exhaled, collected his thoughts, and donned a wry smile. "Oh, nothing. But, you know, this makes the second time you cost me some; you know that, don't you?" Sunny said fervently.

Elvis took a quick look away, then refocused again on Sunny; a light smile came over his face. "I think you better thank God I saved you from the first broad," he said whimsically.

Sunny shook his head and walked away, trolling through his shirt and pants pockets trying to find a smoke, and then realizing he had none.

"Damn, this is frustrating," he blurted out. He walked back over to Elvis. "Look, can I ask you a question?" he quipped. "Since you cost me tonight, how about you say a prayer to eliminate these temptations of having to smoke?"

Elvis smiled again. "You know what to do." he said.

"No, I don't know what to do. That's the reason I'm asking you," he demanded.

"Just do what Jesus did," Elisha stated abruptly.

"You still love to patronize me, don't you, after all this time we have spent together," Sunny said despondently.

"Just trying to help ya," she replied smacking away at her chewing gum.

"Ok, Sunny, what did Jesus say to Satan in the desert?" Elvis inquired.

"I have no idea. Wasn't it something like, 'Get away from me, Satan,' or something like that?" he asked sarcastically.

"Close," Elisha blurted out.

"Ok, Miss Smarty Pants. What was it then?" he retaliated.

Elisha gave Sunny a quick look over, removed the chewing gum from her mouth, cleared her throat, and shouted, "AWAY WITH YOU SATAN FOR IT IS WRITTEN YOU SHALL WORSHIP THE LORD YOUR GOD, AND HIM ONLY YOU SHALL SERVE." The few remaining people that were in the restaurant came trickling out the door, startled by the loud outburst. Neely and Alonzo began laughing as Elisha quickly looked around, shocked and embarrassed by her own outburst.

Sunny chuckled, amused, and quipped, "Yeah, I think that outburst would have scared anything into oblivion."

"Actually that is exactly how you're supposed to say it. You have to forcefully say it with conviction, just like how Elisha did it," Elvis remarked.

"Now, do it the way she did it," said Neely.

"What? Are you kidding me? Yeah, and then have someone call the cops on us for disorderly conduct," Sunny scoffed. Alonzo peered through the window. "Looks like everyone is gone, now. It's just the wait staff inside."

Neely looked back at Sunny. "There you go. Now you can say it without having to scare anybody off."

"Forget it, I'm not doing it. It's stupid," protested Sunny.

Elvis put his hand on Sunny's shoulder and guided him away from the others. "Look, Sunny. I'm telling you this as a brother in Christ. This is serious business. Satan is real, you know that. You have to get tough with him if you don't want him to rule your life through temptations and desires."

"There's no way you can get rid of temptations and desires. You will always have them," Sunny retaliated.

"I know that, and Satan will always tempt you, but you can get control over the temptations by speaking with authority over the temptations. Then, each time you do this, the temptations will become less and less. Satan will flee from you if you resist him and draw closer to God," Elvis confirmed. He pulled Sunny in closer and gave him a hug. He leaned away slightly to look him in the eye. "I love you, brother." He put his arm around Sunny, and then led him toward the others. Elvis leaned in closer to Sunny again and whispered, "You have come a long way in this short time. Your life has changed drastically, and I'm proud of you."

"Thanks, man." Sunny leaned in and gave Elvis a light hug. Elvis pulled away and then smiled. "Now let me hear you tell Satan where to go,"

Sunny inhaled deeply, and then blurted out, "AWAY WITH YOU SATAN. FOR IT IS WRITTEN YOU SHALL WORSHIP THE LORD YOUR GOD, AND HIM ONLY YOU SHALL SERVE!" Sunny immediately leaned forward and placed his hands on his knees.... "Woo, man. Yeah, that felt good." He threw his fist up in the air. "Hell Yeah," he shouted.

They all clapped with approval. Elisha ran to him and gave him a huge hug. "I knew you could do it. That wasn't so hard, was it?"

Sunny smiled and clutched Elisha's shoulder firmly. "No, actually it felt good. My life has changed. I just want to thank all of you, especially you, Elvis, for not giving up on me. You know, I was a hard project. I was stubborn and set in my ways, and I know it had to have been frustrating for you," Sunny confessed.

Neely walked up to Sunny and hugged him, as well as Alonzo.

"Thanks to all of you. Now, let's go grab a beer." Everyone laughed, and then the cheer lulled into silence, each of them realizing the end was near.

Elisha broke into tears and ran up to Elvis. "Elvis, I don't want you to leave. I love you. We all love you. How are we going to live without you?"

"You will live without me for a short while, but I promise you it won't be long," he said cheerfully.

"What do you mean not for long?" Elisha murmured.

"The end is near. That's why Jesus gave me another chance and sent me here. He gave me another chance to redeem myself, but also to redeem the world. I was fortunate of that."

"How long will it be?" Elisha said with desperation.

"The signs are already here. It's on the news every day. Just keep looking up because Jesus will take you up sooner than you expect."

Elisha stepped back as Neely and Alonzo drew closer to Elvis. She looked at him with anticipation thinking he had something to say. It became deafly quiet again. Then, suddenly, a loud clap sounded.

"Ok, guys, we're closing up. You guys have to move along," shouted the manager of Marlowe's. "Thank you all for coming out." He walked up to Elvis and gave him a firm handshake. "Thanks. Good luck with your show tomorrow night." He turned and walked back inside.

"Neely, can you get us in the stadium tonight?" Elvis asked.

Neely, a little caught off guard, said reluctantly, "Yes, but why do you ask?"

"Do you mind if we all take a ride to the stadium?"

Neely glanced down at his watch. "Do you realize its 10pm and we all have a big show tomorrow?"

"Yes, I realize that, but I'm feeling inspired. Would you all like to go?" They all exchanged looks and agreed on the impromptu field trip.

⥪ ⥭

The sapphire girdle illuminated across the opulent exterior of the stadium which was highlighted by luminescent finials, amidst two sapphire-toned pillars. A fountain cascading imperial cerulean waters flowed eloquently against a dusky firmament. The sultry August heat wafted over the Elvis disciples in rare spurts, but each one cherished its temporary relief from the perspiration gushing from their bodies. Elvis continued to remind them of the presence of God once they entered the stadium. Each step became heavier to everyone but Elvis. He experienced some type of spiritual awakening.

"You guys bear with me. We're almost there." Elvis' optimism was not as contagious as he would have liked it to be. He felt from within that his new-found vitality was destined, and God was trying to tell him something. On the eve of the biggest moment he ever experienced. He had a craving to get close to God and have his disciples to share in the exposition. He was in a rheumatic state, Only God could hear his thoughts as they resonated loudly in his mind. He knew that this prayer would be like no other prayer. That voice in his mind spoke to him like a roaring lion. "I have wrestled with savages before. My strength lays in you, Lord. I glorify your name. The journey is just beginning. Lead me to you." He suddenly turned. The disciples sat exhausted on the ground against the two sapphire toned pillars. "How did you all get so tired all of a sudden?"

"Elvis, the humidity is killing me. I'm just going to sit up front here and keep a look out for you," Neely politely demanded.

"I'll stay here with Neely," Alonzo asserted. Sunny lazily stood up and glanced over at Elisha who leaned against the pillar, her white polka dot dress resembling more of a wet mesh with a coal splotch, unmasking her titillating figure. Elisha removed her black heels and rubbed her feet, trying to work the newly formed callous from the bottom of her foot. The silvery light from the finial accentuated the arch in her foot and showered her in beauty.

Sunny veered toward Elvis as he forcefully withdrew his lustful eyes away from Elisha. He leaned in on Elvis' shoulder. "This is so hard to take. My eyes are so lustful. If I keep looking at her like that I'm going to get in trouble," he whispered softly in Elvis' ear.

"Come on, buddy, let's go inside," said Elvis as he guided him toward the gate. Alonzo looked over at Elisha as well. He had the look of a dog salivating at a bone. His eyes were wide as they ogled the woman in distress.

"Hold on a second guys. I'm going with you," Elisha inserted. She picked up her heels and trotted off as Alonzo looked on at her apple-shaped fundament quivering beneath the filmy, sodden cloth. He immediately looked up at the heavens. "Forgive me of my carnal thoughts, Lord."

A sea of blackness surrounded Elvis and his group. With each minute, it seemed as if the darkness gave way to light. The lines in the field came more into view. The seats in the stands grew brighter; Elvis kept his eyes wide open to allow more light in. He led Sunny and Elisha to the center of the field. The three of them stood in silence, taking in the scene; the azure haze surrounded the upper level of the stadium; it descended downward evolving into a misty coral along the stage. The coral meshed with the lavender hue from the upper level, creating a heavenly presence that enveloped the entire bowl. Elvis, Elisha, and Sunny stood in awe and revered the majestic presence before their eyes.

Several hours passed as Elvis had his head firmly on the ground in a praying position, one fist clinched full of grass, and the other with his palm facing the heavens. "Lord, my soul is sorrowful for my past life. You are the redeemer and I have been redeemed. You have given me new life through your death on the cross. Have mercy on my soul. Give me the strength to finish this journey. The night has come quickly, and I ask you fervently to sustain me with your Holy Spirit."

Another hour passed as Sunny and Elisha were sleeping off to the side, not far from Elvis. Alonzo still outside the stadium snoozing next to a pillar, and Neely dozed off in his escalade. A lull lingered in the air; the souls were at rest, except for the fervent one lying face down in the middle of the field. A dark shadow crept by Neely and hovered over him like a watchman, the shadows eyes wanting to take the helpless soul. Only the car door glass separated him from death. The shadow crept up to a resting Alonzo and hovered over him, and breathed in his nostrils, Alonzo tossed and turned his body but didn't awake, the shadow continued toward the dome.

Elvis' body started to relax. He felt a deep sleep come over him as his eyelids fell heavy. He sprawled flat on his belly. The moonlight glimmered over the shadow figure that eased in behind Elvis. A cool breeze rushed over Elvis. The breeze smelled like ammonia, jolting his senses. Elvis turned as a loud voice sounded, "We meet again!"

He rose to his feet as the shadowed figure came in closer. His eyes cut through the dark air like a laser beam. "Who are you?" Elvis snapped with bewilderment.

"You thought you killed me, but I live, and now, it's your turn to die."

"Zorzi!" Elvis shouted.

A loud laugh resonated through the arena. Elvis quickly looked to his left and then to his right. "Where are Sunny and Elisha?" he pleaded.

Another laugh echoed, reverberating through Elvis' mind like a shout in the valley. The cool breeze became instantly warm.

"How are you still Alive?" Elvis rasped.

"You fool! I am destined to die only by the sword of your savior."

"What do you mean?" Elvis exasperated.

You haven't been paying attention. You should have been prepared, especially after the good angel warned you of my return."

"What good…" Elvis hesitated for a moment. "Oh, the angel that visited me by the river." Thinking to himself.

"You might want to take your warnings more seriously, Lion Man."

"You're no different than all the clones that follow your government. If the fools would only read their own good book that their Lord provided for them, they wouldn't fall prey and burn in the lake of fire."

"You will burn, too," Elvis shouted.

"Go meet your God, fool," The black shadow boomed.

Just then, three loud shouts fired from the shadow figure, hitting Elvis squarely in the chest. The thrust propelled Elvis' body backward and onto the ground. His head whipped against a hard metal object from the concert stage, knocking him unconscious.

Receding back into the shadow, Zorzi turned slowly toward Elisha. He grew stronger, panting louder and louder with each long stride. His heart thrusting, he began to pant louder, transforming from a shadow figure to a beast. Growing more excited, his protruding eyes honed in on the exposed Elisha. He roared like a Lion, grabbed Elisha, and shook her violently. She awoke, screaming in horror at the sight of the shadowed beast. Its hand struck her hard across the face. She yelped and fell to the ground. The beast ripped the damp garments from her limp torso. Salvadating immensely, his tongue slithering like a snake, his eyes protruding from the his eye sockets, his finger nails suddenly grew longer. The beast clawed at her exposed torso, as Elisha hollered in pain. The beast grew taller, towering over her like a giant. It grabbed Elisha and shook her like a rag doll. She instantly passed out. He grew angry and howled like a wolf, his blood racing violently through its demon-possessed body. He took hold of his pulsating phallus moved in over her exposed body. As the beast was about to enter her, a loud shot rang out, followed by another, then another. The beast howled, then groaned and fell to the ground with a loud thump.

"Oh, my God! She's dead!" Sunny wailed.

He ran to her and rolled over her nude, lifeless body. He burst into tears.

Elvis turned slowly to his side and grabbed his chest. "No blood," he murmured. He grabbed his head and grimaced.

"Thank you, Lord Jesus," he said. Suddenly, he heard Sunny weeping over Elisha. He slowly got to his feet and slumbered over to them.

"What happened?" said Elvis as he gasped for air trying to catch his breath.

"That beast." Sunny gestured. "He was trying to rape Elisha."

Elvis looked over at the grizzly body covered in blood. "What? I thought it was Zorzi. It even said it was Zorzi. How did it get so big?" He quickly turned his attention back toward Elisha. He placed his head down on her chest. "I can't hear her heart beat."

Elvis placed his hand on Elisha's chest. He lowered his head and closed his eyes. "Lord, I'm commanding all the angels in heaven in the name of Jesus to bring life back into Elisha, now." Sweat poured from his face as he continued with his plea.

Neely and Alonzo entered the field from the other side.

"Woo. What the h..." Neely jumped in shock and instantly fell back on Alonzo. They both went tumbling to the ground.

"Wow!" Alonzo lay on the ground totally mesmerized by the angelic figure hovering over the praying Elvis.

Elvis took his hand and placed it softly under Elisha's chin, then gently turned her head toward him. Her eyes opened and grew wide. Astonished, she rose slightly, confused as she looked down at her nude body. She quickly covered her breasts with her arms. Elvis tore his shirt off and covered her breast. He gave her an intense hug.

"You're ok, now," he uttered.

"What exactly happened?" she murmured. Elvis pointed toward the black figure lying on the ground.

"Who is that?" she asked.

"It was trying to rape you," Sunny uttered softly.

"Rape me?" She cried.

Elvis held her once more as Sunny leaned in toward her. He placed his hand on her shoulder.

Neely and Alonzo made their ways over to the trio. The pair hovered over the group huddled on the ground.

"Is she ok?" Neely bent down and offered a prayer as he reached out to touch Elisha. Alonzo followed suit and knelt down.

After Neely was done with his prayer, Elvis glared at the black figure. "What is it?" he questioned. Elvis stood up slowly and walked toward the figure. He placed his hand on it. Turning it slightly, the head slumped toward its left shoulder. "This isn't Zorzi," Elvis uttered.

Neely walked over to Elvis. "What exactly happened?"

"This beast tried to rape Elisha," replied Elvis.

"Could it be a Nephilim?" inquired Neely. Sunny walked over to join them.

"A Nephilim," Elvis answered. He hesitated. "Yes, it very well could be one."

"They are fallen angels who indwelt men. These Nephilim will become more numerous toward the final days, the same as it was before the flood of Noah. These fallen angels leave their natural state and lust after women," said Neely.

"So it could have been that this Nephilim was only here because of Elisha?" probed Sunny.

"I don't know for sure, but that's what it seems like." Replied Neely.

"Then how come it called itself Zorzi?" said Sunny.

"I don't know. Maybe because it knows we are with Christ and they hate Christ."

"They?" replied Sunny.

"Yes. There will be many of them the closer it gets to God's judgment on Earth, which, in our case, will be the final judgment before the return of Christ." said Neely.

"So you're saying maybe this is a fallen angel that took the body of some man?" replied Sunny.

"This is really creepy. I feel like I'm in some sci-fi movie or something." Sunny uttered.

"How did you kill this thing?" asked Elvis.

"My sweet Sister Sadie... I've been packing heat ever since that crazy Zorzi guy tried to kill us," replied Sunny.

"Maybe it was the spirit of Zorzi?" Neely offered.

"Yeah, maybe. He just took on another body to try and plant his seed in Elisha," said Sunny.

"Are you ok?" Alonzo reached out for Elisha to try and help her to her feet. Trying hard to block out the fact that Elisha was half naked, lustful thoughts invaded his mind as he marveled at her nude body; he glanced down at her exposed vulva. He inched in closer to help her, leaning his body against hers. His hand reached around her back to try and hold her upright. A sensual urge raged up inside him as his hand squeezed her buttocks, and his other hand moved between her legs. Elisha pushed him away and slowly eased away, confused. She wandered off to Elvis and Sunny. Alonzo continued to look on at her walking away, ogling. He turned, confused as to where the thoughts were coming from. He felt like there was an evil spirit present; it was alive and somehow had entered him. He knelt to the ground and began praying with fervor.

Elvis looked back at Elisha. He saw her stumbling toward them. He immediately rose and ran to her. He reached around her to hold her steady.

"We have to leave and get Elisha back to the hotel," said Elvis.

"I'll call the police and tell them what happened," said Neely.

"Should I stay here or go with Elvis?" asked Sunny.

Neely thought for a moment. "Maybe you and Alonzo should stay here because the police will need witnesses."

Elvis nodded in agreement and began walking away with Elisha.

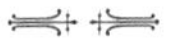

Sergeant Yalom shook Neely's hand as Neely lead him and several officers inside the stadium. He began telling the Sergeant what had happened. They walked toward the field as Neely continued his conversation. Moving briskly toward the center of the field, he turned from the Sergeant and faced the field. "What?" Neely gasped. "What happened to the beast?"

"The beast you were telling me about?" replied the sergeant.

"Yes," replied Neely. "It's gone."

The two continued walking toward the center of the field. Neely knelt down were the beast had fallen.

"Look at this, Sergeant. You can see where it laid," directed Neely.

He desperately needed the officers to believe him.

"Yes, I see that. Something large for sure," replied the sergeant.

"Look, blood spots," the sergeant pointed.

"Yes, like I said, Sunny shot the beast." Said Neely.

"Where is Sunny?" ask the Sergeant.

"Looks like they've fallen asleep." Neely pointed to the slumped Sunny and Alonzo lying on the ground.

"Ok, we're not going to bother with questioning. You guys have been questioned too many times already. I'm just going to have forensics come out and get some blood samples. If anything comes up, I will let you know. Have a good concert today." The Sergeant quickly turned and started walking toward the exit, followed by the two officers.

"Thank you," replied Neely.

Elvis guided Elisha's head onto the soft, satin pillow. "Get some rest. We still have a good ten hours before the concert."

"I'll feel better by then," Elisha whispered. She turned her head softly and fell instantly to sleep.

Elvis took a deep breath, bowed his head, and said a prayer.

Afterward, an uneasiness came over him as he walked to the bath room. He rinsed off his face. He mumbled to himself as he looked into the mirror, "I don't feel tired." But anxiety crept up on him. "Give me peace," he shouted to his reflection.

He poured a tall glass of water and gulped it down. His forehead beaded with sweat. Obfuscating thoughts bombarded his mind. His hands started shaking and his knees became weak. Walking gingerly to the living room, he sat on the edge of the couch. The silence was deafening. The quietness seemed like eternity, and then, suddenly, a rattling sound came from the foyer door. He jumped up from the couch and made his way to the door. Leaning against the wall, he plotted. "Whoever it is, I'll just jump him once he comes in the door." The rattling continued, suddenly it stopped. He reached for the door knob, and it started shaking again. He leaned back against the wall. Staring intensely at the door knob, his arm was raised and ready to strike. Abruptly, it stopped again. Holding his breath, he jerked the door open. Nothing. He furtively looked to the right and then the left. "Is my mind playing tricks on me?" he uttered.

Breaking into a cold sweat, Elvis ran down the corridor. He frantically pressed the elevator button. "I've got to get some fresh air; I feel like I can't breathe." He briskly made his way from the elevator to the lobby entrance. The early morning tourists were stirring.

"Elvis!" a guest pointed to him. Then another noticed him. He quickly made his way to the check in counter.

"Good morning, Elvis. How are you this morning?" said the hotel desk clerk.

"Can you do me a big favor? I left my hat in the room. Can you reach under the computer and give me one of my other hats I left with you guys." "Sure, let me take a look for you. Here you go, Elvis." He quickly grabbed the hat and placed it on his head.

Tipping it toward the clerk, he offered his customary, "Thank you very much." Pulling the hat as low as it would go without covering his eyes, he hastily made his way out the front entrance and onto the street. "Taxi!" he shouted, Can you take me to the arcade?"

⸻

Neely managed to get up at is usual time. It was the biggest day of his promoting career. If the concert went well, it would allow him to reach his career goal. Not to mention, it would set the precedent for the return of Christ. Well aware he was living in perilous times and the end was near, he thought the concert could be God's final warning to accept Christ before the tribulation period. This opportunity was a blessing to him, and he wasn't about to let lack of sleep intervene with his effort to produce one of the greatest spectacles in American history.

With all these thoughts racing through his head, Neely brushed his teeth vigorously as the steam from the hot shower engulfed the bathroom and escaped out to the living room where Sunny and Alonzo were stretched out on a sofa bed. Their bodies rested as if they were lifeless. Sunny's mouth hung wide open while he was snoring, and Alonzo sprawled on his stomach, legs stretched and his left arm dangling over the side of the couch. Neely made his way into the living room and shouted, "Ok guys, get up. We got a concert today." Neither one of them budged. Neely poured a cup of coffee, added a little cream along with some coconut oil, mixed it well, and began sipping it for his early morning fix. He took another glance at the lifeless lumps and let out another call. "Let's get going!"

Grabbing the T.V. remote, Neely flipped on the T.V., and then turned the volume up. Sunny raised an eyebrow and partly opened one eye.

Neely sauntered back to the bedroom with his coffee cup in hand. The mirror was still steamy from the hot shower he had taken moments ago; he proceeded to wipe the mirror until he could see his reflection. Examining his face closely, he lathered up with shaving cream and then took a swipe with a triple blade razor. Suddenly he heard a word from the T.V. back in the living room. "Liberty Bowl Stadium?" he murmured. He quickly turned the water off and walked back into the living room. A half-risen Sunny was leaning up against the sofa bed.

"...where an attacker was apparently shot and then fled the scene. The assailant, appearing to be some sort of Angelic being, attempted to rape a woman. There was another call on the north side of Memphis where an intruder entered a home and raped a woman. This molester was identified as having similar features as the Liberty Bowl attacker. Then a third assault on the west side involved an onslaught by another intruder that raped and killed a woman. The identities of the victims will not be made public until the families have been contacted. However, a missing person report was just made public by the Memphis police. This is coming in straight from a live feed. The name of the missing person is Susan McDonald. She was last seen at Marlowe's Restaurant in Memphis. It is reported that Elvis and his entourage visited Marlowe's last night. Whether they have anything to do with the disappearance of Susan McDonalds is not known. The Memphis police are investigating all three incidents. Back to you, Robin."

At that time, Sunny came to a complete, erect position as he looked over at Neely. "Oh, my God." What do you think happened to Susan?"

"I don't know," sounded Neely. "But I would be willing to bet one of the Nephilims kidnapped her or killed her."

"I can't believe all this is happening," lamented Sunny.

"Well, you can believe it, and it's only going to get worse," said Neely.

He turned and headed back to the bathroom; looking in the mirror once again, he began stroking the cream from his face.

Sunny followed him. "What do you mean get worse?" Sunny delved as he watched Neely shave.

"We don't have time right now, but after this concert I will teach you what God said about the times we are living in now. It's all in the Bible, my friend, all in the Bible." He finished wiping the cream from his face with a towel, he turned swiftly toward Sunny. "Have you accepted the Lord Jesus as your Savior?"

"Yes, I have," retorted Sunny.

"Good, that's all you need to know right now because we could get raptured up into heaven anytime, now."

Neely headed toward the closet and sorted through some pants. He picked dark navy blue, slim-fit trousers and quickly slid them on each leg.

Neely, searched for a shirt and pulled out a violet stripped dress shirt with pointed collars and barrel cuffs. He reached out toward Sunny and gave him a pat on the shoulder. "Don't worry about it right now. We have a concert to go to. You better start getting ready because you guys can't stay here." He glanced at Sunny with a firm smile, and then he walked back toward the bathroom.

Sunny glanced around the room and noticed a bronze-toned Jesus on a wooden cross, and next to it was an empty cross. Mesmerized by its detail, Sunny stood in a trance. Everything raced through his mind. He thought back to the time he first saw the beam and the descending Elvis, the bar scene in the Nevada desert, the incident with Elisha, the black church, the prison, the concerts, and now this.

Neely placed the silver chain with a Star of David around his neck, and then slid his pearl cufflinks into place. He adjusted his collar slightly, splashed a little Givenchy PI on his face, and turned off the bathroom light.

"Come on, we have to got to go." Sunny held his stare for another couple of seconds, then headed toward the living room.

"Come on, Alonzo. Get up," Neely shrieked.

Sunny followed in behind Neely, grabbing Alonzo by the arm. "Come on, man, we got to get out of here." Dazed and confused, Alonzo tried to collect himself in a flash, and then the three of them darted out the door like a bat out of hell. Neely led them down the corridor.

"Where are you guys going?" Alonzo blurted out, trying to catch his breath.

"We're going to the stadium," replied Neely.

"Ah, do you mind if I head on home? I'm not feeling too well."

"Well, actually I do mind. We have a lot of work to do at the stadium," Neely insisted.

Alonzo looked at his watch. Can I just leave for about three hours, then come over to the stadium later?" he implored.

"Sure, just try not to be any later than 3pm," demanded Neely.

"Ok, see you guys later, then." Alonzo turned and headed in the opposite direction.

Alonzo walked out of view and leaned against the wall of one of the condos, panting and trying to catch his breath. He could feel the energy within his body surging. Blood rushed through his veins, and his arms and legs appeared to get bigger.

"What is going on with me?" he shouted, and then looked around to see if anyone heard him. He casually walked along the sidewalk leading away from the condo into the street. Pedestrians walked to and fro as he wandered down the sidewalk. The smell of perfume captivated his senses. The alluring smell ran through his nostrils. He turned to see a woman walking in his direction from behind. Taken in by her provocative attire, a short dress, long, inviting toned legs, he turned his head back around and slowed his pace. His heart beating exceedingly faster. The woman's momentum brought her alongside Alonzo. He glanced over at her and nodded his head. "You're looking good today," he blurted out to her. The woman turned an offered a bewildered glance toward him as she picked up her pace to try to get ahead. A total state of hunger came over him as he watched her derrière sway alluringly beneath her gauzy skirt. His height instantly grew several inches. His blood pulsed wildly, and Alonzo felt a mighty strength rise up in him. He suddenly reached out toward the woman and grabbed her, placing his hand over her mouth and forcing her in an alley away from view. The woman, kicking and clawing frantically, tried desperately to get away. He grew bigger and bigger, and overtook the woman in a rage. His fingernails, having spurted in length, ripped the skirt from her waist. His eyes widened at her exposed haunches. As he manipulated her body, he strengthened, pressing her head into the ground with one hand while the other hand controlled her body. He entered her and maliciously moved.

He howled as his body rapidly convulsed its conclusion. As he fell back to the ground, his panting grew to a faint breath. Alonzo gathered himself, trudged toward the street, the partially-bare woman laid life less in the alley, unconscious. His extremities returned to a natural size and he regained his full awareness. Alonzo continued walking at a normal pace, but his memory eluded him. He didn't know where he was headed or what he was doing. Before he reached his destination, a total state of dejection came over him, and he fell to the ground and lost consciousness.

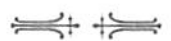

CHAPTER TWENTY NINE

"**LAST ELVIS CONCERT TONIGHT!**" the newspaper headline read. Just below the headline, Elvis stared at the foreboding subtitle.

"LAST DAYS OF USING CASH AS CURRENCY."

"The conclusion of last night's summit meeting at the United Nations in New York came to resolution concerning the currency that will be used to implement the TTP deal. 'We have come to the conclusion that the monetary system that we currently use will not work effectively as a global exchange system. Therefore, we would like to introduce that all cash be turned in for vouchers. These vouchers would be the same value as your cash, except it would be drawn from a bank account. This will allow all transactions through our new electronic exchange system to work more efficiently. We will allow all citizens from each nation to turn their cash in for vouchers by the end of this fiscal year,' said the spokesman of the Secretary-General."

"Amazing," Elvis muttered as he continued gazing at the paper in disbelief.

"Can I help you?" said the waitress.

"Hi, Karen." Elvis tipped up his hat just a bit.

"Ha ha, I didn't recognize you." She slid down beside him in the booth.

"Are you ready for your big concert tonight?" she whispered.

"Ready as I will ever be. Are you coming out?"

"Yes, for sure. I get off at 2pm, and I will head straight over to the stadium," Karen giggled.

"Look. Here is a back stage pass. Show this to the guard so you can get in behind the stage."

"Ok, thanks. I'm so excited." She gave Elvis a kiss on his cheek and got up. "So, the usual, right?" she asked.

"Yes, sweetheart," he replied.

"We interrupt this program for a special live report. Hello, everyone. This is Kyle Everett with WMCA Action News 5. We have the latest on a series of rapes, and one murder that happened late last night through the early morning. Let's go to Robert Smith for the latest."

"Thank you, Kyle. I'm standing outside the Memphis police station where another rape has been reported. This is now the fourth reported rape in just a matter of hours, since about midnight last night. None of the attackers have been positively identified as of yet. The only clue to the attacker's identity is by a statement from Elvis-promoter Benjamin Neely to Sergeant Yalom. Neely stated that the attacker resembled an angelic, beast-like being. This was the first reported incident, but there have been three other rapes, one murder, and one missing persons report since then, and we have reason to believe that they may be linked. Back to you, Kyle."

"Ladies and gentlemen, we would like to switch you over to the national news."

"Hello, and good morning from NBC news headquarters. There have been numerous reports of women being raped across the country. And there have been, it seems like, from what I'm reading here, yet another murder involving a rape that would make five murders and fifty rapes across the country since midnight of last night. This is a strange phenomenon, Bob. Can you explain more about what is going on?"

"Yes, Pat, all of these rapes seem to be by the same attacker, or at least the description of the attacker is alike, but you know as well as I do, it can't be the same attacker since we have attacks reported from several different states."

Elvis took a gulp from the glass of water sitting on the table. He started feeling yet another bout of anxiety coming on. His forehead dampened. Baffling thoughts bombarded his mind once again. His hands started shaking, and his knees weakened.

At the Peabody, the door rattled again as Elisha lay oblivious to the noise. She turned softly to the side, briefly waking, then drifted back to sleep. The door knob resumed rattling.

Elvis' befuddled thoughts turned to urgency as he quickly rose from the table and laid down fifty bucks on the table.

"Elvis," Karen blurted.

"I've got to go. See ya at the concert."

In the suite, the door opened as the dark figure made its way inside. A vulnerable Elisha slept soundly in her bed. The shadowy figure slowly made its way through the living area, then past the kitchen. It started breathing heavier and heavier as it moved closer to the unsuspecting Elisha.

"Excuse me," Elvis blurted after running into a pedestrian.

"Oops, sorry, Sir."

His heart pounded inside his chest from knowing something was wrong. The intuition came over him in vivid form, playing out like a movie. His light jog turned into a full-throttle run toward the Peabody. The beast hovered over Elisha. It drooled as he glared down at the half naked Elisha, her rounded hips, alluring legs, and titillating breasts exposed before it. The panting became louder and louder. Elisha tossed and turned without opening an eye.

"Elvis," said the bell hop.

"Emergency, sorry," Elvis gasped, swinging open the door violently.

He ran toward the elevator and firmly pressed the up button, in rapid succession. The beast exposed its pulsating member and moved over her. Elisha sensed a foul smell. She opened her eyes. "AHH." She screamed.

The beast quickly covered her mouth. "You will be mine, together as one, my bride," the beast growled.

It manipulated her as she tried desperately to wrestle against its mighty strength. She managed to get one leg free, so she violently kicked the beast in the scrotum. It howled with pain and fell back. Elisha quickly got up and started running toward the door. It immediately grabbed her bare leg and pulled her back toward the bed.

The elevator door finally opened. Elvis entered and immediately started pressing the "seven" button. It ascended, and the bell rang. He hurriedly exited and raced toward the suite.

The beast coerced her to the floor, Elisha restlessly squirmed and kicked. Twisting her head back and forth trying desperately to avoid the saliva dripping from its mouth, Elisha perilously fought at the beast's intrusion.

Elvis grabbed the door knob and violently pushed open the door. He dashed toward the beast. Pulling his 9mm from an ankle holder, Elvis unloaded a whole clip into the beast. It hollered and then fell to the ground. Elisha immediately ran toward Elvis.

Holding Elisha tightly in his arms, she wept fiercely.

"It's ok. You're safe." He assured her.

The beast was still wheezing as it lay in its blood.

Elisha turned her head and eyed the barbarian. "Where on Earth are these things coming from?" she exclaimed.

Elisha turned her head and buried it in Elvis' chest.

"I can't stand to look at that awful, disgusting thing."

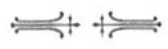

The noon August sun beamed down on Neely as he went over some last minute details with the production crew chief.

"The only thing left to do now is a sound check, and it's a wrap until show time," said the chief.

"That's great. Well I will get back with you shortly before show time." Neely picked up his ringing cell phone.

"Hello?"

"Benji, another Nephilim tried to attack Elisha this morning," said Elvis.

"Is she ok?"

"Yes, she is fine now, thank God."

"Good. Well, you guys be safe, and I'll see you here around 2:30.

You'll have celebrity guests coming to see you before the show."

"We will." Replied Elvis.

"See you later," said Neely.

"See ya." Elvis placed his cell phone down. He gave Elisha another hug. "It's okay." He assured her. Elvis guided Elisha to the sofa. He held her hand softly. "You'll be ok. You're a Godly woman. Did you notice that the prefixes of both our names is 'El?'" Elisha gave him a puzzled look and answered, "No, I didn't think about it."

"Yes, and 'El' is synonymous with 'Elohim.' God as he is referred to by the Jews. So, the prefix to both our names means 'God.'

"That is amazing," Elisha replied.

"The second syllable to my name is 'vis.' It is spoken of as power. Power as in the force of God. Elvis is an anagram for 'Lives.' 'Chaim,' from 'Chai,' is a Hebrew name of life." He pulled the Chai Necklace from his neck and placed it in Elisha's hand. "I want you to have this. It means life. I wore this because I didn't want to miss out on going to heaven on a technicality."

Elisha laughed. "But, Elvis, if it means that much to you, you should keep it."

"I know I'm going to heaven, now, so I don't need it." He smiled and held Elisha's hand firmly. "I had a premonition that a Godly power was in me during my first life. Something kept rising up in me and, at times, I literally thought I was Jesus. My family ancestry is Jewish. I come from a line of Jewish mothers. Therefore, I'm a Jew from direct descent. Jesus, of course, was a Jew. And, now that God as brought me back, everything has come full circle. Now, I understand why I had that feeling as if I were Jesus or a part of him."

"This is so surreal to me. It's like a dream, and sometimes I have to shake my head and wonder if I'm dreaming or not," mused Elisha.

"You're not dreaming." He held her hand tighter. "It's real. As real as I'm sitting here right now talking to you," Elvis said smiling. He grabbed his disguise hat. "Come on. I'm taking you downstairs. You need some fresh air."

They exited the elevator and instantly noticed a large mob outside the hotel. Pedestrians desperately tried to get a peek of the king before he left for the concert. He pulled Elisha to the side.

"What are we going to do?" said Elisha.

Elvis thought for moment, promptly looking around. He immediately took his hat off.

"What are you doing?"

"I don't know exactly why I'm doing this. I just feel led to do it for some reason. Follow me." Elvis took Elisha's hand.

An onlooker quickly noticed them. "Elvis!" the fan gasped. Numerous people turned toward Elvis.

Elisha pulled at Elvis' shirt. "Elvis, I think you're making a mistake," She exclaimed desperately.

"It's ok. Trust me. The Lord will protect us." He held Elisha's hand firmly as the pair walked toward the door.

"Elvis, can you sign this?" a young man yapped.

Elvis touched the young man. "Have you accepted the Lord Jesus as your savior?"

"What?" he said.

"Accept Jesus today." He continued walking.

Another person came up, then another. Elvis was surrounded by a mob of people before he could even make his way to the exit.

"Mr. Elvis," a hotel clerk shouted. He rapidly ran from behind the check-in counter to the door. "Elvis, can you please try to be anonymous? It's going to create too much of a frenzy. Please," he pleaded.

"It will be ok. I promise," Elvis said with a confident gesture.

The clerk instanily ran back to the counter and immediately picked up the phone. "We need police back-up here at the Peabody at once."

Elvis and Elisha made their ways through the front door.

"Elvis, Elvis, Elvis!" Arms stretched out from all directions. Elvis touched as many hands as he could reach while his other hand held Elisha firmly, making sure she didn't drift off in the crowd.

"Accept Christ today. Accept Christ today." Elvis repeated the instruction as he continued to wedge his way through the crowd.

Moments later, police back-up arrived. Officers Dudley and Bailey made their way through the crowd trying to get to Elvis.

"Elvis, we're going to have to ask you to try and stay anonymous. You're causing too much of a scene. It's slowing down traffic," Officer Dudley demanded.

An outstretched hand slipped between the officer and Elisha. Elvis noticed the hand, so he reached out for it and pulled it gently toward him. It was a boy in a wheel chair. His legs were disproportionate to one another.

"Elvis, can you pray for my son? He has an incurable disease," the mother pleaded.

"Oh, brother," Officer Bailey sighed in disbelief.

Elvis bent down toward the boy as numerous hands reached out to touch Elvis on the shoulder. The two officers tried not to allow too many people near him.

"Can you hear me?" asked Elvis.

"Yes," she replied.

"Have you and your son accepted Christ as your savior?"

"Yes," she answered.

"It's important to understand that God hears your prayer just as much as he hears mine. The power of Jesus is in you, now. You can pray with the same authority Jesus did."

The woman wept. "Elvis, I know, but please pray for my boy?"

"I will pray for him, but please understand that you have the same authority to as I do, through Christ Jesus. Do you understand?"

"Yes, yes, yes," the woman pleaded.

"What is your boy's name?"

"Eric." The boy replied.

Elvis leaned in toward the boy as the two officers hovered around him tightly trying to keep people away. He reached out his hand and placed it on the boy's shoulder. "By the power invested in me through my Lord and Savior, Jesus Christ, I command this crippling disease to flee Matthew now, in the name of Jesus."

Instantly, a turtle dove flew in from above and landed on the boy's leg. The boy's eyes widened, and the mother gasped as the amazed crowd looked on. The two police officers looked down as well and watched a miracle take place. The boy's leg began to take shape; one became equal to the other as the dove stayed on the boy's leg. Each leg grew proportionate to the other. The dove quickly departed into the sky. The crowd looked on at the dove as it ascended and disappeared. There was an instant calmness that came over the crowd.

"Get up and walk," said Elvis.

The boy looked up at Elvis. He tried pushing his body out of the chair. The mother reached in to help him.

"No, no. Let him do it on his own," Elvis instructed.

The mother withdrew her hand. The boy eased up out of the chair. The crowd gasped, heads stretched, and eyes peered over shoulders. They tried desperately to see the miracle. Cell phones were in the air recording it. The boy balanced himself and put one foot in front of the other, the small strides got wider and wider.

"Do you believe in God, now?" Officer Dudley smiled at Officer Bailey. Bailey gave him a sly look as the two officers cleared the way, the child continued to walk down the street. Screams and foreign tongues filled the air as the boy made a complete circle among the crowd. He walked back to the outstretched arms of his mother as tears streamed down her face with joy.

The crowd instantly cheered as the two embraced. Officer Dudley looked on in amazement. A bright light descended over the crowd. Everyone squinted, shielding their eyes with their hands.

A thunderous voice echoed over the crowd. "I WILL COME FOR YOU WHO TRUST ME, SOON."

The sound reached everyone standing in the streets, sitting in their cars, walking across the street, and working in the restaurants nearby. Some fell to the ground instantly and started praying. Others looked confused and dumbfounded, milling about aimlessly.

Officer Dudley looked over at Officer Bailey. "This is exactly what I was talking about. The end is near," said Dudley.

Officer Bailey smirked at Dudley. "Your God is a bloody beast wanting to scare and intimidate people." He raised his fist toward the sky and cursed God. Immediately, a bolt of lightning descended from the sky. Officer Bailey's uniform shredded into a thousand pieces. Lichtenberg figures dispersed over his skin in branching patterns. He lay lifeless in the street. The crowd instantly dispersed in different directions. Officer Dudley kneeled down to feel his pulse. Elvis rushed to the slain officer.

"No pulse," Officer Dudley announced. Officer Dudley began to weep silently. Elvis put his arm around the officer.

"I'm sorry." Elisha kneeled down beside them. Sirens resonated through the hot August air. Police cars tried to make their ways to the victim, followed by rescue squads and a fire truck. A small section of the crowd began to disperse, as several fracases broke loose. Several shots rang out. A man fell to the ground. Pandemonium ensued. The remaining crowd dispersed into sections, rioting and looting throughout the area. Several screams revealed a man violently shredding the clothes off a woman. The man forcefully raping the woman in the streets as people ran by and did nothing.

Elvis looked around as he quickly grabbed Elisha's hand. He raced toward the Peabody as quickly as he could. The Peabody had locked its doors. He pounded on the door, but couldn't get in. Elvis took Elisha's hand, and they escaped the chaos. Elvis noticed a man on a park bench, hunched over, clothed in a military jacket, and a hat pulled low over his face. He immediately reached out for him. "Jesse!" he said softly. The man fell to the ground, his face obscured with sweat and dirt. He reeked. Elvis cringed at the offensive odor. "Jesse, is it you?"

The lifeless man lay on the sultry pavement. Elvis shook him several times. Elisha tried to pull Elvis away.

"Hold on a second," Elvis demanded.

"Please, Elvis, the man is dead," she urged. With one hand resisting Elisha and the other hand on the man's face, he shook him again. He rested his head on his chest and heard a faint heartbeat.

"He's still alive."

She moved in closer and kneeled down, resting her head on Elvis' back. Elvis prayed over the man, and he gradually opened his eyes.

"Jesse, is it you?" His face was covered in grit and perspiration. The man nodded softly. "I am," he said faintly.

"Why didn't you want to see me at the Arcade?" The man gradually shook his head again. "I didn't want you to see me in this state."

"Jesse, it wouldn't have mattered. I love you," Elvis said, tears racing down his cheek.

Managing a light smile Jesse said, "I know, I know. I wanted to see you in heaven, not here on earth. I have been praying for you and countless others. I'm an angel, Elvis. My only job is to pray for people. I knew Jesus was going to send you back here," Jesse explained through ragged breaths. "This body is worn, and my time is up here, Elvis," he gulped. "I will see you later, in heaven, my brother." His head fell to the side.

"No, Jesse," Elvis screeched. He sobbed uncontrollably as Elisha comforted him. "Why, why, why didn't he say something to me earlier? He was near me the whole time I've been here." Elvis sobbed.

"It wasn't God's will, Elvis; God had a reason not to reveal him to you until now." Elvis gradually stood up, wiping his eyes and trying to clear the mucus from this throat. He fell to the ground once more and pounded his fist repeatedly on the pavement.

"Why, God? Why?"

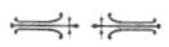

The massive crowd filled the stadium. Sunny peered from the field and was taken in by the gravity of the situation. He could feel the presence of the spirit. A tantalizing feeling came over him. He immediately dialed his phone.

"Hello?"

"Hey, Pop."

"Hey, Sunny. What's you up to, my boy?"

"Nothing much, Pop, just standing in the middle of the Liberty Bowl football field looking at all the people filing in for the concert this afternoon."

"Yes, I have been hearing about it on the news."

"I wish you were here, Pop. I know how you love Elvis," Sunny said as a tear welled up in his eye.

"It's ok, boy. I can enjoy it just as much from my living room."

Sunny noticed a police officer walking up to him. "Look, Pop, I have to go. I was just thinking about you and I wanted to make sure you were going to see the concert."

"I wouldn't miss it for nothing," he replied.

"I love you, Pop."

"I love you too, boy."

"Bye." Sunny wiped his eyes as the officer approached him.

"Hi, Sunny."

"Hi, Sergeant Yalom."

"I hate to bother you. I know you're busy, but we have a missing person and her name is Susan McDonald. Did you know this woman?"

"Yes," replied Sunny.

"When did you last see her?"

"Yesterday evening."

"Do you remember anything at all about that evening that may be the reason for her disappearance?"

Sunny thought for a long moment. "No, she was upset at me is all."

"Why was she upset?" challenged Yalom.

"She was upset because Elvis sort of put her on the spot about whether she had accepted Christ or not."

"Why would she get upset about that?"

"I don't know, really. She said she felt like she was ambushed because I didn't tell her Elvis was going to do a communion at the restaurant."

"A communion? That's a strange place to have a communion," the sergeant scoffed.

"Yeah, well, Elvis wanted it to be a last supper type of thing, you know?"

"Ok, well, if you can think of anything at all, can you call me?"

"Sure, Sergeant Yalom. No problem."

"Good luck tonight."

"Thanks," replied Sunny.

Yalom patted him on the back and walked off.

Sunny habitually reached in his pocket for a cigarette. "Damn," he said loudly, shaking his head in frustration.

"What did Sergeant Yalom want?" asked Neely.

"Yeah, he was asking me about Susan. Did you tell him I knew Susan?"

"Yes, he questioned me a while ago," said Neely. "I told him that one of the Nephilims may have gotten her."

"What do you call them things again?"

"They're Nephilim, or fallen angels. The Bible also refers to them as Sons of God."

"Sons of God?" Sunny questioned.

"Yes, that's another name for them." Inquired Neely.

"Oh, my God!" declared Sunny.

"What?" replied Neely.

"There was a strange man that bumped into me at the barbeque place, when Susan ran out the door. His license plate read, 'Sons of God' on it. He drove away behind Susan." Sunny looked around with a sense of urgency. "I've got to run and get sergeant Yalom."

"Wait, hold on. I'll just give him a call."

Sunny started pacing back and forth. "Damn. Why didn't that hit me earlier?" he murmured.

"No answer," Neely replied.

"I will try and catch him before he leaves. I'll be right back."

Sunny raced across the field toward the exit. He made his way out the gate, took a quick glance around. Nothing. Suddenly, he heard a door shut in the far corner of the stadium. Almost out of view, a police car was just pulling off. He quickly raced toward the car.

"Officer Yalom," he shouted, hitting on his driver's side window.

The sergeant hit his brakes hard and rolled down his window.

"Woah, man, you scared the crap out of me!"

"Sorry about that, but I just remembered something about the other night. There was a strange man that followed her out of Marlowe's Restaurant. And I remember his license plate read, 'Sons of God.'"

"Sons of God," Yalom reiterated. He reach for his walkie talkie pinned to his collar. "Can you give me a license check?"

"Go ahead."

"Sons of God." Said the sergeant.

"The name Zaira Zorzi, 128 Popular Ave Memphis, Tennessee."

"That's Zorzi," said Sunny.

"Zorzi?" questioned Yalom

"Yes, that crazy sounding name is his real name?"said Yalom. I thought Zorzi was just a nickname," informed Sunny.

"Zorzi is dead," answered Yalom.

"Zorzi has accomplices. The guy that tried to kill Elisha and me is one," said Sunny.

"Ok, I will dispatch and officer to check it out. We'll let you know if we find anything."

"Ok, thanks." Replied Sunny.

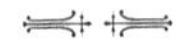

CHAPTER THIRTY

A multitude of people filled the stadium. A band played outside, and a host of entertainers surrounded the perimeter of the stadium trying desperately to earn a buck from pedestrians and concert goers passing by. An airplane streaked across the sky with a banner that read, **"Last Elvis concert tonight...watch it live on Fox Channel 12 Memphis."** A newspaper boy stood outside the event holding up a magazine with the head line, **"Elvis introducing the coming of Christ...God's final warning to the World."**

"Read all about the second coming of Christ right here," the newspaper boy shouted to the crowd. A host of television caravans surrounded the stadium. Countless buses filed in from the rear of the stadium, and different celebrities could be seen exiting the buses. A fence separated the crowd from a line of policemen. Yells and screams echoed from the crowd as the celebrities filed into the rear.

"Hello, Ian Gillian. How are you? Are you excited about meeting Elvis?" the Fox News reporter, Steve Roberts, asked.

"I once had a chance to meet Elvis. For a young singer like I was at the time, he was an absolute inspiration. I soaked up what he did like blotting paper. It's the same as being in school. You learn by copying the maestro. His personality was also extremely endearing. His interviews were very self-effacing, and he came over as gentle, and was generous in his praise of others. He had a natural, technical ability, but there was something in the humanity of his voice, and his delivery. Those early records at the Sun Records label are still incredible, and the reason is simple: he was the greatest singer that ever lived."

"Wow, what a compliment. I hope you enjoy the show."

"Mr. Greg Lake, how are you? It's a pleasure."

"Pleasure to meet you, too."

"What's your take on the king?"

"He is all there in elastic voice and body. As he changed shape, so did the world. His last performances showcase a voice even bigger than his gut, where you cry real tears as the music messiah sings his tired heart out, turning casino into temple. I think the Vegas period is underrated. Would have been nice to see him there, but I'll take Memphis," he laughed.

"Thank you, Greg, enjoy the show."

Sunny stood gazing at the gigantic LED screens hoisted to the left and right of the stage. Shaking his head in amusement at the celebrity guests filing in, he glanced at his watch and made his way backstage.

"I've got to meet some of these guys," he murmured to himself.

A makeup artist prepared Elvis for the show as he stared at himself in the mirror.

"How much longer do you guys have before you're done?" asked Neely.

"Just rapping it up now," replied the makeup artist.

"Elvis, after you're done here I'm going to have you meet some celebrities in the concert lounge area. Is that ok?" "Yes, that's fine," replied Elvis.

Elisha laid a Bible on the makeup table; Elvis looked up at her with a smile and took her hand.

"Thank you," he murmured.

⁂

"Bono." Said Roberts as he gestured Bono toward him.

"Hello, Roberts," said Bono.

"I'm fine, thanks. So, tell us. What's your Elvis connection?" Roberts inquired.

"I think that soul has little to do with the color of your skin or where you were born. It's the same with acting. If the actor believes in the story, so does the public, so I thank Elvis, who is one of my favorite singers in both the RR and RB fields, for doing the music I love the most," Bono replied. He nodded and walked away.

"Hello, Mr. McCartney. How are you?"

"I'm Fine, thank you."

"Wow, such a pleasure to see you. What's your connection to Elvis?"

"I put Elvis up there with Jolson and Sinatra, and I'll go one step further: Elvis was the greatest entertainer of the 20th century. And the 21st century, I might add. But, like Al Jolson, he gave his all when performing. He sang from his heart, his body, the very essence of his total being, when sharing what he felt," McCartney expounded.

"Mr. Crowe." Roberts signed the actor to walk toward him.

"Yes, yes, yes," he replied.

"What brings you out here to see the risen Elvis?"

"life has taught me not to leave anything for tomorrow. I've made a list. Some items are personal, intimate, others are places I have to visit before I die, and seeing Elvis is on my bucket list," he said with a smile as he nodded at Roberts, he waved his hand to the crowd, and humbly walked inside.

The line of celebrities continued to file into the back entrance of the stadium as onlookers tried to get a closer look only to be met by resistance from the police barricading the area.

Mick Jagger, Marty Friedman, Madonna, Elton John, all made their ways into the back entrance of the stadium amidst the jubilant crowd that waved continuously trying to be seen on T.V.

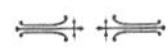

Led by Neely, Sunny, and Elisha, Elvis made his way to the concert lounge to greet the celebrities. One by one, each celebrity introduced themselves to Elvis. Elisha and Sunny stood in awe of the scene. Never had they witnessed such a spectacle.

"The king lives. I can't believe my eyes." A stunned Russell Crowe looked on at Elvis. "I've always told myself that if I had a chance to meet you, there truly is a God, and now it seems I have to make a choice. My choice is to live for God. Cheers mate." Russell stepped back. "May I?" He gestured as if singing in a mic. "Take me down to the river, Preacher, take me by the hand. Take me down to the river; mend the soul of a broken man. Drown me in forgiveness, wash these bloody hands of mine. Take me down to one last river. Let me testify."

Elvis applauded. "Wow, I'm impressed." Elvis gave Crowe a firm hand shake and a hug.

"Hey, had no idea you could sing like that. Not bad for an actor," Bono bellowed.

Crowe put an arm around Bono and raised his drink. "Cheers to a great concert tonight, Elvis."

"Thanks, thank you very much."

A jovial McCartney walked into the conversation. "Elvis, I apologize for John Lennon's comment. The old Rock N' Roll Elvis is back with a vengeance." He smiled

"All is forgiven. That was one of the best afternoon jam sessions I have ever had, Paul. Wow, what a day, and we made history," proclaimed Elvis.

"Yes, what a way to be introduced to America the beautiful, British style. We still rock better than America, but you're an exception, Elvis," admitted McCartney.

"America's best are descendants of Britain, but I do humbly say I must be an exception through Christ my Savior," Elvis conceded.

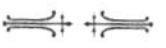

Outside, Roberts continued reporting. "That about raps things up here. I think all the celebrities have made their way inside to visit the king. Back to you, Brenda."

"Thank you very much Steve for the telling interviews, and thank you all for tuning in with us today. We will be live at the Elvis concert until it's over, Oh wait a minute, we have compelling news that has just made its way in from the wire. It appears as if the North America has merged with the European Union to allow the distribution of the one-world currency. New York and London will be the two hub spots for all commerce related to the Transatlantic Union. An exchange for your cash has to be done by the end of this fiscal year, which is the end of this month. An election will be held in November for the Head of the Transatlantic Economic Union between the European Union and North America. We will give you the latest from this as it develops further. Back in a minute after this quick break."

Sunny glanced down at his cell phone. The name "Sergeant Yalom" appeared on the screen.

"Yes, Sergeant."

"I'm afraid we have some bad news," Yalom said somberly.

"Oh, God." Sunny's heart raced.

"It appears Susan was brutally raped. We found her dead lying at the foot of the podium in the First Episcopal Church. I'm sorry to have to break this news to you Sunny."

"Oh, my God. If only she had stayed with us instead of leaving. Did you find out who did it?" questioned Sunny.

"No, but I'm having forensics inspect the crime scene, Now. It appears to be the same type of crime that has been going on around the nation."

"Yes, it sounds like it. Oh, man, her poor daughter. Well, thank you for letting me know, Sergeant."

"Take care, Sunny, and good luck with the concert tonight."

Sunny floundered around in a circle, walked aimlessly for a few minutes, then refocused. It occurred to him the importance of taking heed and reverence to the sovereignty of God. "If only she would have respected the sovereignty of God instead of taking offense to the communion, she would still be here." He shook his head while walking back toward the stadium.

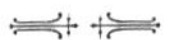

"Elvis, check it out," Neely said, pointing toward the entrance to the concert hall lobby.

"Oh my heavens. Sammy Moore." Elvis took a quick swallow of his coke and walked over to Sammy.

"Sammy." He gave him a hug and laughed plentifully.

"Thank God, that's alright Mama," Sammy said jokingly.

"Yeah, we wouldn't be here today, without Mama, that's alright," Elvis Jested.

"This is truly a miracle from God that you're here."

"Yes, I know it won't be long, now before the return of Jesus. Are you ready?" probed Elvis.

"Ready as I'll ever be."

"Good."

"Can you sign my telecaster, Elvis?"

Elvis laughed without turning his head. He raised his arms in the air. "James..." Elvis trailed.

He turned slowly to meet the gaze of James Burton. "I had to see if all the hoopla was for real or not."

"It's real, I promise you," exclaimed Elvis.

Reaching out to give him a hug, he went on. "Wow, you haven't changed a bit."

"I just need to figure out how to reverse my age the way you've done."

"Ha ha. Only by the grace of God, brother, only by the grace of God." Exclaimed Elvis gleefully.

"We got a telecaster for you on stage. Are you going to come up and play a solo?"

"I guess I will." Said James.

"Ain't no guessing to it; you're coming up." Elvis smiled and looked over at Sammy. "As a matter of fact, the two of you are coming up; I'll give you the cue."

"Excuse us for a second," Neely interrupted.

Neely put his arm around Elvis. "This is it. We're getting close. I'm going to give you the cue to enter the stage. You've got about thirty minutes to clear your mind, meditate, pray. I know God has to be in this show. I got you covered." Neely guided Elvis away as he turned and waved to everyone.

"Thank you all for being here. I can't begin to tell you how much it means to me. May God bless you all, and enjoy the show." Elvis blew everyone a kiss as a soft round of applause, with a few rowdy cheers, followed him to the back. He waved his hand once more before disappearing behind the black curtain that separated the concert lounge from the hall. The long walk back to the dressing room seemed like eternity.

"Can you make sure Sammy and James have seats along the side of the stage? They're going to come up and do a set at some point in the show."

"Sure, I got you covered, Elvis," Neely replied placing his hand on the back of Elvis.

Neely took a step in front of Elvis before opening the dressing room door.

"You have a visitor in your dressing room, Elvis," Neely said calmly.

"A visitor? Who?"

"A former love interest," he said smiling.

Elvis stood dumbfounded. Feeling feverish, his face turned a bit white, a hollowed gaze probed Neely. "Can you say a quick prayer for me before I enter?"

Neely took Elvis by the hand and they lowered their heads.

"Father, give Elvis the words he needs to heal a soul, to comfort and sooth. May the power invested in you through our Lord Jesus be in his words, and your presence be in his spirit and soul. Amen."

"Thank you, brother. I needed that." Neely smiled and gave Elvis a pat on the back. "You'll be fine. Look out for my cue."

Elvis nodded in approval, his hand trembling slightly as he opened the door. The room was dim, a single light from a small table lamp lingered across the make-up counter and fell on the silhouette of a woman with vivid crimson locks flowing eloquently down over her shoulders. The soft light descended on a brimming onyx dress layered with a long-sleeve, a white lace blouse tied elegantly at the neck. Elvis' eyes gazed at the sleekness and refinement of the delightful lady. Her sculpted legs were provocative and infinitely sensual, complimenting her silver cap-toe pumps. She softly placed a black clutch upon the makeup counter and turned toward the spellbound Elvis.

"I could feel your presence; your own unique scent surrounded me. It was eerie. The morning was overcast and dreary, the stillness and deafness surrounded me. I knew you had passed. Today was different. The light from the early dawn awakened my senses. The dew from the shrubs and the grass reminded me of a new-born life, but for an August morning it was uncharacteristically cool. It quickened my spirit and aroused my senses. My curiosity had been running amok since I heard the news of you being alive. I didn't know whether to believe it or not. You know how the tabloids are...always making stuff up to sell papers and advertising space. I kept telling myself it wasn't real, until this morning. It was different. Something inside of me confirmed that you were really alive and breathing. I gave into my curious nature, and driven by an insoluble desire to see for myself whether it was you or not, I came. Now, as I look at you, there is no doubt." She snickered softly with a bit of despair, then cried tenderly. Elvis quickly reached for a tissue from the make-up counter and wiped the tears from her eyes.

"I didn't want to come. I swear I didn't. I knew this was going to happen." Her tears flowed more readily as Elvis reached for more tissues. "You left me alone, battered, confused. I was lost searching for my identity. You were everything to me all that I am and will be. I will love you to the end of time. My heart has mended well, but the scars are still there. It has been forty-two years since that dreary morning in southern California, the worst day of my life. There was something inside of me, always beckoning me that your spirit was alive. The things you said were too deep for me to understand at the time. I actually thought you were crazy and had lost your mind. But, now, I know that your spirit was calling out to God. It was meant for you to come back like this. Everything is in His perfect timing and will. I honestly believe that."

She wept some more as Elvis kneeled down and placed his arm around her. She buried her head in his shoulder and continued to weep. He softly stroked the back of her head and leaned away to kiss her on her damp red cheeks. "Your death made me stronger, and I learned to confront people and to face issues, and take charge of my life, and most of all I learned of my mortality. Because of your death, I have learned to love. I realize you were a victim of your image. You never had a chance to be a normal human, or to grow up to be a mature adult. You never experienced the world outside of your artificial, superficial life of being 'Elvis.' Your passion was entertaining your friends and fans. You are a giving soul. You touched and gave happiness to millions, and it is no surprise to me that God gave you another chance at life."

She rose up in the chair not realizing her body had been crunched over almost in a ball. Straightening her dress and blouse, and giving herself a glance in the mirror, she wiped the tears from her puffy eyes. She smudged her lip stick with a tissue, then turned and looked at Elvis.

He reached his hand out to touch her soft, supple, radiant face and said, "God has given me another chance, and with it, a responsibility like I have never had. To tell the world Jesus is coming soon. You are right. I never did grow up to take on responsibility, and I always ran from it. I was scared of it. I was trapped in a world of not knowing or realizing my true identity. The only world I knew was being a budding star; I did live a superficial life. A life sheltered from the real world. Stardom desensitized my emotions. It caused me to become callous and less affectionate toward others. I wanted to make them happy, but not love them. I was my own world. A lost soul, but searching for an identity, and now I have found it after being at the feet of Jesus, crying for forgiveness. Forgiveness was granted to me because I did accept Christ as my savior many years ago. And I would hope that you have, too. The afterlife is real; we do live on. I'm a living example. Live your life with compassion to others, always, and never be divisive to others. I'm glad that you learned about life through my mistake-riddled life and my untimely death. It goes to show that during the darkest hours, God still guides us through life, and he has certainly guided you. I love you, and I always will love you. We will be together forever in heaven. Continue to live a good life, and help others when you have a chance. I trust that you will put your faith in Christ. This crusade is finally coming to a climatic end, and you will always be my wife. The Bible tells us that after divorce, he doesn't recognize another marriage. We are still husband and wife in his eyes, and we will be husband and wife forever."

He embraced her face with his hands cupped softly around it, he kissed her quivering lips. The lingering kiss catapulted into a loving embrace. They held each other firmly, staring into the eyes of the other.

A light tap sounded at the door. "Elvis, it's time to go on," Neely shouted. Elvis took a quick glance at the door, and then refocused on what he was saying.

"Our souls are intertwined with one another. We are one in Christ Jesus. Your prayers will be mine, and mine yours. Our love will stand the test of time, through the millennium reign of Christ, and beyond thru eternity. It will never relinquish. The fire will continue to burn in our souls for one another." Elvis closed his eyes and held her tightly. The chanting from the crowd grew louder and louder. "Elvis, Elvis, Elvis." His name echoed through the stadium and the breezeways, reverberating through the dressing room. The small light from the trembling lamp created flickering shadows across the walls. A light knock sounded again at the door. "Elvis it's time to go." Neely's voice was faint amidst the thunderous chants. The door crept open allowing the deafening chants to enter the dressing room. Elvis kissed her again and rose gently from his kneeling position. He raised her hand to meet his kiss and gently pulled his hand away. Another tear escaped her eye as Elvis sauntered toward the door. He glanced back at her, winked, smiled, and departed.

A light smile came over her face. She whispered, "I love you," and stared deeply in the mirror. The Elvis chants echoed through her mind. "He is a very special man," she thought.

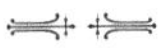

"We are here live at the Liberty Bowl waiting for Elvis to appear on stage. The crowd is chanting his name over and over." The news reporter turned away from the camera to look at the massive crowd.

"As you can see, everyone, well almost everyone, is wearing the white robes that were handed out as people came into the stadium today. All of you can see the magnificent beauty of it. Wow what a spectacle. Everyone is on their feet chanting 'Elvis.' Unbelievable scene here, Brenda."

"How long as the chanting been going on? And how long have the fans been waiting for the king to appear on stage?" inquired Brenda.

"Brenda, Elvis was supposed to start at 5pm and its 5:35, so this massive crowd, and the millions from around the world viewing this live event on television, are waiting anxiously for the arrival of the king. That half an hour seems like eternity, I'm sure. Back to you, Brenda. Oh, wait a minute. They're playing the intro to 'Thus Spake Zarathustra' now."

The camera panned toward Elvis entering the stage. The roar of the crowd was deafening as Roberts turned back toward the camera. Yelling loudly, he announced, "It looks like Elvis is sporting his famous Thunderbird suit, Brenda. We've got to cut away. I can barely hear myself think. It's total pandemonium here." The camera refocused on Elvis as he waved to the crowd. He immediately bent down to hand a young woman a scarf and blew several kisses to the crowd. He reached out for the microphone and started crooning the lyrics to C.C. Rider. The camera panned the audience, showing throngs of people rushing toward the barricade. The crowd became hostile as the masses of people started jostling for position. Elvis quickly recognized the mini fracases breaking out and signaled for the music to stop.

The stadium suddenly became silent when Elvis spoke. The small fights stilled. People looked around, dumbfounded as to what was happening.

"I know you all are excited to be a part of history, but I'm begging you. We have to remain calm. As you all are well aware by now, the only reason I'm here is to warn you that Jesus is coming soon. We must be peaceful and not allow ourselves to get hot-headed." Elvis signaled for another song. Let there be peace tonight …in the Valley. Elvis grinned at his pun on words.

Oh well, I'm tired and so weary
But I must go alone
Till the lord comes and calls, calls me away, oh yes
Well the morning's so bright

As Elvis sang "Peace in the Valley," the empty area in front of the barricade filled up with people wearing white robes. Collectiveness came over the stadium as observers were taken in by the magnificent sight.

"Thank you, thank you very much." He wiped his forehead with a towel and took a swig of water. "Thank you all for settling down. I'm excited like you guys are, and thank you for being here." The crowd applauded like thunder and everyone stood. The clapping continued as Elvis smiled at the crowd.

"Thank you, thank you very much." He laughed heartily as he shrugged his shoulders toward the band and gave an "I don't know," gesture toward them. He walked back toward the microphone.

"Thank you, thank you very much. Please, you can be seated." The crowd finally quieted, but most remained standing.

"As I stated a few minutes ago, all of you should know by now why I'm here. I came down here in a beam of light from heaven about, ah…" He looked at the huge clock on the LCD screen. "About thirty-nine days and sixteen hours ago. My earthly time is coming to a close, yet again. But, as you all know, God gave me another chance, a chance to warn you all that Jesus is coming soon, very soon. So, now is the time to accept Christ as your savior. Not later, but now, and trust me, from a man that has literally seen Jesus, you do not want to wait until after tonight to accept Christ as your savior. We'll give everyone that opportunity before the concert is over tonight. I would like to thank the Memphis Choir for joining us today. And the amazing Memphis Symphony Orchestra. The next song is 'Amazing Grace.'" Elvis signaled the choir director and the band; the piano struck its chords and started the intro to the song as Elvis waited for his cue.

He walked gracefully back and forth on the stage, waving and blowing kisses to the crowd. He bent down and touched the hands of some of the people on the front row.

"Amazing Grace, oh how sweet the sound,

That saved a wreck like me,

Elvis continued belting out the lyrics as he delicately paced up and down the stage. The choir, standing on an incline, blended in with a beautiful chorus line, and he continued with the lead vocals. The orchestra pitted in front of the stage harmonized beautifully as the conductor waved his baton briskly back and forth through the air. The symphony reverberated through the unseasonably crisp August night. People walking on the streets outside the stadium stopped to listen with a joyful ear as the heavenly angels carried the magical melody and its healing sound through the listeners' hearts and souls. Some listeners fell to a knee, bowed, and prayed earnestly. Some stood mesmerized by the tranquility of the moment. Cars pulled over to the side of the road just to hear the melodies. The angels carried the glorious melody through all the streets of Memphis, through all the bars, restaurants, and hotels. Every ear could hear the transforming concordance. A bartender stopped talking to a patron and was instantly magnetized by the healing euphony. The insensitive and lost souls ignored the inflections, and some became extremely agitated, as if it were a disturbing noise interrupting their busy, important lives. The heavenly angels carried onward as the melodies transcended through every household in Memphis. People stood still in their homes and yards to heed the beautiful message transported by the angels from above. The healing diapason entered every house around the world that was tuned into the concert. The hardened souls looked upon the mesmerized listeners as if they were lost space cadets in a foreign land. Not realizing the gravity of the situation, the transformations that were taken place, and the many souls that were healed awaiting the final call of redemption from above ushered in by no other than the risen king. ELVIS!

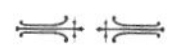

The late afternoon sun gradually transformed the titian sky to a transparent sea of onyx and violet, a painting that mystified the star gazers' imaginations. The stadium stood fast against the eternal backdrop, separated by the alabaster circle that encompassed the confines of the Liberty Bowl. Helicopters swirled above like vultures lurking for their prey. The news stations were in full force, and all of them were covering the concert. The onlookers gazed into the charcoal mural as falling stars trekked across the vast night sky. The moon stood out against the dazzling display. People pointed and applauded.

Elvis wiped the sweat from his forehead after performing "You'll Never Walk Alone." Elvis glanced up at the heavenly canvas and smiled. He reached for a Bible perched on a stack of other Bibles waiting to be tossed into the crowd. He opened it and walked toward the microphone.

"Thank you, thank you very much," he said smiling and waving his hand down to calm the crowd from the thunderous applause of the last song. Thousands upon thousands of camera flashes incessantly flickered throughout the crowd. Elvis sat on a stool that was placed on the stage by a stage hand. He lifted the Bible up to meet his gaze.

"I have a verse from the Bible I would like to share with you tonight. It's one of my favorite verses of all time. So, here it goes.

1 Corinthian 13: 'Though I speak with the tongues of men and of angels, but have not love; I have become sounding brass or a clanging cymbal. And though I have the gift of prophecy, and understand all mysteries and all knowledge, and though, I have all faith, so that..."Suddenly, a loud outburst issued from someone in the crowd near the stage.

"Hey what is this crap all about? This is supposed to be a concert, not a freaking church service." The fan flipped Elvis the bird and started walking toward the back, pushing people out of the way as he headed toward the exit. Another person followed in behind him, then a bevy of other protestors screamed obscenities before the crowd. They all followed the first protestor toward the exit. A host of boos echoed through the stadium, some from the protestors and some directed toward the protestors.

Elvis said through the microphone, "Go forth haters of God…he will give you over to a debased mind." The words pierced the ears of the protestors and, in retaliation, some of them made obscene gestures back toward Elvis.

"What was the commotion about inside?" asked Roberts from Channel 12 news as some people exited the stadium.

"This is a joke of a concert. It's more like a church service. That Elvis is a scam artist." The protestor walked away.

Roberts corralled another fan walking out of the stadium. "What exactly happened in there just now?"

"I don't know, but this so called Elvis character has only performed Gospel songs. He hasn't performed any of the songs that made him the king of rock. This concert has been a total disappointment to me. Total waste of my time being here."

"What about the message of Christ's return?" asked Roberts.

"That's a bunch of hogwash, man. He should keep his religious views to himself. That shit has no place in the public. Those people should be put away in a mental ward or something." The protestor walked away shaking his head in disgust.

"Excuse me, sir… Excuse me," Roberts seized yet another fan walking away. "Why are you leaving the concert?"

"This concert is a joke. If I had known this concert was going to be a church service, I never would have come. I should have known something was up when they were handing out the white robes."

Another walked away before Roberts had a chance to ask another question.

"Brenda, that about wraps it up here. Seems like there are a lot of unhappy fans here tonight."

"It sure looks that way. Thank you, Steve. Stay tuned on channel 12 Memphis with more updates from the Elvis concert."

"We're doing great. Only a few protestors out of sixty-thousand people here tonight," Elvis laughed as he finishes reading Corinthians 13. The crowd went into a frenzy and started chanting his name.

"I'm going to invite a couple of long lost friends of mine to help me with this next song. Come on out here, Sammy and James." Elvis stood in between both men with his arms around their shoulders.

"You think you guys can trade off leads for this next song?"

"What song is that?" asked James. Elvis and Sammy looked at one another and laughed, then simultaneously said, "That's alright Mama."

"I love these guys, great minds think the same. Ladies and Gentlemen, Sammy Moore and James Burton." Elvis squared up behind the mic, looked out among the crowd, grinned and winked at the crowd. James and Sammy trade off leads in a smashing electrifying 5 minutes of back and forth guitar licks. Elvis steps back behind the microphone. Elvis, Sammy, and James came together at the center of the stage and bowed. Elvis hugged both them before they exited the stage. Elvis squared back up behind the microphone. With a wry smile he said, "See what those protestors missed out on by leaving early?" A roaring applause from the audience moved across the stadium. Waves of people stood up yelling and screaming.

"Wise words from the Son of David, and the King of Jerusalem, Solomon."

"I have seen all the works that are done under the Sun, and indeed, all is Vanity and grasping for the Wind."

"If only I would have taken the King's Word to heart previously, my life would have been totally different. Ladies and gentlemen, let this scripture linger in your mind because you don't want to get snared by the material things of this world. You just may lose your soul." Elvis shouted to the crowd.

"I was saved by the blood of Jesus, and it's only by his grace that I'm standing up here talking to you, now. I can't emphasize enough how serious this is. This next song is a tribute to our savior, Jesus Christ."

The conductor raised his baton high in the air and signaled the orchestra to begin. A soft melody started that led into a rich adagio.

One pair of hands formed the mountains,

One pair of hands formed the sea, the chorus blended in softly with a heavenly tone

One pair of hands, healed the sick, the orchestra struck hard with a soothing blend, and the chorus strengthened, rich with power and authority. The orchestra finished with a thunderous rendition. Every mind was stupefied. Every soul was soothed, and every heart transformed. Tears streamed down the faces of thousands of people that stood transfixed on the miraculous event unfolding before their eyes. Masses of people fell to their knees weeping; others called out to the heavens. A heavenly transfiguration occurred in the stadium, forming a bridge between heaven and earth. A bright cloud hovered over the stadium, suddenly an extremely loud roll of thunder ruptured across the sky. A blinding white light illuminated the stadium as every head turned away from the intense ray of light. It immediately left as fast as it came. Everyone peered upward; not a cloud was in sight. Thousands started moving in closer to the stage. The LCD screen showed Elvis with a smile as sweat poured from his face. He raised his hands toward the sky. "Christ, save these thirsty souls that reach out to you." Thousands and thousands lay face down, praying with passion and reverence. Sunny stood amazed at what was taken place. He instantly called his dad.

"Dad, Dad," Sunny said in a panic.

"Yes?"

"Are you seeing this on T.V.?"

"Yes."

"I just wanted to make sure you're not missing this," Sunny said desperately.

"Yes, I'm watching it, boy. It's quite amazing. Please, get back to your show," he pleaded.

"Sure, Pop. I love you." "Thank you, boy. I love you, too," he echoed.

"Bye, Pop." Sunny turned his phone off, and immediately signaled for Elisha to start tossing out the Bibles. They both began to hurl them out over the crowd as countless hands retrieved them. Elvis looked out across the stadium as tears streamed down his face. He signaled toward the choir. The choir began with a glorious hum. Elvis stood firmly with both hand clasped around the microphone. He closed his eyes.

"Oh Lord my God when I, in awesome wonder,

Consider all the worlds thy hands have made,

The choir joined in. "When Christ shall come with shout of acclamation, everyone sang together, Then I shall bow in humble adoration and there proclaim my God how great thou art." The piano merged in with the melody as Elvis and the Choir continued. The piano continued on as the orchestra filled in with flying harmonic scales. Elvis concluded with a resonating final line. "How great thou..." He trailed off again as his voice dropped. He bent over to catch his breath and quickly swayed his upper body erect as sweat flung from his face. He raised his hands up toward heaven and clinched a mighty fist. Jubilance filled the stadium, as did deafening cheers, screams, and complete adoration.

"Thank you, thank you very much." He wiped the sweat from his forehead with a towel. "Whew. Ha ha. Wow... Invigorating. Thank you, Lord," he murmured. Elvis grinned at James sitting off on the side of the stage.

"Hey James, can you play 'Johnny Be Good,' with the guitar behind your head? I would love to see that again," he said laughing. "Come on up here." James hurled himself up on the stage again, grabbed his telecaster, wrapped the strap behind his neck, grinning at Elvis, then suddenly twirled the guitar behind his head and played 'Johnny Be Good.' The crowd burst out with energetic cheers. Sunny jumped up and down on the side of the stage with excitement as Elvis looked on grinning, pacing back and forth waving to the crowd. He hurled a couple Bibles to the crowd and handed a couple scarves to some girls down near the stage. James slung the guitar back around in its normal position and imitated Chuck Berry's duck walk.

Elvis laughed hysterically and tossed a few more Bibles out, shaking his head. James quickly laid his telecaster on its stand and waved at the crowd as he bustled off the stage. Elvis gingerly walked toward the microphone.

"Ha... Ha... amazing stuff, amazing stuff. James I love you, brother."

Neely gave him a cue from the side of the stage and pointed toward his watch to finish up. Elvis' face turned a bit solemn as his eyes panned across the sea of white robes. "Ladies and gentlemen, I guess we have to bring this to a close. I've got a flight to catch to the Nevada desert." The cheers and the exaltation exploded throughout the stadium. Elvis took a quick glance toward the sky as the stars continued to streak across the sky and the moon turned a bit more maroon. He swallowed hard realizing what was happening.

"I hope you all have accepted Christ here tonight and all the millions watching. Tonight is the night. Please accept him now before it's too late."

The crowd became quiet as Elvis cleared his throat."John 17:4: Jesus said, 'I have glorified You on the earth. I have finished the work which You have given Me to do. And now, O Father, glorify Me together with Yourself, with the glory which I had with

You before the world was.' And ladies and gentlemen, likewise with us, we will be reunited with the father here tonight." Elvis started sobbing with emotion as tears streamed down his face. "My last song tonight will be 'He Touched Me,' then I'm going to leave you with the quartet as they sing 'Sweet, Sweet Spirit.'" The choir began their melody as the piano softly blended in. The quartet sung low over them as Elvis joined in. Shackled by a heavy burden neath a load of guilt and shame…Elvis continues until the end of the song.

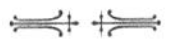

"It looks as if this concert is coming to a close. Elvis is singing his last song, Brenda. I can't begin to tell you the energy that was in this place tonight. Absolutely amazing, and I have never experienced anything like this before in my life. Speaking from a personal standpoint, this by far is not only the best concert I have been to, but the best spectacle I have ever witnessed. Unbelievable, simply unbelievable is all I can say. Back to you, Brenda."

"Thank you again, Steve, for your outstanding coverage of this historic concert. I would like to turn our attention to perhaps a more gloomy side. It is reported that we are experiencing and unprecedented meteor shower. The sky, as you can see here from our live cam, the sky is just filled with millions upon millions of falling stars across the atmosphere. Not to mention, if you look to the left of the screen, you will see a bloody moon. Here at the station, we have experienced heavy winds and a very uncharacteristically chilly cold front sweeping across the region. We will keep you up to date on this development as well as the concert tonight. Back in a moment after a word from our sponsors."

"Something happened and now I know,
He touched me and made me whole."

Elvis hammered out the last words of the song as his voice buckled underneath his passion. Sweat profusely flowed from his face. He walked tenderly back toward the microphone, trying desperately to catch his breath.

"Thank you, thank you very much, and may God bless you all."

The quartet started to sang "Sweet, Sweet Spirit" as Elvis took his final walk around the stage, touching countless outstretched hands. Elisha and Sunny continued to toss out Bibles as Elvis handed out his remaining scarves. People began to cry with uncontrollable emotion. Most of the crowd pushed toward the stage hoping to get a closer glimpse of the king before he left. Elvis reached out to as many hands as he possibly could. He blew a final kiss toward the crowd as he walked gracefully off the stage. Neely handed him a towel to wipe his sweat-drenched face.

"Elvis, we have a helicopter that will fly you to the jet. Follow me," Neely said urgently. Sunny and Elisha fell in behind Elvis as they headed out the back of the stadium. The helicopter was in the distance. Neely led them up an incline toward the helicopter. He began to yell over the loud sound. He looked at his watch.

"You should be able to make it in time, barring the weather. I heard its really getting nasty." Neely leaned in toward Elvis and hugged him, then gave Elisha and Sunny a quick hug.

"Thank you guys for everything. It was quite a ride. Thousands and thousands, perhaps millions of people, came to Christ tonight. It was awesome." He shouted and gave them a thumbs up as the trio headed toward the helicopter and climbed aboard. The pilot shut the door as they all buckled themselves in and waved goodbye to Neely. The helicopter ascended, twirled around, and took off in the direction of the airport. Neely continued watching as the helicopter eventually went out of sight. A sad feeling came over him; he shut his eyes and said a small prayer for their safety. Opening his eyes, he smiled and headed back inside the stadium.

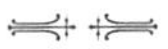

After boarding the plane, Elvis, Elisha, and Sunny made themselves comfortable as the plane engine revved up, then gradually lined itself up for takeoff. Moments later, they were catapulted into the night sky, which was increasingly highlighted by streaking stars and a crimson moon that appeared to be larger than before. The plane settled in above the clouds with a cruising speed of six-hundred fifty miles per hour.

"Ok, you all are free to leave your seats now," said the plane coordinator. Sunny stretched his legs, got up, and instinctively reached for his pocket again for a smoke.

"Holy crap, I can't believe I'm still doing that," he said out loud.

"You should be getting used to that by now," Elisha retorted.

"I can't ever get used to not smoking. It's the toughest thing I have ever been through."

"Some habits are hard to break, especially the chemical addictions, like cigarettes," said another passenger on the plane.

Sunny looked over at the guy who was dressed in a dark suit and tie. Sunny gave him a quick look over, "he looks a little shady" he murmured under his breath. He was sitting next to a woman wearing a red mini skirt and a transparent white halter top. He took a second look, then turned is head away, desperately trying to control the lustful thoughts that normally bombard his mind during moments like that.

"I have the mind of Christ, I have the mind of Christ," Sunny kept repeating to himself as he walked to the bathroom. Elvis was meditating with a Bible in his hands and his eyes shut. Suddenly, the plane shifted violently to one side. Elvis was thrown instantly to the floor, and Elisha managed to grab a safety bar that kept her from falling in the lap of the blond. Sunny tumbled in the bathroom as his head struck the edge of the mirror.

"What in the hell is going on?" he wailed. The intercom broke in.

"We are experiencing some strong winds and very violent lightening. Please, stay in your seat and buckle your seat belts." Sunny stumbled his way back to the seat as the lovely woman sat across staring at him. Elisha couldn't help but laugh because she knew Sunny was fighting off temptations. Sunny turned his head toward the window. The plane shook violently again as it began rocking back and forth. The scantily dressed woman grabbed herself in fear that something may fall loose. Sunny tried desperately to focus on something else.

"Are we going to make it to the beam, Elvis?" Elisha looked at Elvis with an expression of panic written on her face.

"Have faith. We will make it," he said. Elvis held Elisha's hand and prayed silently as she looked at him. The plane straightened out and began to steady itself again. Elisha exhaled deeply and closed her eyes. "Thank you, Lord," she whispered. The intercom broke in again. "This region is experiencing extremely bad weather. We are currently flying over the northern part of Texas." The plane shook violently for a short period, but it eventually settled down once again. Sunny finally gave in and said something to the scantily clothed woman.

"Where are you guys flying to?" he asked. The woman didn't answer back. She turned away to stare out the window.

"Oh well. Weird people, I guess," he thought to himself. He pulled a magazine from the chair in front of him and began strumming through the pages going back to front as usual. Suddenly, in his peripheral vision, he noticed that the man next to the woman handed her a device, and she put it in her purse. His heart started racing as he tried to pretend like he didn't see anything. He remained calm, pretending like he was reading the paper, but tried to keep an eye on the woman's purse. The woman moved her hand inside the purse. Sunny edged up in his seat as his heart felt like it was going to burst out of his chest. He looked around the plane quickly. Elvis and Elisha were meditating quietly.

"Oh, my God, what am I going to do?" he thought. The woman's hand remained in the purse.

"It could be a bomb. Why is she leaving her hand in the purse? I've got to do something, quick." He glanced around, then immediately sprung up from his seat and launched himself toward the woman, ripping the purse from her hands. The man beside her jumped up from his chair and lunged toward Sunny, trying desperately to wrestle the purse away. The woman got up from her chair and pulled a sharp device from the bottom of her heels and rushed toward Sunny. Elvis opened his eyes from a deep meditation and noticed the woman hurling herself at Sunny with the device; he quickly got up and grabbed the woman's arm just in time before it struck Sunny's back. He immediately pushed the woman back as she lost her balance and fell to the floor. Elvis urgently grabbed the man and tried to pull him off Sunny. Elisha looked up and noticed the fracas. The woman began running toward Elvis with the sharp device in her hand, and Elisha stuck her leg out and tripped the woman. She fell to the ground. Elisha rushed up and grabbed the weapon that fell from the woman's hand.

"Give that to me, you bitch," blurted the woman. Elisha swiftly ran the blade across the woman halter top, and it sprung loose, exposing her breasts. The woman reached out again, trying to grab the blade, and Elisha slashed the sharp device across the woman's wrist. She bent down immediately in pain to try and stop the blood from spurting out. Elisha grabbed the woman's hair and jerked her head back. She ran the blade across her neck. Blood squirted out and ran down the woman's exposed breasts. The blood-soaked woman fell to the floor and started to quiver violently. Elisha immediately jumped in to help Elvis pull the man off of Sunny. The man, Elisha, and Elvis' momentum caused them to fall backwards. Sunny noticed the sharp device lying on the floor covered in blood. He instantly picked it up and ran it across the throat of the man.

The man grabbed his throat in agony as blood spurted relentlessly and began to saturate his black suit. Elisha and Elvis stood up from the fall as the two passengers bled to death on the floor. Blood seeped down the floor of the plane and eventually ran underneath the entrance to the cockpit. The plane coordinator immediately opened the cockpit door. She stood in shock at the scene. "What on God's earth happened?" she said in horror.

"I don't know, exactly. It happened so fast, but these two people tried to kill Sunny," said Elvis.

"They have some type of explosive device on them," declared Sunny.

"The woman had some sharp razor, and I saw her trying to use it on Sunny," Elisha proclaimed.

"Ok, everybody remain still. Where is the explosive device?" asked the plane coordinator.

"The device was in the lady's purse," Sunny replied. The coordinator walked over to the purse and opened it carefully.

"Yes, I see a device." She placed the purse to the side out of the way.

"Let's just keep this purse here out of the way until the police have a chance to observe the crime scene. We will contact the authorities immediately."The coordinator walked back to the cockpit and closed the door behind her. Standing dazed, Elvis collected himself enough to sit down. Elisha and Sunny took seats as well. They peered down at the two helpless people dying.

"What do we do?" exclaimed Elisha. Elvis took a deep breath.

"There's nothing we can do, now. They will handle everything once we land."

"Who are these people, and how did they get on the plane?" asked Sunny.

"I don't know. It is a commercial flight, so apparently someone booked a flight just like Neely did." Elvis got up and frisked the pockets of the man. He pulled out a wallet from the man's pants pocket.

"Matthew Mercendell," Elvis murmured. He rumbled through the wallet. "Zion Tabernacle Church," Elvis uttered softly.

"That's one of Zorzi's guys, and that's where Susan was murdered," blurted Sunny.

"I guess they stop at nothing. These people must have known I was a Jew," said Elvis.

"What does being a Jew have anything to do with it?" Sunny challenged. Elvis put the wallet back in the dead man's pocket, and returned to his seat. "Esther with Haman," Elvis said leaning back in the seat to try and get more comfortable. Sunny leaned in toward Elvis. "Who is Haman?"

"One of the first recorded people to try and kill the Jews," replied Elvis.

"Why did people want to kill the Jews?" Sunny inquired passionately.

"You don't know about Hitler?" Elisha blurted.

"Yes, of course I do," Sunny replied with a bit of haste in his voice.

"It's the same thing. Evil people hate the Jews," demanded Elisha while she gazed in her makeup mirror to adjust her eyelash that had come loose from the scuffle.

Sunny hesitated briefly. "Why do evil people hate the Jews?" Elvis reached for a Bible that was situated on a seat near him and handed it to Sunny.

"Because they are God's chosen people. Jesus was a Jew, and all lineages from the tribe of Judah are Jews. God gave them a larger piece of land than any other tribe. It's all in here. Get to know your God." Sunny gazed at it with a new found curiosity.

"I had no idea the Bible was this deep,"

"Oh, it's deep alright. It's infinite because God is infinite. The human mind can't come close to understanding everything about God, but knowing the Bible, you can open your eyes to the truth."

"Are the Jews a race?" questioned Sunny.

"No, not at all. They are a culture set aside by God," said Elvis. Elisha laughed. "You mean you didn't know that, Sunny?"

"No, I know absolutely nothing about religion. My father was saved a number of years ago, but he never told me any of this."

"Yes, knowing God is very important to your faith. That's why you have to read the Bible. You can't just carry it around and not read it. You can know God by reading the Old Testament and know Jesus by reading the New Testament. They are equally important, and each is dependent on the other."

The plane violently shifted to the side, and Sunny reached out to prevent himself from falling on the bloody bodies lying on the floor. The intercom blurted out, "We're approaching strong winds. Everyone buckle up. We're approximately forty minutes from touchdown." Elisha gazed out the window as flashes of light mingled with dark clouds encompassing the plane. She immediately began to pray. Sunny looked on in amazement pondering his new-found revelation. Elvis braced himself and glanced back at the two of them, smiling. "We're going to be fine. Don't worry." The lights inside the plane began to flicker as the plane shook more violently. Elisha looked in horror at the two dead, bloody bodies that slid on the floor to and fro with the movement of the plane.

She shouted out, "This is sick; I can't bear to look at this." She fiercely closed her eyes, concentrating as if trying to force the visual presence from her mind. She tremored as a cold chill went down her spine.

The chilly, damp air circulated throughout the cabin, creating a lingering musky scent, Elisha started to dry heave. Her complexion became ghostly white. She grabbed the chair in front of her and moaned incessantly. Elvis sat next to her and offered a reassuring hug. The plane continued to sway forcibly back and forth.

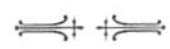

Slick Earl the Pearl looked at himself in the rear view mirror of his 1964 Chevrolet Corvair, adding a little more grease to his slicked-down jet-black hair.

"That's it. Perfect," he said gazing at his smile highlighted by the two golden teeth. He looked down at his watch once more. "They ought to be arriving any minute." He stepped outside of his Corvair, lit a smoke, and then took in the view of the shooting stars and the maroon moon. "What on earth is going on tonight?" he murmured. Suddenly, he heard sirens in the distance.

"What the f…?" he mumbled. A line of blue lights ascended along the airport landing strip, followed by the fiery red flashing lights from several fire trucks, with several T.V. station vans following. They all streamed in at once along the edges of the runway. Earl jumped in his car and immediately raced to the scene.

"What's going on officer?" probed Earl.

"Please step back from the runway," demanded Deputy Andy. Earl grinned at the quirky looking officer.

"I'm picking up Elvis, and I need to know what is going on."

"Elvis' plane has to make an emergency landing. It seems as lightening has struck an engine," Deputy Andy explained. A roaring sound could be heard in the distance. Deputy Andy and Slick Earl the Pearl gazed up into the star-stuck sky. The plane swayed back and forth seemingly trying to straighten itself for the landing.

Earl shouted out, "Oh, my God, are they going to make it?"

"Let's hope so," said Deputy Andy. The plane came closer and closer, losing altitude at an alarming rate. The roar of the plane grew louder as it slammed into the runway with a deafening howl. Metal on asphalt sparked streams of fire from the belly of the plane. The landing gear crushed beneath the weight of the plane as it continued sliding across the runway. It tilted to one side, ripping the left wing from its body. The nose of the plane plowed into the pavement. The plane caught fire as it circled to a stop; the fire trucks raced toward the flames and immediately started thrusting water on the inflamed wreckage of twisted metal and debris. Earl the Pearl stood helplessly as he gazed at the wreckage. The fire turned to black smoke as the flames were being extinguished. A trail of black smoke ascended into the coral sky. Suddenly, amidst the smoke, the cabin door cracked open. A host of emergency workers reached out toward the door.

Elisha descended, along with Sunny, Elvis, and the flight coordinator and pilot. Police held back the T.V. reporters as they desperately tried to get closer. "Elvis, Elvis, will you make it to the beam on time?" yelled a reporter. Elvis lethargically looked around trying to get his thoughts together, suddenly from a distance, a beam of light descended from the sky. A distant thunder could be heard.

"We must get to the beam now," yelled Elvis.

"We will escort you toward the beam," shouted Captain Andy. As he gave Elvis the stern eye. The Captain raced toward his vehicle. Sunny, Elisha, and Elvis followed Earl the Pearl to his Corvair. The police car raced ahead as the Corvair followed along with a host of other police cars. The effulgence of blue lights flashed, racing to the bright white beam in the sky. Captain Andy's car veered off the road toward the beam with a crash and a thud. Slick Earl the Pearl's Corvair streamed in behind.

"Ouch," Earl shouted as his car bottomed out and smashed the desert ground. Ripping and streaking its way toward the beam, he desperately tried to avoid as many boulders as he could, but could only grimace each time a rock would clang up against the car. Sunny reminisced about his first visit toward the beam as his head repeatedly hit the ceiling of the car.

"De'ja'Vu," Sunny snickered to himself. Captain Andy's police car veered off to the right as the Corvair zoomed past. The blinding light engulfed the car as Earl the Pearl slammed on the brakes, and the car came to a sudden halt.

"I can't see," Earl shouted out. Elvis exited the car, followed by Elisha. Elisha squinted and looked toward Elvis. Elvis looked back at her, fighting to see her figure standing in the midst of the blinding light.

"What may I do for you before I am taken away?" Elvis asked.

Elisha said, "Please, let a double portion of your spirit be upon me." Elvis placed a necklace with an amulet around Elisha's neck. He looked down at Elisha and embraced her, cradling her head with his hands. He said softly, "As the Lord lives and as your soul lives, I will not leave you!" He gave her a soft kiss, lowered his hands, turned, and walked toward the beam.

"Elvis!" she shouted. "When will I see you again?"

He turned slightly. "You will see me again in heaven." Elvis waved as the beam encapsulated him. The beam vanished, leaving a sea of blue police lights flickering across the desert plains.

"What the..? Elisha? Sunny? Where are you?" Earl the Pearl exclaimed.

ABOUT THE AUTHOR

I'm a professional writer and I enjoy writing novels, movie scripts, poems, short stories, and blogs. My blogging site is www.heartwinners.wordpress.com I'm also a wedding photographer at www.weddingchurchphotography.com. I have an internet food business as well at www.heartwinners.com. I presently reside in Raleigh N.C. and I currently attend East Carolina University pursuing a degree in University Studies. Upon graduating I will seek a lateral entry position in teaching at a Public or Private School system. The beach and the mountains are my two favorite places to get away for relaxation and fun. I love to meditate on the Word of God daily and I'm devoted to Jesus Christ as my Lord and Savior. My life goal is to win hearts to Jesus Christ, and expose the Word of God to others, to allow a life changing transformation to take place in their hearts and lives. More information about my ministry can be found at www.livingstonesspiritualhouse.org and the ministry 24 hour a day prayer hotline is 800-865-7822. More information and social media about my novel "Elvis is Alive" can be found at www.elvisisalive.org

Made in the USA
Coppell, TX
18 October 2020